THE LAST
PUMPKIN
PAPER

THE LAST PUMPKIN PAPER

A Novel

BOB OESTE

RANDOM HOUSE

NEW YORK

Library of Congress Cataloging-in-Publication data is available.
ISBN 0-679-44837-3

Printed in the United States of America
on acid-free paper
23456789
First Edition

FOR KIRSTEN

"At the core of the Hiss case was the conflict of two irreconcilable faiths—godless communism versus freedom of divinely created and inspired man."

—Donald Hodel, secretary of the interior, designating Whittaker Chambers's farm a National Historic Landmark, May 1988

"I conducted that investigation with two [characterization deleted] Committee investigators—that stupid—they were tenacious. We got it done. Then we worked that thing. We then got the evidence. We got the typewriter. We got the Pumpkin Papers."

—Richard M. Nixon, speaking to John Dean, White House Transcripts, February 28, 1973

PROLOGUE

November 12, 1989

The Lincoln Tunnel was empty up ahead. I hit the supercharger, felt the jolt as the T-bird shot forward, watched the fluorescent lights flash by faster, heard the whine echo off the tiled walls. Headlights in the rearview dropped back out of sight.

The Boss sat hunched in the bucket seat next to me, wavy gray hair fluttering in the cold wind from the hole in the ragtop, herringbone topcoat collar turned up over his blue flannel shirt. He was grinding a fist into his palm, rocking back and forth, cursing nonstop.

"Goddam lying sonofabitch! Goddam pinko commie bastard!" His eyes darted around. "You'll stop me if I try to kill him, right, Joe?"

"Right, sir."

"Because I damn well should, make no mistake. The commie bastard thinks he's above it all, thinks he can sit back playing Goody Two-shoes while the goddam country goes down the tube and he wrecks my career in the bargain. Well, we'll just see about that!"

I guess now we would. Hell, we had no choice. Not that I wouldn't have rather been home in Key West enjoying my so-called retirement, maybe sitting on the porch with a fruit-a-bomba shake, maybe out at the high school watching the Fighting Conchs risk heat stroke, all for fleeting fame and the fickle heart of a sweet Conchette.

But Key West was a month ago now, wasn't it? A month since I drove up the Jersey Turnpike, parked the T-bird in the lot off Chestnut Ridge Road, and walked into the Boss's office for what was supposed to be a one-night bag job back at the farm.

Didn't end up that way, that's for sure. I'd been on the run for the past month, out of the country for most of that, awake for two straight days. I helped spring my old commanding officer from jail, got arrested by an ex-Nazi commie Indian, had my hair parted by a CIA sniper, and was damn near trampled to death by a stampeding herd of a hundred thousand crazy Krauts. Oh yeah, and after forty-one years I was a half hour away from cracking the Alger Hiss case.

Which is what brought me here, hurtling into Manhattan at midnight next to a former president of the United States . . .

THE LAST
PUMPKIN
PAPER

1

October 12, 1947

The plane landed at night, so I never did find out if the new La
Guardia Field was as swell as Closky said. This wasn't how I pic-
tured coming home after three years, I can tell you that much. Not
that I was sore about missing the ticker-tape parade—hell, I missed
most of the war anyway—but so far things were turning out pretty
crummy even by government standards. The rain didn't help much
either.

Closky heaved himself into the backseat next to me. I inched away.
He reached up front and waved a crumpled copy of *Time* magazine
in the cabbie's face, pointed his fat finger at a line of small print.

"Right here, pal. Rockefeller Plaza. Number nine."

The cabbie gave a half salute. "Okay, Colonel."

"Wait a minute, Victor, we're not going to stop at a hotel first,
maybe change out of our uniforms?"

Closky flipped his officer's cap onto the back shelf, wiped the rain
off his face with his sleeve, tugged his rumpled Eisenhower jacket

down over his gut. "Change, Joey? You know something I don't? We're traveling light, remember?"

Traveling light. That's one way to put it. Five A.M. Sunday the MPs stuff me in Closky's Ford outside the PMO at Oskar-Helene-Heim, drive us straight to Tempelhof, C-54 gassed and ready, we leave Berlin without so much as an *Auf Wiedersehen*. Talk about your bum's rush. I was still trying to figure it all out.

"So I guess this means those letters you flashed at the MPs yesterday were fakes, right?"

Closky cocked an eyebrow, pulled a couple of folded papers out of his tunic pocket. "Fake's one of those funny words, Joey. What's fake, what's real? I've been chomping on that nut for a while now. You ever crack it, let me know."

The cab was a '41 Dodge, smelled like stale smoke and wet GI wool, back vent stuck shut but I finally managed to knock it open with my elbow. Cold breeze felt good as the cabbie found high gear on Grand Central Parkway. Closky leaned over, shoved the letters through the vent. I caught a glimpse of what looked like General Clay's signature as the papers fluttered in the wind. Then he let them go.

I spun around, wiped a spot clear in the fog on the rear window, watched the letters swirl away and disappear in the dark. When I turned back I saw the skyline.

"Got enough lights on, that's for sure."

Closky grinned. "Hey, this ain't Berlin, Captain. You don't have Uncle Joe Stalin next door with his finger on the light switch. Not yet, anyway."

I cranked the window down and stuck my head out, felt the rain sting my face. Empire State, Chrysler Building, a hundred others, all lit up like New Year's Eve. No ruins, no bomb craters, not so much as a bullet hole. Not one. And the traffic. Geez. Maybe Germany was just a bad dream after all.

Closky slid a Pall Mall out of his pack. "Listen, Joey, I don't want to say we're calling off our manhunt. Let's just put 'er on hold for a while, okay? Way I figure it, the Führer's not goin' anywhere. We got other fish to fry anyway."

4

"Namely?"

"Truman, for one. Send the little pissant back to that damn tailor shop in Missouri or wherever the hell he came from. Get somebody who knows what we're up against and has the guts to do something about it."

"What, somebody like Dewey?"

"Dewey, hell. Somebody like Strom."

"Yeah, well, I guess if we can't find Hitler . . ."

He was different, all right, and it was giving me the willies. Oh, he was still the Colonel. Still my pal, still Victor. Same fat, pink face, same huge dome of a head, same Eisenhower jacket with the phony fruit salad plastered all over his chest like some Russian field marshal. But he was different, and it wasn't just the crew cut. It was something inside him, something that went *snap* a couple nights back. The night the boy died. Not that anybody would ever care about that now.

We crossed into Manhattan on the Queensborough Bridge, headed west on Fifty-ninth Street till we hit Fifth Avenue. The streets were slick and shiny. I shot another glance over at Closky. He was tapping the Pall Mall on his Zippo, staring out at the rain, thinking—well, thinking what?

Guess if I was him I'd be thinking about what life was going to be like now that I'd lost my job as head of one of Berlin's top spy outfits, lost my corner on the Kraut black market, lost my pipeline to undernourished German boys, lost just about everything I'd built up over the past three years. Yeah, I guess I'd be thinking about that.

The cabbie swung around the block, pulled into the plaza off Forty-eighth Street. Closky started to toss his unlit smoke over the front seat, then remembered where he was and pulled out a couple greenbacks instead. He yanked the name tag that said CLOSKY off his pocket flap, switched it for a new one I couldn't read in the dark. We got out, ran across the sidewalk in the cold rain and in through the big revolving door.

The lobby was empty except for a guard at the desk. Closky looked down at him. "We need to go up to Editorial on twenty-nine," he said. His voice was soft, but there was always an edge in it

5

that kept folks from asking him to say things twice. The guard shook his head.

"Closed till tomorrow at nine, sir."

Closky smiled, looked around the empty lobby like that was the biggest joke in the world. His voice got even softer.

"Is it really possible you don't know who I am?"

The guard didn't answer. Closky leaned over the counter. "Listen, pal, I can see you're doing a real fine job here, okay? Now, if you want to make sure I tell my *Uncle Henry* about it, you'll phone Editorial and say I'm on my way up. Then you can go back to your goddam crossword puzzle."

For the first time I caught a glimpse of Closky's phony GI name tag. It said LUCE.

The guard swallowed hard. He picked up the phone, jerked a thumb at the elevators. "Cars are self-service, sir. Push-button."

We got in the elevator and the door slid shut.

"So tell me, Victor, does Henry Luce really have a nephew in the army?"

Closky winked. "He does tonight."

"I figured that. But you still haven't told me what the hell's going on."

"Simple. We're going to throw the Committee some fresh meat."

The Committee? Holy hell. I knew Closky worked for the Committee early in the war. I also knew they didn't exactly part friends. Of course, that was before the Boss came on board, so maybe things were patched up now. Guess I was about to find out.

The car eased to a stop at the twenty-ninth floor, doors rumbled open. A shaft of light fell on the dark wall, grew into a square. Heavyset guy stepped out of the shadow, stared at the floor. I kept waiting for him to look us in the eye, but he never did.

"Hello, Victor."

He was older than us by a good twenty years, I'd say, mid- to late forties, teeth as bad as any I'd seen in Berlin. Brown hair, high forehead, collar tabs pointing every way but down, rumpled tweed jacket with a pipe stuck in the side pocket. Looked like Central Casting's idea of a magazine editor, all right.

The two of them shook hands. Then Closky introduced us.
It was the first time I ever heard the name Whittaker Chambers.

October 14, 1989

I parked the T-bird in the lot off Chestnut Ridge Road, popped the rear deck, and cranked the top up. The trip from Key West took two days, half of which felt like I spent it on the Jersey Turnpike. Couldn't even catch the Series on the radio, since they start the damn things at night now, even on Saturday. All goes to show I wasn't getting any younger, but then of course neither was the Boss.

Maybe that's why GSA fell for his sob story about the commute to New York, chauffeur or no, set his new office up in a Disneyland replica of the Pitti Palace here at the Dutch end of Jersey. Pint-sized copy of Michelangelo's David guarding the parking lot, ersatz stucco walls, columns at the entryway, big Renaissance windows. Gran Sasso at Saddle River, Elba-on-the-Passaic, end of the line for a Machiavelli manqué. *Sic transit,* eh?

Well, at least I wouldn't have to worry about the car in this neck of the woods. I locked 'er up anyway, checked my hair in the side-view, rubbed the tangles out of my beard, brushed the Cheez-It crumbs off my new Harry Truman shirt. Sun going down now but it was still pretty bad, even in October. My cheeks were sore, stung when I touched them. Plus my neck hurt like hell. Arthritis, believe it or not. I crunched a few Tums, then popped a couple Advil, washed it all down with a last half swallow of warm Tab.

Johnny was supposed to meet me out front, or at least that's what he said when he called a couple days back. Maybe I was early. I checked my watch. Then the door opened.

"Hi, Joe."

Jesus, Johnny in a blue suit? The kid filled it out pretty good too, square shoulders to match his jaw, trim gut, long legs. Bulge under his pocket hankie made a certain impression too.

"Howdy, kid." We shook hands. I clenched my teeth and waited for the bones to stop crunching. Johnny was close to forty now, lines on

7

his tan face, maybe even a touch of gray in his short blond hair, but he wasn't going down without a fight. "Still keeping in shape, eh?"

"Have to, Joe. Part of the job. He doesn't use Secret Service, you know."

We walked up the front steps.

"Yeah, I know. Only one who doesn't. How was China?"

"Not bad. Deng got an earful about Tiananmen, I guarantee you that. Press cut us some slack for once too."

I'd seen the papers. All the usual Elder Statesman bullshit, as the Boss would say. "So you've been with him what now, three years?"

"Just about. Since Blunt retired." Johnny lowered his voice. "Not that we advertise who's on the payroll now."

I rolled my eyes. "Yeah, I know the drill. 'Everybody remembers the Boss, nobody remembers me, and he likes it that way,' right? Makes us all more useful, I guess."

Johnny nodded. "Also makes us dread answering the phone."

He led the way in the front door to the office where the Perillo Tour girls worked, then into the hallway, under the fake Florentine chandelier, past the bronze statue of some Greek dame with a tambourine, up the big curving staircase that led to the office. All the art was phony, of course, but what do you want for 140 grand a year in federal rent subsidies? Johnny tugged open the big oak door and we went in. The outer office was empty, door to his private study stood open.

He was cranking out a book again, I could see that much. Notes and papers scattered over his Charles de Gaulle replica desk, a dozen legal pads covered with that unmistakable scrawl, fresh leaf of surplus government bond clamped in Rose Mary's old IBM. Behind him, tall window that overlooked a skating rink across the street, next to the window bookshelves and framed eight-by-tens from better times, Boss with Elvis, Khrushchev, Henry, Mao.

I tapped on the door frame. He looked up. Seventy-six years old now, hair a lot grayer, jowls lower, eyes still not at rest, still darting around like some damn trap was about to snap shut. Starched white shirt open at the collar, blue silk tie loose, sleeves rolled up. End of a long workday. He stood up and grinned.

"Goddammit, Joe, I knew you'd come."

8

I wasn't so sure about that, but here I was. "Good to see you, Mr. President."

Richard Nixon came out from behind the desk and we shook hands. "Damn straight it is. How was the trip up?"

"Not bad. Maybe a little too much sun."

"Don't tell me you're still driving that old black bomb of yours." He winked. "An Edsel, isn't it?"

The Nixon sense of humor. I'd almost forgot after a half dozen years. "No sir, it's a Thunderbird. '58."

"Right, right. Don't build 'em like they used to, that's for goddam sure."

He nodded at the door and Johnny stepped over to close it. Looked like we were cutting the small talk short a lot quicker than usual. Nixon pointed at a couple of armchairs, then went back and sat down. I took the cue. Johnny disappeared for a second, came back in with a silver tray, coffee for the Boss, Tab for company. My throat was parched and the cold pop felt good.

Nixon fished an eight-by-ten out of the heap on his desk. He stared at it a long time. Finally he tossed it over.

"Remember that one, Joe?"

I remembered all right. Karl Mundt, Ed Hébert, John McDowell, and, off to the left in his shirtsleeves again, sheaf of papers in one hand, running the whole show even back then, even at thirty-five, freshman congressman Dick Nixon. Stripling and Mandel in the back row, behind them Closky in his new Palm Beach suit and crew cut and, if you looked real close, well, modesty forbids, but geez, was I ever really that skinny? I tossed the photo back.

"Day after the cruise, right?"

Nixon nodded. "December 2, 1948. Hell of a time. Hiss case dead in the water, Dewey down the toilet, country on the brink of a commie takeover, and what do you political Einsteins do? Send me on a goddam cruise. Jesus Christ."

I grinned. It wasn't quite the way I remembered it, but what the heck. "Well, okay, but flying you back on that Coast Guard plane after we sent you the wire was just the right touch. Turned out pretty dramatic."

"Dramatic my ass. You know, when the reporters in Miami told me about the goddam pumpkin patch, I thought it was some dumb bastard's idea of a joke."

Nixon tossed another photo across the desk. It was the famous one, Stripling holding up the microfilm while Dick eyeballs it through a magnifying glass like some cartoon private eye.

Nixon leaned back. His chair creaked. "Know what was on that film? A goddam navy manual about what color to paint fire extinguishers. No kidding, that's all it was. Of course, when Strip told the press it was instructions for a 'technical device' they damn near thought we'd found plans for the goddam A-bomb. Stupid sonsofbitches."

Johnny cleared his throat. "It wasn't all fire extinguishers, sir. There were the cables from Sayre at State, too. Plus the trade agreement with the Nazis in '38, plus the cable from Paris about Jap plans for China. Heck, you had the bastard dead to rights."

Nixon stood up, started pacing. "Sure, sure, dead to rights, you think I don't know that? So Hiss was guilty, what the hell else is new? But the microfilm was chickenshit, every damn bit of it. Even the cables and so forth were chickenshit, make no mistake about that."

He sat back down, folded his hands, leaned across the desk and stared at me. Finally he said, "You were there, weren't you, Joe? That night at the farm?"

So that was it. Some damn loose end for his next book. Hell, I drove two days for this? I felt the Tab start to churn in my gut but I kept my voice calm.

"Yes sir, I was. That was the day Closky served Chambers the phony subpoena. We drove up from D.C. with him that night."

He leaned closer, bored in on me like he was back on the Committee and I was some poor commie tailor from Cleveland. "And how many cans of film did Chambers give you, Joe?"

Oh, for— "Well, you know that, sir. He gave me three."

Nixon rocked back in his chair, took a deep breath, stared at the ceiling. "Three, eh? Yeah, I guess he did. Matter of fact, I know he did." Then he slammed his fist down on the desk. "But goddammit, the sonofabitch had four!"

The ice cubes jumped in my glass. Maybe he thought I would too, but I didn't. Hell, if anything was water under the bridge at this point it was the Hiss case. At least to the rest of the world it was, and that was fine with me. In here, well, maybe folks danced to a different tune. I glanced over at Johnny. The look on his face told me he'd heard this song before, probably more than once.

Nixon was on his feet again. "Oh, sure, you're going to ask why he held it back. But don't forget, Chambers and Hiss were a pair of goddam pansies from the word go, and don't let any sonofabitch tell you any different. It was a lovers' spat, for Christ's sake, and for all the harm Chambers wanted to do his ex-boyfriend Alger, he never wanted to go too far. That's why he gave us all the goddam evidence piecemeal."

Nixon slurped his coffee, slammed the cup down in the saucer. He was warming up, I could see that all right, and there wasn't much you could do but let him blow off steam.

"First he swears Hiss is a Communist, right? But when that doesn't do the trick he swears Hiss passed secrets to the goddam Russians, and when even *that* doesn't do it all of a sudden he 'remembers' the sonofabitching microfilm and so forth. And that was enough to coldcock Hiss, so Chambers finally called it quits."

His voice dropped to a whisper.

"But he still has more. He still has the bombshell, the most explosive piece of evidence he could possibly have. Only he doesn't need it so he doesn't use it." He gave an exaggerated shrug, held his arm up, wrist limp, took a couple swishing steps around the room, high falsetto. *"And Whittaker doesn't care because Whittaker's already got what he wants!"*

Hoo-boy. Johnny was nodding but his eyes were someplace else. I figured I'd better bring us back on track. "Sir, not to put a damper on this, but you're talking like we can all drive down to the farm and ask the poor bastard about it. But Whittaker Chambers died what, thirty years ago?"

He flashed a grin like he was waiting for that very question. "July ninth, 1961. But before he went, Joe, you know what he did? He wrote me a letter. That's right, the sonofabitch wrote me a letter."

He tapped on a desk drawer. "I'll show it to you in a minute, see what you make of it. But first I'll tell you what I think."

Nixon's shoulders gave just a hint of the old twitch that always meant something was up. His voice dropped back down.

"I think Whittaker Chambers had a document that would rewrite the history of the twentieth century. I think he had a piece of evidence so damning he could have used it to blackmail either the United States or the Soviet Union, take your pick. And right before he died I think he hid it someplace where it would tick away like a goddam time bomb. And I think it's about due to go off."

Geez, this rang a bell. How many times did Closky tell me there was more to Chambers than met the eye? Looks like it rubbed off on poor old Dick. Still, it didn't make any more sense now than it did then.

"Even if that's the case, sir, what makes you think you're going to find it now?"

"Because the world is changing, Joe. The ground's shifting right under our goddam feet. Christ, pick up a newspaper, young kids gunned down in China, Hungary lifts the Curtain on Austria and fifty thousand East Germans pop their corks, hell, the whole damn world's going crazy." Nixon rested both hands on the desk, leaned down toward me. "Besides, I'm not going to find it. You are."

He reached behind his desk, pulled out a battered brown calfskin briefcase. "Remember this, Joe?" He ran his hand over the cracked leather. I smiled. Of course I remembered. Good old Dick.

"Now listen. If you come up dry, you won't need any of this. A little cash, maybe, sure, but not the rest of it. If I'm right, though, and I'm pretty goddam sure I am, then you'll need what's in here." Nixon clicked the briefcase open, pulled out a fat manila envelope. "I won't bore you, Reed can help you sort it out, he's going with you."

I shot a glance at Johnny. He gave me the thumbs-up. "Bags are packed, Joe, ready to roll when you are."

"Whoa now, fellas, wait a minute. Last time Johnny and I did a job was six years ago and that damn near got me killed. I'm officially retired and I got the papers to prove it. I can even ride the bus for free."

Nixon slipped the envelope back in, clicked the latch shut, set the briefcase down on the desk in front of me. "Spare me the bullshit, Joe, I know how old you are. I also happen to know you're worth a dozen men half your age. Besides, what am I going to do, call in some wet-behind-the-ears government recruit for a job like this? You think I could get one, even if I tried? I hate to admit it, boys, but my authority with those little shits is exactly zero."

Whew. I knew government had gone to hell in a handbasket the past half dozen years or so. Warring factions, rogue agents, mutinies. Even a handful of us left who still answered to the Boss now and then.

"Listen, it's a long story, Joe, so I'll stick to the basics. First stop, Allenwood Federal Prison."

"Allenwood? But why in hell—"

"Now, don't argue with me, goddammit. All you have to do is go visit an old friend, maybe take him out for a little fresh air . . ."

Nixon's blow-off lasted a good half hour, and twenty minutes after that we were back out on the parking lot. Johnny had changed into his chinos and alligator shirt for the trip, canvas overnight bag in one hand, shovel in the other. I was just about to ask him what he really thought about all this when I saw the car.

"Oh holy, holy hell."

There was a three-foot gash in the ragtop, driver's side door leaning open. My head spun around. Nobody. Then I ran over and looked inside.

The cooler was still on the floor, ditto my kit bag and Rand McNally. Quarters for the Garden State Parkway scattered on the console, untouched.

Johnny pointed to the hole in the dash, cut wires hanging out. "What kind of radio was it?"

Ah, hell. So much for catching the Series. "A Volumatic."

"A what?"

"A '58 Volumatic. Good luck finding tubes for it is all I can say."

Johnny shook his head. "Joe, do you really think somebody broke into your car to steal a thirty-year-old AM radio?"

Guess not. "Red herring, huh?"

"No kidding. They took the radio to make it look like a run-of-the-mill break-in."

"Rather than—"

"Rather than a bugging. Or a search."

I looked down at the beat-up briefcase in my hand. "I'd say they were a little early for a search."

We went over the T-bird inside and out, but we came up dry. So maybe it was a search. Or maybe just a calling card, food for thought. Whoever it was, I knew they wouldn't be far off our tail when we hit the road.

I threw Johnny's stuff in the trunk next to the case of Tabs, tossed him the keys. "Listen, kid, I'm bushed. How about taking the first shift?"

Johnny shot me the high sign, slid behind the wheel. He cranked it, put it in gear, and we pulled onto Chestnut Ridge, headed back through town. We stopped for gas at the Sunoco station, then shot over Route 17 down to the Garden State. It was late afternoon and cooler now, wind blowing down through the hole in the top, loud fluttering of ragged edges as he shifted into overdrive.

I reached under the seat for the red-and-yellow cracker box, held it out for Johnny. "Cheez-It?"

Johnny grabbed a handful, stuffed them in his mouth. When we finally reached the parkway I slipped him a quarter and he tossed it in the hopper, picked up the Garden State south. Traffic was light. Johnny plugged in the fuzzbuster. I flipped the Rand McNally open to Pennsylvania to scope out the route.

"Listen, kid, maybe I've just spent too many years on my porch in Key West, maybe I really am gettin' old, but even after that little speech at the end there I'll be damned if I can figure out just what he thinks we're looking for, much less why he thinks we'll find it after forty-one years."

Johnny shrugged. "He thinks we're looking for the last piece of the puzzle, some final bit of evidence that'll prove once and for all Hiss was a spy, Chambers was a saint, and you-know-who was right all along."

"Yeah, I got that much myself. The last Pumpkin Paper. One more jewel in the crown of our Elder Statesman's rehab program, eh? Well, I guess there's worse ways to spend the weekend. Only problem is exactly where to look."

"Maybe that's where the Colonel comes in."

Geez, calling him the Colonel again, are we? Promoted himself to three-star general when he got his Doctor o' Divinity back in '78 near as I could recollect, not that it mattered now. Besides, I couldn't imagine Closky would want to help us much with anything. But then with Closky you never knew.

Just outside Paterson we picked up I-80 west for the Delaware Water Gap. I reached in the cooler, popped the top on a cold Tab. My gut wasn't quite ready for another one, but I figured I could use the kick if I was going to take the second shift.

So we were back on the Hiss case after forty years. Terrific. Not exactly a time of my life I was proud of, although it's not like we railroaded the guy either. Not exactly. Sonofabitch was guilty of something, as Closky used to say. Still, I wasn't too thrilled to be stirring up that particular can of worms again. I tried to sound casual.

"So seriously, Johnny, what's the deal? Some new angle on the case I don't know about?"

"Probably not. Most of the old ones give you enough to chew on anyway."

"Such as?"

He shrugged. "Such as the simplest one. Chambers was telling the truth and Hiss was really a spy. Buy into that and you can spend the rest of your life working out the bugs in Chambers's story. Not to mention the question of Hiss's motive."

"Simple. FDR made him do it."

Johnny laughed. "Yeah, that's one of my favorites too. Roosevelt wants to help Stalin beat Hitler so bad he orders somebody at State to pass secrets to the Commies, starting in 1937."

"Right, and naturally he picks somebody so dumb they pass documents with their own initials on them."

"Naturally. So how about a different theory, say maybe the one where Hiss's wife made him do it for dark reasons we can only guess

15

at. Matter of fact, some people thought Prossy was the spy and Hiss was covering up for her."

"Yeah, great theory. All you needed was a shred of proof."

Johnny shrugged. "Okay, so cut to the part where we assume Hiss is innocent and Chambers is lying. Is he lying because he's crazy? Is he lying because he's gay and Hiss spurned his advances? Or is he lying because he never left the Communist party after all, Russians put him up to it to smear the Democrats and make Truman look bad?"

I shrugged. "Take your pick."

Johnny shook his head. "Of course, what rational motive could Chambers possibly have for framing Hiss? Even if he was still in the Party, why would the Communists want to make Truman look bad if it would've brought in somebody worse? And if he wasn't, would he really throw away his big-money job at *Time* magazine, risk a perjury conviction and wreck his personal life just to settle an old grudge? That's the part that never made sense to me."

Welcome to the club. Of course, if the kid knew the whole story it would make even less sense. But I'd be damned if I was about to get into that now, even if the statute of limitations on all the crap Closky and I did back then ran out long ago. I just didn't want to think about it.

But now I guessed I'd have to, at least for a few days. I reached in my pocket, pulled out the photocopy of the letter Nixon gave me before I left. It was dated July 5, 1961.

> Pipe Creek Farm
> Westminster, Md.

Dear Mr. Vice-President:

Remembering your many kindnesses I have at last steeled myself to inform you of an aspect of the Case that has remained a secret until now.

You may recall my statement years ago to the effect that success in the art of concealment lies in choosing a hiding place which is at once completely natural and completely unexpected. The overly conscientious practice of this art is, I fear, ultimately

16

to blame for the recent, bitter defeat suffered by you and, dare I say, by our nation.

It is too late to change any of that now, of course, but if you wish I could fly to California next week to discuss this matter with you.

Signed, "W." Four days later, of course, Chambers was pushin' up pumpkins. July 9, 1961. I folded the letter back up. "You've seen this before, right?"

Johnny nodded. "Lots of times, Joe. He showed it to me again right before you came up."

"What do you make of it?"

Johnny shrugged. "Could be nothing. Chambers had a gift for melodrama."

"Also had a gift for bullshit. Can't say there was ever anything real natural about a pumpkin patch in December."

"Well, you got a point. Unexpected, yes. Natural, no. But it sounds like he's talking about something different here, doesn't it? Maybe a document he hid somewhere else, maybe hid too well. Maybe even something that would've given Nixon a shot in the arm in '60 like the Pumpkin Papers did in '48."

"Yeah. But what-oh-what could that have been?"

I checked my watch: 6:15. We'd be crossing the Delaware at Stroudsburg in another ten minutes. I reached for the radio knob, grabbed empty air. Bastards. There went the pregame show in Frisco. I leaned back and tried to relax. At least the Advil was kicking in and my neck didn't feel too bad. Sun going down dead ahead like a big fat orange, air dry and cool, trees a bright gold. Not a bad time of year for a drive. I looked at the letter one last time, then stuffed it back in my pocket and shut my eyes.

"Guess we'll have to ask the Colonel."

August 2, 1948

I'd been back in the States for a couple months when I finally traded in my khakis for a double-breasted suit, got handed a stack

17

of papers that didn't quite spell Discharge, bought myself a gray '41 Hudson with a radio and heater for a hundred bucks cash and drove down to D.C. to start a respectable nine-to-five job on the Hill. One way or the other you're working for the government. Never got much chance to be called Captain before they started calling me Assistant Investigator, whatever that meant.

Well, it meant something, I guess, or at least it meant I got to see California for the first time ever. Flew out that fall in a speedy DC-6 to help Dutch and his pals put the kibosh on movie scripts about hard-up farmers, grouchy Negroes, and whatever else played straight into Moscow's hands. And believe me, if I ever thought my army uniform put the fear of God into a Kraut or two over in Frontier Town, well, that was small change next to the shuffles and yassahs I got in Hollywood by flashing a simple Committee ID.

Oh, and then there was the campaign, of course, not that any California Democrat stood a chance against Dick Nixon that year. Closky couldn't let it rest, though, went through a fair amount of taxpayers' money riding back and forth in the Super Chief no less, planting bugs in Zetterburg's HQ and printing up phony flyers that made the Dems out to be Commies or worse.

The manslaughter rap was a dead letter now too, deader than Closky's poor little friend what's-his-name, and if you ever asked him about it you got a smirk and a shrug. Word had it Nixon made Closky talk to a couple GI shrinks, for all the good that did, hell, maybe it did some good, or maybe he just started keeping his crew cut a little shorter, I don't know.

As for Mr. Big, well, I'd seen ex-comrade Whittaker Chambers exactly once since last fall. That was in March when he gave a deposition to Mandel and the boys. All that was going nowhere fast too. Which is what had Closky's dander up again this morning, I guess, that plus the heat and humidity that came in the package deal with August in Washington.

We were sitting in the House cafeteria under a ceiling fan that was moving so slow flies were taking rides on it, poking at our waffles, Closky smoking the last of his Berlin Pall Malls. His white shirt looked like it turned to crepe paper about ten minutes after he put it on, tie loose and flecked with GI syrup, new Palm Beach suitcoat drooping over the chair next to him like a Dali pocket watch.

"You want to know why they're not calling him to testify, Joey?" Uh-oh. "Why, Victor?"

Closky stuffed his smoke out in a piece of waffle. "Because he's too hot to handle, that's why. He's going to start naming names, big names. Truman's scared shitless, so's Hoover. Hell, you think they haven't put the word out to keep him on ice?"

"But geez, Victor, Chambers already talked to the FBI, didn't he?"

Closky snorted. "Well, of course he's talked to the FBI, that's the whole point—he's told his story to half the government and nobody wants to hear it. Started off telling it to Adolf Berle at State in September '39. Berle buttonholes our late great president during a wheelchair croquet game on the White House lawn, says, 'Listen, sir, I've got this contact who's sitting on proof the whole damn government's full of Commies.' You know what our refined and noble leader tells him?"

Here we go again. "What?"

"Well, he gives his croquet ball a whack, or at least as much of a whack as you can sittin' down, then he says: 'Tell your contact to go fuck himself.' No shit, those were President Roosevelt's exact words, I got that straight from Berle in Berlin last year."

"So you really think there's a cover-up?"

Closky's face turned a darker shade of pink, eyes bugged out, crew cut bristled. "Do I think there's a cover-up? Jesus, Joey, hell yes there's a cover-up. Chambers has something big, something real big, believe it, not just on the Commies and fellow travelers and liberals and Demos either, hell, even the Committee wouldn't touch him at first."

"You mean back in '39?"

"Yeah, '39 and again in '40 we took the story to Martin Dies and he jumped on it like an Idaho farmboy on a Paris whore, then all of a sudden he got cold feet. So we took it to William Allen, ditto. We took it to the Bureau and they claimed they didn't believe it. Hell, they had Berle's original notes and they *still* wouldn't buy it. Levine and Ben Mandel even peddled the story to Walter Winchell, for

19

Christ's sake. Winchell checked with the White House and five minutes later he wouldn't touch it either. So the fix is in, Joey, don't kid yourself."

I grinned. "Maybe they all just decided Chambers is full of crap."

Closky just about popped his cork. "What are you, nuts, Joey?" He set his fork down, laid a sweaty hand on my arm. "Hell, boy, don't tell me they got to you too?"

He was kidding, I think, but then with Closky you could never tell. I kept my voice calm. "Victor, for Pete's sake, how would they get to me? Who could ever pay me as much as you do?" I winked.

He backed down a little. "Well, but if not now, when? The Nutmeg Mata Hari herself testified yesterday, gave 'em a little taste of it, named Harry Dexter White at Treasury, Bill Remington at Commerce and two dozen others. Every damn bit of it hearsay, of course. Which means we need a backup, we need corroboration. Chambers has got to be due up next."

The Nutmeg Mata Hari? Papers were calling her that, I guess. Real name was Elizabeth Bentley, ex-commie courier in a flower-print dress and dark glasses, Vassar girl long since gone bad, only now she was trying to take half the government down with her. Tough act to follow but Closky was right, Chambers was the logical choice. Unless, of course, the fix really was in. And maybe it was; stranger things had happened.

All of a sudden Closky sat up straight, looked over my shoulder, tapped my arm. I turned around. It was Ambassador Kennedy's son, skinny guy not much older than Closky, skin dark yellow from some damn disease nobody talked about. He had a *Post* under one arm, Nordic blonde on the other. Guess there was something to that love and death stuff after all. Then again, maybe it was just his old man's dough.

"How's, ah, how's the French toast, boys?"

Closky grinned. "Not bad, Congressman. I'd stay away from the sausage, though."

"Thanks for the tip. Listen, I've said this to your boss and I'll say it to you, I'm, ah, I'm with you all the way on your fight against

Communists in government. It's a bipartisan effort. Keep up the, ah, good work."

We stared at him. Finally Closky nodded. "We'll do our best, sir. Might take a while before we get the really big guns out, though."

He flashed a toothy grin, huge ivories gleaming white against the jaundice. "Oh, I wouldn't say that. Tomorrow's supposed to be a pretty big day, I hear."

Closky's eyebrow shot up. "News to us, sir. We haven't even issued the subpoenas for tomorrow yet."

He winked, wagged a bony finger at us. "I'm, ah, surprised you don't know your boss better by now. First he leaks it to the papers, then he tells you to issue the subpoenas. Makes for a better show that way."

He flipped the newspaper open, dropped it on the table between us. We both looked down. Small headline below the fold, bottom of page 1:

COMMITTEE CALLS NEXT WITNESS
TIME EDITOR TO TESTIFY

2

October 14, 1989

The guard at Allenwood didn't much care for my Harry Truman shirt and Bermudas, frowned at the ponytail and beard too. I brushed the Cheez-It crumbs off and they fluttered down to the linoleum. I told him it was warmer yesterday in Key West, flashed my Florida driver's license, and he finally stamped my hand and waved me through. On the other side of the metal detector I picked my watch, keys and pocket change out of a little wooden box. The other guard was checking Johnny's phony signature against his phony ID. Finally he handed it back.

"He'll be out in a few minutes."

We walked over to a beat-up vinyl couch next to a Coke machine. Maybe a dozen prisoners were scattered around the room, low voices, tired wives, long tables. The guards were out of earshot.

"So how long you been working this particular scam, Johnny?"

"Well, he needs family to get out on the weekend furlough program. And Victor doesn't have any family. We came up with this last spring; he's been out twice since then. Once just to see if we could do it, once to talk to the Boss."

"Aha. So Victor's the one who put the hair up Nixon's ass about the Hiss case. I should have known."

Johnny shook his head. "You'd think so, wouldn't you. But Victor's not like that anymore."

"Oh come on, Victor's Victor."

"Well, in some ways he is. You'll see."

I looked across the room toward the big metal door. So far, *nada.* When was the last time I saw him? Miami, spring of '84 I guess, five years ago now. Trademark Palm Beach suit, platinum toupee shellacked to a high gloss, bounding down from the stage to shake my hand. Hell, they loved him back then, or at least twenty million of 'em did, steady viewers, loyal Victor o' Christ Prayer Partners, scales still glued to their eyes tight enough to give him sixteen percent in the Florida primary. That was before the roof fell in. Mail fraud, wire fraud, conspiracy, you name it, twenty million Prayer Partners left holding the bag. Front page of *The New York Times,* August '85, white shirt open at the collar, red silk tie gone for once, shoelaces gone too, I guess, shackled hand and foot, federal marshal on each arm, game grin for the cameras one last time, just like Saint Peter, boys, he said, Closky *in vincoli,* Closky in chains. Judge told him this time they'd be putting him away for a while.

The door opened. A beefy black guard came out, black overnight bag under one arm, other one leading a withered old bald guy dressed in somebody else's rumpled brown Goodwill suit, clothes as loose as if they were hung on a peg. Geez, was this joint a jail or a nursing home?

The guard steered the old guy between the tables. For some reason they were headed our way.

It was the eyes, of course. Hell, it was always the eyes. Empty baby blues, sure, eyes that looked right through me now even up close, but I knew them all right, knew the eyes and knew the big dome of a head. Hair gone now, smirk gone too at last, not much else left. I reached out and put my hand on a bony shoulder. My voice caught.

"Hello, Victor."

He didn't answer, didn't move except for a head that never stopped bobbing, kept his eyes on some spot about ten feet behind my head. Johnny stepped up, gave him a hug for the guards' benefit, patted his arm.

Nothing.

I couldn't help it, I was staring at him while Johnny scribbled a fake John Henry on a half dozen papers. Finally the guard at the metal detector took the overnight bag from the black guy, unzipped it and ran the beeper through, poked around, zipped it back up, gave it to Johnny. The black guy patted Closky on the back, smiled. "You try to keep these boys out of trouble now, Reveren'. We'll see you Sunday night."

Closky still hadn't said anything, let Johnny take his arm and shuffled on down the hall. They buzzed us through the first security door, then the second and we were outside.

I sucked in the fresh air and wiped my face on my sleeve. The night air felt sharp and cool.

"You okay, Joe?"

"Yeah. Somethin' in my eye."

I walked to the car on autopilot, popped the rear deck, took the overnight bag from Johnny and flipped it in the trunk, slammed the lid down. Johnny opened the door, pushed the seat up and helped Victor climb in the back. Then we both got in and I cranked it and headed back out past the towers and fence. I kept it in low for a long time, gas pedal floored, engine howling, tach at the redline. Over my head the rip in the top fluttered like cards in bike spokes.

Johnny reached in the cooler, pulled out a granola bar. "He's actually lookin' better, Joe, believe it or not. First time I saw him here they brought him out in a wheelchair."

I didn't say anything. Johnny peeled back the wrapper, gnawed off a slab. "I couldn't even take him out in the car, just pushed him around the grounds for a while. He seemed to like it, I don't know."

Johnny was talking about Closky like he wasn't even there. It was giving me the creeps. Finally I couldn't stand it anymore.

24

"Jesus Christ, Johnny, what kind of crazy bullshit is this? We come out here to spring Victor for some big job and he's in this kind of shape? And I'm supposed to be happy he's not in a wheelchair? Hell, what's he going to do if we run into bad guys, drool on them? This is unbelievable, it's just—"

The words were sticking in my throat and I couldn't say any more. I wanted to say it wasn't fair, wasn't right for the poor son-ofabitch to end up like this, even if he was Victor Closky, and it sure as hell wasn't right to keep somebody like that in jail, I don't care what he did.

Johnny finished his granola bar, stuffed the wrapper in the ashtray. "He's not always this quiet, Joe. He has good days and bad days."

I slammed the gearshift up into third, let the clutch pop off my foot, floored the pedal again. "Right, well, I'm sure he does, Johnny, I'm sure he has some real fine days now and then but somehow I have a funny feeling we're not going to see him get up and recite Homer in Greek any time soon."

It was getting dark as we headed down US 15 along the Susquehanna. Sign said sixty miles to Harrisburg, maybe another forty or so after that to the Maryland line. Figure we hit the farm sometime after midnight, which was just about right for the job we had in mind.

I switched the headlights on and settled back for the drive. Green glow from the dash, white lines flashing by. I reached in my shirt pocket, popped the last of the Tums. For a long time we didn't say anything.

I guess it was a half hour south of Harrisburg when I noticed the headlights. They were fifty yards back, keeping their distance just a little too tight for a little too long to suit me. I took it up to 75. The lights kept up. I nailed it there for a minute, then eased it back down to 55, then 50. They started to catch up, then drifted back again. Ah, hell, when it rains.

"Looks like we got company, kid."

Johnny slumped down, eyeballed the sideview.

25

"How long?"

I checked the clock. "Ten minutes."

"Cop?"

"Doubt it, but let's find out." I shoved the eight ball up into third and watched the tach jump. When it hit the redline I pulled back down into overdrive and let the speedometer needle tick off the eighties. Johnny checked the mirror again.

"He's keeping up."

"What a surprise." The fluttering canvas over our heads sounded like a motorcycle engine. The air was icy cold. I shot one last look back, then reached under the dash and switched on the supercharger. I felt the jolt, then heard the howl as the blown high-octane boosted us up to 105. I kept it there.

We flashed by a couple of semis like they were running in reverse. Left lane was clear ahead but how long could that last? Sign put us five miles north of York.

"He's right on, Joe."

"No kidding." I knew the old T-bird could do more, a lot more, but with traffic I couldn't risk it. In a couple minutes we'd take the exit, see where that put us.

We flew by one last truck, then I eased up on the gas and drifted into the right lane. Ramp came up faster than I judged and I wound up slamming the eight ball into second and we took it with the engine screaming and the tach over the red.

Luckily it wasn't a loop, just a straight shot downhill to a red light at a Sunoco station, traffic island in the middle of a three-way stop. I clicked the blower off and coaxed her down to 50 just in time to flash by a DO NOT ENTER sign on the wrong side of the traffic island, run the light and shoot up a hill on I-83 Business. Beat-up Datsun coming on the right slammed on the brakes, leaned on the horn. I took it back up to 75 as we flashed by a Dunkin' Donuts, up over the crest of the hill and down past a cemetery.

Johnny was sitting up, hands on the dash. "Hey, Joe, you don't think the local cops are gonna get touchy about this, do you?"

I was feeling the rush. "Hell, Johnny, what are we, five miles from the Maryland line? We'll outrun the sonsofbitches."

"Joe, for Pete's sake, this isn't the forties anymore, they all work together now, they got computers."

Computers. Least of my worries. I downshifted again as we came up on a steel girder bridge. It was narrow but I took it at 60, bounced over some railroad tracks and shot straight onto York's main drag. Car was a block behind us and closing fast. Up ahead, a string of red lights like Christmas morning.

I hit the brakes, shot a glance in the mirror. "You make out what he's driving, Johnny?"

Johnny sat back, checked the sideview. "I don't know. European sedan?"

"What, a Kraut?"

"No, I don't think so. Looks like a Citroën."

"You're shitting me. I'm driving my ass off and we can't shake a Citroën?"

Johnny shrugged. "Must be a custom job."

We were smack in the middle of downtown now, and if you ever thought Friday night in York PA was dead, guess again. I figured if nobody looked too close we might pass for a carful of kids in a hot rod cruising George Street for action. I was weaving in and out of traffic now, the Citroën a half block back playing copycat. I slowed for a red light, then ran it. The cars behind me stopped and cut off the Citroën. Just before I turned off the main drag I saw him pull out after us.

"Joe, you ever think of stopping to see what he wants?"

"No. Why, what do you think he wants?"

Johnny didn't answer. We bounced over another set of railroad tracks and I hung a left.

"Shouldn't you be doubling back?"

"Ah, but he's expecting that. I'm gonna shoot out on George Street, head south again and fox him."

I went down one more block, hung another quick left, then a right. I kept it in second and took it up to 50.

Johnny checked the mirror. "There he is."

I looked up again. Sure enough. "Now, how in the hell—?"

We were in the rough end of York now, nineteenth-century row houses, gingerbread trim, half of them boarded up waiting for the gentrifiers to trickle down from Harrisburg. Good luck.

"This is bullshit, kid. We come to the end of this I'm gonna get back on the Interstate. We'll just outrun his ass, traffic or no."

Pair of gas stations up ahead told me the on-ramp couldn't be too far off. I held it at 60. One last red light that didn't want to change.

Sign at the corner said YORK HOSPITAL EMERGENCY ENTRANCE. Hey, maybe if I leaned on the horn they'd cut us some slack. I gave it a couple of toots and gunned it good. Clear view of the intersection. Diet Coke truck bearing down on the right, saw me coming, pulled his air horn. I bumped the blower on with my left knee, felt the jolt and we shot on through.

"Hang on, kid."

The air horn didn't stop. I heard brakes, then the crash. For the first time Johnny turned around to look out the back. I eased off the gas.

"How bad?"

Johnny craned his neck. "Pinned him to a pole. No fire yet."

"Lucky boy." I took it down to 50. Up ahead I caught the sign to pick up 83 again. I checked the dash clock. Five minutes since we jumped off at Exit 10.

"Hey, kid, I think we made better time going through town than on the bypass. We ever get back to Jersey, remind me to call Triple-A and tell 'em."

Johnny didn't answer, just slumped back in his seat. Finally he said, "You know, Joe, for a guy in his sixties you've got pretty good reflexes."

"Thanks, kid, but it's mostly the Tab." I shot up on the on-ramp and back onto the Interstate. My heart was pounding and my shirt was wet, but for the first time in a month my neck didn't hurt.

Then I remembered Closky. I looked back over my shoulder. He was still sitting in the corner where Johnny plunked him down two hours ago, staring straight ahead.

He hadn't said a damn word.

"We're ruined." Mundt slumped in his chair, head down. He was running for the Senate from South Dakota that year, so you could take the "we" however you wanted. Mundt lit a fresh smoke from the butt of the last one, rubbed his nose, flicked an ash on the mahogany someplace near the ashtray.

Then he said it again, quieter. "Ruined."

We were back in the steamy hot Committee room after morning hearings over at Ways and Means. A half dozen congressmen were slumped on various chairs trying to look like they hadn't just gotten a whole bazaar full of rugs pulled out from under them. Strip and Mandel sat together on a couple armchairs by a window, Closky was wedged in the corner behind a little typing table.

So Chambers finally got his day in court, but it wasn't turning out like we planned. Oh sure, he named names, fairly big ones too. Only trouble was, one of those names belonged to a high-class lawyer, FDR's ex-fair-haired boy, right-hand man at Yalta and first secretary general of the U.N., fellow name of Alger Hiss who didn't much like being called a Commie, and he took a day off from his new job as head of the Carnegie Endowment in New York to come down to the District and say so. Sat up straight, looked us square in the eye, spoke out loud and clear, swore he'd never even heard of a Whittaker Chambers much less been part of his commie spy ring and, well, folks believed him. Hell, why shouldn't they? All of which made the Committee look like a bunch of horse's asses.

Ed Hébert spoke up. "You want my two cents, we should wash our hands of the whole damn mess. Turn it over to Tom Clark at Justice and let him worry about it for a change." Hébert had his own ax to grind, of course, sly Demo from deep in the Bayou who still hadn't got used to the Boss's knack for drawing the spotlight.

Then Rankin chimed in. "It's sloppy staff work, is what it is. Hell, you boys shoulda known Chambers was full of shit from day one. You ever hear of background work? You ever hear of corroborating testimony? Hell."

Stripling and Mandel didn't flinch but they were seething, I could see that. Hell, so was I. Two days ago there wasn't a congressman in this room who wasn't chomping at the bit to go public with Chambers's testimony. Now that it was blowing up in their face it was all our fault.

Then I heard it. Over in the far corner, echoing off the high ceiling. I stared over. Everybody else was looking too.

Closky was sitting up straight at the little table. His white suitcoat was cleaned and pressed, bright red tie and hankie to match, huge pink face shiny with sweat, crew cut down another eighth of an inch since last week. He had his GI Zippo out and was flipping the top open and clicking it shut. Over and over again. Flip. *Click.* Flip. *Click.* Finally he shut it for good, slipped it back in his pocket. When he looked up he was staring straight at Nixon.

"We turn this over to Justice," Closky said, "and we might as well hang up our gloves and go home. Because number one, I guarantee you we try to hold another hearing the whole country's going to say, 'Why don't those sorry amateurs let the Justice Department do its job? That Committee can't tell shit from Shinola, let alone the difference between a lying communist sonofabitch and an honest American like poor old Alger Hiss.'"

He was right about that and everybody knew it. Nobody said a word. Closky kept staring at Nixon, like they were the only ones in the room.

"And number two, far as Justice goes, that's just putting the fox in charge of the henhouse. Hell, Justice had Chambers's testimony nine years ago and they sat on it. We give it back to 'em they'll sit on it some more. Meanwhile the Commies are getting a free ride."

Mandel chimed in. "Okay, Victor, but what are we going to do for evidence? It's our man's word against Hiss, and our man is a sleazy, fat little ex-Communist and Hiss is the tall, dark and handsome all-American boy. Besides, you want to try and *prove* somebody was ever a Communist, good luck."

He had a point. Hell, Mandel was an ex-Commie himself, spent ten years as business manager of the *Daily Worker,* and the only reason we knew it was he confessed. Besides, proving anything wasn't the Committee's cup of tea; we usually made do pretty well with innuendo.

Closky picked up a stack of transcripts, balanced them on his hand. "Hell, Ben, I know we can't prove Hiss was a Communist. So what? The way I read these, we don't have to. All we have to do is prove he *knew Chambers.*"

He shook the papers in his hand, set them down again. "If we can prove Hiss knew Chambers—at all, even the slightest bit—we've got him on perjury. Period."

Stripling pursed his lips. "I hate to say it, but Closky's right. One way or the other, we got ourselves a prima facie case of perjury here. Chambers says they were close friends in the Communist party, Hiss says he never laid eyes on him. One of them's lying and I'll lay odds it's Hiss. All we have to do is prove *that.*"

Finally Nixon stirred. He cleared his throat and stood up. I settled back in my chair.

"First of all, just let me say with all due respect to my esteemed colleague from Mississippi that I fully recognize the hard work our staff puts in here each and every day. Without them, we'd all be in hot water, let there be no question about that." He nodded toward our table.

Good ol' Dick. Never one to bite the hand that feeds him, that's for sure. Closky started to answer from across the room but Nixon cut him off, pacing now.

"As for Hiss, well, I will say I didn't much care for the tone of his answers. He was a little too mouthy, a little too careful to suit me. You all know how I asked him straight off who suggested he come down here to Washington and we practically had to get the thumbscrews out before he'd admit it was Felix Frankfurter. Now, why would he want to hide something as simple as that?" Nixon rubbed his jaw while he paced like he was trying to figure that one out. Then he stopped short. "And come to think of it, he never actually said he didn't know Chambers, did he? He always said he didn't know anyone 'by the name of Whittaker Chambers.' "

Nixon nodded toward Mandel. "And sure, Ben, we may never be able to prove Hiss was ever a Communist, that's just one man's word against another's, but we should damned well be able to get corroborative testimony that proves whether or not the two men knew each other. And let me add, if Hiss is lying about not knowing Chambers, he might also be lying about whether or not he was a Communist."

Stripling spoke up. "I'll tell you something I don't much like. We've been hearin' a smear campaign against Chambers since we first announced he was testifyin'. 'Chambers the alcoholic, Chambers the homosexual, Chambers the mental patient.' It's exactly the kind of character assassination that's typical for your Communists to employ."

Nixon nodded, waved his hand like all that was too obvious to mention. "Listen, there's a simple way to get at this. We'll form a subcommittee. We'll question Chambers in private. We'll ask him everything he knows about Hiss—personal habits, family, hobbies, quirks and so forth. If Chambers is telling the truth he'll be able to tell us a great many things like that. Then we question Hiss on the same points and see if it matches up."

At first Mundt and Hébert didn't go for it, but the rest of them talked it up and pretty soon it was settled. Nixon wanted the subcommittee to meet Chambers sometime in the next few days. He offered to chair it himself, Hébert and McDowell to go along for the ride. Guess that meant another weekend shot.

I looked over at Closky. His fat pink face was shiny with sweat, white Palm Beach suit gleaming in the sunlight that streamed in the high window. He was fiddling with his red silk tie, biting his lip. I knew that look. He was doing all he could to keep a big fat grin from spreading all across his face.

October 14, 1989

We left I-83 for 216 west, crossed the Mason-Dixon line twenty minutes later, flashed past a MARYLAND WELCOMES YOU, DRIVE GENTLY sign. The road got worse but the fuzzbuster was quiet so I kept 'er at a smooth 85.

"Listen, Johnny, one thing I never asked, but probably should have. This a government job we're on, or is Nixon freelancing again?"

"Hard to say, Joe. We both know he's got more up his sleeve than writing books and posing for snapshots at the Great Wall with Deng. Always did. But things are different now, the funding's all private."

"Yeah, except the federal pension, rent subsidy, staff allowance—" Johnny waved me off. "That's all peanuts, Joe. Couple hundred thousand a year, maybe half a million tops. I'm telling you, the man's got backers again, big ones too. Folks that never liked the raw deal he got in '74 and want to set it right somehow, maybe even help him get back in the ring next year."

"Back in the ring? Are you serious? What's he going to do, run for governor of Jersey?"

"Something like that. Maybe something bigger. You heard of the Committee to Repeal the Twenty-second Amendment?"

I shook my head. "Comeback of the Century, if it works."

The voice from the backseat was reedy and thin. It was real quiet, too, but it got my attention quick.

Just like it always did.

"Will you two shut the fuck up?"

I felt my face light up like a Christmas tree, even let out a laugh, turned around to stare at him and damn near ran off the road, couldn't stop grinning. "Holy hell, Victor, you can talk!"

"Of course I can talk, who the fuck do you think I am, Philomela?"

I laughed again. "Hell no, I just thought—I mean, I guess Johnny and I thought you were worse off than you are."

"Yeah, well, there's worse off and then there's worse off. Listen, what kind of car is this anyway?"

I looked at him in the rearview mirror. "It's a T-bird. A Ford Thunderbird. Told you I'd give you a ride in it someday, remember?"

"Pretty fast for a Ford. Thought it was a goddam Studebaker."

I winked at Johnny. "Hey, c'mon, Victor, you haven't been out of action that long, have you?"

We drove for a while in the dark and Victor got quiet again, Johnny pulled out the Cheez-It box and passed it around. All we needed was a harmonica playin' "Home on the Range." Jesus, here we were, all three of us, together again like it was some damn movie, and we even got away from the bad guys and everything was going to be okay. Man, he had me going there for a minute, he really had me going.

"So who do you think they were?" Johnny asked.

"Beats me. Know anybody around here with a real strong interest in a forty-one-year-old spy case?"

"You mean like the Maryland Historical Society?"

"I don't think they drive that fast."

I eased on back to 65. Everything was settling down inside me now. Figured I'd kill some time on the back roads for the next hour to make sure folks had time to turn in, maybe shoot for getting there by one A.M.

Then I felt a tap on the shoulder.

"Hey, pal, what kind of car is this anyway?"

My gut knotted up. I glanced back. Closky's head was bobbin' around in the dark like some damn lost chicken. I looked over at Johnny. He shrugged.

Closky poked my shoulder again. *"Hey, what kind of car is this anyway?"*

I swallowed hard. "It's a Thunderbird, Victor. A Ford Thunderbird."

I glanced up in the mirror. He was nodding. "Pretty fast for a Ford. Thought it was a goddam Studebaker."

I didn't say anything, just kept the pedal down and the needle on 90. Hell, maybe it was nothing. Maybe he just repeated himself a lot now, maybe his memory played tricks now and then.

Or maybe this was all a real big mistake, maybe I should've told the Boss to take a flying leap and stayed home in bed. Too late now. So much for the Comeback of the Century.

"Look familiar, Joe?"

I guess it did. Hadn't been out this way since December '48, drove up from D.C. with Closky on a night that changed history, such as it was. I wondered if he even remembered that.

We were on 496 now, probably a couple miles yet. Well, let's just get it over with, come up dry and find some gentle way of telling the Boss he's full of crap so we can all go back home. I knew the way, or at least I knew the way until it was time to park and switch to shoe leather. But that's where Closky comes in, right? I almost laughed out loud. The whole thing was so damn pathetic it was making me sick.

Johnny slouched down, eyed the sideview. "What about our company?"

I checked the mirror again, shook my head. "What, you think they got all-night body shops in York? Besides, if he's back there he's been driving with his lights off for the past half hour."

We were almost to the farm now. Somewhere in the pitch dark off to the right was Pipe Creek. I kept one eye on the odometer and slowed down when we were a mile south of Bachman's Valley.

"Did we pass it?" Johnny cranked the window down.

"No, I don't think so."

I slowed down some more. Then I saw it. Turnoff on the right, green road sign flashing in the high beams. EAST SAW MILL ROAD. I eased it on down and took the turn nice and slow.

"So who's home, you figure?"

I shrugged. "Well, his son lives in one house on the property down the road, daughter lives in another. Third one belongs to an ex–state senator."

"And that's the one we want?"

"That's it, unless you want to check with the Colonel back there."

I pulled onto the grass shoulder, killed the engine and lights. I figured the job shouldn't take but a half hour tops.

Johnny zipped up his jacket, pushed the door open. "Guess if we rile anybody we can tell them we're shopping for our Halloween jack-o'-lanterns."

"Right, kid, we'll tell 'em that. Listen, help Victor out of the back there before he asks me if this is a Studebaker again and I shoot him, okay?"

I climbed out and clicked the door shut, handed Johnny the flashlight.

"Hang on to this but keep it off. We'll try to do without."

I stretched, peeled the shirt fabric off my back. When the cold air hit the wet cloth it felt like somebody shoved an ice pick down my spine. Geez, the old body really was falling apart, wasn't it? I stretched again and shook it off, walked around to the other side and helped Johnny pull Closky out of the backseat.

"*Where the fuck are we?*"

"Shhh. We're at Pipe Creek Farm, Victor. Got a little late-night business here."

Closky's voice dropped to a loud whisper. "Pipe Creek Farm? No shit? What, we're going to see Chambers again?"

"No, Victor, I don't think so. Just a little business, a little loose end the Boss wants us to tie up. Then we're going home."

"Oh."

I opened the trunk. "Here, why don't you carry this shovel?"

"I can't see it."

"It's right here, hold out your hand. Got it?"

"Yeah, okay. Listen, the film's not buried though. It's inside a goddam pumpkin."

"Right, right. But there might be something buried, okay? So we're just going to go see."

I took the lead and we started up the hill. The driveway was asphalt now, I could tell that much, even in the dark. Sky was overcast, no moonlight, no nothing. We'd gone maybe fifty yards up the hill when I realized I couldn't see a goddam thing.

"You still back there, boys?"

Nothing. I turned around to listen.

All of a sudden I heard a noise like somebody whacked a sledgehammer on a church bell, then a shriek, then Closky's voice yelling "Jesus Christ" over and over again.

I wanted to shut him up but I had to find him first, stumbled toward the sound of his voice and almost fell. Then Johnny switched on the flashlight and swung the beam around.

We spotted Closky on the ground about twenty feet away. He was sitting up by the side of the drive, hands over his face, moaning. I rushed over, bent down, hands on his shoulders.

"Shhh, Victor, you're gonna wake the damn dead. What the hell happened?"

Johnny ran over and shined the light on Victor's face. There was blood on his head.

"Oh holy shit."

I whispered. "Quiet, will you guys, hell, it's a little blood, he banged his head on something, take it easy or you're going to wake somebody up." I pulled a clean hankie out of my Bermudas and pressed it on Victor's forehead. "You're okay now, Victor, just relax. What the hell happened?"

"Banged my head."

"See, he banged his head. He's okay."

"Banged it on what?"

"Hell, I don't know, let's just all pipe down and see if everything's still quiet."

Johnny killed the light and we sat there for a couple minutes in the dark listening to each other breathe. No porch lights, no barking dogs, nothing.

"Okay, let's see what the hell it was. Where's the flashlight?"

Johnny switched the light on again, swept the beam around the ground in front of us.

"Right there, look. A metal pole."

"It's a sign."

We walked closer. At the top of the pole was a gray-and-black metal plaque. Johnny aimed the beam at it.

FARM OF WHITTAKER AND ESTHER CHAMBERS

has been designated a National Historic Landmark by the Secretary of the Interior. This site possesses national significance in commemorating the history of the United States of America.

"Oh holy hell. Turn off the goddam light."

"What's it say?"

"Nothing, Victor. It says we're here."

"Shit, I knew that."

"Yeah, so did I. Come on, take your shovel. It's just ahead."

My eyes were used to the dark by now and I could make out the outline of the old red barn on the right, and just past that the two-story clapboard house built after Chambers's old place burned down. By some miracle the lights were still out. I led the way around to the back of the barn.

"Okay, kid, hand me the light."

The white pine trees were bigger of course, and the old pump was rusty, but the wood slat fence was still there. The pumpkin patch had gone to weeds, no hint of history here, not so much as a ceramic-and-neon Hummel pumpkin courtesy of Dutch's old Interior Department.

Closky limped over to the pump, started to raise the handle. It creaked. I grabbed his arm.

"Shhh. Too much noise, Victor."

Closky leaned over, whispered in my ear. "I'm thirsty."

I patted his arm. "We'll get something on the way back. Rusty old pump probably doesn't work anyway."

I pushed the gate open and we walked a few steps into the little yard. Except for the crickets it was still dead quiet. For a long time we stood and didn't say anything. Finally Johnny spoke up.

"Well, Joe?"

I was dreading this part, but orders are orders, I guess, even if I wasn't officially working for the Boss anymore. Besides, the sooner we got started the sooner we could call it quits and go home. I reached out and touched Closky's bony arm again. Well, here goes.

"Listen, Victor, we need a little help here. We don't have all night and we don't want to dig up the whole goddam yard. You were with him and I wasn't, remember?"

"What, you mean when he gave us the film?"

"Yeah, this is the barn over here, see, and that's the water pump, and over there's the stand of white pine and the fence where he made me wait. But you were with him, remember? So the question is, can you remember exactly where he stood when he picked up the microfilm? In other words, where was the hollowed-out pumpkin sitting in relation to the barn and the fence?"

38

The wind was picking up, sky was clearing, half-moon shining down through fast-moving clouds. I could see Closky's face now, head bobbing, looking around. Hell, did he even know what I was talking about? Yeah, he knew all right. He had to know. Closky stared at the barn, then back over toward the water pump. Finally he took a couple steps toward the fence like he was pacing it off, looked around again, then took a half dozen steps away from the barn toward the far corner of the yard. He stood still. He held the little shovel by the handle and jammed it into the ground.

"Right here."

I nodded at Johnny. He handed me the light, walked over, pulled out the shovel and started to dig. First he took out a neat slab of sod and laid it to one side. Then he started down. After a few minutes he stopped.

"Listen, Joe, tell me again why we think there's still something here after forty-one years."

"Because Richard Nixon thinks so, and we think exactly what he thinks, okay? Just shut up and dig till you hit China. We come up dry we can always tell him we said hi to Deng."

Johnny took up another half dozen shovelsful. I clicked the light on and poked the beam around the hole.

"Nice, rich soil."

"Yeah, maybe they oughta plant pumpkins again." I switched the light off.

"Seriously, Joe, how far do you want to take this?"

"Oh hell, I don't know, I'm ready to pack it in when you are. He told me if there was anything at all it would be here, period."

Johnny stuck the shovel in the dirt and walked over to the fence to take a breather. I followed him.

"Of course Victor could be a foot or two off."

"Yeah. Or a yard or two. Or a mile or two."

In the moonlight I could see Closky's stooped figure shuffle over to the shovel, pick it up and start poking the ground.

Johnny started over but I held his sleeve. "The hell with it, let him dig for a while."

We stood by the fence. The air felt real cold now, chilly breeze fluttering my Harry Truman shirt. Geez, was it really forty-one years since I stood on this spot in my suit and topcoat, cold and foggy December night, start of a long story I figured was played out long ago. It was, too. Had to be. Hell, if this wasn't a waste of time I didn't know what was.

"Listen, Johnny, what say we fill the damn hole back in and get the hell out of here."

"Yeah, I guess. Looks like Victor's way ahead of you, though."

I looked over at Closky. Sure enough, he was shoveling the dirt back into the hole. Good. Now we could forget the whole damn thing. Check into a motel someplace, run Victor back to Allenwood tomorrow, drop Johnny off in Saddle River and I could be back in Key West in time to catch Game Three on the Trinitron. I walked over.

"You want me to finish that for you, Victor?"

"Nah, I can handle it. Change of pace from sweeping out my fuckin' birdcage every goddam day."

"Yeah, well, I guess you heard we're headin' out, right?"

"Might as well, we're done here."

"Right. Here, I'll get that." I bent down and laid the sod back in, then stamped it down. "You want to carry the shovel again, Victor?"

"Okay. You want to carry this?"

He reached into his pocket and held his hand out. I heard something rattling but couldn't see so I switched on the light.

His bony hand was shaking from the cold. The rattling noise came from what he was holding.

It was a battered old aluminum canister the size of a salt shaker, wrapped in black electrical tape, covered with fresh dirt.

Johnny shook his head. His voice was a whisper.

"It's not possible, Joe."

We all stared at the canister for what must've been a full minute. The kid was right, of course. It wasn't really possible. It couldn't be. Not after forty-one years.

I grabbed the canister from Closky's hand, shoved it in my pocket and we left.

3

August 7, 1948

We pulled up to Penn Station at the Seventh Avenue carriage entrance. Closky paid the driver a buck with a ten-cent tip. Up ahead McDowell, Hébert, and the subcommittee chair were climbing out of the lead car. We formed up again on the sidewalk.

"Anybody for lunch at the Savarin?" Hébert's Cajun palate on overtime again. Sounded good to me.

Nixon checked his watch, shook his head. "Not if we're going to make the four-fifteen. Let's just head for the lunchroom."

Hébert frowned. Nixon led the way through the big columns that were supposed to look like the Brandenburg Gate, except somebody overdid it and put six Kraut eagles on top instead of the horses and chariot. When we got inside we marched across the main waiting room and followed the smell of burgers in onions up the steps to the arcade. The huge lunchroom was pretty packed but the three bigwigs managed to claim the last empty table. Closky and I settled for a pair of stools down near the six chromium coffee urns that always reminded me of the boiler room on the *Titanic*. I ordered a burger and coffee. Closky spent a good minute staring at the counter boy, finally ordered a tuna sandwich.

"Geez, he was great, Joey, wasn't he? What a mind, what a grasp of detail. God, the man's a genius."

"What, Chambers? He had answers, that's for sure."

"No kidding. And that damn bird, what was it called?"

I checked my notes. "A prothonotary warbler."

"Right. That's the kind of thing a man knows when he's telling the truth, Joey. Mark my words, I can spot a phony a mile away and Chambers is no phony."

I sighed. Okay, so maybe I was impressed too. We grilled Chambers for two and a half hours up in an empty room at the Foley Square courthouse, fired questions at him one after another and he never flinched. Either he really knew Hiss or he was a hell of an actor working off a hell of a script. Still, a lot of things didn't add up.

"What about the stuff he got wrong?"

Closky finally took a bite of his sandwich. "Like what?"

"Victor, are you serious? Not that I'd mention it to the Boss at this point, but you know, stuff like claiming Hiss is deaf in one ear. He isn't. Or that he walks with a mince. He doesn't. Or Hiss's height, for God's sake. Chambers said Hiss was five-eight. He's six feet tall. Now are you telling me Chambers met Hiss twice a week for two years, stayed at his house for days at a time, shared his every secret, and he can't even guess the guy's height within four inches?"

Closky frowned. "Let me tell you something, Joey. I don't blame you for asking questions, okay? I'm not going to chew out your ass every time you call a shot like you see it. I respect that. But okay, let's take something like Hiss's height. You're right, it's crazy for Chambers to be that far off. But sometimes the truth is crazy. Because look at it the other way. Say Chambers was coached, say the whole thing's a commie frame-up and he memorized all that crap about Hiss's hobbies and family and houses and apartments and furniture. Don't you think he'd memorize his goddam height too? I mean, wouldn't that be one of the very first things he'd get straight? But he didn't, he was wrong about it, and if you want my

42

opinion, that just makes it all the more convincing he's telling the truth."

Well, I wasn't going to win this argument, I could see that much. Chambers gets the details right, it proves he knew Hiss. He gets the details wrong, it proves the same thing.

"So what's the next step, grill Hiss?"

"Nah, not yet. First we'll want to talk to that other Commie Chambers fingered, the guy from Treasury, Harry White."

"Pretty big fish though, U.S. head of the IMF. Hard to believe he's a Commie too."

Closky chuckled. "Don't let 'em fool you, Joey, the sonsofbitches are everywhere. We've just got to be smarter than they are, that's all. Once we sweat some answers out of White we'll get ready to go after Hiss. Check the leases on those apartments, the kennel on Wisconsin Avenue where Hiss boarded his cocker spaniel, title transfer on the Model A, the whole bit. See what we can dig up to confirm Chambers's testimony before we make horses' asses out of ourselves on the television."

"Sounds like now you're not so sure about Chambers after all."

"Well, Joey, there's gut feelings and then there's business, know what I mean? Right now I'd just about bet the farm on Chambers, but I'd want to have proof in my hand before I put the Boss in front of those cameras." He winked. "Plus I'd make sure it was Chambers's farm."

I flagged down an apron, got a refill on my coffee. "So where do you see this heading, Victor? You serious about wanting Strom in the White House this fall or is that just hot air?"

Closky brightened up. "Hell, it's a four-way race, any number of ways your Dixiecrats could win, mathematically speakin'." He pushed his plate aside, flipped the place mat over, pulled out his Parker pen. Hand flew across the paper, outline of the U.S. "Look, Thurmond takes the Deep South, right? Let's get optimistic and give him a few border states. Dewey takes New York and Pennsylvania. Give Truman Missouri if he's lucky. Wallace, well, is it too crazy to say he takes California? So nobody gets an electoral majority and the vote goes to the House."

"And the House elects Strom Thurmond president of the United States?"

Closky didn't answer; he was hunched over the place mat shading in the old Confederacy. Then he shaded in Arizona and New Mexico for good measure, lighter shading on Kentucky and West Virginia. Finally he looked up.

"Look, I'll level with you, Joey, at this point I'd settle for Dewey. That gives us Dulles at State, Brownell at Justice, much more favorable climate for the intelligence business, no question about that. Any luck we can start bringing the boys over from Berlin in December, bring the files over too, maybe set up shop right down in the District. Or maybe across the river in Virginia, I don't know yet."

Wait a minute. "Bring the boys over? What, you mean like Blunt and those guys? Are you serious, they're still around?"

Closky grinned. "They're still around and they've still got the files. Just waiting for us to settle in over here, waiting for the climate to shift. Waiting for the word from me."

I couldn't believe it. I guess somehow I thought this was it, thought the espionage game was over, thought we'd been kicked out of paradise or hell or wherever it was we were to end our days as second-rate Committee investigators snapping photos of Commies under beds. And for sure I thought Closky got his wings clipped permanently after that trouble with the boy. Now he tells me the whole damn Berlin operation survived, plus he still had the pull to set it back up over here.

"I'll tell you the key, Joey. The key is we nail Hiss or White or whoever the hell we and let folks chalk the win up to that man over there." He nodded across the room. Nixon was just getting up. "That'll make him big news, national news, probably even put him in the Senate two years from now just like he said. I know how it's going to work, Joey, believe me, I know exactly how it's going to work. Scripture summed it up, whither he goeth, we're gonna go, where he lodgeth we're gonna lodge, his gods are our gods, you name it. The man is goin' places, Joey. And so are we."

44

I looked across the room. McDowell and Hébert were putting on their topcoats. Nixon was standing by the table, not moving, staring at us. Finally he held a hand out and waved us over.

We got up and followed him.

October 15, 1989

Finding a microfilm machine in suburban Maryland first thing Sunday morning wasn't the easiest thing in the world. Johnny wanted to drive straight down to D.C. but I figured there had to be someplace closer than that, and a quick check of the phone book proved me right. Main branch of the Baltimore County public library had Sunday hours, somebody's tax dollars at work.

We followed the motel clerk's directions down Route 45, crossed the Baltimore Beltway into Towson, hung a left at a Wendy's and pulled into a big concrete garage that said LIBRARY PARKING. I locked the T-bird up on the third level. Johnny grabbed the briefcase, I helped Closky climb out of the backseat and we headed inside.

On the way past the newspaper rack I shot a quick glance at the sports page in the morning *Sun*. A's beat the Giants five-zip in the Series opener at Oakland. Five-hitter for Stewart, wasted effort by Jack Clark. Serves 'em right for leaving the Polo Grounds.

Meanwhile Johnny got a handful of dimes from the librarian and sat down at the microfilm reader. He clicked the machine on, fan came up with a loud hum. Then he peeled the tape off the canister, pulled the film out, started winding it onto an empty spool.

Last night at the motel Johnny and I argued for a good half hour about breaking the seal on the canister, finally figured what the hell, switched off the lights and took a chance, snuck a peek at what we thought was an exposed roll of forty-one-year-old Kodak microfilm. But damned if the film wasn't brand-new. Already developed too, if you can believe that. So whatever it was, it wasn't something Chambers left behind in '48.

Johnny was still winding the film onto the big plastic spool, shaking his head. "I still say this is some kind of hoax, Joe."

"Guess we'll soon find out." I glanced at Closky. He was sitting in an orange vinyl chair reading *National Geographic*. "I'll make sure Victor has enough magazines, you print out the copies." Closky seemed happy enough. That morning at Friendly's he put away more pancakes than any man or beast I'd ever seen, but then I guess he didn't get much of that at Allenwood. Slept pretty good last night too, at least for the four hours or so we managed to cram in once we found the Econo-Lodge off 695. Wish I could say the same for myself, but every joint in my body ached and the Breakfast Combo Number 2 wasn't sitting quite right either. Maybe I was just keyed up.

Johnny finally got the film threaded, cranked it and pulled up the first page. I looked at the screen. First thing to come in focus were fat black letters at the top of the page:

GEHEIME KOMMANDOSACHE

"Secret Command Matter." The highest East German security classification. What the hell?

Johnny dropped in a dime, hit the PRINT key. The hum got louder, the machine clicked and whirred, spat out a hard copy. Johnny cranked the reel up a frame, popped in the next dime.

I glanced at the first couple pages. Account numbers, columns of figures, dates, names of a half dozen Kraut companies I'd never heard of. Intrac, Zentral-Kommerz, Transinter, Gerlach, Forgber, Genex. Then some kind of code references: B-Geschäft, C-Geschäft. "B-Business" and "C-Business," whatever that meant.

"Any idea what this is all about, kid?"

Johnny plunked another dime in, hit the key. "Well, Genex is the East German outfit that imports consumer goods from the West and sells them at Intershops for hard currency. Gerlach and Forgber I never heard of, but from what I can see here it looks like they're into scavenging microelectronics and other high-tech goodies in the West. Which means they work for Stasi, most likely."

Holy hell. The dreaded Stasi. East German State Security, *Staatssicherheit*. Private army of aging party boss Erich Honecker. Gestapo in cheap windbreakers, the Kraut KGB. Just what we needed.

"Any dates on this stuff?"

Johnny pointed to a blurred line in the corner of the screen. "15 June 89." Two months ago.

"So you figure these are actual Stasi documents?"

"I think so, because—"

"Hey, where the fuck's the bathroom in this place?"

Uh-oh. From across the room a librarian coughed, glared over at us. So much for keeping a low profile.

I walked over to Closky, patted his arm, tried to shush him. He shook me off.

"Get off of me, you goddam retard. Where the fuck are we anyway?"

I kept my voice down. "We're in a public library outside Baltimore, Victor. We're printing out the film we got last night at the farm."

He nodded his head about a dozen times. "Good idea. Don't want it to go bad."

"Right. Come on, I'll show you where the bathroom is." I took him into the men's room and waited outside the stall.

So the stuff was East German. Go figure. Nixon sends us out to Chambers's farm looking for a codex to the Pumpkin Papers and we turn up this. No doubt a can of worms all its own, but at least it was a new can of worms. No need to bring up all that old Hiss crap now, no need to tell Johnny about it, no need to even think about it. Fine with me.

I popped a couple Advil, cupped my hand and washed them down with water from the sink, dried my beard with a paper towel. Face in the mirror looked every minute of my sixty-four years, long hair and beard gone to gray now, fat red face lined and leathery from too much sun in too many Key West summers. I pulled myself up straight, stretched my neck until I felt it crack. Ah, hell. At least my Harry Truman shirt was clean.

Couple minutes later Victor shuffled out, started to wash his hands. Then he stopped, looked at me in the mirror.

"Where the fuck are we, anyway?"

"Library, Victor. We're printing out the film, remember?"

"Oh right, right."

When we got back to the machine Johnny had a stack of about a dozen pages piled on the table. I leafed through them.

"You been reading these?"

"Yeah. So far it's all high-level stuff, series of memos from East Germany's so-called Office of Commercial Coordination, KoKo for short. Shady financial deals, mostly. Sale of weapons to third-world countries, sale of political prisoners, fines on foreign drivers, et cetera."

"You were about to tell me why you think they're Stasi documents."

"What? Oh right, look, here's a memo from Mann to KoKo deputy director Günter Schmidt dated July fifth."

"Who's Mann?"

"You're kidding, right? *Genosse Generaloberst* Alexander Friedrich Mann. Came out of nowhere a half dozen years ago to mastermind East Germany's shadow economy. Supposedly the brains behind the billion-mark credit they finagled from West Germany a couple years back. CIA claims Honecker secretly named him a three-star general in Stasi even though his true rank in the so-called People's Army is only major. But the really interesting thing is that nobody's ever—whoa, wait a minute."

"What's up?"

Johnny pointed to the screen. "Wow, look at this, Joe. 'Mann to Schmidt, 3 August '89. *Geheime Kommandosache.* Subject, external debt of the German Democratic Republic.'"

"Which officially doesn't exist?"

"Right. But which unofficially, according to this, is twenty-point-five U.S. dollars with a bullet. Jesus, *twenty-point-five billion.*"

"Puts them in a league with what, Haiti?"

"If they're lucky. Man, these guys are in trouble."

"Well, we all knew that. Hell, pick up the papers and there's pictures of East Germans climbing over the wall at the West German embassy in Prague, sprinting across the Hungarian-Austrian border, lining up for exit visas in Warsaw, you name it."

"Yeah, but this is different. They can fix that if they want to, crack down on dissent, seal off the borders to the Socialist Brotherlands with a couple thousand Vopos, maybe even machine-gun a few more wall jumpers. But they can't take the debt service on twenty and a half billion bucks out behind Stasi HQ and shoot it."

Good point. "Okay, Johnny, I give up. Who buried this can of film at Chambers's farm and how in hell did Nixon know it was there?"

Johnny dropped in another dime, hit the PRINT key. The machine whirred. "First question, I don't know. Second question, the Chinese told him."

"The Chinese? What, all of them?"

"I don't know, all he told me was he heard it in Beijing two weeks ago. And from the time he got back he barely stopped pacing, said we had to get you and Victor back on the payroll ASAP to clear things up."

I stared at the screen. Me and Victor. Good choice. "And why would the goddam Chinese happen to know about this as opposed to, say, the goddam Hottentots?"

Johnny heaved a sigh. "Because they heard it from the East Germans. Honecker's deputy Egon Krenz flew over with half the Politburo for Communist China's fortieth birthday party the week before last. Guess since the Russians called off the Cold War the East Germans are odd man out in Europe now, so they're cozying up to the last bastion of the True Faith."

"Birds of a feather. And what, Nixon was there same time as Krenz?"

"Well, just about. Actually, they invited him but he wouldn't go for the fortieth anniversary, said it would've looked like he supported the massacre and all that. So they let him come the week after, by which time Krenz was back in Berlin. But Krenz left a message, and Nixon got it."

"The message being what, exactly? The contents of the microfilm? Or where it was buried, or both?"

"Good question. He was vague about that."

49

"Terrific. You see what I'm getting at, right, kid? I mean, it makes a big difference whether the East Germans lost this stuff and want it returned or whether they planted it at Chambers's old farm as some kind of message."

"I don't know, Joe. If somebody stole this film I can't picture them hiding it at Chambers's farm. It's gotta be a plant, gotta be a message aimed at us."

"Maybe." I tried to work it out in my head. The East Germans come to China, fine. They have a secret message for a soon-to-be-visiting U.S. elder statesman, viz, Richard Nixon, fine. So Krenz tells Deng and Deng tells Dick. But tells him what, exactly? "Send your boys to Pipe Creek Farm, have them walk ten paces and dig three feet down and you'll get a big surprise"? We did that and got one, all right.

"Hey, wait a minute, Joe, check this out."

I looked down at the screen. Personal memo out of KoKo HQ dated two months ago. My German was a little rusty, but it wasn't hard to figure out what the kid was getting all excited about.

MINISTRY OF FOREIGN TRADE
OFFICE OF COMMERCIAL COORDINATION
WALLSTRASSE 17-22   1020 BERLIN

17 August 1989
To: Mann
From: Schmidt

GEHEIME KOMMANDOSACHE

Loyal Comrade Lieutenant General!
    Your note of 3 August is alarming in the extreme. Clearly radical measures are called for to preserve the financial and political sovereignty of our Republic. I again call your attention to Comrade Tjaden's rumored possession of the so-called K-Document (K for our old friend Karl, I presume?) If such a document exists, it is high time we made use of it. Urgently recommend you exert your influence to elicit favorable response from Tjaden.

Johnny pointed at the screen. " 'Karl'?"

I didn't say anything. Johnny turned around. "Joe, don't you get it? 'Karl' was Chambers's code name in the 1930s communist underground."

I got it all right, I just didn't like it. "Also happens to be the name of a couple hundred thousand Krauts."

"Right, but we didn't find this film on their farm, did we?"

Well, he had a point there, much as I hated to admit it. Damn. Five minutes ago I had myself convinced I was off the hook, figured whatever this crap was it wasn't the Hiss case. But now I wasn't so sure.

"Listen, Joe, I may be jumping the gun here, but I've got an opinion on this. I think this so-called K-document is the one we're looking for. I think the East Germans have got it, and I think they got it from Chambers, say maybe in '59 when he flew to Vienna to meet Arthur Koestler. I also think somebody from over there planted this film at the farm, then had Krenz tip off Nixon so we would find it. Somebody who wanted to send us a message."

I mulled that one over for a sec. "Somebody with a sense of history, sense of irony?"

"Right. Plus maybe a sense of humor."

"Yeah, that too I guess." I could even think of one guy who filled that bill, one guy in the world who would've picked that particular way to send us a message. But it didn't make sense. You don't get messages from a dead man.

I pointed at the other name on the screen. "Any idea who 'Comrade Tjaden' is?"

Big frown now, smell o' burnin' wood. Johnny got up, walked over to a catalog computer, slapped a few keys, checked the screen and disappeared into the stacks. A minute later he was back, leafing through a fat red book. He set it down on the table.

"Bingo."

The book was open to a photo of a Dutch passport dated 1935. Head shot of a young guy, mid-twenties maybe, wavy hair and glasses. Face rang a bell but I couldn't place it. The name under it was Marten Tjaden.

Johnny tapped the page with his finger. "Only he wasn't Dutch, he was German. The passport's a phony, cover for the underground head of the Greater Berlin Communist Youth League, young

Rhinelander about to get himself busted by the Gestapo and spend ten years in the Brandenburg-Goerden penitentiary. Russians sprung him in '45 and he went on to make a name for himself, eventually wrote this book."

"Okay, kid, I give up. Who the hell is it?"

Johnny flipped back to the title page.

The book was called *From My Life*.

It was the autobiography of Erich Honecker.

Johnny reached under the chair, pulled out the old calfskin briefcase. "Looks like we'll be needing this after all, Joe." He clicked the latch open, slid the envelope out, unfolded the flap.

I peeked inside. Passports, driver's licenses, Social Security cards, everything you'd need for a long trip. That plus the money. Small bills and traveler's checks, phony Eurocards sharp as any the boys in Documents ever turned out. I didn't see any plane tickets, but something told me they were in there too. We were still funded, all right.

Johnny gathered up the printouts and slipped them into the briefcase next to the envelope. He snapped the latch shut. I glanced over at Closky.

"Guess they'll be missing him back at Allenwood tomorrow, huh?"

"Yeah, assuming he didn't leave a dummy in his bunk."

"Let's assume he didn't. You figure government's gonna cover this one for us?"

Johnny shrugged. "If we pull this off it won't matter. If we don't pull it off, it won't matter either."

Philosophy. Always my favorite subject.

Johnny checked his watch. "You willing to trust your car to long-term parking at Dulles?"

Ah, hell. "Sounds like we'll be catching the rest of the Series on AFN."

Johnny winked. "It won't be so bad, Joe. They got TV over there now."

I shook my head, muttered a curse, walked over to Closky, slipped the *National Geographic* out of his hands. He didn't say anything. I tugged on his baggy sleeve. "Up 'n' at 'em, Victor, time to go."

He looked up. "Why, where we goin'?"

I kept hold of his sleeve, leaned down, looked him in the eye. "Berlin."

For a second his eyes looked clear, glimmer of recognition in the baby blues. Glimmer of satisfaction, almost. Then it was gone and his head started that bob and weave again.

"They lift the blockade yet?"

I sighed. "Yeah, Victor, they did. Forty years ago. C'mon, we'll stop on the way to the airport and buy you a new suit."

Johnny led the way out the library door. It was chilly in the parking garage, loud hum of a heat pump behind a cyclone fence in one corner. I popped the rear deck on the T-bird and tossed the briefcase back in the trunk. I was about to slam it shut when I saw the car. Next level down, just visible between the guardrails. Green Citroën, passenger-side door smashed in, glass busted.

Then I heard the voice.

"You can leave that open."

German accent. We both spun around.

Two beefy young guys Johnny's size, close haircuts on big Nordic heads, a blond and a redhead, nylon windbreakers and ersatz chinos. Faces bruised and cut, blond guy's left eye swollen shut. For some reason he was the one with the gun, Makarov 9mm from the look of it.

I played for time. "Looks like you boys had a little accident. Hope your boss isn't too burned up about the car."

They weren't laughing. The redhead pointed at the trunk. "We'll take the briefcase, Grandpa."

Grandpa my ass. I damn near slugged him, pistol or no. Johnny didn't move. Closky was making some kind of gurgling noise.

The guy with the Makarov took a step toward us. "Now!"

All of a sudden Closky let out a shriek, grabbed his chest, slumped against the car. The two Krauts looked at him. Johnny took the cue, aimed a kick that sent the pistol skittering down the concrete slope. Blondie started after it but I made a lunge and tackled him. Guess I was about to find out if the Boss was right about guys half my age.

We both got up and he landed a punch in my gut, then a glancing blow off my jaw that just missed connecting for the KO. I figured the plan was to let him pummel me until Johnny could finish off his buddy, then come bail me out. So far the first part was working.

I aimed a weak punch at his good eye but he ducked away, then came back with a couple of quick jabs in my left side that knocked me off balance. He connected again and I went down hard and a second later he was on top of me. He jammed his forearm across my neck to pin me to the concrete. A jolt of pain shot down my spine as he brought his other arm up for the blow to my face we both knew would send me out.

Then I heard the *gong*.

His face got a dumb look before he collapsed on top of me, nose pressed against mine, dead weight. His breath came out with an *oof*. It stank. I rolled over and shoved him off, stood up.

"Thanks, Victor."

Closky threw the shovel back in the trunk.

"Don't fuckin' mention it." He pointed at Johnny and Red over in the corner. "Ain't over yet, though."

"Damn near." The red-haired Kraut was already staggering when Johnny landed a kick in the groin that doubled him over, then came up with a knee to the chin. I heard his jaw snap and watched him crumple to the ground. Johnny stood over him for a second, breathing hard. Then he turned to me.

"You okay, Joe?"

I rubbed my face on my sleeve. Touch of blood but not much. "Yeah, thanks to the Sultan of Swat here."

Closky grinned, dusted his bony hands.

We went through their pockets while they were still out cold. Car keys and cash, maybe a couple hundred bucks. Then we checked the Citroën. No surprises there either. Diplomatic plates, D.C. registration in the glove box to the embassy of the German Democratic Republic on Massachusetts Avenue.

I handed the registration card to Johnny. "Okay, kid, tell me this. If the papers were a Stasi plant aimed at us, how come these goons want them?"

Johnny frowned. "I don't know. I'm still trying to figure out how they found us."

We looked at each other. Then we both thought of it at the same time, ran back up the slope to the T-bird. We opened the doors and climbed in.

"Okay, where didn't we look?" Johnny slammed a fist down on the dash, leaned forward. He popped the glove box and pulled the flashlight out, shined it into the hole in the dash where the Volumatic used to be, reached a hand in, lost an arm up to his elbow. Nothing. Then he reached in farther, gave a yank. When his hand came out he was holding a black metal box the size of a cigarette pack.

Closky caught up with us, leaned down, poked his head in the window. "I always thought they were bigger."

Johnny shook his head. "Art of concealment, gentlemen. Completely natural, completely unexpected."

August 16, 1948

"That goddamned Hiss! He's a lying sonofabitch!" Dick Nixon pounded a fist on the table, face red, but with a grin spreading fast across his dark jowls.

We were in the Committee's private office next to the hearing room after a late-afternoon session that went into overtime and then some. Looked like Hiss was finally starting to lose the edge off his sass after Nixon grilled him for two hours straight on the Amazing Disappearing Ford, the missing apartment lease and a hundred other holes in his story. Now claimed maybe he *did* know somebody who looked like Chambers after all, fella by the name of George Crosley who sublet an apartment near Wardman Park from him back in the summer of '35.

Nixon picked up the phone, asked for long distance. He put his hand over the receiver, winked. "A lying son of a— Yes, Operator, I'd like to place a station-to-station call to Westminster, Maryland." He recited Chambers's number from memory. "Thank you, Operator." He looked at Closky, held up an index finger.

"Good evening, Mr. Chambers, this is Richard Nixon. I hope I'm not calling too late. Good, good. Well, we've just finished speaking with Mr. Hiss and I have two brief questions for you. First, did you ever stay in his apartment on Twenty-eighth Street? You did?" Big grin, thumbs-up. "All right, second question. Mr. Hiss claims the man he's calling 'Crosley' had a wife with a very dark complexion. Did Hiss ever see Mrs. Chambers, and is it possible she is the woman he's alluding to?" Bigger grin this time, hand slapping the table. "I see. Well, that's very good news, Mr. Chambers. We'll be talking again soon. Right. Good-bye."

Nixon hung up. "Sonofabitch, he really *does* know him! The case is cracked, boys, now all we have to do is get the two of them together to prove it. The sooner the better, too."

"Not scheduled till the twenty-fifth," I said.

Nixon frowned. "Yeah, I guess you're right. Wouldn't hurt to move it up a little, though. Don't want to give the bastard the chance to build his story, get his ducks in a row and so forth."

He thumbed through the latest pile of transcripts. The secretaries were bringing them in a couple dozen pages at a time, fast as they could type them up from the steno notes, but it wasn't fast enough for the Boss. He'd keep us here all night if he had to.

"What I'd really like to do is nail the whole goddam crew, White, Remington, Wadleigh, every one of the goddam commie sonsofbitches. Then we'd be getting somewhere."

"Won't be easy," Closky said. "They're all taking the Fifth. Except for White and Hiss."

Nixon rubbed his jowls. "Yeah, that makes it tough all right. Of course, White's playing the same game as Hiss, flat-out denial of everything Chambers said, which means if Hiss cracks we've got a shot at White too."

"Or vice versa," I said. Actually, White was probably as big a fish as Hiss, bigger maybe. Co-author of the Morgenthau Plan, assistant secretary at Treasury who helped dream up the World Bank, now the U.S. director of the IMF. Hard to believe he was a commie spy too, but he was on Chambers's list with everybody else.

Closky slurped down a mouthful of Nescafé, balanced the mug on a pile of transcripts. "We handled White bad on Friday, though, sir. Thomas never should have badgered him like that. Hell, reading his doctor's note out loud, cracking wise about him playing Ping-Pong with a bad heart, making him sound like a goldbrick just because he wanted to take a breather. It wasn't smart, it was bad PR, it'll just stir up sympathy for the old bastard."

Nixon shrugged. "The hell with it, he'll get over it." He tapped a finger on the transcript, leaned back in his chair. "You know what I'm thinking about, boys? I'm thinking about that goddam car. Now, Chambers told us in New York that Hiss gave his old Model A to the Commies when he bought his new Plymouth. Drove it to a commie service station and just dropped it off. Now, today Hiss claims he gave the car to this 'Crosley' fellow, a near-total stranger, mind you, and let me say a stranger who just stiffed him on two months' rent, but now Hiss can't remember the details, can't even remember if he actually did it or not."

I shrugged. "Of course, even Chambers admitted the car was a piece of junk, old '29 Ford, not worth much."

Nixon shook his head. "What's the goddam difference? I don't care how old the goddam thing is, if I gave somebody an automobile in 1935, I would goddam well remember it today, I can tell you that much."

We went on like that, Nixon sifting through the transcript, preaching a homily on every line like it was holy writ, Closky and me taking notes for the next go-round, all of us slugging down cold Nescafé to keep our eyes on the page. The big window was open, fan on the sill blowing in wet night air that was almost starting to turn a little cool.

It must've been close to midnight when Nixon finally decided to wrap it up. He rubbed his eyes, clicked off the desk lamp. For a minute I thought he was going to put his head down right on the big green blotter.

Before he did, though, there was a knock at the door. Nixon grumbled "Come in." It was Bert Andrews, Washington correspondent for the *Herald-Trib* and Nixon's personal messenger boy, printed every scrap of secret testimony we tossed his way. So far the relationship was working out pretty good.

Nixon stood up, walked over and shook Andrews's hand. He pointed at the transcript on his desk. "Got some hot new stuff here,

Bert, but I can't give it to you this time, they'll smell a rat. I'll have to go with Carl Levin, maybe funnel it to him through the FBI."

Andrews shrugged. "Don't worry about it, Congressman, I'll pick something up next time. Listen, you heard Babe Ruth died, right?"

Oh hell. I'd seen that one coming, I guess, death watch outside Memorial Hospital for the past week. Still, it hit me in the gut. Nixon was shoving papers in his briefcase. "Who?"

Andrews shot Closky a glance. Closky shrugged. "Babe Ruth," Andrews said. "Okay, so you're not a big Yankee fan, but I thought you'd at least be glad the old Bambino's gonna take up some ink on page one tomorrow."

Nixon still didn't look up. "How so?"

Andrews frowned. "You mean you fellas really haven't heard the news? What, no teletype in here? Not even a radio?"

Now he finally looked up. "What news are you talking about, Bert?"

Andrews looked at all three of us. Then he zeroed in on Nixon. "Harry White. He's dead too."

Nixon's face went blank. "Bert, if you're joking—"

Andrews shook his head. "No joke, Congressman. He had another heart attack this afternoon up at his place in New Hampshire. Only this time it was fatal." He winked. "Must've been all that Ping-Pong."

Nixon sank down in his chair. "Oh my God."

Closky shook his head. "See, I *told* you Thomas screwed up. Making fun of his weak heart, now the old guy keels over and it looks like we drove him to it. Which we probably—"

"Shut up, Victor." Nixon stood up, started pacing. His face was white, fist grinding into his palm, veins on his hands about to pop. "Goddam commie Jew bastard. Goddam sonofabitch. Sonofabitch couldn't have died a week ago, no, he had to wait till after we grill him so he can make us look like goddam grand inquisitors and ruin my career in the bargain. Shit. This is going to be all over the goddam papers tomorrow. No offense, Bert, but all those Hebrew bloodsuckers that run the press are going to play this one like a Jewball *Uncle Tom's Cabin*, make no mistake. Damn. Hell."

Closky shrugged. "So hold the hearing tomorrow."

Nixon's head spun around. "What?"

"Hold the goddam hearing tomorrow. Hell, you can even hold it in New York if you want, Hiss and Chambers are there already and that way Hiss won't have time to figure out what's up. We rent a hotel room, call Hiss up on some phony pretext and let him walk smack into an executive session. So okay, White gets the headlines this morning, but we knock him off page one the next day. And if our headline says HISS ADMITS KNOWING CHAMBERS, well, this time next week folks are going to be saying 'Harry Dexter who?' "

Nixon was still pacing. He looked at his watch. "Right, right. Okay, let's do it. Pope, get on the horn and book us a suite in the Commodore on Forty-second Street. First thing tomorrow morning I'll call Chambers at *Time* magazine and tell him to meet us in the hotel lobby right after work. Then I'll round up McDowell and Thomas, they can go up with us. Who else? Stripling and Ben of course, plus a stenotypist. Oh, and once we get to New York, we can call Hiss. Victor, you handle that. Tell him we just need to see him for a few minutes, *don't* tell him Chambers will be there, don't tell him a goddam thing, let it be a shock like you said." He turned to Andrews. "Bert, you can have this one, but you've got to promise you'll keep it under your hat until six o'clock tomorrow night."

Andrews grinned. "No problem, Congressman. Just keep the pipeline open."

October 16, 1989

I could feel the Pan Am frozen breakfast churning up in my gut and my head was pounding in time with the windshield wipers as Johnny nudged our silver rental Mercedes through rush-hour traffic on Kantstrasse. The cold, misty drizzle the Berliners don't bother to call rain still hadn't let up, not even after forty-two years.

Geez, what was it about this place that got me so worked up? What did I think, the MPs were going to pull us over, nail me on a forty-year-old AWOL charge and slap me back in the damn stockade as a sixty-four-year-old buck private? No, it wasn't that. At least I didn't think so.

"Pretty crazy town, eh, Joe?"

Crazy is right. We were stopped for a red light at the Zoo station, sidewalks packed with Krauts in suede coats and silk scarves stifling a collective goose step as they surged across the street and down to the Kudamm to fling their dough around in upscale shops. I cracked the window, took in the damp air mixed with the greasy smell of bratwurst frying from a stand at the corner. Over by the Zoo station entrance a Turk in a GI fatigue jacket was screaming broken German at a scrawny little blonde with a dirty face. He slapped her and she started to cry. Then the light changed and we pulled away.

"I love this place, Joe, it's exciting, know what I mean? You got all this action but you got history too. Memorial Church over there with the busted-off tower from the SS's last stand, Zoo Palace, where Goebbels cried at *Gone with the Wind,* Frederick the Great buried out there somewhere, the whole bit. Then the other side across the Wall, a different world. It's wild, you know?"

"Yeah, it's wild, kid. Look out now, that's Hohenzollerndamm coming up. You want to turn right and park it wherever you can."

Hohenzollerndamm was a broad boulevard that started downtown and ran all the way out to the Grünewald. Up at this end it was lined with big old gray stone row houses with ironwork balconies, 1870s *Bürger* mansions built with French money after the Prussian War, most of them carved up for apartments now. The one we wanted was in the next block.

Johnny found a spot and hit the brakes. He backed in, turned off the wipers and killed the ignition.

"Nice park job, kid. Most of your Krauts usually end up on the sidewalk. Come on, let's help Victor out."

Closky shoved the back door open. "I can get out myself, I'm not a goddam cripple."

Closky was wearing the ersatz Palm Beach suit we bought him at the Chevy Chase Woody's yesterday. Still looked pretty sharp, even after sleeping on the plane, which is more than I could say for myself. At least the drizzle in my face was waking me up. Remind me to buy a raincoat. I pulled a comb out of my back pocket, ran it through my beard.

We locked the car and headed down the wide stone walk to Number 3. I tugged the heavy wooden door open and we ducked into the vestibule out of the drizzle. Inside it was still chilly, smelled musty and damp, stairwell roughly the size of a grain elevator, smooth hardwood banister curving up, worn red carpet that looked like it felt the scuff of jackboots in its day.

Johnny switched the briefcase to his left hand and grabbed the railing. He took a deep breath. "Fifth floor?"

"Yeah. If I collapse just send me up with the coal man."

My legs were stiff as hell from the eight-hour flight and Closky stopped on every third step to catch his breath but somehow we made it. I pressed the buzzer. "He knows we're comin', right?"

"Hope so. Hell of a shock if he doesn't."

The door creaked open. I wasn't ready for the snow-white hair, but not much else was different since I last saw Ed Blunt at the Key Biscayne Hotel in '83. Still a big bear of a guy, even in his late sixties. Same lumpy face, same big grin.

"Welcome to Berlin, sirs." Blunt shook my hand, then Johnny's. "Sorry I couldn't pick you up at the airport, but you-know-who wanted me near the fax machine." He winked at Johnny.

Then he turned to Closky and his face dropped. His voice got quiet. "Colonel?"

Closky and Blunt were the same height, same bulk too once upon a time, back before Blunt got religion and Closky had it sweated out of him in stir. Now here they were, two old men with a long shared past. Closky nodded and stared, blue eyes searching Blunt's craggy face like radar, dead silence.

Then Closky's face lit up, almost like he was taking off a mask. For the first time since we picked him up at Allenwood, he smiled. He stuck out his hand.

"Well, hello, Sergeant," he said. "Long time no see."

Blunt just grinned. He held the door and waved us in.

It was warm inside at least, tile oven cranked up near the door. Past that it looked pretty much like I'd always heard, combination junk shop, IBM showroom and antiques store. Beat-up sofa and huge stuffed chairs probably original equipment from the age of the first Wilhelm, big mahogany armoire and carved wooden desk, likewise early *Kaiserzeit*. Couple old radios from the thirties, table model perched on top of a big console, shiny black typewriter and an adding machine, scattered bits and pieces of scrap metal you could either melt down for Mauser bullets or build a mechanical man from, depending on your mood. Guess Blunt hadn't lost his touch.

Oh, and a photocopier and, sure enough, a fax machine, desktop computer, modem, couple more boxes of streamlined beige plastic I didn't even recognize, all of it linked up in a spaghetti of wires that twisted over the furniture, under the threadbare carpets and across the floor. Johnny stepped over a heap of cable, headed for a big box in the corner. "This is new, isn't it, Ed?"

Blunt nodded. "Color photocopier. Not a bad piece of machinery. 'Course, you gotta play with the final product, but it'll do in a pinch." He reached into a stack of papers on the desk, handed me a document with a flourish. "*Bitteschön.*" It was an East German passport. I ran my fingertips over the cover, felt the grain on the ersatz blue leatherette. Not a bad job. Then I looked inside. Blunt's photo and a fake name.

Blunt shrugged. "Gets me on the bus for free here in the West, anyway. Damn things aren't good for much else these days."

I handed the passport back. "Didn't know you were still working."

"Well, I'm officially retired, but you gotta keep busy."

"Tell me about it. This time last week I was drinking a fruit-a-bomba shake out on my porch in Key West, all of a sudden the phone rings and here I am."

"Yeah, I get those calls too, Joe. Doin' our part for the Comeback of the Century, right?" Blunt winked. "Listen, can I get you folks anything?"

I rubbed my head, stretched my neck till it cracked. "Coffee would help if you got it."

Blunt made a face. "I'm not much on caffeine anymore. No sugar, no alcohol. None of that poison."

Terrific. "So what do we have?"

"*Mineralwasser.* But it's good stuff." Blunt opened one of the dirty French windows, blast of cold air shot in and the noise of traffic on Hohenzollerndamm got louder. He reached out on the stone window ledge and grabbed a green bottle. Then he slammed the window shut, set up four glasses and poured a shot in each. He handed me a glass. I tasted it. Lukewarm and flat. So much for pleasantries.

"Listen, Blunt, how up-to-speed are you on all this?"

Blunt shrugged. "Well, I know you want tickets to Disneyland, which I'm workin' on. I also know you're carrying some hot papers, although when the Boss faxed me about it yesterday he used a code I'm not up on. Somethin' about diggin' up the pumpkin patch at Whittaker Chambers's farm." Blunt laughed.

I nodded to Johnny. He handed me the briefcase. I clicked it open, pulled out the file and gave it to Blunt.

"It wasn't a code, Ed. We really did dig up a roll of microfilm at Chambers's farm. In the pumpkin patch."

Johnny chimed in. "In an aluminum canister sealed with electrical tape."

Blunt shook his head. "Somebody's pulling your chain."

"No kidding. Any idea who?"

Blunt pulled a pair of thick GI specs out of his shirt pocket, slipped them on, eased himself into a soft chair by the window. He started to read, then stopped and pointed at the old leather briefcase.

"That what I think it is?"

"Yeah. Sentimental sonofabitch, isn't he?"

Blunt rolled his eyes, tilted the paper toward the light. I sipped my mineral water as if it would do a damn thing for the pounding in my head. Johnny wandered over to study the electronics, Victor was fiddling with the knobs on one of the old radios.

"Hey, Sergeant, what the hell year is this *Volksempfänger,* a '36?"

Blunt glanced over at Closky. "It's a '37, Colonel; '36s had the brown Bakelite knobs."

Closky nodded. "Either way they're not worth shit. All they can pick up is Kraut stations. You can rig 'em to get BBC, though."

"Yessir, you sure can." Blunt turned back to the papers for a couple more minutes, whistled as he thumbed through the stack. Then he set them down. "Well, you're right. This is a very hot batch of papers here. Amazingly hot."

"That's what Johnny said. I was looking for a second opinion. Guess I got one."

"Guess you did. This K-document supposed to be the Chambers connection?"

"Yeah, assuming Schmidt's 'old friend Karl' is Chambers."

Blunt shrugged, glanced back at the paper. "Might make sense. Honecker's Party code name in the thirties was Tjaden, Chambers's was Karl. Then again, Schmidt might be wrong. Could be something else entirely. Lots of things start with *K*, 'specially in German." I sighed. "Tell you what, Blunt, if it'll make you feel any better I'll do some digging, okay?" I reached up on the shelf behind his chair, pulled down a battered German-English dictionary, flipped it open to the *K*'s and started running my finger down the columns. *Kabarett, Kabel, Kabine, Kabinett, Kabuse* . . . The Caboose Document? Nah.

Johnny walked back over and sat down. "Whatever it means, *K*'s the code for it, all right." He pointed to one of the papers. "See, it starts here. Schmidt brings it up first on July thirty-first, says if the debt situation gets any worse they might have to 'locate the K-Document.' Then on August twenty-first Mann calls it *Plan K*. Doesn't sound like either one of them knows where the damn thing is."

Kantate, Kantine, Kanzlei . . . Hm. Chancellory Document? "Nor do they seem to know *what* it is."

"Right." Johnny turned to Blunt. "But see, Ed, we're assuming Erich Honecker's sitting on something he got from Whittaker Chambers, maybe when Chambers flew to Vienna in '59. Something Chambers held back when he handed over the Pumpkin Papers in '48."

Blunt frowned. "Which in turn were already ten years old at the time. So whatever it is, it's over fifty years old."

Johnny shrugged. "Maybe."

Blunt shook his head. "Well, pardon my French, sirs, but what the hell kind of fifty-year-old intelligence document is going to be worth jack shit today? Except maybe for historical interest."

Kapital, Kapitän, Karat . . . "We've been mulling that one. You know Victor always told us Chambers had something big but wasn't letting on."

Blunt looked over at Closky. His voice got quiet. "Yeah. Something on FDR, right? Like maybe the president knew about Pearl Harbor in advance, or he made a secret deal with Stalin to trade eastern Europe for a free hand in the Pacific after the war, all that stuff. That's old news, Joe. It'd be explosive to have proof, sure, but it's not the kind of thing Honecker could use to blackmail anybody, East or West. Besides, the guy's days are numbered, he'll be out to pasture in a month."

Karbon, Karfunkel, Kartell . . . "Why do you say that?"

"Lot of reasons. Last week he cancels his trip to Denmark. Then he pardons all the poor saps Stasi picked up at the fortieth anniversary demo. Then he finally makes a statement about the refugees, real compassionate, no fire in his belly. The guy's run out of steam, he's used up."

Kastration, Katastrophe, Katzenjammer . . . "Or maybe he's just desperate enough to pull the document and use it. Whatever it is."

"Whatever is right. But of course that's why you're here."

I set the dictionary down. "That's exactly why. We want to see General Mann."

Blunt grinned. "Six months ago, I'd have said you're crazy. Two months ago, even. Now, well, I switch on the GDR news and all of a sudden they're saying, hey, maybe *perestroika* ain't such a bad idea after all. Then you show me this and I see why." He tapped the paper. "I also see a man desperate enough to sell his grandmother for hard currency."

"Meaning Mann."

"Meaning Mann." He peered at me over the top of his specs. "Assuming, that is, you really believe in such an animal."

"What do you mean?"

"I mean nobody's ever seen the sonofabitch. Or if they have, they don't talk about it. Popped up out of nowhere five years ago, no record of him anywhere before then, least not in any files we can find, which ain't exactly the usual career path for a Stasi lieutenant general. Some folks think he's a composite, something Stasi dreamed up to give a little flash to an outfit with a reputation for churning out gray-suited bureaucrats with faces to match. Mann's not like that, he's more of a wheeler-dealer, a rule breaker, does whatever he can to bring in hard cash for the workers' paradise."

"So you think he really exists?" Johnny asked.

Blunt shrugged. "If he does, he's ready to deal. Good and ready."
I stuck my finger in the page, stood up, walked over to the window.
The Wall was out there somewhere, couple miles up the street and
over to the left. This time tomorrow we'd be crossing it. Question
was, how? I looked back at Blunt.

"Okay, Ed, so what's the plan? Fiberglass poles at dawn? Trumpets in our rucksacks? Catapults? You must be cooking something
up since you got the word from Jersey HQ."

Blunt fished in his pocket, pulled out a plastic bag with a half
dozen toothpick-sized carrot sticks. He slid one out, took a nibble,
huge jaws grinding like the mills o' God. Finally he swallowed,
dabbed his lips with a hankie.

"Well, you figure you want to do it quick and dirty. Because basically Mann's outfit does three kinds of business, most of it crooked
and all of it aimed at getting hard currency into the state treasury.
One, they sell politicals. Two, they buy Western goods wholesale,
sell 'em at the Intershops at jacked-up prices. And three, they skim
shipments of GDR products they're supposed to be sending to the
Socialist Brotherlands and sell them to the West."

"What about the Catholic charity scam?" I flipped the dictionary
back open. *Kilowatt, Kimono, Kindergarten . . .*

Blunt grinned, tapped the papers in his lap. "Ah, your so-called
C-Geschäft, right? Pilfering the Church poor box to buy electronic
surveillance equipment for Stasi, supplying the big kahunas at
Wandlitz with their Citroëns and Johnnie Walker. Rhymes with
B-Geschäft, by the way, ransomin' your politicals from Bautzen at
seventeen thousand marks a head. All that gets too complicated for
our purposes, we just want to get you in with a plausible cover story.
The simpler the better."

Kipper, Klang . . . "I thought somebody *wanted* us in."

"Somebody does. Somebody else probably doesn't. Either way
you can't just hop off the U-bahn at Friedrichstrasse and say 'Take
me to your leader.' You've got to follow the rules."

Klumpen, Klunker . . . "Fine. Tell us the rules."

"Rule One: You got to see Mann. Rule Two: Nobody ever sees
Mann." Blunt grinned. "Not nobody, not nohow. So what I'd recom-

mend for starters is a little outfit called IMES GmbH Import-Export. Tiny part of Mann's far-flung Office of Commercial Coordination. I'll try to get them to courier over an invitation you can flash at the Vopos, but if that don't work out you can just cross on a one-day tourist visa. Shouldn't matter, really, long as you've got the Colonel with you."

Koitus, Kokain— "Wait a minute, Blunt. No way we're taking Victor in the shape he's in. That's just asking for trouble."

"Asking for more trouble if you don't. He's the one they want to see."

I thought about that for a half second. "And why the hell would anybody want to see him?"

Geez, listen to me, now I was doing it. Talking about Closky like he wasn't even there. I looked over at the poor old guy. He was leaning against the radio, big head swaying back and forth, tapping his foot to some forties tune. Terrific.

Blunt picked out a fresh carrot stick. "They want to see him because they know him. Worked with him in '84."

"Disciples for Dollars, remember, Joe?" Johnny asked.

Disciples for Dollars. Count forty-one or so in the seventy-two-count indictment that sent Closky up the river in '86. "Yeah, but—"

"Ah, that was the beauty of it, sirs. Disciples for Dollars was a front. The Colonel never did get a single political out of a single Zonal jail. All the dough went to IMES."

Johnny and I stared at Blunt.

"See, Honecker set the shop up in '82, then passed it on to Mann in '84. Started off selling GDR-made AKMs to both sides in the Iran-Iraq War, branched out to Jordan and Egypt, Angola, Mozambique, Ethiopia, all your usual suspects. By that time they weren't just talking light weapons either, they added tanks to the menu. T-62s, plus a few '72s. Rumor has it you can even pick up a MiG-21 if you got the cash and a taste for vintage aircraft."

"I take it Victor wasn't in the market for vintage aircraft in '84," I said.

Blunt stood up, opened the French windows again, pulled in a fresh bottle of mineral water, unscrewed the top with his huge paw. He wet his lips, capped the bottle and set it down on the table.

"Correct. He was in the market for small arms. Remember those reports a few years back about your Sandinistas and your Contras shooting at each other with GDR-made AKMs? Well, Honecker was shipping them to Ortega out the front door while Mann's outfit was selling them to the Colonel out the back." He winked. "That's irony."

Blunt nibbled off another end of a carrot stick. "Plus, it's also our ticket in. Because the guy in charge of IMES is the same guy the Colonel dealt with on the weapons deal in '84. Deputy director of KoKo, your pal from the papers here, Comrade Günter Schmidt."

I stared back at Closky. "Günter Schmidt knows *Victor*?"

Blunt nodded. "Small world. Now, you gentlemen up on the latest Warsaw Pact firepower?"

Johnny shrugged. "There is no latest, is there? Makarov 9mm's been around since the early fifties. Simonov and Dragunov still make those snipers' specials last I heard, popular item with the young Saxon boys in the guard towers across town. Then your Kalashnikovs."

Blunt nodded. "One of which happens to be produced locally." He reached for a folder from a stack on the windowsill, pulled out a crumpled paper. "Old government spec sheet, accurate enough for our purposes."

He handed me the paper. I was still trying to come to grips with the fact that our only hope on this job was a demented sixty-nine-year-old ex-spook-turned-preacher whose plaque-encrusted brain was playing a permanent loop of the year-in-review for 1948. I pushed the thought away, skimmed the paper quick. *Kalashnikov submachine gun, modernized (AKM)*. Knockoff of the Soviet model, but with a plastic stock and pistol-grip and pressed steel housing to bring the weight under four kilos. Leave it to the Krauts to build a better mousetrap. Otherwise standard Rooskie issue, thirty short 7.62mm rounds, effective single-shot range four hundred meters. Et cetera. I handed the paper back to Blunt. He stuffed it in his pocket.

"Mann's got a warehouse up in Kavelsdorf near Rostock. Word has it he's keeping twenty thousand or so in crates to ship out as needed."

For the first time in twenty minutes Closky turned his head toward us. "More like twenty-five thousand."

What the hell? Blunt just nodded. "Okay, sir, twenty-five thousand. Anyway, let's assume we can get you a fifteen-minute chat with Schmidt at KoKo HQ. You talk a little arms deal, you flash a little cash, get him good and antsy. Then you use your considerable talents to bore your way up."

I didn't get it. "Look, Blunt, why all the hocus-pocus? Why can't we just drive over and make Schmidt an offer for the goddam thing?"

Blunt's eyebrows shot up. He damn near spit his carrot stick across the room. "Geez, Joe, are you serious? Because it's touchy. It's hot. You don't even know who planted the film. You get over there and let slip to the wrong Zonal individual you're in on a Socialist state secret this size, you won't ever cross back again. Ever. And that's if you're lucky."

"But Schmidt *wants* to sell the damn thing," Johnny said. "That's clear from the microfilm."

"Maybe he does. Maybe he already has. Maybe he's got a better offer and you'll just be a nuisance that knows too much."

I sighed. "Okay. So what's our offer?"

"No word on that yet. Not from the Boss, anyway. You got some walkaround money?"

Johnny tapped his suitcoat pocket. "Yeah, but it's nowhere near enough if we're shopping for the document of the century."

"It'll get you in the door. That's probably all you'll need, things bein' what they are. Fact is, the Politburo's scared shitless. Last night a hundred and twenty thousand people hit the streets in Leipzig, Vopos just stood and watched. Ten thousand in Dresden."

Johnny nodded. "Yeah, we saw it on a TV screen at Tegel. *Aktuelle Kamera* on *DDR Eins*. Took us ten minutes to figure out we weren't watching a West German broadcast."

"So you think this is good for us or bad for us?" I said.

Blunt frowned. "Definitely good. They're scared, they're desperate, they're not thinking straight. So it's good." He thought a minute. "Dangerous as hell, but good."

"Terrific. Meanwhile, we're in the market for small arms. You think I can still pass for government?" I straightened the collar on my Harry Truman shirt. "Or maybe a Miami drug dealer?"

Johnny stared at me. "Joe, you look like a Miami drug *user.* The beard's gotta go. The hair's gotta go. You can grow it out again when you get back to Key West. *If* you get back to Key West."

"Geez, you guys are the soul of optimism this morning, aren't you? If I didn't know we were takin' Victor along I'd really be worried."

Blunt looked over at Closky. He was banging a fist on the old radio, muttering under his breath. Blunt stood up, walked over, gently pulled Closky's hand away. Then he leaned over, spun the dial until it was playing Glenn Miller again. Closky relaxed.

It was going to be a long week, I could see that much. I opened the dictionary again to give it one last shot, flipped through to the end, ran my finger down the column. *Kupfer, Kuppel, Kur, Kürass* . . . Oh the hell with it, I'd check it later. The dictionary was almost shut when it caught my eye. Next-to-last page. Last word in the column.

Kürbis. "Pumpkin."

The Pumpkin Document. *The Pumpkin Papers.*

August 17, 1948

The room was crowded and hot. McDowell and Nixon sat with their backs to the open windows overlooking Forty-second Street, lamp table jammed between their chairs as a jury-rigged speaker's rostrum, Gideon Bible under a stack of files. Stripling dragged out a third chair, hot seat for Hiss if the poor bastard ever showed up. I moved over on the sofa to make room for Chambers once he came in from the adjoining bedroom where Closky was keeping him on ice. I checked my watch: 5:30.

So this was it, just like Closky called it, the Big Confrontation nine days early, our boy and their boy mano a mano on the fourteenth floor of the Commodore Hotel. I glanced over at Nixon. His upper lip was shiny with sweat.

All of a sudden there was a knock on the hall door. Mandel opened it and in walked Hiss, his pal from the Carnegie Endowment a half step behind. Hiss was forty-three years old, looked like Clark Gable with a shave and an ear-tuck, tall and slim in his new eighty-dollar suit, light brown hair combed up in a sharp pompadour. Of course Closky hadn't told him what was up when he phoned this afternoon, but Hiss figured it out pretty quick.

He studied his watch, then looked up. "This will obviously take more than the ten or fifteen minutes I was led to believe. Would it be possible for someone to call the Harvard Club and leave word that I won't be there for my six o'clock appointment?"

At the words *Harvard Club* Stripling pursed his lips. Nixon smirked, nodded at the phone. Hiss's pal walked over and made the call.

Hiss coughed, cleared his throat. "I would like to make one comment. On my way downtown from my uptown office, I learned from the press of the death of Harry White, which came as a great shock to me, and I am not sure that I feel in the best possible mood for testimony. I do not for a moment want to miss the opportunity of seeing Mr. Chambers. I merely wanted the record to show that."

We all stared at him, nobody said a word. Hiss shifted his feet.

"I should also like to add that yesterday I was told that those involved in these hearings were going to take an oath of secrecy. Yet the first thing I read in this morning's *Herald-Tribune* is a story by Carl Levin referring to my testimony that could only have come from the Committee. It certainly did not come from me."

Nixon's eyes darted around. "Mr. Hiss, if you get in touch with Mr. Levin, I am sure you will find he obtained the information from sources outside the Committee."

Right. Nixon saw to that when he laundered the story through his friends at the FBI. McDowell didn't know any of that, of course. His face got red.

Hiss was about to say something else but Nixon gave a nod and Mandel got up and opened the door to the bedroom. Closky poked his big head out, looked around like a kid about to sneak out of school, then held the door open and stood aside as Chambers shuffled in, head down, arms limp at his sides.

He didn't look much like a champ, but when did he ever? Same rumpled tweed coat he'd had on his short, fat body since the middle of last fall, same shirt too it looked like, same hangdog look, puffy face pale and sweaty, eyes on the floor, hair like it came straight out of the salon de cowlick.

Nixon perked up. "Sit over here, Mr. Chambers." Chambers eased himself onto the couch next to me. I nodded at him. Nixon shuffled some papers, then wanted Chambers on his feet again.

"Mr. Chambers, will you please stand? And will you please stand, Mr. Hiss?"

They both stood. Hiss wouldn't look at Chambers, though, just kept staring straight ahead out the window.

"Mr. Hiss, the man standing here is Mr. Whittaker Chambers. I ask you now if you have ever seen this man before."

Hiss slowly turned his head. He drew himself up to his full six feet, head back, nose in the air, towered over Chambers. The creases on his slacks were sharp and clean, white shirt starched and smooth, burgundy bow tie in a flawless knot, pompadour perfect as a wave under a Bernini nymph.

Hiss didn't even bother to address Chambers, turned back to Nixon instead. "Can he speak? Will you ask him to say something?"

Nixon nodded. "Mr. Chambers, will you tell us your name and your business?"

Long pause. At first I thought he wasn't going to answer. Then he said, "My name is Whittaker Chambers." Trademark Chambers mumble. I was three feet away and could barely understand him.

Hiss took a step toward Chambers, stared into his fat face. His voice was almost kind. "Would you mind opening your mouth wider?"

Chambers seemed to droop lower in the heat, new rumples forming in his tweeds even as he stood there, double chin oozing over his wrinkled collar like a melting candle. He stared at the floor.

"My name is Whittaker Chambers. I am a senior editor of *Time* magazine."

Hiss turned to the Committee, the look on his face like the whole thing was just too pathetic for words. "May I ask whether his voice, when he testified before, was comparable to this?"

Nixon frowned. "His voice?"

"Or did he talk a little more in a lower key?"

McDowell tilted his head back, smoothed his mustache, looked over at Nixon, shrugged. "I would say it's about the same."

"Would you ask him to speak a little more?"

Nixon nodded. "Read something, Mr. Chambers. I will let you read from—"

"It is possible he *is* George Crosley," Hiss said, "but I'd like him to talk a little longer." He turned to Chambers. "*Are* you George Crosley?"

"Not to my knowledge. You are Alger Hiss, I believe."

"I certainly am!" Satisfied smile for the crowd.

Chambers shrugged. "That was my recollection."

Nixon slid a copy of *Newsweek* out from under some papers on the lamp stand. He leaned forward in his chair and passed the magazine to Chambers. Chambers flipped it open, started reading aloud.

" 'Tobin for Labor. Since June, Harry S. Truman has been peddling the labor secretaryship left vacant by—' "

Nixon interrupted. "Just a moment. Before we proceed any further, I think Mr. Chambers should be sworn."

Hiss smirked. "Now, that *is* a good idea!"

The stenotypist pulled out the Gideon, and Chambers took the oath.

Nixon glared at Hiss. "Mr. Hiss, let me say one thing. When I suggested Mr. Chambers be sworn, I was addressing the Committee. Under such circumstances I do not wish, nor will I tolerate, any interruptions from you."

Hiss stiffened. "In view of what happened to Mr. White after his treatment before this Committee on Friday, Mr. Nixon, I think there is no occasion for you to use that tone of voice in speaking to me, and I hope the record will show what I have said."

For a second they both glared at each other. Finally Nixon rubbed his dark jowls, gave a slow nod, looked over at the stenotypist. "The record shows *everything* being said here today."

Whew. Chambers mumbled a few paragraphs from *Newsweek*. Hiss's gaze locked on his fat face. Finally Hiss asked if he could interrupt.

"The voice sounds a little less resonant than the voice I recall of the man I knew as George Crosley. The teeth look as though there has been considerable dental work done since I knew George Crosley, which was some years ago. I believe I am not prepared, without further checking, to swear an absolute oath that he is George Crosley. Would it be possible to ask him, for example, what dentist performed the work on his teeth?"

Oh, for— Nixon raised his eyebrows, looked at Closky. Closky winked, heaved his huge bulk up out of the chair, tightened the knot on his red silk tie. He walked over to Hiss, stood right in front of him.

"You know, Mr. Hiss, from the minute I came into the room with Mr. Chambers here—from the minute you walked over and asked him to open his mouth—you've been making it sound like your whole identification is based on what this man's *teeth* looked like! And yet here's a fellow you knew for months, right? You knew him so well he was even a guest in your house—"

"Would you—"

"Let me finish. He was a guest in your house, you gave him your old Ford, leased him your apartment, and yet the only thing you want to check on are his dentures, is that it? There's nothing else about his features that would make you say, 'This is George Crosley'? Is that your position?"

Hiss's face turned bright red. He took a deep breath, stared at Closky. "Is your preface through? May I answer?" Closky smirked, nodded. "First of all," Hiss said, "I would not call Crosley a guest in my house. I have described the circumstances. If you wish to call him a guest, that is your conclusion."

Closky shrugged. "Okay, forget the word *guest*. He was *in* your house."

"I saw him at a time I was seeing hundreds of other people. Since then I have seen *thousands* of people. He meant nothing to me except under the circumstances I have described."

Closky nodded. "I guess I'm just a little concerned, is all, because of the statement you made before this Committee and a couple hundred other people last week that you'd never seen, heard, or laid eyes upon this man, and now you say it's possible that maybe you *did* know him."

Hiss's face got red again. "I did not say I have never seen *this man*. I said, so far as I know, that I never knew anyone who called himself *Whittaker Chambers*."

"You never knew him under his communist code name of Karl?"

"I certainly did not."

"You never associated with him as a member of an underground communist cell?"

"I did not."

"You never belonged to any such group?"

"I did not."

"Never knew Mr. Chambers was a member?"

"I did not."

Closky smirked. Hiss tugged at his bow tie. He was sweating, feeling the heat in more ways than one, I could see that much, but he still had some fight left in him. He turned to McDowell. "May I ask the Committee if I might cross-examine the witness at this time?" McDowell gave the okay. Closky sat down, snickered, rolled his eyes. Nixon frowned.

Hiss clasped his hands together, paced back and forth in the tiny area between the sofa and the chairs like he was getting ready to address a jury. Finally he turned to Chambers. His voice was strong and clear.

"Did you ever go under the name of George Crosley?"

Chambers shook his head. "Not to my knowledge."

Hiss took a step back, rubbed his chin. "Did you ever sublet an apartment on Twenty-eighth Street from me?"

"No, I did not."

"Did you ever spend time with your wife and child in that apartment?"

76

"I most certainly did."

Hiss did an exaggerated double take. "You did or did not?"

"I did."

"Would you tell me how you reconcile your negative answers with this affirmative answer?"

For the first time Chambers looked Hiss straight in the eye. A flicker of emotion passed over his fat face, just the hint of a twinkle in his droopy eyes. "Very easily, Alger. *I was a Communist and you were a Communist.*"

Bingo. Hiss jumped back like somebody pushed him. "Mr. Chairman, I don't need to ask Mr. Whittaker Chambers any more questions. I am now perfectly prepared to identify this man as George Crosley."

Wow. McDowell spread his hands. "Well now, Mr. Hiss, do you positively identify—"

"Positively. I have no further questions at all. If he had lost both eyes and taken his nose off, I would be sure."

McDowell turned to Chambers. "Mr. Chambers, do you positively identify this man as Alger Hiss?"

Chambers was still sitting on the couch. He didn't look up. "Positive identification."

Hiss shot across the room, fists clenched. "May I say for the record at this point that I would like to invite Mr. Whittaker Chambers to make these same statements out of the presence of this Committee without their being privileged for libel? I challenge you to do it, and I hope you will do it damned quickly!"

He leaned down toward Chambers. Oh holy hell. I stood up between them, started to touch Hiss's arm. He shook me loose, screamed at me. "I am not going to touch him! Get your hands off me! You are touching *me*!"

I let go. Stripling stood up. "Please have a seat, Mr. Hiss."

Hiss's face looked almost purple, eyes bugging out. He was breathing hard. "I will sit down when the chairman asks me, Mr. Stripling, when the chairman asks me to sit down!"

McDowell rapped on the lamp table. "I want no disturbance."

"I don't—"

McDowell was shouting now. "Sit down, please!"

Finally Chambers looked up at Hiss. At first his fat face was blank. Then a smile spread over it, a crooked, taunting smile tailor-made to send Hiss into a rage.

But it didn't. Hiss glared down at him, half in horror, half amazed. The words came out slow through clenched teeth.

"Why are you doing this to me?"

5

October 18, 1989

Johnny eased the Mercedes into the short line of cars off of Friedrichstrasse. We were a good fifteen feet outside the Free World by now but the Vopos hadn't worked their way down to us yet. I leaned over the front seat and checked the rearview. Beard gone for the first time in fifteen years, hair cropped too. Serious, dignified. A businessman. I straightened my tie.

Johnny stuck his head out the window, stared at the Wall. "Well, there it is, Joe. Five meters high, four-meter concrete slabs with a one-meter-diameter metal pipe up top all the way around. Runs for ninety-nine and a half miles, total circumference of West Berlin, twenty-three-point-six million cubic feet of concrete, stone, and cinder block. There's your security zone, sanded and swept to make footprints show up, fifteen meters. Then your forty-meter patrol area, then your tarmac road for the motorized patrols. Along the way you've got some two hundred and forty-seven observation towers, one hundred and thirty-five shelters, two hundred and sixty dog runs, assorted tank traps, flares rigged to concealed trip wires, night-vision TV cameras, mines, and so forth. Wild, isn't it? Man, what a town."

Yeah, what a town is right. Closky was sitting in the backseat next to me, raincoat folded on his lap, crisp off-white suit tailored to his frail frame, red silk tie in a full Windsor knot. He was reading the *Bild-Zeitung.* Hadn't said a word since we left the hotel. Probably better that way, at least till we got through the checkpoint.

I slipped the new passport out of my suitcoat pocket, eyeballed it for the tenth time. Photo matched the guy in the mirror all right. Hair gray at long last, eyes still hazel though. DOB 24 November 1924, New Jersey, USA. Close enough. I ran my fingers over the embossed red-and-blue "Issued in Washington, D.C." stamp, felt the give of the eighty-pound stock on the slightly worn pages, flipped back through the visa section. Hong Kong, Singapore, Tripoli, Amsterdam. Geez, this guy really gets around, doesn't he? I closed the passport and tilted it to let the gold eagle catch the light. Fine piece of work, I'd give him that much. Good old Blunt.

Meanwhile a pair of Vopos in gray raincoats were working on the car ahead. Hood open, trunk open, backseat out, then the custom-built dolly with the mirror on it run underneath to check for unwelcome company strapped to the tailpipe. I remembered the drill from my last visit fifteen years ago. Looked like it was just about our turn.

"Damn, I wish Blunt could've got us that letter."

Johnny shrugged. "Don't worry about it, Joe. They get a couple hundred cars a day through here. It's just as well if we don't stand out."

"You sure it makes sense to keep the money on you?"

"I told you before, they search the car, not us. This isn't the Blockade anymore, Joe, this is détente. What the heck do you think Nixon went to China all those times for?"

"As a matter of fact, he went to piss off the Russians, which is partly why these guys aren't exactly throwing confetti and waving little American flags to welcome us in."

Okay, so I was a little nervous. Last time I crossed this line on a real job was over forty years ago. Things were simpler then. Hell, I was a kid, younger than Johnny was now. Nothing could happen to you at that age. Besides, having Closky along back then would have actually done some good. Now, Christ, who knew what could go wrong?

Finally the car ahead pulled out and the Vopo waved. Johnny eased us up a couple yards, then put it in park and shut off the ignition. The Vopo leaned down to the window. He looked about twenty.

" 'Tag. Ihre Ausweise, bitte."

Saxon accent? Less likely to jump the Wall if they're not locals, I guess. The kid's eyes darted around. Don't tell me he was nervous too. Of course, why shouldn't he be, twenty thousand people marching in Dresden last night, Party types on the tube talking about "rapid and significant changes," whatever that meant. Nobody dead so far at least, which is more than you could say for Frisco after the quake yesterday. Nixon was right, the whole damn world was going nuts.

I handed Johnny our two passports and he passed all three of them out the window to the kid. He gave our photos the Vopo Stare, then did the same to us. Finally he stuck the passports inside his coat pocket and handed us three one-day GDR visa applications with a correct Bitteschön. I sighed. He disappeared inside, no doubt to check our passports against the database of the GDR's Top Ten Million Most Wanted.

"Sure could've used that letter, eh?"

Johnny shrugged. "This is routine, Joe. That guy couldn't care less who we are. We'll be through in ten minutes." He turned around and pointed at the form. "For 'Purpose of Trip' just put 'tourism.' I'll fill out Victor's and he can sign it."

Five minutes later the kid was back.

"Steigen Sie aus, bitte!"

Great. We got out. It was a light rain, just enough to bead up on our new white Wertheim trench coats. Closky wore his German-style, draped over his bony shoulders like a cape. He leaned against the car, face buried in the newspaper. Drops of rain plunked down on the open page but he didn't seem to mind.

"Machen Sie die Türe auf, bitte!"
We opened the doors. The Saxon kid poked his head in the front seat, opened the glove box, slammed it shut again. Then his partner moseyed over and ran the mirror-on-a-roller-skate under the car. The kid checked the back. Clean so far.

"Kofferraum aufmachen!"
What gives, pal, no *Bitteschön* this time? Johnny popped the trunk and the Vopo stuck his head in. He lifted up the panel to the spare tire, dropped it down again.

Finally he took our visa applications and disappeared back inside. We slammed the trunk down and shut the four doors. Nobody told us to get back in the car yet so we played it straight and stood in the rain. I stared back across the border to the guard shack at Checkpoint Charlie a hundred feet away. A bored MP stared back. I waved. He didn't move. A limp Old Glory dripped in the rain.

Looked like the MP had company too, skinny dark-haired guy in a wet gray suit and sunglasses coming out of the guard shack. He stood on the street staring at us, assuming he could see anything with those shades on. But now hold on a minute. It couldn't be, but—

I nudged Closky. "Hey, Victor, that guy look familiar?"

Closky's head came up slow. He stared toward the MP shack for a second, then turned back to his paper. The expression on his face never changed.

Before I could say anything to Johnny our Vopo came back out. He looked around one last time. Then he walked up to Closky.

"Die Zeitung bleibt hier!"
This time Closky didn't look up. Oh holy hell, Victor, just give him the damn newspaper. The Vopo grabbed Closky's paper, snatched it out of his hands. *"Westzeitungen dürfen nicht in die Deutsche Demokratische Republik eingeführt werden!"*

Now Closky's head jerked up. His eyes got big, face flushed. He answered in English. His voice was loud and shrill.

"What the fuck are you doing with my paper, pal? I was readin' that paper!"

"Oh Jesus, Victor—"

Closky took a step toward the kid. "Goddam retard took my paper! I was readin' that paper!"

The second Vopo charged over, shot a look at the first one, nodded. He switched to English. "All three of you will come inside!"

Ah, hell. Why in God's name did we let Victor have the paper in the first place? We knew we couldn't take it across the checkpoint. Now what?

We followed the Vopo across the tarmac to the cinder block steps that led up to the guardhouse. Guess I should have brought a snack.

Then I heard Closky's voice again, quieter this time.

German this time.

"Sang Se, iech will net indiskret sei, ober wo komm' Se aigntlich her?"

Saxon dialect, no less. What the hell?

The Vopo stopped on the steps, stared down at us. *"Wie bitte?"*

Victor smiled. "Where you from, Lieutenant? *Wo komm' Se aigntlich her?"*

I guess the kid was too surprised not to answer. *"Aus Plauen."*

"Was Se net sang! De Familie von meim Vader kommt aus Blaue!"

Closky's pop's family came from Plauen? That was a new one. The kid didn't look like he was buying it either. Still, the Saxon dialect was right on the money. Closky poured it on.

Saint John's Church still under restoration? No kidding. And the old castle ruin? It's a law court and lockup now, right? Oh, and the linen mill, my goodness, Opa worked there till he dropped but of course that was under capitalism, no doubt conditions are better now, et cetera, et cetera.

The Vopo turned to Johnny and me, switched back to English. "Listen, you must know you are not supposed to bring such newspapers into our Republic. Keep it in the car." He handed the rolled-up paper back to Closky, stared at him for a long time. Then he pulled a rubber stamp out of a pouch on his belt, stamped our passports right there in the rain and handed them back. *"Einreise genehmigt!* Entry permitted. Currency change through that door."

We looked at one another. Then we dashed up the second set of steps into the low-lying, prefab building next to the guardhouse. Inside it was cramped but at least there was no line. A pimply-faced clerk in a cheap uniform scowled at us from behind a counter, shook us down for twenty-five Westmarks each in exchange for a fistful of worthless Zonal scrip. A minute later we were back outside.

The Vopo nodded, shot Victor something that almost passed for a smile. Then he signaled to his pal and the first barrier came up. We hopped back into the Mercedes before they changed their minds and Johnny started her up, eased her forward through the maze of concrete and cinder block. Sharp right, then a sharp left. You couldn't go more than a couple miles an hour but that was the idea.

Finally we passed the last Vopo and found ourselves back on Friedrichstrasse, same street we got off a half block back in a different world. I turned around and looked out the back window. The Wall was a hundred feet behind us. The guy with the sunglasses was gone.

"What did I tell you, Joe, simplest thing in the world."

"Yeah, kid, piece of cake." I turned to Closky.

"Victor, are you out of your goddam mind? Telling him your family came from Plauen, laying that Saxon dialect on him, you're damn lucky he didn't arrest you for Deserting the Republic, or whatever the hell they call it."

Closky stared at me for what seemed like a full minute. Finally he shrugged, tapped the newspaper. "Didn't want to lose the paper, Joey. Middle of a story."

Joey. *Joey.* The sonofabitch knew my name. First time he'd said it since before Allenwood, first time in five years. *Closky knew my name.* Jesus.

Johnny pulled up to the light at Leipziger Strasse and checked his watch. "Listen, Joe, we're a little early. How about if we run up to Unter den Linden, take the long way around? We'll still make it by four."

Closky knew my name. I couldn't get over it. I shook my head to clear it, took off my glasses and rubbed my eyes. Finally I said, "Let's save it for the ride back. This is business."

Johnny switched on the blinker. When the light changed to green he turned right.

"Not exactly rush hour."

He was right about that, at least. Even at mid-afternoon the broad boulevard was nearly empty. A dirty green Trabant sputtered by on the left, cloud of oily blue smoke shooting out a rusty tailpipe. Architecture a mix of bullet-pocked Wilhelminian row houses and vacant lots. Looked like all that brown coal was taking its toll on the century-old house fronts too. Then again maybe the sulfur dioxide crust was the only thing holding the damn things up.

A couple streets later the high-rises started, huge blue-and-silver blocks that were supposed to look like the future that worked, but of course it wasn't and they didn't.

"Reminds me of public housing," Johnny said.

"Exactly what it is. Real existing socialism."

Closky snorted. I stared over at him but he didn't look up.

We rumbled across Gertraudenstrasse at Spittelmarkt. Looked the same as forty years ago, street probably hadn't seen a repair crew since then either. Up ahead it curved to the left, ran along the Spree for a while. Wasn't any cleaner on this side, that's for sure. I looked for a street sign.

"This Wallstrasse?"

"Yeah. Märkisches Museum up ahead, FDGB headquarters next door."

"And our buddy Mann?"

"Across the street. Right up here." Johnny pulled into the left lane, slowed down. He turned into a half-empty parking lot, stopped next to a guard shack. A Vopo stepped out.

"Not another carwash routine."

Johnny shook his head. "Relax, Joe, these guys know we're coming."

Sure enough, the Vopo checked our license plate against a clipboard and waved us in. Johnny parked next to a late-model Citroën sedan.

"You done this before, kid?"

"Not exactly this, not for a while. But Victor has."

I glanced over at Closky. He reached into his suitcoat pocket, pulled out some kind of black-red-and-gold ribbon, pinned it to his lapel. A metal disk hung from the ribbon, hammer-and-calipers emblem of the German Democratic Republic. I leaned over and read the inscription. *Held des Sozialismus.* "Hero of Socialism." Holy hell.

We got out and headed for a side exit. I reached for the handle but before I could grab it the door swung open. A second Vopo stood inside, nodded.

"You are expected," he said in English. We followed him up a flight of metal stairs and down a long gray corridor lined with unmarked doors of cheap veneer. He stopped at the last one, came to attention, knocked.

"Herein!"

The Vopo opened the door and waved us in. The room was big, picture window that looked south over the Wall toward West Berlin. At first I couldn't figure out what was odd about the place. Then it hit me.

Nothing was odd about it. Looked exactly like an office down the street in the West, every square inch of it furnished right out of Wertheim's *Hauswarenabteilung,* sleek Swedish desk and bookshelves, pseudo-Bauhaus brass floor lamp, Chagall prints on one wall. And why the hell not? This was the outfit that did billions of marks worth of business with the West, right? Figures some of it would trickle down here.

A pudgy guy in a French-cut suit came out from behind the huge desk, stuck his hand out. He looked about Johnny's age, late thirties maybe, small round glasses, thinning brown hair. I don't know where he bought his suit, but it wasn't the one-size-fits-all Polish polyester from Kaufhaus Centrum, I could tell that much. I stuck out my hand but he walked straight past me.

"Welcome back to our capital, Reverend Closky. It's good to see you again."

What the hell? Closky shook hands, face blank, didn't say a word. Finally the guy turned to us. "I am Schmidt.

He motioned us to a set of Barcelona chairs grouped around a low marble-topped coffee table and we sat down. A white porcelain Kaffee-Hag pot sat in the middle. He poured four cups.

"I think you'll find the coffee to your taste."

His name might have been phony, but there was nothing ersatz about the java. No doubt Mann laid in a couple tons of A&P French Roast down in the basement just for entertaining. I took another sip and waited for him to get down to brass tacks.

"I understand you are visiting our capital on business again, Reverend Closky."

Closky just stared at him. I didn't know how long Schmidt would keep nattering before he figured out Closky wouldn't answer, so I jumped in. "That's correct, Herr Schmidt. We represent a client interested in a business transaction with your government." Schmidt glanced at me, then looked back at Closky like he was waiting for his okay. Finally I couldn't stand it anymore.

"Look, Herr Schmidt, I can see you're used to doing business with Victor here. I respect that, I've done business with him myself. But surely you know he's had something of a reversal of fortune."

Schmidt spread his hands. "The internal affairs of capitalist countries are of no concern to the government of the German Democratic Republic. We are, however, aware of Reverend Closky's status as a political prisoner in the United States. Frankly, I am delighted to see that status seems to have changed."

"We're delighted too, Herr Schmidt, although we're not sure exactly how long his new status is going to last. We brought him along because we understand you insisted on it."

Schmidt leaned back in his Barcelona chair. The leather creaked. He spread his arms. "The direct approach is usually the best, gentlemen. The German Democratic Republic has always favored pragmatism in dealings with the Nonsocialist Economic Sphere."

"As long as there's money to be made, I guess."

"Yes, yes, the money. It comes from Iran, it goes to Miami and changes hands three or four times, it comes through New York and back again, eventually reaches the CIA. Then it reaches us."

I smiled. "I hope you don't think we're CIA."

Schmidt sighed. "I would of course be flattered if you were, but I understand that you are not."

I nodded at Johnny. Start simple, keep it subtle. He reached into his inside pocket. Schmidt stiffened, then relaxed as he saw a fat envelope come out. Johnny ripped open the sealed flap. He counted out thirty-five crisp thousand-dollar bills.

"That's thirty-five now and thirty-five on delivery," Johnny said. "Total order of four hundred GDR-made AKMs at a hundred and seventy-five dollars apiece."

Schmidt eyed the dough, nodded slowly. "Now, you do understand our holdings include much more than just weapons. We have Meissen porcelain, gold medals from the Sarajevo Olympics, Havana cigars. And Western goods, too, of course, all very reasonable. Ladies' wristwatches from Cartier, Chanel cosmetics, an excellent '82 Château Bellevue—"

"Maybe you could mail us a catalog."

A sour grin.

Johnny got us back on track. "It's possible we would be interested in something more. But we would need to speak with Herr Seidel. Or better yet, with General Mann himself."

Schmidt's eyebrows shot up. "Herr Seidel is in Westberlin on business. And *Herr Generaloberst* Mann—" He smiled and shrugged the way the Japanese do when they don't want to say no. For a few minutes we just sat there. Good opening, kid. Let's keep it low-key now. Come at it from a different angle.

I was just about to say something else when I heard it. A soft click, just one, but it got my attention like a gunshot. I looked over at Closky. He was sitting erect on the edge of his chair, right hand stuffed in his side pocket. Another click. Then his hand came out, bony fingers clutching an ancient silver GI Zippo. Closky's yellowed thumbnail flipped the lid up, his wrist flicked it back down again. His hand was shaking, but that thumbnail never missed. Finally it stopped. Closky looked up.

His head was still for once, eyes focused, staring straight at Schmidt. When he finally spoke his voice was quiet, but it had that edge back in it that used to make folks listen. And Schmidt listened.

"Schmidt, you are wasting my time. Do you think I sat in stir for three years just to come here and listen to you jack your jaws about antique machine pistols and cheap wristwatches? Because if you do, you're even more full of shit than Mann himself."

Schmidt froze. We all did. Closky stood up, walked over to the window. His limp was gone. He turned around and took a deep breath, even seemed to fill out his coat a little more. Geez, did he gain weight in the past couple days?

"Now, that thirty-five thousand on the table, that's peanuts. You know it and I know it. Thirty-five *million* would be peanuts. Because the fact is, your so-called German Democratic Republic has run up a debt to the West upwards of twenty *billion* U.S. dollars. Am I right about that?" He turned to Johnny. "That's right, isn't it? That's what I heard you say?"

Johnny stared at Closky. His voice was quiet too. "Twenty-point-five."

Closky turned back to Schmidt. "Fine, twenty-point-five. Quote that number to Mann, whoever the hell he is, okay? Tell him you got it from Victor Closky. Tell him we have it on paper." He reached into his inside pocket, pulled out an envelope, waved it in the air. "Tell him at that rate he can sell every piece of equipment in the goddam Nationale Volksarmee and you're still looking at default on your external debt by early 1991 at the very latest."

His voice was getting louder and he was pacing now, phony Palm Beach suitcoat flapping behind him, arms waving just like they used to do on TV, face bright red. He stopped, spun around. A grin spread across his face. His head looked like a skull.

"When that happens, Schmidt, your precious Showcase of Socialism will collapse in a heap of shit that's going to make the goddam Polacks look like a bunch of Swiss bankers. After which Mann's going to be wearing a striped suit he didn't buy from Cartier. And tell him I know what *that's* like, and he won't take to it. I didn't."

Closky stood still right next to Schmidt's chair. He was breathing hard, hand resting on Schmidt's shoulder.

"Now, Mann's got one item in his store that we want, and one item only. He knows what it is. But he doesn't know *where* it is. Only one man on earth knows that." Closky leaned down until his face was a foot away from Schmidt's. The grin disappeared. "Erich Honecker." He reached into his pocket again, set something down on the marble-topped table with a loud click. It was an aluminum canister. "You tell Comrade Honecker he can put it in here if he wants. Don't worry, it'll fit. And you can tell Mann from me we're offering *two billion* U.S. dollars. Five hundred million into Honecker's personal account at the Swiss Bankverein Lugano up front on your verbal say-so. Five hundred million when the document is in our hands. And the second billion when we cross the checkpoint into West Berlin. Total, two billion. That won't get you out of hock but it'll buy you a good chunk of time, maybe five years, maybe ten if you're smart."

I stared at Closky. Two *billion* dollars? Was he nuts? Hell, Nixon could buy himself the governorship of Jersey for a lot less than that. Senate seat too, for that matter. Maybe even—

Schmidt cleared his throat. I held my breath, waited for him to call in the Stasi goons or push a buzzer that would open a trapdoor straight to Siberia. But he didn't. Finally he said, "Perhaps it would be best if you met with Herr Seidel after all. We could get you an appointment tomorrow—"

"*Tomorrow?*" Closky's face turned bright red. He looked like he was ready to explode.

The phone rang. Schmidt picked it up. He listened for a minute. His eyes got big. He said a single word: "*Nein.*" He said it like somebody who just heard his whole family got wiped out in a car crash. Then he hung up real slow. For a long time he stared at the phone without moving.

Finally he looked up at us. His voice was almost a whisper.

"This meeting is terminated."

August 21, 1948

The drive up from Washington in Closky's new Plymouth took close to two hours. It didn't feel as humid once we got outside the District but it was still hot, even with the windows down and doing 60 up the blacktop that cut through the rolling Maryland farmland. Closky had the radio on and was singing "A Tree in the Meadow," warbling the tenor obligato to Margaret Whiting's soprano, damp white shirtsleeves rolled up, red silk tie fluttering in the hot wind, sweat glistening on his scalp at the roots of his crew cut.

I'd just finished scanning the first couple pages of the *Herald* to see if we'd gotten any mileage out of Dick's latest leaks to Bert, but so far just about everything was taking a backseat to the news from Berlin, most of it bad. Russians still weren't calling it a blockade, not even after two months, still claimed "technical problems" were keeping the access routes shut. Meanwhile the airlift wasn't coming close to putting food on the table, so the black market was back in full swing, which was just the excuse the Rooskies needed to play Jesus at the Temple. Yesterday they raided the booths at Potsdamer Platz, fired into the crowd, arrested some twenty-five hundred Krauts, it sez here, commie goons even dragging some of our own boys back across the line into the Zone.

I held the paper up. "Looks like we got out of Frontier Town just in time, eh, Victor?"

Closky glanced at the headline, frowned. "All I know is, I'd like to see those goddam Commies try to shut *me* down if I was still over there. I'd like to see them try that." I sighed. Victor against the Red Army. Would've been close, I guess. I held my arm out the window to let it dry. Closky stuck a Pall Mall in his mouth, clicked his Zippo on, steered with his knee as he cupped the flame. I figured I'd change the subject.

"So you really think Chambers is going to open up, Victor?"

Closky shrugged, snapped the lighter shut. "Fact of the matter is, if we don't get some action soon, we're cooked in November. Truman's out raising hell in that damn train while Dewey's sitting on his porch up in Albany with his thumb up his ass. We can still piss this election away, Joey, don't kid yourself. We need a bombshell, and so far Chambers isn't giving us bombshells. He's giving us BBs."

True enough. It was still one man's word against another's, and even if Hiss cracked, the charges against him weren't serious

91

enough. But I couldn't imagine it was going to cost Dewey the election.

Closky downshifted to second as we came up on a turnoff. "Can you make that sign out, Joey?"

I leaned forward. "East Saw Mill Road?"

"Bingo."

Closky took the turn, then drove slow for a hundred feet or so until he found the driveway hidden among the trees. He put it in low and the car whined up the dusty, rutted dirt road that led to a red barn next to a stand of young white pine. Just past that was a beat-up frame farmhouse. We rumbled across the packed dirt yard between the barn and the house and Closky nudged the Plymouth into the shade.

Chambers was standing on the porch. He was wearing overalls and a red-and-white-checked cotton shirt.

"Looks like he owns something besides that damn suit after all," I said.

We climbed out of the car. Closky ignored Chambers, walked over to an old iron pump with a metal cup chained to it. He worked the handle until the water gushed out with a creak and a whoosh, filled the cup and drank it down. Water dripped off his chin, spotted his tie. I stared out across the field. Up at the top of the ridge a car was headed south toward Westminster, too far away to hear. Heat off the blacktop made it shimmer. This side of the road the yellow-green field sloped down to a little pond, then up to the hill where the barn was. Back of the barn to my right was a vegetable patch behind a wood slat fence. Pretty good-sized green tomatoes. I walked over for a closer look. Pumpkins.

"You comin', Joey?"

I followed Victor over the packed dirt yard to the farmhouse porch. Chambers stared at the ground. His shirt was wet.

"Hello, Victor. Hello, Mr. Pope. You seem to have brought the Washington weather with you."

He held the screen door open and we went inside. The little farmhouse was dark and hot. German Bible on a table by the window, stuffed raven poking out of a plaque on the wall. It wasn't Georgetown, that's for sure.

Closky loosened his tie. "You still commute to New York for the week?"

"Yes, but not for much longer, I'm afraid. My notoriety is beginning to strain my relationship with Mr. Luce somewhat."

Chambers pushed a couple old wicker chairs together and we sat down. He pulled a pipe and a tobacco pouch out of his overalls and started stuffing it. For about a minute nobody said anything. Finally he looked up.

"It's not working this time either, Victor."

Closky shrugged. "Let's give it a chance."

"I gave it a chance in 1940. You took me to see Martin Dies. You said when he heard my testimony the Committee would turn the State Department upside down."

"Yeah, well, that didn't work out, did it."

Chambers sighed. "No, it didn't. The administration was far too interested in protecting its own. What makes you think it will be different this time?"

Closky grinned. "One reason. Gentleman from California. He's a sharp cookie, make no mistake. He's out to stir folks up, make a name for himself."

"I am aware of that. I had rather expected you to say that he cares deeply about the communist threat facing our nation and is prepared to go to any lengths to combat it."

Closky frowned, rubbed his crew cut. "Well, hell, you want me to say that, Whittaker, I will. Don't think it matters all that much as long as you're willing to swear under oath what you told us back then."

"I will tell the truth."

"The truth being what, at this point?"

Long pause.

"I was a member of the Communist party from 1924 to 1937. In the 1920s I was editor of the *Daily Worker*. In 1934 I received orders to go underground." His voice was flat, like he was reciting from a script. The whole time he talked his eyes never left the floor. "The apparatus was headed by Nathan Witt, an attorney for the National Labor Relations Board. Later, John Abt became the leader. Government attorney Lee Pressman was also a member . . ."

Chambers hesitated.

"And Hiss," Closky said.

Chambers didn't look up. His voice was a mumble. "And, of course, Alger Hiss."

It was the way he said it that bugged me. Shifty-eyed, mumble-mouthed, not exactly the ring of truth. For the first time I spoke up. "You know, Mr. Chambers, a big part of the problem is you just don't *sound* believable. I hate to say it, but there are times I wonder about it myself. Lot of men on the Committee feel the same way."

Chambers still didn't look up, kept his voice a monotone. "How can you not believe me? What motive could I have for lying? What could possibly induce me to jeopardize my family's future, risk losing a thirty-thousand-dollar-a-year job at *Time* magazine? Why would I do it?"

"Yeah, well, I understand Mr. Luce has actually been pretty generous with your legal fees and so forth. Doesn't seem like you're jeopardizing a whole heck of a lot."

Closky shifted in his chair, leaned forward, waved me off. "Listen, Whittaker, I hate to say it too, but Joey's got a point here. We need to *convince* folks you're telling the truth about Hiss. We do that and we grease the skids for Truman but good. Clean house in Washington once and for all, sweep out the whole rat's nest of Commies, fellow travelers, liberal Democrats, you name it. Public opinion's shifting, folks are starting to think Hiss really is lying, I swear they are. But we need you to help it along. Don't hold back, for God's sake, if there's anything at all you haven't told us, anything that would strengthen your case, let go of it now."

The wicker caning creaked as Chambers settled back in his chair. "I assume you're talking about espionage?"

"Of course."

"I've already told you the purpose of the group at that time was communist infiltration of the government. But espionage was certainly one of our eventual objectives."

"Yeah, I know you told us that. But did you ever reach that objective? Did Hiss ever pass information to the Russians, either through you or anybody else?"

Chambers frowned. "Only to the Russians?"

"Why, who else you got in mind?"

Chambers stared at the floor. He was quiet for so long I almost thought he was going into one of his trances. Finally he spoke. "If someone told you, hypothetically speaking, that a high government official established unauthorized contact with, say, the Germans in 1939, would you wish to pursue it today?"

Closky laughed. "No, frankly, I would not, because hypothetically speaking, if anybody tried to help the Germans beat Russia I say more power to 'em, would've saved us the trouble of dropping the A-bomb on the Kremlin, which we're gonna have to do sooner or later anyway."

I cleared my throat. "Jesus Christ, Victor—"

"Relax, Joey, we're among friends. Besides, even if that wasn't true, fact is we're not going to get any mileage from rooting out Nazi symps in the government, hell, none of 'em are going to be liberals anyway, and if it doesn't give the New Deal a black eye it's no use to us. Period."

Chambers puffed on his pipe. Smoke hung in the hot, wet air, didn't move. "Even if the man were a member of Congress today?"

Closky cocked an eyebrow. "Are you saying there might be proof that a current member of Congress passed secrets to the *Nazis*?"

"Perhaps. Or perhaps conducted unauthorized negotiations."

"Wow. No shit. Really? Republican or Democrat? Wait a minute, don't answer that. Forget it. It would just muddy the waters. I don't want to hear about it."

That caught me off guard, but Closky was probably right. Any one of a dozen guys could fill that bill, half of them on the Committee itself. Hell, what was that book Rankin was always hauling out at the hearings? *Who's Who in American Jewry*? The whole damn outfit was shot through with bigots, anti-Semites, Ku Kluxers and assorted other folk more partial to Krupp than the Kremlin. What else was new?

Closky shook his head. "Look, let's get back on track here. I'm asking you to search your memory, search your heart if you have to, and tell me if the Ware-Abt-Witt gang ever graduated from infiltration to espionage. Soviet espionage, okay?"

Chambers sucked on his pipe but it was out. "Espionage, Victor, is a very perilous and very confusing business, especially espionage of the Soviet variety. Often one has difficulty in determining if it is even taking place or not." He reached for a box of matches on the table. Closky pulled out his Zippo, flicked it on, held it sideways. Chambers put his hand on Closky's, sucked the flame down into his pipe. "Thank you."

Then Chambers said, "Much as you had difficulty in Berlin."

Closky froze. "Meaning what, exactly?"

"Boys are usually trouble, Victor, you should know that by now. That little fellow last year, for example, was a member of the KJVD sent by the Russians to keep an eye on you. You had no choice, I suppose."

"What the hell are you talking about?"

"Your little friend. The boy who had the unfortunate accident. He was a communist spy, of course."

"Communist spy my ass, he was the son of a Gauleiter, for Christ's sake."

"Youthful rebellion. Many of the young men in our apparatus were the sons of reactionary elements, as we used to call them."

Closky's face was bright red, shiny with sweat. His eyes were bugging out. I'd seen him like that before, and it was trouble.

Closky stood up. "Look, I can see we're wasting our time here. You give it some thought, all right? Think about it real hard. You come up with anything else, Whittaker, you call me."

I was half running to keep up as Closky stormed across the dirt yard. We got back in the car and slammed the doors. I stared at him.

"Kai Beckmann was a member of the Communist Youth League?"

Closky switched on the ignition and pressed the starter. "So what if he was? Do you think I would have killed him for it? It was just an accident, all right? It was a fucking accident."

Closky slammed the gearshift up into reverse, backed onto the driveway and hit the brakes. Chambers stood on the porch staring at us. Closky dropped it into low, gunned it and popped the clutch. Dust and pebbles flew out of the spinning back wheels as the car fishtailed down the driveway. My head damn near hit the roof as we bumped over the gutter back onto the blacktop. Closky gunned it again and took the turn onto 496 south. He tore his tie off and threw it onto the backseat. His hands were squeezing the steering wheel like he was trying to twist it off.

"How could he know, Joey? How could he possibly know?"

October 19, 1989

Blunt warned me about the mineral water and rice cakes for break-fast this time so I made sure I filled my thermos at Kaffee-Hag on our way over. The rain had slowed to a drizzle overnight but the inside air still felt damp, even with the tile oven cranked up. Johnny and Blunt had a half dozen morning papers spread out on the work-table and were picking them apart like they were the Dead Sea Scrolls. Both TVs were on, one set of rabbit ears pointed east and the other west. And Closky was, well, he was back in his trance, ear leaning against one of the *Volksempfängers* listening to Glenn Miller on AFN.

Blunt looked up from the paper, took off his glasses. "What time did Schmidt get the phone call?"

"For the tenth time, Blunt, four o'clock. Maybe five after."

He nodded, tapped the newspaper. "Well, that's what it was, all right. Talk about bad timing."

I stood up and carried my coffee over to the worktable. Head-lines were variations on a theme, but the best entry in the Original Fiction category, as usual, came from our pals at *Neues Deutsch-land*:

COMRADE ERICH HONECKER RESIGNS
FOR REASONS OF HEALTH

On the 18th of October the Central Committee of the Socialist Unity Party met for its eighth session. As the first item of business, Comrade Erich Honecker asked to be relieved of his duties for reasons of health. Voting unanimously to grant his request, the Central Committee relieved Comrade Erich Honecker of his duties as General Secretary of the Central Committee, as a member of the Politburo of the Central Committee, from the office of Chairman of the State Council and as Chairman of the Defense Council of the GDR. The Central Committee expressed its gratitude for his long years of service to the Party and to the German Democratic Republic.

On recommendation of the Politburo, the Central Committee unanimously elected Egon Krenz, member of the Politburo and Secretary of the Central Committee, to the position of General Secretary of the Socialist Unity Party.

I glanced at the other papers, but you didn't need Woodward and Bernstein to figure out *Neues Deutschland* was full of crap. Hell, if Honecker resigned for reasons of health, Nixon was just enjoying a long Jersey vacation.

I poured some more coffee into my thermos cap. "So much for the theory that Honecker was going to pull the K-document to save his skin."

Johnny crunched a rice cake. "Maybe he never got the chance. Or maybe he'll still try it, shoot for a comeback."

Blunt shook his head. "Honecker's washed up, I called that one yesterday. This clinches it. Only question now is whether you can get back in, and whether anybody's left to talk to if you do."

"So we're assuming the guys who cashiered Honecker can't locate the K-document on their own," I said.

"Pretty safe bet. Of course, now that they've got him on ice who knows how it's going to play out? Or who else will try to get to him?"

I looked over at Closky. He was sitting on a wooden chair next to the old radio, volume low, head to one side, tapping his foot to the music. Since we left East Berlin last night he hadn't said a word. Finally I couldn't stand it anymore.

"Victor."

I walked over and snapped the radio off.

"Victor!"

He looked up at me, eyes blank.

Johnny got up, walked over. "Ah, leave him alone, Joe, he's in one of his fogs."

"Like hell he is. Victor, I know you can hear me, so let's cut the crap, okay? This isn't a casting call for *The Three Faces of Eve* here, it's just you and us, and I think it's about time you give us some goddam answers."

"Joe—"

"Oh, bullshit, Johnny, the guy's been yankin' our chain since we left Allenwood. Hell, if he's got some kind of dementia I'm Napoleon, it's an act, it's gotta be. Look, you heard him yesterday, he took over the goddam meeting like it was forty years ago, spilled the beans just like he always does, even had Schmidt buffaloed until that damn phone rang. He's heard every word we've said in the past three days and he was probably in on the whole damn thing from the start." I leaned down, put my nose two inches from Closky's face. "Weren't you, Victor?"

For a few seconds I just watched his head bob, listened to him breathe. His eyes burned into mine. He knew, all right. Finally he said, "You're fuckin' A."

I stood up. I kept my voice as calm as I could. "Why don't you tell us about it?"

Closky smiled, a real smile this time, not that crazy grin. "Okay, Joey, I will. Remember a fellow we used to call The Wheel?"

I stared at him. The Wheel. Yeah, I remembered. How could I forget? Even thought I saw the sonofabitch at Checkpoint Charlie yesterday, but there was at least one good reason why I knew I didn't.

"Died in '64, right?"

Closky shook his head. "November '65, if you believe the FBI. But never mind that. Remember how you used to bug me about him, and I always told you not to worry because it didn't mean anything?"

"Yeah . . ."

"Well, it meant something."

Johnny waved for a time-out. "Wait a minute. Who's The Wheel?"

Blunt grinned. "Geez, The Wheel. That's gotta take you back, doesn't it, Joe?" He turned to Johnny. "Willie the Wheel, a.k.a. Willie the Wheelman, a.k.a. Guillermo Marco. Big fish in the Chicago outfit, worked his way up from getaway driver in the bootleg days to high-level influence peddler in the forties and fifties. One of Chicago's men in Washington. Did us a favor once when we came up short on some hard evidence we needed at a Committee hearing, right, Joe?"

Johnny stared at me. "Joe, is he serious? The Committee got evidence on Hiss from the Chicago *Mob*?"

Blunt rolled his eyes. "Here we go again."

I sighed. "Yeah, Johnny, it's true. So the Committee didn't always play by the rules. So what else is new?"

"*This* is new, Joe, what you're telling me here is new. Jesus." Johnny looked around at the three of us. "Okay, so I'm the only one here who wasn't with you in '48, but I know the Hiss case inside out—geez, I've been getting it rammed down my throat every day for the past three years. I've read every book on the subject, every newspaper article, talked to half the guys that were there, and nobody ever said anything about the Mob. Now, how do you explain that?"

I looked at Blunt. He shrugged. "Because nobody else knows," I said.

"Except us," Blunt added.

"And now you." I smiled.

Johnny stared at me. Victor turned the radio back on. I lost my temper, yelled at him. "Will you shut that goddam thing off, Victor?"

He ignored me. Ah, hell. "Look, Johnny, it was a long time ago, all right? We cut a few corners, took a few shortcuts, but it didn't change anything. Hiss was guilty and we sent him up the river. We got a little help, but it was small change. Besides, what did you think we were, Boy Scouts?"

At first Johnny didn't answer. Finally he said, "No, Joe, I didn't think you were Boy Scouts. And it's no skin off my nose who you took a favor from forty years ago, that's not the point. You think I'm getting all worked up about ethics? About scruples? Look at me, Joe, how do you think I earn my living? Who do you think I work for?"

We all stared at Johnny, waited for him to calm down. I reached out and patted his arm. "It was small change, kid. A couple guys buttonholed me on a street in Georgetown, put me in a car, a man I didn't know gave me a single document. That was it."

Johnny raised an eyebrow. "The document being—?"

All of a sudden Closky snapped off the radio and stood up. "Are you assholes through yet?"

The words hit me like a punch in the gut. I set my coffee down. Johnny didn't say anything. I looked at Closky. "Yeah, Victor, I guess we are."

"Good. Now listen, I've told you this before and I'll tell you again, we're running a business here. You got a business, you got competition. Sometimes you eliminate them. Sometimes they eliminate you."

What could we say? He was back, who knew for how long. Closky's bony hand gripped the table, he leaned forward. His red silk tie was crooked and loose, white suitcoat rumpled, big head bobbing like it was on a spring. But his eyes were clear, and that told me all I needed to know.

"Victor, are you saying we've got competition looking for the K-document? Competition that drives Packards and wears chalk-stripe suits and two-tone shoes? That kind of competition, Victor?"

Closky shrugged. "Maybe. See, boys, The Wheel helped us out in '48, helped us out more than you could ever know, more than you *want* to know. Until '65, that is. FBI tried to arrest him and he pulled a gun. There was a fight and he had a heart attack. Lot of that going around."

Closky's bony hand pushed back a wisp of white hair. "So we won't be seeing much of him anymore. But he had a son, Jack. Born 1940. Young punk, worked Chicago in the late fifties, came on

101

board for the Bay of Pigs in '61, settled into the corner of the Company where they no speaka da *inglese*. Lacks his pop's old-world manners. Big trouble."

"And what makes you think he's trouble for us?"

"Because he's here. We saw him standin' out in the rain at Checkpoint Charlie yesterday, remember?"

Holy hell. "You mean the guy in the suit and sunglasses?"

"Bingo. It was him. And we'll see him again, mark my words. I made sure of that when I put on that little show with the Vopo."

I didn't like the way this was heading. Didn't like it one bit. Hell, I signed on for a weekend gardening job to give the Boss a shot at the Trenton statehouse and here I was back in Frontier Town mixed up in something that took in government and the Mob and the CIA and Christ knew what else, something that went back so far and so deep it was just possible we might never find our way back out. And Victor was loving every damn minute of it.

Closky clicked the radio on, leaned back in his chair. "Point is, Joey, once all this crap with Honecker works itself out, they're going to call us back over there. That might take a while, though. In the meantime, stay alert. Because on a job like this, you don't know who you're going to run into."

He closed his eyes, head started a slow bob and weave. I reached out and grabbed him by both arms, shook him until his eyes opened again. I pushed my face close to his and we stared at each other a long time.

"Goddammit, Victor, you know, don't you? You even know what the goddam K-document is, you're just not going to tell us."

He smiled and closed his eyes. I gave him one last shake and let him go.

6

August 24, 1948

I parked the Hudson just past the canal on Wisconsin Avenue and set the hand brake, headed up the alley on foot. Closky wasn't kidding about the neighborhood. Guess our funding wasn't what it used to be. Out past the warehouses the Potomac flowed on, a hot and muddy brown.

I'd skipped breakfast to make it on time and already regretted it. My gut was churning, head pounding. Temp at eight A.M. was already in the eighties, humidity off the charts. I tugged my tie loose, popped the collar button.

When I got to the top of the alley I saw a familiar-looking '46 Ford sedan parked alongside Closky's Plymouth, next to that a big OD deuce-and-a-half, sloppy brush strokes on the door where the army star used to be. Couple of Negroes in rumpled fatigues were heaving crates out the back, big NCO with a Berlin garrison shoulder patch shouting orders with his mouth full, oversize thermos in one hand, couple of doughnuts in the other. Looked like the army hadn't changed much. The sergeant turned around.

His big lumpy face was smeared with powdered sugar, tie crooked, sandy hair poking out under his service cap, uniform jacket open at the waist, shirt half untucked. I recognized him straight off. Geez, had it really been a year?

"Morning, Sergeant."

Ed Blunt snapped to something that passed for attention and shot me a half salute. Then we both laughed and I held out my hand. He shrugged and shook it.

"Good to see you, sir. Heard you made captain at the end there. Congrats."

"Well, thanks, I guess. Actually I've been off active duty since January first."

"What, ready reserve?"

"Something like that. See you're movin' up in the world yourself, got yourself another rocker. How's it feel to make master sergeant before you're thirty?" Blunt grinned, patted the chevrons on his baggy uniform sleeve. "Feels pretty good, sir." Then he looked around, voice dropped to a whisper. "Actually, the Colonel told me to sew 'em on last week. Orders haven't come down yet, but I figure any day now."

Aha. "Yeah, no doubt. So what have you been up to the past year? I always figured you guys scattered to the four winds after we went on the lam."

Blunt stuffed half a doughnut into his huge mouth, shook his head. "Wasn't easy, but we stayed together. Espionage went down the toilet but we kept the cash flow going. Sold off most of the Colonel's art. Even got ourselves mixed up in the airlift. Supply and distribution, that kind of thing. For a while I thought we were going legit, then I found out a half dozen guys were taking a cut for their trouble. CARE packages, if you can believe that."

"You're shitting me. You guys were skimming off of *CARE* packages?"

Blunt's face got red. "Well, you got to live, sir, know what I mean? Of course, when the Colonel found out he blew his stack. Shut the

104

operation down just like that, fired half the personnel and sent 'em back to their units. That's when I heard the rest of us were coming over here. Guess he wants to keep an eye on us. Funny, we didn't think he'd be that touchy about something like that."

It was funny all right. Closky could lie, cheat and steal with the best of them, robbed Uncle Sam blind while he was in Berlin, ran a black-market scam that probably did a dozen things he could've been court-martialed for, maybe even shot for treason. But let him find out you're swiping Hershey bars out of the gaunt hands of Berlin brats and the guy pops his cork. That didn't surprise me. What surprised me was he could still do something about it, even from over here. What was next?

"So listen, Blunt, what kind of show you figure we're going to run here now? This sure as hell isn't Berlin."

Blunt bit off half of the second doughnut, wiped the powdered sugar on his uniform sleeve. "Berlin's a state of mind, sir, know what I mean? Least, that's what the Colonel always says. Besides, we got a job to do, we're going to do it. I looked the files over on the plane, seems simple enough. Track down a title transfer for a Model A Ford in '35, right? Verify some apartment leases in the District for '35 to '36. Check out the records at a dog kennel over in George-town. Excuse me—"

Blunt shouted at a Negro PFC toting a pair of filing cabinets on his back. "Easy on those, they're Abwehr, can't replace 'em. Second floor."

The Negro staggered past us, fat drops of sweat plopping down on the cracked concrete like hard rain. I peeled my seersucker suit-coat off, draped it over my shoulder. "What if the documents we need don't turn up?"

Blunt unscrewed his thermos, poured himself a refill of coffee doped with so much cream it looked almost white. "Things like that, sir, they always turn up. Always. If they don't, well, we make 'em turn up. Part of the job." He reached up on the tailgate and pulled down a good-sized brown bag soaked with grease spots. Blunt stuck his hand in and came out with a couple of honey-glazed doughnuts clamped together in his huge paw, chomped down on two at once. Somehow he still managed to talk, glaze chips flying from his fat lips.

"Fact is, sir, we made a lot of mistakes in Berlin. You and the Colonel got out by the skin of your teeth last year, we both know that. Sure, you had pull, never would have got out if you didn't, but they were the wrong people. Way wrong. Like that crazy Indian art dealer out at the Wannsee, remember him? Plus all that black-market crap, all the dollars and Reichsmarks and contraband nobody could ever keep straight, we were playing too fast and loose with the rules. Plus it got worse when the Colonel left. Now we're home. Now we're going respectable. We even got a committee of Congress covering our ass, if you'll pardon my French. At least that's the word I got." Blunt stuffed the other two doughnut halves in his mouth, gulped down the coffee.

All of a sudden the door next to the loading dock flew open, slammed against the brick wall. It was Closky. His white shirt was wet and streaked with dirt, sleeves rolled up, fat face shiny and pink. He stopped and held the door from slamming shut. A second later Nixon darted out, double-breasted pinstripe suitcoat buttoned up tight, snap-brim hat tugged down over his eyes, glancing around like he was ready to dodge a flashbulb or a bullet, whichever came first.

Closky shot me a wave. "Mornin', Joey, welcome to the new HQ. I'll show you around in a minute."

Nixon barely nodded at me, brushed past Blunt straight for the Ford. He opened the door, then turned back to Closky. "You sure about this, Victor?"

Closky grinned. "This and anything else you've got in mind, sir. It's what we do."

Nixon frowned. "Because if you aren't, you damn well better tell me now. We can't afford to screw this up."

Nixon climbed in the car, slammed the door. He shoved the key in the ignition, then stopped and rolled the window down.

"Oh, and Victor."

"Sir?"

"I was never here this morning, got it? Never saw this goddam place, never even heard of it. It doesn't exist."

Closky leaned his hands on the window ledge, winked. "What doesn't exist, sir?"

Nixon grinned. "Go to hell." Closky saluted and Nixon shot him the V sign. Then he started the car and gunned it, backed out onto South Street. We watched him drive off.

Closky opened his top shirt button, loosened his red silk tie, wiped the sweat off his face, jumped up and let out a whoop.

"We can't miss now, boys. In for a dime, he's in for a dollar. Come on in, Joey, I'll show you the setup."

He started in the warehouse door. I looked back at Blunt, shrugged and started in after him. Then I turned back.

"You wouldn't have another cruller there, would you, Sergeant?"

Blunt turned the bag upside down, shook it. A shower of crumbs floated down onto the asphalt. "Sorry, sir, I'll save you one tomorrow."

November 2, 1989

The sixth-floor cafeteria in Wertheim's was crowded and hot. I hung my umbrella on a stand-up table in the corner and started in on my potato pancakes and applesauce, sipped on a Schultheiss in a plastic cup that dripped onto the front page of the *Neues Deutschland* I'd picked up at the Europa Center.

Looked like things were hopping over in the Zone these days, which may have been why Schmidt or Mann or whoever was in charge there now wasn't returning our calls. Monday before last, 300,000 East Germans hit the streets in Leipzig, did it again a week later, and two days after that Krenz promised every GDR burgher a passport and a visa. I wasn't holding my breath on that one, although he sure didn't waste any time issuing one to himself. Flew to Moscow yesterday, it sez here. Not that there was much to discuss.

COMPLETE AGREEMENT IN MEETING
OF GORBACHEV AND EGON KRENZ

Moscow (Nov. 1)—The unshakable fraternal ties between the German Democratic Republic and the Soviet Union were further strengthened today at meetings of the CPSU Central Committee. President Mikhail Gorbachev and General Secretary Egon Krenz announced jointly that perestroika will lead both countries to new successes in the perfection of socialism. Stressing the continued importance of the close, comradely relationship between the Soviet Union and the GDR, Egon Krenz called for a "great spiritual renewal of our socialist society."

In response to a comment by a correspondent for the US magazine "Time" Egon Krenz stated: "Under the leadership of Erich Honecker much good was accomplished in the GDR. I have no need to feel ashamed of my role during this time."

Et cetera, et cetera. Who says they only print bad news? I wiped a couple spots of applesauce off my trench coat, pushed the paper away and looked around. Still no sign of the Mafia or the CIA or the Bund or any of the other jokers Closky told us to be on the lookout for.

Closky. Don't remind me. A dozen times in the past two weeks I'd convinced myself the Alzheimer's routine was an act, all that fiddling with those damn Nazi radios, dressing up in Blunt's old Eisenhower jacket and strutting around the room singing Andrews Sisters tunes. But then he'd come out of one of his trances and start talking about things like the "real reason" Honecker built the Wall back in '61 (don't ask) and I'd start to wonder again.

Oh, and the Giants lost, of course. Two-week layoff while the grounds crew filled in the Great Candlestick Fault probably didn't help. First Series sweep since '76. Guess I didn't miss much after all.

I mopped up the last of my applesauce with half a potato pancake and stuffed it in my mouth. Then I polished off the Schultheiss, tilted my head back to get the last drop out of the little red cup.

When I set it down I found myself staring at a pair of Ray-Bans flecked with drops of rain, wiry dark-skinned guy in his late forties with a GI haircut and a fancy wet three-piece suit. It took a second for it to sink in. Same wavy dark hair, same rough olive skin too. And the nose, Jesus. Couldn't see the eyes behind the Ray-Bans, but come to think of it Marco Senior never took his shades off either.

He set his Schultheiss down next to my empty cup, grinned at me. *"Ein Schweinewetter, nicht?"*

I answered in English. "Helps if you wear a raincoat. They got 'em downstairs. *Herrenabteilung,* ground floor. Hundred-fifty marks."

Another grin. He shook the rain off his coat sleeves, tugged at his collar, looked around at the crowd behind him like he could really see through those lenses. "Maybe you're right. 'Course, it's probably a lot nicer back in Key West this time of year. I hear they have those good fruit shakes down there. Plus the cheerleaders at the high school." He winked. "Easy life. You ought to consider going back."

Closky was right, he wasn't as smooth as his pop but it sounded like they made him do his homework. "I'll give it some thought. They're not cheerleaders, though. Majorettes. Big difference. Might want to change that on your master file."

He took a sip of his Schultheiss, set it back down. "You know, they always told me you were the biggest wiseass going. I guess they were right."

I shrugged. "Guess they were. That what you wanted to tell me?"

He gave a cockeyed grin, stretched his neck. With the glasses on he looked like Ray Charles. "Listen, Pope, I don't know what you and your senior citizen friends think you're doing here, but you're in the way, big time. You're screwing our system. There's shit going on here you don't want to get mixed up in."

I didn't know what he was talking about so I tried for a shot in the dark. "You mean a busy guy like you still has time for the Hiss case after all these years? Your pop would've been touched."

He stared at me. "Time for what?"

"The Hiss case. You know, Alger Hiss, Whittaker Chambers. Your pop helped us out with it in '48, I figured you were carrying on the family tradition. We appreciate that."

His face was blank. "What the hell are you talking about?"

Was he playing dumb? "Oh, come on, pal, we're all grown-ups here, all on the same side, okay? I met him in '48, he helped us put some evidence together and it nailed Hiss and that was great. But it never really cracked the case, never flushed out everything Chambers had. Now it turns out some of that made its way over here and you're looking for it. Fine, so are we."

He hunched over, looked around to his left and right, tugged at his wet suitcoat collar. His voice dropped to a hoarse whisper. "Are you out of your fuckin' mind? The *Hiss* case? You think we're out here puttin' our goddam necks on the line for the goddam *Hiss case*? You think Stasi would ever collect two billion dollars for the solution to the *Hiss case*?" He snorted, shook his head. "Man, I always heard you government guys were a bunch of fruitcakes and old ladies, but this beats all. The Hiss case." He looked around like the Krauts were going to join in on the joke. "Jesus, Mary, and Joseph."

He leaned across the table, put a hand on my arm, held it tight.

"Listen to me, Pope. Listen real good. You're in over your head. Way over. Get out of Berlin, get out of our hair before you and that idiot Closky end up dead. You hear me?"

I heard him all right, but all of a sudden something over at the doorway got my attention quick.

He was there and gone so fast it didn't even hit me until after he disappeared. Big guy, full head above the crowd. Broad, flat face half covered by a wide-brimmed floppy hat like Göring used to wear. And the skin on his face, geez, was I dreaming that? Red-and-white checkerboard, bad skin graft over long-healed burn scars.

I stared into the crowd. "Holy hell, is *he* with you?"

Marco turned around. "Who?"

It couldn't be. I knew it couldn't, knew I'd been locked up in Blunt's place too long breathing fumes from that damn tile oven and listening to too many of Closky's cockamamie speeches and songs. Holy hell. I stepped away from the table, shoved my way through the crowd, craned my neck.

Nobody.

But wait, there he was again, back toward me now, headed out of the cafeteria into the store. Damn. I had to get a good look at his face, had to settle it just for my own sake.

"Hey, where you goin', Pope?"

"I'm takin' your advice, okay? I'm leavin'."

"Like hell you are." He reached for my arm. I grabbed my umbrella and brought the handle up quick and hard, caught him in the chin. I heard something snap and hoped it wasn't my umbrella handle. I jabbed him in the gut and he doubled over, then I brought my knee up in his face. He was still on his feet but I gave him a shove and he went down quick. The Krauts started screaming and I sidestepped through the narrow aisles, muttering *Verzeihung*, ignoring the shouts and curses. I got out just in time to see the hat disappear down the escalator.

I tried to run down after him but there was a crowd between us that wouldn't budge. I leaned over the rail and spied him three floors down and moving fast. I looked back. No sign of the Ray-Bans.

When I got to the bottom I raced through the ground floor and out the big glass doors into the rain and rush hour crowd on Joachimstalerstrasse. It was five o'clock and already getting dark, traffic noise louder on the wet streets.

Which way? Guy his size couldn't be too hard to spot, even at dusk. I looked around. Bingo. There he was again, headed north across Kurfürstendamm against the light. That made it good odds he wasn't a Kraut, but then I was pretty sure of that already.

He was quick for a guy his size. By the time I reached the Kudamm myself he was a half block ahead of me. The sidewalk in front of Kempinski's was so crowded I couldn't manage more than a slow jog, but after the scuffle it was enough to wind me. I slowed down and tried to keep him in sight.

Did he even know I was back here? He didn't look around, just kept twisting and turning and slipping through the crowd like some damn football player. At Kantstrasse he crossed on the diagonal. Cars honked, and somewhere a cop whistled. Krauts on the side-walk pointed and shouted *pfui*, which they'll do for your jaywalkers but not your genocides.

My heart was pounding and my chest ached but I broke into a run and shot out into traffic. I could see where he was headed now and knew if I didn't catch him soon he'd be gone for good.

111

Sure enough, when he reached the sidewalk he ducked straight into the Zoo station entrance. There were at least a dozen dark stairways and concourses in there and it was anybody's guess which one he'd head for.

I shoved my way through a crowd of commuters, broad-jumped over a couple of drunks on the ground, looked ahead through the dingy tunnel.

He was gone.

A skinny teenage girl in a GI field jacket was leaning against a pillar.

"You see a big guy in a rain hat come through here a minute ago? White hair, scars on his face?"

She shrugged. I reached in my pocket, pulled out a crumpled twenty-mark bill, shoved it in her hand. She pointed up the stairs to the S-bahn.

"*Da hoch.*"

I could hear a train pulling in and took the steps two at a time. When I got to the top I froze.

Two trains. One on each side of the platform. Both with their doors open.

West to Spandau. East into the Zone.

I had a hunch, but before I could play it I heard the loudspeaker crackle out a *Zurückbleiben* and the doors on the eastbound train slammed shut. I ran over anyway because I knew it had to be that one, ran alongside the old brown-and-red wooden car as the ancient electric motors shoved it forward, tugged at the door handles but they wouldn't budge. I finally stopped when I couldn't keep up anymore, leaned on my knees breathing hard, looked in the windows as the train rumbled past.

Nothing.

Then I saw him. Last car. Standing up, hat pushed back. Broad, scarred face like a stone mask. Did he see me?

Message from a dead man.

I watched the train disappear out the station hall and down the elevated track, listened to the rumble fade as the red lights got small until the back of the train was a tiny dot at the Tiergarten station a half mile away. I thought about racing downstairs and hopping a cab but it was hopeless, he'd be past the Lehrter Bahnhof and across the border before we even got out of the downtown traffic.

I took it slow back down the stairs, caught my breath as I headed straight down to the U-bahn, hopped a southbound redline car for the two stops back to Spichernstrasse.

Ten minutes later I came up the steps at Hohenzollerndamm. It was dark but at least the rain was letting up. I walked along the wide stone sidewalk back to Number 3, pulled open the heavy door. I stared up at the five flights of shabby red carpet, took a deep breath and started the climb.

When I got near the top I could hear Closky belting out "Don't Sit Under the Apple Tree." I shoved the door open. Closky was dressed in a baggy wool World War II uniform, U.S. army, full-bird colonel. Now, where in hell did he get that? Blunt had his Eisenhower jacket on and was playing the accordion. Jesus.

Johnny jumped up. He was the only one dressed normal, if you call an alligator shirt and chinos normal. "Joe, where the heck have you been? Look at this, we're going back over tomorrow, we've got a meeting with Seidel."

He was waving a piece of fax paper at me. Blunt played a fanfare on the accordion, grinned. "Came through an hour ago. Looks like all systems are go."

For a long time I just stared at them. Finally Closky noticed that the music had stopped and piped down. Johnny shoved the paper in my hand.

I handed it back without looking at it. I had to tell them, of course, but even when the words came out of my mouth I still wasn't sure I believed it myself.

I told them anyway.

"I just saw George Two Moons."

August 24, 1948

After Closky's grand tour I headed back out the alley to Wisconsin Avenue. Temperature was ninety-five degrees, figured it would probably be twice that inside the Hudson. I peeled off my seer-sucker sport coat, slung it over my shoulder.

So the whole damn Berlin operation was salvaged after all, packed up in a C-54 diverted from the airlift and flown over for delivery to an abandoned warehouse right here on the Union side of the Potomac. Unbelievable. From what Closky just showed me it looked like most of the files made it over, maybe half the staff. Said we'd be adding personnel after Dewey's inauguration. Also said once that happened we'd have our hands full.

I was mulling it all over when two goons in dark suits stepped into the alley from the concrete steps that led up to South Street. Their hands were empty, but from the lay of their suitcoats it looked like they might not stay that way for long. Goon Number One stepped in front of me. His partner stood to my right.

"You Joe Pope?"

"Sounds like you already know."

They took that for a yes. "Our boss wants to talk to you."

"Sounds great, fellas. I'm just headed back to the office. Tell him to meet me there in a half hour."

"He wants to talk to you now."

Goon Number Two nodded up the steps. I looked around. Blunt and Closky were out of sight, probably not even outside anymore. Oh holy hell. I shrugged and went with them.

At the top of the hill a two-tone Packard sedan with Illinois plates was parked with the motor off. Goon One opened the back door. I looked around again and thought of making a run for it. Goon Two smiled and reached inside his suitcoat, shook his head real slow.

I got in.

I wasn't alone. The guy in the backseat was a sharp dresser but he wasn't on his way to the Harvard Club, I could tell that much. Two-tone shoes, chalk-stripe suit, hundred-dollar Stetson on the seat between us. I looked at his face. Late forties? Low-slung jaw, pock-marked olive skin, good-sized honker, clean-shaven, eyes covered by dark glasses.

He didn't look at me, stared straight ahead. His voice was raspy and thin.

"Communism is a terrible thing, isn't it, Mr. Pope? They don't believe in God, don't believe in private property, nothin'."

I stared at him. He opened a silver cigarette case, held it open. "Smoke?"

I waved him off. He snapped the case shut, slipped it back in his pocket. "And now we find there are even Communists at the highest levels of our government. Shocking, Mr. Pope, don't you think?"

I still hadn't said anything. Whatever this joker's game was, he sure didn't need me to make conversation.

"That's why I wanted you to know how important your work is. I mean the committee you work for, that's real important. All those congressmen fighting to weed out the Reds. And yourself, of course. You're a fine young man, Mr. Pope. A real fine young man."

He looked at me and grinned. "But you got problems."

Well, he was right about that at least, although I still didn't know what the hell he was aiming at. Figured I had no choice but to hear him out. "I'm listening," I said.

"Good. That's real good, Mr. Pope, I'm glad you're listening. That's important too. Now, tomorrow you've got a public hearing where you're going to confront a high-level Communist with testimony from his former associate. Real detailed testimony. Of course, since all Communists are liars, he'll deny everything and you're back to square one. You need evidence."

"We're working on that."

"I know you are, Mr. Pope. But the hearing is twenty-four hours away and so far you've come up dry. Let me help you out, okay?"

He reached into his suitcoat pocket, pulled out a white business envelope with the flap pasted shut.

"You might want to keep that sealed until you get back to the Hill. I can drive you if you like."

I held the envelope in my hand, stared at it. "Thanks, I'm parked around the corner."

"Then I'll wish you a safe trip. Watch out for traffic."

I looked at him. "Why are you doing this?"

"Communism, Mr. Pope. It's bad for business. Real bad. I see a chance to weed it out, I do it. My duty as a citizen. Yours too."

115

"I'll do my best."

"I'm sure you will, Mr. Pope. Especially if you put what's in that envelope to good use. You do that, and maybe we can end this thing before poor Mr. Hiss has to have a heart attack too, know what I mean?"

I stared at him, felt the blood drain out of my face. "I don't think I caught your name."

For the first time he turned to look at me. "Just call me The Wheel. Everybody else does. I see you're in trouble again, I'll be around."

November 3, 1989

This time Closky played it straight and we cleared the checkpoint in ten minutes. Johnny took us up Friedrichstrasse to the center of town, then cut a left on Unter den Linden. Dead end at the Brandenburg Gate was just ahead but we hung a quick right at the French embassy and headed up to Zetkinstrasse. I was sitting in the front seat, trench coat crisp thanks to a one-hour dry cleaner at the Europa Center. Looked like they even managed to get the applesauce stains out. So I was ready for action, I figured.

"Pretty crowded for a workday."

Johnny was right. The sidewalks were packed with East Germans and they weren't exactly carrying soccer pennants. Guess whatever they had brewing in Leipzig was starting to spill over to the Hauptstadt, banners and all. Here and there a pack of Vopos in long gray coats huddled on a corner, watching folks pass. Even the rain was holding off, skies a lighter shade of gray for once, good day for a demo.

Johnny pulled the silver Mercedes up outside the parking lot behind the U.S. embassy, switched off the ignition. With the heater off the car got chilly fast. I turned my collar up.

"Now we wait?"

Johnny nodded.

I pointed to the parking lot entrance. "And somebody's going to flash their headlights at us from over there?"

"That's the plan." Johnny grinned. "Of course, we might want to watch for smoke signals while we're at it."

"Ha, ha."

"Seriously, Joe, he was alive the last time you saw him, right?"

I sighed. "How many times have I told you this story, Johnny? Yeah, he was alive all right. His face was burned to shit and he was singin' his greet-the-great-spirit chant but he was alive."

"So you didn't actually *see* him die. Which means it could have been him."

I shrugged. "Guess so." Geez, listen to me. Last night I was convinced it *was* him, hell, I knew it was, saw his face through the window, he looked at me, stared right at me like he knew I was there. Now, well, I wasn't so sure. Because for the past six years I'd had myself convinced George Two Moons was dead, and it would take more than a glimpse of a guy in a crowded elevated train to change my mind.

"You think he was partners with Marco Junior?"

Closky kicked the back of my seat. "I already told you George wouldn't hook up with that greaseball, dead or alive. And last I checked, he was dead."

"Right, Victor. Thanks. But you still haven't told us why Marco laughed at me when I said we were trying to crack the Hiss case."

Closky didn't answer, started humming instead. Some Negro spiritual, couldn't place it.

I turned back to Johnny. "So anyway, no, I don't think they were together, but then I only saw the big guy out of the corner of my eye. When I looked over, he'd already turned around. Then I saw him again on the train."

"Headed east."

"You could put it that way. Of course, he could've just hopped that particular train for the hell of it. Could've got off at the Tiergarten stop or the Lehrter Bahnhof. Wasn't necessarily headed over here into the Zone."

Johnny laughed. "You still call it the Zone?"

I frowned. "What the hell do you call it?"

Johnny shook his head. "Joe, you're living in the past, I ever tell you that? It's one of the things I love about you."

"Go to hell." We sat there for a while and waited. It was a back street, just a block off the main drag but pretty quiet. A couple cars came and went, little East German jobs that left oily clouds of smoke hanging in the air for minutes afterward, but that was it.

Then a big Citroën pulled around the corner, drove up slow across the street. Green sedan, two guys up front, two in the back.

Johnny's hand moved toward the ignition. His voice was quiet. "This doesn't look right."

A second car pulled up behind us, Volvo this time, four more guys. That made it eight to two, three if you count Victor. Where did we leave that damn shovel, anyway? Trunk of the T-bird, long-term parking at Dulles, half a world away. Damn.

I checked the sideview. "Hats?"

Johnny shook his head. "No hats. No suits."

Across the street all four doors opened at once. Four oversized blond goons headed our way. Same chinos as back in Baltimore. Same windbreakers, too.

Johnny's voice was a whisper. "*Stasi.*" His hand was on the ignition now.

All of a sudden Closky reached over the seat, clutched Johnny's shoulder, shook it hard.

"Drive, you dumb sonofabitch, drive! Get us the hell out of here!"

Johnny jumped in his seat, twisted the key. The motor cranked, didn't catch.

Two of the guys were reaching in their windbreakers when they heard the car crank. They were halfway across the street and broke into a run. One of them pulled a gun.

"Oh holy crap." Johnny switched it off, cranked it again. It caught. He gunned it and slammed the gearshift down. Tires squealed and we shot out into the street.

I looked back. The guys in windbreakers were running back to their car. The one with the gun stopped, aimed it our way. I ducked but nothing happened. When I looked up I saw the second car starting after us, driver of the Citroën waving the shooter back in. The Volvo was a half block behind as Johnny took a left to bring us back to Unter den Linden, for all the good that would do.

"Johnny, what the hell are you doing? We're in East Berlin, remember? There's no place to go."

Closky cuffed me on the ear. "Shut up, dammit!"

"Ow! Victor, what the hell—"

"I said shut up." Closky leaned up behind Johnny's ear. "Take a left here. Follow it till I tell you to turn again."

Johnny spun the wheel and the tires squealed. We fishtailed back out onto the main drag headed east, straight into the heart of town. By the time we flashed through the intersection at Friedrichstrasse a block later he had it up to 110 kmh. I tried to decide whether I'd rather end my days rotting in a Stasi jail cell or splattered on a Litfasssäule between the B-Z posters and the ads for the Berliner Ensemble.

"Listen, Joe, we may not live through this, so how about answering a question for me?"

I reached back and tugged the shoulder harness across my gut, clicked it shut. "Since you put it like that, shoot."

"What exactly was it you got from Willie the Wheel back in '48?"

I almost laughed. "Holy hell, kid, you telling me you don't have anything more pressing on your mind at the moment? Like maybe how you're going to drive this car through a fifteen-foot-high concrete wall? It was small change, okay? Water under the bridge."

Humboldt University was coming up on the left, crowd of students crossing the street. Johnny leaned on the horn. "Okay, so it was small change. In a half hour we'll either be dead or serving ninety years to life at Bautzen, so why don't you just break down and tell me what it was?"

Oh, what the hell. "All right. Keep your hands on the wheel, okay?" Johnny grinned.

I leaned back in the seat. "It was the title transfer to Hiss's Model A." It took a second to sink in. Then Johnny's eyes got big.

"The title transfer, Joe? The fucking *title transfer?* That's the document you think was small change?" He damn near ran off the road, finally took his eyes off me when I grabbed for the wheel, put us back in the center lane. He couldn't stop shaking his head.

"Jesus, Joe, you guys *nailed* Hiss with that document at the August twenty-fifth hearing, you crucified him with it, even laughed at him when he claimed he couldn't remember signing it and now you're telling me after forty-one years the goddam thing was a *fake?*" I braced my feet against the floorboards, checked the shoulder harness, didn't say a word, didn't want to get the kid any more riled than he was. All we needed now was for him to remember what happened to poor Marvin Smith and he'd probably drive straight through the glass walls at the Palast der Republik.

Johnny banged a palm on the steering wheel, slapped his forehead. "And Marvin Smith, holy cripes, Joe, remember *that?* Buddy of Hiss supposedly notarizes the damn thing at the Justice Department, then swears he doesn't remember doing it and two weeks after that he's dead of a broken neck? You think that was small change too?"

Johnny finally stopped shaking his head, took it back up to 100 kmh as we flew by the Neue Wache. The guard was changing, twenty-year-old NVA boys in white gloves and Russian helmets goose-stepping down the sidewalk just like old times. I looked behind us. The Citroën was a couple blocks back and holding steady. Johnny didn't seem to care.

He leaned on the horn again, swerved around a crowd outside the rebuilt cathedral. "I mean, it changes everything, doesn't it, Joe? At the very least, it means Hiss was *framed.*" He thought for a second. "It might even mean he was framed by the goddam *Mob.* Jesus Christ, Joe, why would he be framed by the Mob?"

I sure didn't feel like getting into this now, so I trotted out the party line. "Johnny, it doesn't change a damn thing. There were links between government and those guys going back to forever, okay? They rolled out the welcome wagon for us in Sicily in '43 and we let 'em alone during the Occupation, they helped us flush out Commies in the unions and Hoover looked the other way in Vegas." Then I told the same lie I'd been telling myself for the past forty-one years. "Besides, it wasn't a frame-up, the title transfer was real. Victor checked it out."

Of course the kid didn't buy it anymore, why should he? Why should anybody? He laughed. "Oh, Victor checked it out, did he? That's great, Joe, that's a real vote of confidence. Victor checked it out. I don't know what that's like, it's like a goddam—"

Johnny swerved again, this time to miss a bus as he took the curve into what used to be Stalin Allee. Pastel-colored high-rises now, Showcase of Socialism. There was traffic here but not much, couple dozen Trabis and Wartburgs sputtering along in low gear. Big crowd out on Alexanderplatz, though. Then it thinned out again as we passed the Hotel Stadt Berlin and headed under the S-bahn overpass and up Prenzlauer Strasse out to—well, out to what?

I figured it was time to get that straight, at least. "Listen, Victor, you know we don't have enough gas to make China, right?"

No answer. I felt a breeze. Then I turned around just in time to have my eardrums split by the pop of a .45. Closky was leaning out the back window, left hand holding on to the seat, right hand aiming an ancient semiautomatic at the Citroën and Volvo. He fired off three more rounds and my ears started ringing.

"Victor, for Christ's sake, what the hell are you doing? Where did you—Johnny, Victor's got a goddam *gun,* where the hell did he get a *gun?*"

"Probably from Blunt's junk pile. Don't worry, he won't hit anything."

Closky turned his head sideways. "Like hell I won't!" He stuck it back out, wisps of white hair fluttering in the wind. "Lousy Commies!" *Pop.* Another round. The Volvo swerved.

"Victor, Jesus—" I lunged over the seat, made a grab for him. He pummeled me with his left fist but his arm was weak, it didn't hurt much. I was in the backseat now and pulled him in. He fired the last two shots into the air.

"That was seven, right, Johnny? That was seven?"

Damn well better have been. Closky's face was bright red, eyes big, wisps of hair settling down now. "You made me miss, you goddam retard." He punched me again and I backed off. Then he turned around and flopped back in the seat. He was half crying. I looked out the back window. The Volvo was pulling over, Citroën still headed our way.

"I could've had both of them, Joey. I could've taken them both out."

I stared at him, rubbed my neck. My heart was pounding. "Yeah, Victor, I guess you could have."

He handed me the gun, wiped his face on the sleeve of his ersatz Palm Beach suit. "Let's not fuckin' talk about it."

I pulled the slide back and eyeballed the chamber. Empty. I slumped down in the seat. Johnny hadn't turned around, kept the speedometer nailed at 120 kmh as we headed north up the broad empty boulevard into Prenzlauer Berg.

I gave Closky a hard look, shouted into his ear. "Okay, Victor, so what's the plan? Safe house in Treptow? Dump the car outside town and hike to the coast for a midget sub pickup? You tell me."

Closky stared back at me. "Plan, Joey? Hell, I don't have a plan. Never did." He grinned. "I just hate to see you make it easy for those commie sonsofbitches."

Well, for—

I tapped Johnny on the shoulder. "You hear that, kid?" He heard all right. He was already easing off the gas, shaking his head. "I don't believe this."

We pulled over outside an old hospital across from the Elias-Kirche near Ernst Thälmann Park. Johnny took it out of gear and set the emergency brake. For the first time I noticed he was sweating.

The Citroën pulled up behind us with a screech, doors flew open and the goons piled out, guns drawn.

I buzzed my window down and tossed the .45 out. It clattered on the paving stones. I opened the door real slow and climbed out, hands over my head. Johnny did the same. Closky stayed in the car. He was singing "America the Beautiful."

122

Three of the Stasi boys were holding Makarovs on us. The fourth one stood in front of them with his hands at his sides.

His eye looked pretty good but he still had a bandage around his head. Guess Zonal medicine wasn't as good as you read in the papers.

"Now," he said, "you will give me the briefcase."

7

August 25, 1948

The caucus room of the House Office Building was packed, every seat filled, folks jamming the aisles. When the big double doors opened you could see the crowd out in the hall, hoping for the chance to get in. It was hot as hell, and the television lights didn't help. Not that we minded the extra attention. First congressional hearing ever shown live on the television, and it probably wouldn't be the last.

Dick Nixon sat at the far right end of the raised Committee table, fiddling with his microphone. Congressmen and other folks were milling around nearby. I saw Joe Kennedy's son step up on the platform, lean down and say a word to Nixon. He looked sicker than usual in the television lights, skin yellow and drawn, suitcoat hanging off his skinny frame. He was one non-Committee Democrat on our side at least, although I still hadn't figured out why.

At ten o'clock sharp Closky brought Chambers in, led him to a straight-backed chair in the spectator section behind the press tables just below the Committee rostrum. A little girl was in the seat next to him, maybe seven years old, box lunch on her lap. When Chambers sat down, the girl's father got up and switched seats with her. Looked like Chambers was going to be a tough sell, but we knew that already.

Hiss sat a couple rows back next to his lawyer. I was at the far end of a table we shared with Strip and Ben Mandel. Closky heaved himself into the chair next to me, mopped his crew cut with a red silk hankie, jabbed me in the ribs.

"Keep your eyes and ears open, Joey, this is going to be beautiful."

"Victor, I can't believe you're going along with this. The guy as good as said White's heart attack was no damn accident. He said Hiss might have one too."

Closky leaned over, whispered in my ear. "Don't worry about it, Joey. The Wheelman's strictly a lobbyist now, okay? Represents some Chicago business interests, that's all. Gets a little overdramatic sometime, doesn't mean a damn thing."

All of a sudden something clicked. "Chicago? Wait a minute, we're not talking about the guy who got Tom Clark to let Paul Ricca out of Sing Sing last year, are we? The guy who works for Ricca's lieutenant, what's-his-name?"

Closky frowned, nodded at the television cameras, leaned closer to my ear. "Shhh. Yeah, what's-his-name is right. Giancana, okay? Sam Giancana. And no, it was Murray Humphreys who did that, but they work together. Believe me, they're going to come in damn handy for Campaign '50, so let's not rock the boat now."

I couldn't keep quiet. Hell, there wasn't going to be a Campaign '50 if we didn't get through Campaign '48. "And it doesn't bother you that we're about to introduce evidence we got from some goddam gangster into a congressional hearing? Even if he was pulling my chain about Harry White, and I'm not convinced he was, how do we know the paper's not a forgery?"

"Shhh. For Christ's sake, keep your voice down, there's microphones all over the place." He laid a fat hand on my arm. "No, Joey, it doesn't bother me. And after a while it won't bother you either. Because I checked it out yesterday and it's the real McCoy, okay? I went to Motor Vehicles, I went to Cherner's up on Florida Avenue and it's all legit, so let's not worry about where it came from."

Before I could say anything else Thomas rapped the gavel and the crowd piped down. Hiss took the oath and sat down at the stand. Stripling stood up to face him.

"Mr. Hiss, you are here in response to a subpoena served upon you on August seventeenth at the Commodore Hotel in New York City, is that correct?"

Hiss cut a sharp figure in his gray plaid suit, pompadour shining in the TV lights, hands folded on the table. He shot Strip a friendly smile.

"Mr. Stripling, as I told the subcommittee that day, there was no need to serve a subpoena on me. A subpoena was *handed* to me. I had already told you I would be very glad to be here on August twenty-fifth."

"You are here in response to a subpoena, however?"

"I *received* the subpoena. Yes, Mr. Stripling."

"You are here in *response* to it. Is that correct?"

Another smile. "To the extent that my coming here quite voluntarily after having received the subpoena is in response to it, I would accept that statement."

Well, this was going nowhere fast. Stripling asked Hiss and Chambers to stand and had Chambers sworn. Then he started the warm-up.

"Mr. Hiss, I ask you if you can identify this man."

"I can identify him, Mr. Stripling."

"As who?"

"As George Crosley."

Then it was Chambers's turn. "Mr. Chambers, do you know this man?"

"I do."

"Who is he?"

"Alger Hiss."

"Thank you, Mr. Chambers. You may sit down."

Stripling turned back to Hiss. "Mr. Hiss, would you relate to the Committee the circumstances under which you first met the person you have identified as 'George Crosley'?"

Hiss folded his hands on the table again, leaned forward. "Mr. Stripling, I have already, in an effort to be helpful to the Committee, given the best recollection that I have. As I said at that time, I have had no opportunity to consult records. Some of the records, I find, are not available to me. I believe they are in the custody of the Committee—"

"Just a moment, Mr. Hiss. What records have you attempted to obtain which were in the custody of the Committee?"

"I have attempted to get the records with respect to the Ford automobile that I owned. I am informed that the records are not in their normal, official location but are in the custody of the Committee."

"That is absolutely untrue. The Committee *has* obtained a copy of a document from the Department of Motor Vehicles of the District of Columbia. However, the original document is still in the files."

Hiss shook his head. "I am told, Mr. Stripling, that the original document is no longer in the files. I tried to have my counsel have access to it."

Stripling frowned, shot a glance in Closky's direction. "When did you try to secure the document?"

Hiss's lawyer piped up. "A representative of mine tried to get this document yesterday afternoon. He was told that it was photostatted at some time prior to yesterday but the document itself had been taken from its normal place yesterday."

I gave Closky a nudge. So it all checked out, eh?

Thomas told Stripling to have one of us run over to Motor Vehicles during the lunch recess. Hiss's lawyer muttered something and went back to his papers.

Then they were off again, this time trying to sort out the apartment lease business, Nixon and Hébert chiming in on cue, Hiss serving up a couple dozen "to-the-best-of-my-recollections" until

127

they finally figured out that if Hiss really did sublet his Twenty-eighth Street apartment to Chambers in 1935, it couldn't have been for more than a month or so, tops. Because Hiss left the joint on May 1 and Potomac Electric turned off the power on June 29. Which made you wonder if Hiss ever sublet the place at all. But it made you wonder even more about the Amazing Disappearing Ford. The question being, if Chambers only sublet Hiss's apartment for less than two months—and stiffed him on the rent to boot—why the hell would Hiss give him a car in the bargain?

But that's exactly what Hiss claimed he did, as Stripling was about to let folks know.

"Now, Mr. Hiss, I should like to read from your testimony before the Committee on August sixteenth, page fifty-three, referring to 'Mr. Crosley.' "

Strip picked the transcript off the Committee table and turned to face the camera. He read:

MR. STRIPLING: What kind of automobile did that fellow have?
MR. HISS: No kind of automobile. I sold him an automobile. I had an old Ford that I threw in with the apartment. I had been trying to trade it in and get rid of it. It was an old, old Ford we had kept for sentimental reasons. We got it just before we were married in 1929.
MR. STRIPLING: Was it a Model A or Model T?
MR. HISS: Early Model A with a trunk on the back, a slightly collegiate model.
MR. STRIPLING: What color?
MR. HISS: Dark blue. It wasn't very fancy, but it had a sassy little trunk on the back.
MR. STRIPLING: You sold that car?
MR. HISS: I threw it in. He wanted a way to get around, and I said, Fine, I want to get rid of it. I have another car, and we kept it for sentimental reasons, not worth a damn. I let him have it along with the rest.

"Now, Mr. Hiss, is that the testimony, according to your best recollection?"

Hiss leaned forward. "That testimony was according to my best recollection at the time I gave it, and that is why I gave it. But as I have also testified, I have not yet been able to get the records from the Motor Vehicle Bureau."

Stripling ignored that one. "What did 'Mr. Crosley' do with this car, do you know?"

"I frankly do not recall. It is possible he used it. It is even possible he returned it to me. I really would not be sure of the details."

Stripling pursed his lips. "Well, as a matter of fact, Mr. Hiss, you sold the car a year later, did you not?"

Hiss hesitated. You could almost see his Adam's apple bob, almost hear the gulp. "Not to my recollection."

"You do not recall selling the car?"

"I have no definite recollection."

Stripling took a deep breath, turned to the speaker's rostrum. "Mr. Chairman, I should now like to refer to the testimony of Whittaker Chambers, which he gave on August seventh in New York City. Reading now from that testimony:

MR. McDOWELL: Did they have a car?—referring to Mr. and Mrs. Hiss.

MR. CHAMBERS: Yes, they did. When I first knew them they had a car. I am almost certain it was a Ford roadster. It was black, and very dilapidated.

MR. McDOWELL: Do you recall any other car?

MR. CHAMBERS: It seems to me in 1936 he got a new Plymouth.

MR. McDOWELL: What did he do with the old car?

MR. CHAMBERS: The Communist party had in Washington a service station, or it may have been a car lot. That is, the owner of this station was a Communist. I never knew who or where it was. It was against all the rules of the underground organization—and I think this investigation shows how wise the Communists are in such matters—for Hiss to do anything with the old car but trade it in. But Hiss insisted he wanted the car turned over to the open Party so it could be of use to some poor organizer in the West or somewhere. Much against my better judgment, Hiss finally got permission. My understanding was that Hiss took the car there and simply went away and the owner took care of the rest for him. I should think the records of that transfer would be traceable.

MR. McDOWELL: Where was that?

MR. CHAMBERS: In Washington, D.C., I believe. Certainly somewhere in the District.

"Now, Mr. Chairman, I have here a certificate of title, District of Columbia, Director of Vehicles and Traffic. It shows that on July 23, 1936—more than a year after Mr. Hiss claims he gave the car to 'Crosley'—Alger Hiss in fact assigned the title to the Cherner Motor Company. I now ask that Mr. Hiss step aside and that Mr. Victor Closky take the stand."

Well, here we go. Closky punched my leg under the table, stood up and straightened his tie. The television cameras swiveled to catch him, followed him as he walked to the rostrum, red electric eyes burning into Closky's baby blues. He raised his hand and took the oath, back straight, fat gut sucked in, crew cut fresh, face shiny and pink under the hot lights. He was eating it up, I could tell that much.

Stripling cleared his throat. "Mr. Closky, will you state your full name and occupation?"

"Victor Horace Closky. Assistant Investigator for the House Committee on Un-American Activities."

"Thank you. Now, Mr. Closky, I hand you a photostatic copy of an assignment of title, as recorded in the District of Columbia, and I ask you to give the Committee details of your investigation regarding this document."

Closky took the paper, held it in his hands without looking at it. "Well, the space on the back here, called the certificate of title of a motor vehicle, as issued by the Director of Vehicles and Traffic for the District of Columbia, shows that on July 23, 1936, a Mr. Alger Hiss sold a car to the Cherner Motor Company, 1781 Florida Avenue NW. There's no record of any money changing hands."

"Now, did you proceed to the Cherner Motor Company with a subpoena and examine all of their sales records for this date?"

"I did."

"In the records you obtained, is there any evidence of a subsequent sale of a 1929 Ford roadster on that same date?"

"No, there is not."

"Now just a moment, Mr. Closky. Going back to the assignment of title, does the photostatic document reflect that the car was sold or assigned on the same date that Mr. Hiss turned it in to the Cherner Motor Company?"

Closky cocked an eyebrow, slightest hint of a grin. "Absolutely. The assignment of title shows that on the same date—July 23, 1936—the car was sold to a William Rosen, of 5405 Thirteenth Street NW."

"Did you go to that address?"

"I did."

"Was there any indication that a William Rosen lived there in 1936?"

"No, there was not. The current resident has owned the house since 1933 and has no knowledge of a William Rosen."

From the far end of the Committee table Nixon leaned toward the microphone, interrupted. "Just a moment, Mr. Stripling. I understand, Mr. Closky, that this car was transferred by Mr. Hiss on what date?"

Closky looked up at Nixon. "July 23, 1936."

"That is, a full year after the transfer to Chambers is supposed to have taken place?"

"Yes, sir."

"Is that in the handwriting of Mr. Hiss?"

"We ran a check on it, sir. Based on a comparison with known handwriting specimens of Mr. Hiss, the signature appearing on the back of the document was written by Alger Hiss."

Nixon rubbed his jaw. "I see. Do the files of the Committee on Un-American Activities disclose any information concerning the William Rosen who gave this address?"

Stripling fielded that one. "There are two William Rosens, and we are now checking. We find no William Rosen who ever resided at this address. May I clear up one other point?"

Nixon nodded. Stripling turned back to Closky.

"Now, Mr. Closky, do you have the sales slips of the Cherner Motor Company for the date on which this car was sold to William Rosen, as well as for the day after and the day before?"

"I do."

"And do any of these sales invoices reflect the sale of a 1929 Ford roadster to a William Rosen?"

"No, they do not."

"So in other words, although the assignment of title shows that the car was sold by Mr. Hiss to Cherner Motor Company on July 23, then resold to William Rosen that same day, the invoices of the Cherner Motor Company reflect no such transaction, is that correct?"

"That is correct."

"Is it possible that an invoice has been lost or is missing?"

"No, it is not."

"Why is that?"

For the first time Closky checked his notes. "Because the invoices are numbered in consecutive order. The first invoice for July 22, 1936—the day *before* the sale—was number 7880, and the last for that date was 7897. On the following day, the day of the transaction, the first number was 7898 and ends with 7909. The day after the transaction, they run from 7910 through 7923. Every one of them— from 7880 through 7923—is accounted for."

"Mr. Chairman, at this time I would like to recall Alger Hiss."

Closky handed the photostat back to Stripling, nodded at the Committee and stepped down. The cameras followed him for a couple seconds, then swung around to Hiss.

Closky sat down next to me, pulled out his red pocket hankie and wiped his face. He leaned over and winked, whispered in my ear.

"How'd I do?"

I whispered back. "Terrific."

Incredible. Nixon's dream come true. Nail Hiss on perjury, he said, and now here we were about to do just that. Because if what Closky said was true, then Hiss not only lied about giving his car to Chambers, he actually sold it a year later in a secret deal to a guy at a phony address. Hell, if he'd been trying to act like a Commie he couldn't have done a better job. Maybe he wouldn't have to have a heart attack after all.

Stripling hold the title in his hands, walked over to Hiss's table.

"Mr. Hiss, I show you this photostatic copy of assignment of title, title number 245647, for a Ford used Model A 1929 roadster, and the numbers are A-2188811-9-19-33—that was the date on which it was originally registered in the District of Columbia. The tag, I believe, was 245647, in the name of Alger Hiss, 3411 O Street NW, Washington, D.C. Now, Mr. Hiss, is this your signature which appears on the reverse side of the assignment of title?"

Stripling stepped around behind the chair, held the paper over Hiss's shoulder in front of his face. Hiss leaned forward, stared at it without touching it.

"Mr. Stripling, it certainly looks like my signature to me." He paused, then looked back over his shoulder at Stripling. "Do you have the original document?"

Stripling pursed his lips. "No, I do not. The original document cannot be removed from the Department of Motor Vehicles."

"Could it be subpoenaed?" Hiss asked.

Thomas interrupted. His bald head gleamed in the klieg lights. "Mr. Hiss, can't you tell from the photostat what this signature is? Whether it is your signature or not?"

Hiss looked at the paper again. "It looks like my signature to me, Mr. Chairman."

"Well, if that were the original, would it look any more like your signature?"

That got a laugh. Thomas grinned, scratched his head. Hiss gave a weak smile.

Then Hébert piped up. "Mr. Chairman, in order to give Mr. Hiss every opportunity, I suggest we issue a subpoena to the Motor Vehicle people and let them come here with the original. It will just be a matter of hours, and he will have to admit it is his signature."

If that got under Hiss's skin he didn't let it show. "The reason I asked was that we had not been able to get access to the original, you see. I just wondered what had happened to it." That weak smile again.

Well, this was making me a little nervous. What the hell did happen to the original? And just exactly what was it I got handed yesterday?

"We will try, and Mr. Stripling, you try at noontime," Thomas said, "if we ever reach noontime."

Stripling nodded. "I think we can reach it this way. Do you recall ever signing the assignment, Mr. Hiss?"

"I do not at the moment recall signing this."

Stripling leaned over Hiss's shoulder, held the paper closer. "Is this your handwriting? 'Cherner Motor Company, 1781 Florida Avenue NW.' Did you write that?"

"I could not be sure from the outline of the letters in this photostatic copy. That also looks not unlike my own handwriting."

"Could you be sure if you saw the original document?" Mundt asked.

"I could be sur*er*."

More laughs.

Stripling stood up, walked around in front of the big table. "Now, Mr. Hiss and Mr. Chairman, yesterday the Committee subpoenaed before it W. Marvin Smith, who was the notary public who notarized the signature of Mr. Hiss. Mr. Smith is an attorney in the Department of Justice in the Solicitor General's office. He has been employed there for thirty-five years. He testified that he knew Mr. Hiss. He does not recall notarizing this particular document, but he did testify that this was his signature."

Nixon leaned toward the mike. His face was shiny with sweat, gleaming in the bright TV lights. "Mr. Hiss, you know Mr. Smith, do you not?"

Hiss nodded. "I do."

"Well, now, on the basis—in other words, you would not want to suggest now that Mr. Smith might have violated his oath as a notary public in notarizing a forged signature?"

Hiss shook his head. "No, definitely not."

Slightest trace of a smile on Nixon's face. "Then, as far as you are concerned, this *is* your signature?"

"As far as I am concerned, with the evidence that has been shown to me, it is."

"All right. You are willing to testify now that since Mr. Smith did notarize your signature as of that time, that it is your signature?"

"On the basis of the assumptions you state, the answer is 'Yes.' "

Well, everybody in the damn room knew what that meant, or thought they did. It meant Chambers was telling the truth when he said Hiss sold the car in a shady deal back in '36, maybe even sold it to a Commie. It meant Hiss lied to cover that up. Or, it could mean something else entirely.

It could mean the photostat was a fake, and Hiss had just let himself get buffaloed into buying it. But then, who knew the damn paper didn't come from the Department of Vehicles and Traffic? Who knew where it really did come from?

Nobody. Just me and Victor. Holy hell.

Hébert hunched forward, suitcoat stretched over his bull neck and broad shoulders. "Mr. Hiss, now that your memory has been refreshed by the developments of the last few minutes, do you recall the transaction whereby you disposed of that Ford you could not remember this morning?"

Hiss stared at Hébert. His voice was calm. "No. I have no present recollection of the disposition of the Ford, Mr. Hébert."

"In view of the refreshing of your memory that has been presented here this morning?"

"In view of that, and in view of all the other developments."

Hébert shook his head. "You are a remarkable and agile young man, Mr. Hiss."

8

November 4, 1989

I spent the night alone in a damp basement cell at Stasi HQ in Normannenstrasse. My neck ached, my gut felt like hell, and whatever
good the cleaners at Europa Center ever did my new coat was turning out to be a wasted effort. Plus whoever cleaned my pockets out
last night took away my Advil. I sat up on the narrow cot and rubbed
my head. At least the hair and beard were coming back, even if it
was gettin' a little late in the game to feel much like Samson.

So now what? Was the whole thing a trap, lure us over here just
to slam the cuffs on and stick us where the moon don't shine to cut
a deal with the government or whoever's calling the shots now?
Maybe that was it. Or no, maybe it was even worse than that, some
damn Zonal scheme to make us talk about the K-document and
when they find out we don't know jack they eighty-six us to Bautzen
or Gorky or some damn place. Ah, hell.

What would I be doing back home this time of year, anyway?
Early November, temps dipping down to the low eighties. Out on

136

the porch with a carry-out bag of conch fritters and a homemade fruit-a-bomba shake. Or maybe over at the high school watching the Fighting Conchs win the hearts of this year's crop of young Conchettes, lithe blondes goose-stepping on the sidelines in white cowboy boots and crimson-and-gray wool skirts.

Yeah, well, all that's there and this is here. I ran it through my head one more time. Nixon goes to China. He gets the word from Egon Krenz about buried treasure at Pipe Creek Farm. We go there, we get tailed, Stasi as it turns out. We shake them, dig up a canister some wiseass has rigged to look like a Chambers original from '48. Only it isn't from '48, it's from '89, inside peek at the state of the union here on the wrong side of the Elbe, that plus a strong hint the last remaining Zonal asset is a misfiled Pumpkin Paper with a two-billion-dollar price tag. We come after it, and Stasi comes after us. That was it, right? Except—

Before I could think about it any more the cell door clanged open. It was Blondie again, looking like he at least had a better night's sleep than I did. I wished him a *Guten Morgen* but he didn't answer. Still peeved about that whack in the head, I guess. He nodded toward the door.

"*Herr Generaloberst* Mann wishes to see you."

Holy hell. Mann himself, eh? Looked like we'd managed to push the right buttons after all. Now we'd see if it did any good.

A couple more goons kept us company as we walked down the hall. My legs were stiff but I'd be damned if I'd do them the favor of falling down on the concrete floor so they could kick me back up again.

At the end of the hall they shoved me into an elevator and pulled the cage shut. No numbers to light up but after what felt like a couple floors the doors opened and they shoved me out again. Carpet on the hall this time, doors covered with cheap wood veneer. We stopped in front of one that said KONFERENZZIMMER.

Blondie knocked and a voice boomed out "*Herein!*" He opened the door and nodded. I stepped in. No shove this time. Guess you don't shove guests into the company of *Generaloberst* A. F. Mann.

Windowless room, long oak table. Couple prints on the wall, Picasso from the look of 'em, half dozen antique Biedermeier china closets packed with Meissen porcelain. The place looked like the storage room for a goddam museum. Johnny was sitting at the table facing me, Victor next to him. They didn't look much better than I felt but at least I could smell coffee. The battered old briefcase was on the table in front of them. Johnny gave a slight nod. I followed his eyes.

We weren't alone. Our host stood with his back toward us at the end of the long table, staring at an oil painting on the far wall. Caspar David Friedrich? Never mind that now.

Jesus. Big guy, six-five at least. Field gray NVA uniform, silver-and-gold lieutenant general's insignia on red epaulets. Thick white hair cropped close.

He turned around and raised his hand.

"Kla-how-ya, Six Pope!"

The burns on his face never did heal right. They looked worse than mine, a lot worse. And of course he didn't die in '83, how could he have? How could he ever?

Comrade Lieutenant General Alexander Friedrich Mann.

A.k.a. George Two Moons.

He kept his arm up. Finally I raised mine.

"Kla-how-ya, Boss Tyee!"

September 7, 1948

Okay, so it wasn't Berlin, but then what the hell was. Closky's new digs took up most of the second floor of the old warehouse, big window looking down over tar-paper roofs to the hot and muddy Potomac a block or so away. Lining the wall on either side of the window were a dozen wood filing cabinets that made the trip over last month. God knows what was in 'em. Stacked up on top, the balsa wood plane models that used to hang from the rafters back in Dahlem Dorf, some of 'em glued together by Göring himself, to hear Closky tell it.

Nixon claimed he wanted to hear the ball game, so Closky had the radio on. Static crackled from a thunderstorm not too far off, then the play-by-play came through again. Walter Masterson just struck out Vic Wertz to end the third. Nats keep this up they were going to give the Browns a run for sixth place.

We were drinking Cokes in our shirtsleeves but it didn't help much. Old electric fan pushed the Pall Mall smoke around. Nixon was fanning himself with a manila folder, face bright red from sunburn after a long Labor Day weekend on the Maryland shore. He set his feet on Closky's desk next to the Hell-on-Wheels ashtray, took a long pull on his Coke, stuck the bottle down between his knees. He wasn't listening to the game, I could tell that much.

"It was a goddam outrage is what it was. I told Chambers as much when he called me Friday night after the broadcast."

Closky shrugged, lit another Pall Mall. "Whittaker said it himself, sir. It's a war. Spivak and them are on one side, we're on the other."

"If it's a goddam war, what do you suggest we do to win it?"

Closky rubbed his crew cut, wiped his pink face on a damp shirtsleeve. "Already half done. With Chambers going public on 'Meet the Press' last week the shoe's on the other foot. Papers are starting to put the heat on Hiss, want him to put up or shut up." He held up a copy of the New York *Daily News*. Headline: WELL, ALGER, WHERE'S THAT SUIT? Closky grinned. "By the time this goes to the grand jury it shouldn't be too hard to convince twelve men Hiss perjured himself."

Nixon pulled out a hankie, dabbed the sweat off his forehead, winced when he struck sunburn. "What if Hiss really does sue?"

Closky grinned. "Oh, he will, sir, no doubt about that. But not right away. See, I got this guy figured, Hiss is a careful one. Only this time he's going to be too careful. What he *should* do right now is slap a suit on Chambers today, right now, right this minute. Bang. Then folks'd believe he's telling the truth. But he won't, he'll piss around and talk to his lawyers, play Hamlet in front of the bathroom mirror while he's workin' on his pompadour. Meanwhile all your liberal news types that've been giving the sonofabitch a free ride up till now, well, they're going to start to wonder—"

Nixon cut him off. "Well, all I can say is, they're going to start without me, because I've got to haul ass out to the goddam West for the sonofabitching campaign."

139

I took a long sip of my Coke. "Thought you had it locked up, sir. Heck, you won both primaries. Only ones running against you are the Progressives, and they've got about as much chance of winning as Norman Thomas."

Nixon rolled his eyes. "Not *my* campaign, Pope, Jesus Christ, the other Republican campaigns. New York, Missouri, Minnesota, I'm booked all over the goddam joint. I can't let everybody else go down the toilet just because they don't have the organization we do."

Or the dough, I guess. One thing you could say about Dick Nixon, he was funded. Not sure how much of it went to pay Closky's rent, but enough did, no doubt. Closky leaned forward. "Look, sir, why don't you at least do this. Write a letter to Foster Dulles, tell him what we know so far. Lay it all out for him, the whole story from the inside, Hiss's phony act at the Commodore, the Model A, hell, tell him Dewey can use it in the campaign."

Nixon shrugged. "I'm not so sure he gives a shit at this point."

"So give him a little something extra. Make sure he knows Hiss tried to cover up to get the Carnegie Endowment job, didn't even tell him the FBI questioned him in '47. Maybe slip him a few details that didn't come out in the hearings, like the two grand the Russians paid Elizabeth Bentley for espionage."

Nixon frowned. "Are we sure about that?"

"Hell yes, we got that straight from the Bureau, they're still sitting on the cash. Right, Joey?"

I nodded. "That's a fact, sir. We even saw the report."

Nixon stood up, arms folded across his chest, started pacing. "Okay, so we pump some information to Dulles at the national campaign, maybe spice the pot with some inside dope nobody else has." He stopped, spun around. "What if it never gets to Dewey?"

Closky frowned a minute, then snapped his fingers. "Carbon copy to Bert at the *Trib*. Personal and confidential. He'll make sure it gets where it'll do the most good, I guarantee you that."

Nixon nodded. "You're damn straight he will. Only question is whether Dewey will ever see fit to use it. You know, I have a lot of respect for the sonofabitch but sometimes I get the feeling he's never going to take the goddam gloves off and really start punching. Now, if *I* were running for the goddam presidency—"

I polished off the last of my Coke, set the empty bottle down on Closky's desk. "He's hanging back, sir, no question about that. Doesn't want to be left holding the bag if Chambers ends up getting indicted instead of Hiss."

Nixon snorted. "Well, he damn well better not hang back too far or we're going to end up pissing this election right down the goddam hopper. Jesus, what I wouldn't give for one piece of hard evidence. A goddam piece of paper, a piece of physical—" He stopped at the window, stared out across the muddy brown river. Then he turned around. "Listen, I don't guess you and your dago friends are any closer to finding that goddam Ford, are you?"

Closky shook his head. "Trail ends at Cherner, sir. We came up dry on that one."

Nixon picked the green bottle up off the desk, downed the rest of his Coke in one gulp. "Well, hell. There's something fishy about that goddam car, boys, mark my words." He set the empty bottle down. "Something fishy about the whole goddam case."

The door opened a crack and Blunt stuck his head in, powdered sugar on his lips.

"Phone, sir, on the Committee line. Marvin Smith."

Closky picked up the phone, held the receiver out. Nixon frowned, shook his head. Closky covered the mouthpiece. "It's the Committee line, sir. Same as if you were in your office. He doesn't know the call came here."

Nixon hesitated, eyes darted around, then his arm shot out and he grabbed the receiver out of Closky's hand.

"Hello?" Eyes back and forth a couple more times before they settled. "This is he. Yes, Mr. Smith, of course I remember you."

I looked at Closky. He shrugged. Smith was Hiss's ex-pal at Justice, guy who notarized the title transfer on the Model A in '36. Except that as of last week he didn't remember doing it. Maybe something happened to jog his memory.

Nixon leaned forward in his chair, switched the radio off. "I see. Can you tell me the nature of this information?"

Closky's eyebrow shot up. Nixon took out his hankie, blotted his upper lip. "I see. Well, I could send a couple of my investigators over there now if that would be convenient." Nixon looked at us, jerked his thumb up, waved his finger around in the home run sign. I stood up and straightened my tie. Closky pulled his feet off the desk, snuffed out his Pall Mall in the ashtray.

"All right, Mr. Smith, they'll be there shortly." Nixon hung up, got to his feet.

Closky tugged on his Palm Beach suit jacket. "What's up?"

"Maybe nothing, maybe a whole lot. Smith says he's got something else to tell us about the title transfer, something he's just come across."

"He won't say what it is?"

"Not on the phone." Nixon glanced at his watch, then looked at Closky. "On second thought, Victor, how about if Pope makes the trip on his own. We've got to be back on the Hill at four." He turned to me. "Campaign business. Why don't you haul ass over to Justice now and see what the hell he's got. Phone if it's a bombshell. Otherwise we'll see you tomorrow."

9

November 4, 1989

"I am sorry I cannot welcome you in the accustomed manner, with blankets and a true potlatch. But the coffee is fresh. Bought from the PX at Oskar-Helene-Heim yesterday. Nescafé. Brewed it myself. *Skookum.* Strong."

I stared at him. My voice was a whisper. "*You* are General Mann?"

The old, scarred face softened, just the hint of a smile around the dark brown eyes. Then it was gone. He turned to Blondie, nodded toward the door. "*Schon gut, Strohmeyer. Warten Sie im Auto!*"

Blondie glanced at us, hesitated just a split second before he snapped to attention and saluted. "*Jawohl, Genosse Generaloberst!*" He spun on his heel and stepped out the door, closed it behind him.

George Two Moons gestured at a chair opposite Johnny. I sat down, eyeballed the coffee. Two Moons nodded. I raised the antique Meissen cup to my lip and took a sip. Sonofabitch was right, it was Nescafé all right, but it was hot and strong and felt good going down. If I could get it past my gut it might even do my head some good.

Two Moons folded his arms. "Our last *klatsch* was far from this house, Six Pope. I truly did not think I would see you again."

"You saved my life, Chief. Looks like somebody did you the same favor."

Two Moons nodded. "The glorious and heroic Soviet navy. Unshakable fraternal ties, international class struggle *und so weiter.*"

I stared at him. Even seeing him in that damn commie uniform I couldn't take it in. "You're joking, right? I mean, last time we talked your politics was somewhere to the right of Rudolf Hess. You had a swastika armband made of wampum. You had tears in your eyes because you never got to meet the Führer."

He shrugged. "*Macht nichts.* Yin and yang, one side or the other, all is government now, *wa.*"

From across the table Closky muttered "Amen." Then the two of them stared at each other and burst out laughing, Closky's high-pitched cackle and Two Moons's baritone guffaw and next thing you know Closky was on his feet and Two Moons came over and they fell into each other's arms like the long-lost pals they always were. I looked at Johnny and he rolled his eyes.

Closky raised his coffee cup. "To the glorious and heroic Soviet navy, boys. Long may she wave!"

Two Moons bellowed out *wa* and the two of them linked arms, Closky's frail frame schunkeling along with the Chief's, booming baritone and wailing obligato, *la lutte finale, auf Chinook bitte:*

> *Nesika skookum pee toma-a-a-l-l-a*
> *kopet mamook puk-puk*
> *Internationa-a-a-l-l-a*
> *potlatch man muck-a-muck!*

Closky let out a whoop and brought the cup to his lips, gulped the Nescafé down, dark streaks of hot coffee dribbling down his chin like blood. The Chief clapped him on the back and nearly knocked him across the room, caught him by a pipecleaner-sized arm and waltzed him back to his seat. Closky fell into the Biedermeier chair, laughing and humming.

I stared at Two Moons. Last time I saw him was what, six years ago, summer of '83, as if I could forget that. Time before that, October '47, right here in Berlin. Had a black-market operation out on the Wannsee that made Closky's setup look like a mom-and-pop store. I took another look at the loot spread out in the room. *Plus ça change.*

"Looks like you're back in the art business, Chief."

Two Moons nodded, snapped to attention. "*MfS Zentrale Arbeitsgruppe VII/13—Kunstfahndung, jawohl!* Ministry for State Security, Art Detection Work Group." He winked. "*Aber natürlich,* this is a different kind of business, Six Pope. Much of the wealth is confiscated from criminals. Antisocials, traitors to the Republic, tax cheats. A simple procedure. Assess value of object, compare with value at time of acquisition. Tax the difference. If it's a family heirloom the tax is one hundred percent, plus fines. *Hyas chickamin, viel Geld.* Thus in most cases the tax is exactly equal to the value of the object. If they cannot pay we confiscate the object as compensation."

From across the table I could hear Closky whisper, "Brilliant."

Two Moons stepped over to a marble-topped counter, poured himself a cup of java from a Mr. Coffee. He took a loud slurp, set the cup down. "From museums it's simpler. State-employed art historians declare certain works *museumsunwürdig.* Yearly quota."

Museum-unworthy? Sounded like the damn Nazis. He was right, maybe it was yin and yang. "The point being?"

"Sell to the NSW for hard currency. Much we keep. Some of my colleagues are connoisseurs of the Biedermeier, as you can see." He made a sour face. "*Chacun à son goût.*"

"I take your point, Chief, but I have a feeling you didn't bring us here to talk about art."

Two Moons spread his hands at the loot scattered around the room. "Art is many things. Sculpture and paintings, porcelain and silver, rare prints and books, weapons ancient and modern." He paused. "Also rare documents."

Now we were getting somewhere. "We wouldn't be talking about rare documents filed under *K*, would we, Chief?"

Two Moons's scarred face turned back to stone. "If I knew where they were filed I would not have called for you."

Johnny finally finished his coffee, piped up from the end of the table. "So it *was* you that planted the film at Chambers's farm and gave Krenz the message for Nixon in Beijing. Weren't you taking a chance he wouldn't figure it out?"

"Better than take the chance it would be intercepted. Even Krenz was only a code-talker. He did not understand. Only your Nixon would figure it out. And only you would be sent."

This was the part I wanted to know. "So what exactly was the message? What did Krenz tell Deng to pass on to Dick?"

Two Moons held his hands out, looked up at the ceiling like he was going into one of his potlatch chants. "*Der . . . Kürbis . . . blüht . . . noch.*"

I stared at him. "That was it? '*Der Kürbis blüht noch*'? 'The pumpkin still blooms'? Are you serious? And Nixon figured it out?"

Two Moons nodded. "Your Richard Nixon is *wake pelton*. He is no fool. And he knows that, for him, *der Kürbis* is the source of all that is good."

I took a sip of coffee and mulled that one over for a few seconds. "Okay, but, George, if your boys planted the film at Chambers's farm in the first place, how come they risked their necks chasing us to get it back?"

"First chase, to make sure you got there. They put *Wanze* in your car to track you, then stayed in sight to light *piah* under your asses."

Johnny frowned. "Okay, but the next morning? Even once we had the film they were *still* after us. It doesn't make sense."

"Makes perfect sense. You were to see film, then lose it. I could not risk your showing it to others. You were to see it, then come. *Wa*. Strohmeyer is a boy, *tenas man, kultus mamook*, bad job." He was quiet for a few seconds, then nodded his big head, spread his hands and grinned. "But look, you have come anyway, so all is well. *Ende gut, alles gut, nicht wahr?*"

I guess so. "So what's next?"

146

He touched his hand to his temple. "Next, I will share with you my *kumtux*, my knowledge. Then you will share yours. Together we are *skookum*. Together we will find the paper. And your government will buy it. For two billion dollars, *wa*."

Closky nodded, slammed a fist on the table. "Amen!"

September 7, 1948

By some miracle I found a parking spot right in front of the Natural History Museum on Constitution Avenue, backed the Hudson in and locked 'er up. Felt good to be out on my own for once, even if it was only because everybody else had something better to do. On the drive over from Georgetown I tried to think what Smith might want. Best I could figure was he'd had a brain wave about Hiss and was finally ready to swear he did remember notarizing the title transfer after all. That wasn't exactly news to the rest of the world, but it would sure as hell be a load off my mind if I could convince myself the damn thing came from somewhere on our side rather than a syndicate printing press in a Chicago basement.

It was cooler inside, thank God for that. Solicitor General's office was on the first floor, dark marble corridor on the west side of the building. I found a door with Smith's name on it, tapped on the frosted glass and walked in. I could smell hot GI coffee, heard the buzz of big floor fans and the clatter of a typewriter. A middle-aged secretary in green print dress sat at a desk behind a Royal standard, raised an eyebrow. She stopped typing. I took my hat off.

"Joseph Pope, ma'am. House Committee on Un-American Activities?"

The eyebrow came down. "He's expecting you." She nodded toward a second door. I opened it and walked in.

Smith stood up. He was in his late fifties, slim guy with nickel-frame specs and thinning gray hair, matching gray pinstripe with a double-breasted jacket he kept on in spite of the heat, blue silk tie. Open window behind him looked out onto Tenth Street. Fan on the sill shoved the hot air around, tissue streamers fluttering in case you thought you were still hot. Not bad digs, but I guess that's what thirty-five years with the civil service will get you.

I stuck my hand out. "Afternoon, Mr. Smith, I'm Joe Pope. We met at the hearing last week."

Smith nodded. "Have a seat, Mr. Pope. I hope the traffic wasn't too bad."

I smiled. "Not at all." We both sat down. I pulled my notebook out of my seersucker jacket pocket, unscrewed the cap on my pen. "I'm told you have some information to supplement your testimony of August twenty-fourth."

Smith stared at me across the desk, folded his hands. "I do, Mr. Pope, but I'm not sure what to make of it. You see, I honestly didn't recall Alger ever coming here to have that title notarized. I still don't. Maybe he did for all I know, but it was twelve years ago and I just didn't remember."

"I understand, sir. Mr. Hiss testified to the same effect."

Smith frowned. "And you think he's lying?"

I shrugged. "Not my job to think about stuff like that, Mr. Smith. That's what the congressmen get paid for."

Weak smile. "I'll be honest with you, Mr. Pope, at first I thought he was. He'd have a reason to, after all, wouldn't he? So I went through my papers for 1936, every scrap I had on file. I keep all my old appointment calendars and I checked the month of July for that year, not because I would have written down something so mundane but in the hopes that reading what else went on that month might jog my memory."

"And?"

"It didn't. Not a bit. But after I testified I decided to poke around a bit more. I didn't stop in July of '36, I kept on through the year and into 1937. Still nothing. Nothing in 1938 either. Then I came to this."

He picked up a slim eight-by-ten wire-bound book, opened to the first page. It said "Year at a Glance, 1939." He opened it to July, spun it around for me to see. I leaned across his desk. He tapped a finger on the page.

"These are my appointments for July 23, 1939."

I frowned, leaned over. "Three years to the day after the date on the title?"

"Correct."

I scanned the page. Black ink, neat penmanship, Palmer method. Then I saw it. "July 23. Twelve o'clock: *Lunch G. Crosley.*"

Smith leaned back in his chair. "He said he was a journalist with *The New Republic* or some such. He was researching an article on pending Supreme Court litigation."

"G. Crosley." Hiss claimed Chambers called himself George Crosley when he knew him back in the thirties. So far he couldn't find anybody to back him up. But was this really the same guy?

"Do you remember this 'G. Crosley,' Mr. Smith?"

"I do and I'll tell you why. He stopped by at noon sharp, offered to buy me lunch. That sounded fine to me and we chatted briefly before starting down the hall. We'd only gone a few steps when he suddenly noticed he'd left his hat in my office. I offered to go back with him but he brushed me off and ran back to get it himself. He wasn't gone but a minute."

"And he came back with his hat?"

"He came back with his hat. But no sooner did he get outside than he had another sudden recollection. Looked at his watch, slapped his forehead, apologized and told me he'd forgotten a dentist appointment across town. At the time I remember thinking that from the look of his teeth he must have forgotten more than one. In any event, he rushed off and I never saw him again. I'll grant you it was odd, but I didn't give it much thought and eventually forgot about it."

"Until—"

Smith picked up a copy of Monday's *Post,* flipped it around on the desk. He pointed to a photo under the fold on page 1. "Until I saw this. That's his picture right there."

It was Chambers, of course. "You never noticed the similarity before?"

"I never *saw* him before, or his photo either. He wasn't present when I testified last week. So I didn't make the connection until today."

I looked around the office. "Mr. Smith, where do you keep your notary seal?"

Smith tugged open his center desk drawer, held the seal up.

"And you kept it there in 1939 as well? Unlocked?"

Smith nodded. We both knew what that meant. Holy hell. "Mr. Smith, are you willing to repeat what you just told me under oath before the Committee?"

"Of course. That's why I called you."

I checked my watch. There was just one more thing to do. I thought about calling the office from here but nixed the idea, figured I'd nail it down myself.

"Sir, I'm going to get this information back to the Committee right away. Then we'll call you to set up an appointment for your testimony."

Smith stood up and I did the same. We shook hands. He smiled. "You're not going to put me on the television, are you?"

I grinned. "Not my department either, sir. We'll call you though, okay?"

I slipped my hat on and ducked out the door. I thought about driving straight back to the Hill and breaking the news but figured if I really wanted to do this right I'd get my ducks in a row first. What the hell, might even get some ink for breaking the case myself.

I sprinted across Constitution Avenue and climbed into the car, unlocked the ignition and pressed the starter. Quickest way was probably straight up Sixteenth Street, but that meant fighting traffic around the White House. What the hell, I decided to chance it.

I started going over it in my head again. July 23, 1939. A month before the Hitler-Stalin pact. Six weeks before Chambers goes to Berle at State to blow the whistle on Hiss et al. *Exactly* three years after the date on that damn title transfer. It could only mean one thing. Or so I thought.

Traffic along Pennsylvania Avenue wasn't so bad after all and once I got onto Sixteenth it was a straight shot past all the big apartment buildings up to Meridian Park. Finally got a breeze coming in the window to cut the heat. I switched the radio on but the Nats weren't playing so I settled for Doris Day and Buddy Clark warbling "Love Somebody." I hummed along.

The more I thought about it, the better I felt. It was a lucky break, all right. In fact, it was damn near unbelievable. JUNIOR G-MAN CRACKS BIG CASE. Maybe even get my picture in the paper. What would Closky say? He'd be sore as hell, I bet. Nixon too, for that matter.

When I hit Florida I took a sharp left and drove another couple blocks, squeezed into a space in the alley off U Street. I set the hand brake and switched off the ignition. If I was lucky I still had a couple of blank subpoenas in the glove box. Bingo. I unscrewed my pen and filled one out in a hurry, glanced around, forged Chairman Thomas's John Henry. So far, so good.

I climbed out of the car. Biggest Ford dealer in the District turned out to be a little yellow brick building wedged into the triangle between Florida, California, and Eighteenth. I brushed past the sharks in the sales department, headed straight for the big cheese in the back. His door was open. I rapped on the glass anyway.

"Mr. Cherner?"

Leon Cherner looked up from his paperwork, took his glasses off. "Yes?"

"Joseph Pope, sir. House Committee on Un-American Activities. My colleague was here a couple weeks ago and I know you were kind enough to come over and testify yourself on August twenty-seventh. Looks like we've just got one more loose end to tie up." I stepped over to his desk and handed him the subpoena. He slipped his glasses back on and read it.

"July 1939?" He shrugged. "Not sure what good it will do, but you're welcome to look."

Cherner stood up, walked over to a metal filing cabinet against the back wall. He gave the drawer a tug, fished out a faded yellow folder, handed it to me. "Help yourself."

I thanked him and started flipping through the file. Sales receipts for July 1939, Cherner Motor Company. Numerical order by date. July 21 . . . 22 . . . 23, 1939. Busy day. Looked like a good dozen transactions. *Purchase of 1936 Chevrolet, trade-in. Purchase of 1934 Ford Tudor, cash sale.* My heart was pounding and my mouth felt dry. What if I was wrong? *'35 Plymouth. '31 Nash.* For a second it occurred to me Smith might be lying, made the whole thing up to save his buddy Hiss. Then I saw it.

Invoice Number 10996. July 23, 1939. *1929 Ford Roadster, Model A. Serial number A-2188811-9-19-33.* Cash sale. $25. Purchase from A. Hiss. Holy, holy hell.

I looked around. Cherner was gone.

I folded the receipt and stuck it in my pocket. Then I closed the folder and put it back, slid the drawer shut.

Cherner wasn't outside either and I didn't look for him. I got back in the Hudson, took a deep breath and cranked it. Closky had left a half pack of smokes on the front seat, and for the first time since the war I lit one up. It tasted like hell and even made me cough but at least it calmed me down some. I checked my pocket to make sure I still had the receipt, then I looked at my watch. Ten after five.

I felt like I was about to bust if I didn't tell somebody, but Nixon and Closky were out of reach and I sure as hell wasn't about to tell Stripling or any of those jokers. What the hell, Nixon wanted to see me tomorrow, he'd see me tomorrow. It would wait. It would have to. I turned left on Sixteenth Street and headed back home out Route 29 to Silver Spring.

November 4, 1989

Blondie was waiting out in the car just like the Chief told him. One thing you could say about the Krauts, East or West, they sure as hell knew how to take orders. When he saw us coming he hopped out and snapped to attention. Two Moons held his hand out.

"Die Schlüssel, Strohmeyer! Ich fahre selbst heute."

Blondie's hand shot into his windbreaker pocket, pulled out the keys and slapped them in Two Moons's huge paw. *"Jawohl, Genosse Generaloberst!"*

Two Moons turned to Closky. "Best if you sit in the back with Tenas Six. Pope can ride up front with me. Much to explain."

Closky nodded and climbed in the back, Johnny after him. I followed orders myself and got in the front. Blondie shot me a glance but he was too good a Prussian to do more than that. He clicked his ersatz Hush Puppies and turned on his heel, disappearing inside the building.

The Chief's car was a new 500 SEL, smelling of leather seats that creaked no matter how still you sat. Two Moons cranked the engine and put it in gear, big V-8 gurgling like the Packards on a PT boat as he eased us past a saluting NVA guard and onto Normannenstrasse. If I thought traffic was light downtown, it was like a pedestrian zone out here. Sidewalks were crowded though, even at mid-morning, crowds headed in for more action. A couple people were carrying signs. I caught a glimpse of one. WIR SIND DAS VOLK. "We are the people." Good luck.

I looked over at Two Moons. If he noticed the restless peasants he didn't show it. Gray NVA officer's cap pulled down to his dark aviator glasses, white hair cropped short Prussian style, scarred face a stone mask. I figured now was as good a time as any.

"You know, George, I can't help thinking about the last time you and me took a ride together."

Two Moons nodded. "I remember, Six Pope. August 1983. Tenas Six was in the backseat as now. Victor was with us too, but *kopa wind*"—he pointed to the Blaupunkt—"on the air. You drank much *piah chuck*. I had the privilege of driving your car. Fine machine." He sat up straight, held his arm up like he was reciting an oath. " *'No man, say the Indians, could see the Thunderbird except in flashes as it flew swiftly through the clouds with arrows of lightning bolts tucked beneath its wings!'* "

I stared at him. "Kwakiutl legend?"

"No. Ford Motor Company press release, April 1954. Bob McNamara. Good man, knew his business." He winked. "Something for you in the glove box, by the way."

I clicked the dash open and reached inside. Familiar-looking red-and-yellow box. I pulled it out.

Cheez-Its.

Two Moons grinned. "Also PX at Oskar-Helene-Heim. Knew you were coming. More in the trunk. Not sure how long you'll be here." I stared at the box and shook my head. Good old George. What the hell. I tore the top open, slipped a cracker in my mouth. Fresh and crunchy. I reached around best as my neck would let me and offered them to the back. Johnny waved me off, Victor reached in and grabbed a handful, stuffed them in his mouth. Yellow dust settled on his Palm Beach lapels, clouded his Hero o' Socialism medal. I turned back to check the road.

We were headed west into town on a wide, potholed street called Adler-Gestell, I could tell that much, ran alongside an S-bahn line to our right. Off to the left we were passing the abandoned Johannisthal Airport, just beyond that the Wall. I figured we were headed downtown, maybe back to KoKo HQ. We'd find out soon enough. Meanwhile, I hoped Two Moons stayed in a talkative mood.

"Point I wanted to make, Chief, was that back in '83 you weren't exactly singing the Internationale or praising the heroic Soviet navy. I've got to wonder how in the hell you managed to end up here. When did you trade in your buckskins and swastikas for that damn monkey suit? In other words, what the hell is a seventy-year-old, ex-government Kwakiutl Nazi doing on the Stasi payroll in 1989?"

Closky piped up from the back. "Don't tell him the whole story, George, we'll be here all goddam day." I turned around again and my neck felt like one of Dr. Guillotin's crash dummies. Closky grinned, shot me the thumbs-up.

Two Moons must've seen me wince because he reached into his coat pocket, handed me a white plastic PX drugstore bag. I looked inside. Tums and Advil. Hallelujah. I snapped the roll in half, peeled off the foil and popped them. When they hit my gut you could almost hear the hiss.

Two Moons reached into another pocket, pulled out an opened stick of Bazooka, chewed off a plug. "Soviet navy plane flew me to Moscow, September 1983. Personal meeting with Comrade Andropov. Thanked me for foiling plot against heroic Socialist Motherland. Proclaimed me Hero of the Soviet Union. *Wa.*"

Closky gave the back of my seat a couple of kicks. "Hear, hear."

"Based on experience in Berlin after the war, sent to Socialist Brotherland as economic adviser. Much success, *hyas kull chickamin.* But now—"

He waved a meaty hand at a crowd of five hundred or so folks in what I figured was Treptower Park. What was it Brecht said in '53? Maybe the government should dissolve the people and elect a new one.

Johnny piped up. "Now you're looking at default on your debt service by mid-1990."

Closky was still kicking my seat. "Might make it to '91."

Two Moons shook his head. "We need *kull chickamin,* hard currency. *Devisen.* Strauss's billion-mark credit helped, but more must come. That is why I brought you here. You will help me find the document and we will sell it to government for two billion dollars, *wa.*"

Two Moons eased off the gas, flipped on his right blinker. I checked the street sign coming up. Eisenstrasse. Never heard of it. We rumbled over a bridge that crossed the Spree to the north. Guess we weren't headed downtown after all.

Two billion. Jesus Christ. Blunt was right, it didn't make sense.

"I've had time to think about this, Chief, and what I think is the whole case is a crock. It's got to be. Because whatever the document is, it's going to be at least fifty years old, right? What could possibly be in it? What did Hiss give Chambers in 1938 that would be worth ten cents today?"

Two Moons didn't answer. "Any more Cheez-Its left?"

I flipped the box open, passed it over.

"Besides, who in government's even *got* two billion dollars these days? Nixon? I mean, I know Johnny here says he's still funded but geez, the guy's renting an office from Perillo Tours, can't even afford real art. At least you've got that much, George, hell, compared to him you're a regular Renaissance prince."

Closky tapped me on the shoulder. "Money's never a problem in government, Joey. Never. Don't let that Jersey office fool you, he's still funded all right. And as long as he is, we are too. It'll come from somewhere, trust me."

Comforting thought. Two Moons switched on the headlights as we headed through a short tunnel under the Ostkreuz S-bahn junction. We came out near a park, bare trees and a dreary brown lake, too small for the Weissensee though. We braked for a traffic light and I squinted to read the street signs. Leninallee and Ho-Chi-Minh-Strasse. Terrific. Puts us in any one of ten countries between the Elbe and the Mekong Delta. Guess things had changed since '47.

The light switched to green and Two Moons gunned it and the tires squealed, thick smear of Michelin rubber on Berlin paving stones. Now the Weissensee on our left, no doubt about that, no doubt about the direction either, north out of town toward Bernau. We were in the part of East Berlin that made the Empty Quarter look like Times Square. Straight shot out Bernauer Strasse, big empty chuckholed six-lane boulevard past endless rows of bullet-pocked workers' flats, every half mile or so a shabby VEB grocery store with empty cans stacked in a dusty window.

Finally we came up on a sign: SIE VERLASSEN BERLIN, HAUPTSTADT DER DDR.

Good riddance. We crossed the line and left four-power territory for the Zone proper. A mile later Two Moons picked up the Auto-bahn loop, snaked west along the Berliner Ring for a quarter mile, then merged left onto the on-ramp for the old spur north to what used to be Stettin, 120-mile trip to nowhere since the Poles took the town over in '45. Concrete road surface full of potholes big as bomb craters, looked like it hadn't seen a repair crew since Hitler first took a shovel to it in 1934. Didn't stop Two Moons from airing it out, though, speedometer reaching 160 kmh now and then. At this rate we'd hit the Baltic coast in just over an hour if we didn't blow a tire first.

"Kind of cold for a day at the beach, George."

No answer.

After about five minutes I spotted a green-and-white sign. When we got close enough to read it I knew where we were headed. Johnny tapped my shoulder and pointed.

"Wandlitz."

156

Of course. Wandlitz. Also affectionately known to the common folk as Volvograd. Combination Versailles, Forbidden City and Levittown, home to the local commie elite since the '56 Hungarian unpleasantness made 'em too jittery to spend the night in town.

Two Moons took the exit at a steady 100 kmh, tires squealing as we curved around the overpass and down onto a bumpy two-lane blacktop that headed west through the north German pine barrens. A few minutes later he hit the brakes again, pulled off on the shoulder and made a sharp right turn north on a road into the woods.

For the first time in the past hour and a half the road was smooth, fresh macadam in a neat line past a dozen signs of the I'd-go-back-if-I-were-you variety. A military-style gate and guard shack were just ahead.

Johnny leaned over the seat, tapped my shoulder. "Wandlitz, Joe. Geez. Not sure anybody from our side's ever been here."

I nodded. Of course, George was from our side, or used to be, but let that pass. For the first time since we left the East Berlin city limits Two Moons slowed down. A sharp-looking NVA sergeant in white gloves and jackboots strutted out of the shack, eyeballed the car and gave a crisp salute. Somewhere inside the shack his partner must have hit a button, because the gate swung open in front of us. We drove through.

Inside the compound were tennis courts, landscaped gardens, row of Bavarian-style ersatz ski lodges stretching off to the right, low-lying office buildings dead ahead. Home to some three hundred Party types last I heard, twice that number of Stasi flunkies to bring 'em their morning coffee, shine their shoes, and run errands into the Non-Socialist Economic Sphere to buy their groceries.

We pulled into a driveway next to a long, three-story glass-and-concrete building. Only sign I could see was a big blue *P* for parking above what looked like a garage entrance.

Two Moons tugged off his aviator glasses as we headed onto the concrete ramp and down into the dark. Three levels down he steered off the ramp and into the parking area. Could've been an underground parking garage anywhere, I guess, except for the NVA guard who snapped to attention and shot us another white-gloved salute as we drove past. Two Moons touched the patent-leather bill of his cap, steered down a row of Citroëns, pulled into an empty space marked POLITBURO. He shut off the engine, pointed at the dash.

"You won't need the Cheez-Its."

Did he really trust us or was he just crazy? I looked around. Of course, even if we wanted to try something, where the hell would we go? I climbed out of the car and opened the door for Closky. Johnny and Two Moons got out the other side, stretched. Two Moons tossed his Bazooka pack onto the front seat, slammed the door.

"This way, *meine Herren.*"

The click of Two Moons's jackboots echoed off the low concrete ceiling as we followed him down the line of cars. He stopped at the corner.

"You already know that some Party members' taste runs to the Biedermeier. Comrade Honecker is somewhat more modern, but no less a collector. Much wealth."

We turned the corner. Johnny let out a low whistle.

It was much wealth, all right. Couple of 500 SLs, an old bathtub Porsche, Jaguar E-type, black ZIL limo. Down at the end a few U.S. jobs, '55 Packard, '58 Fairlane, '60 Impala. Beautiful cars, every one of 'em. All in mint condition too. Geez.

"These all belong to Honecker?"

Two Moons nodded. "Twenty-three fine *piah-chicks,* including the sedans and limousines for everyday use." He held his hands out at the row of parked cars. "Twenty-two of them you see here. One you don't."

He turned around. At the end of the garage was a gray metal overhead door. No signs, no markings. Heavy padlocks on a hasp at each corner. Two Moons reached into his pocket, pulled out a key ring. His huge frame bent down, unlocked one padlock, then the other, slid them out of the hasps and set them aside. Then he reached inside his greatcoat, pulled out a little black box with a keypad, angled it to the overhead lights, typed in a dozen digits. He looked at us.

"I have said I will share my *kumtux,* my knowledge. It begins here."

Two Moons aimed the box at the garage door, hit a button with his thumb. From inside there was a clank and a thud, then a loud whir as the door went up real slow.

It was dark inside, smelled like damp must and motor oil. We followed him in and he reached against the wall, clicked a switch and a fluorescent light flickered on.

Inside was a single car. Erich Honecker's personal fleet, *piahchick* number twenty-three.

Or was it number one?

Holy hell.

All four tires were flat, windshield cracked. Olive-drab paint chipped and peeling, dark blue showing through underneath. Faint remnant of Cyrillic letters stenciled on the driver's-side door, CCCP-something-or-other.

We stepped closer. My heart was racing. *Model A . . . slightly collegiate model . . . saucy little trunk on the back . . .*

Two Moons lifted the hood. Johnny elbowed his way to the front, stuck his head in.

"Looks like a Skoda carburetor, Joe. Fuel pump off an old Studebaker. Somebody did a job to keep her running, all right."

I didn't answer. Two Moons knew what I was really looking for, pointed to the serial number on the engine block. Forty-one years ago a skinny kid with an ax to grind learned it by heart, never forgot it. I bent over, stuck my head under the hood.

2-1-8-8-8-1-1.

I read the number three times, digit by digit. *Do you recall the transaction whereby you disposed of that Ford, Mr. Hiss . . . ?*

I ran my finger over it, felt each number stamped into the cool metal plate in Dearborn exactly sixty years ago. It was real. . . . *I have no present recollection of the disposition of the Ford, Mr. Hébert.*

I stood up and tried to stretch my neck, rubbed my head and eyes, stared up into Two Moons's big, scarred face.

"How, George? How did Alger Hiss's Model A Ford end up in Erich Honecker's garage?"

Two Moons reached up on a high metal shelf. He took down a small cardboard box, checked the label, tucked the box under his arm. Then he switched off the light.

He looked down at me and shrugged. "Why don't we go and ask him?"

September 8, 1948

Nixon hung up the phone. His face was white, hands shaking, upper lip shiny with sweat.

"Marvin Smith is dead."

It hit me like a punch in the gut. Closky didn't budge.

"When?"

"This morning. Hour ago. Fell down a circular stairwell at the Justice Department. D.C. cops are calling it a suicide."

I felt sick.

I pointed to the yellow carbon paper on Nixon's desk. "We still have the receipt. And we can subpoena Smith's appointment book. It's got Crosley's name in it for the same date as that receipt. That's the link we need right there."

Nixon held the receipt in his hands, stared at it. "Shit."

When I first told him about Smith's story he damn near hit the roof. Hell, why not? It meant Hiss might be telling the truth after all, at least about Chambers calling himself Crosley and about giving Chambers the damn car. And if it also meant the title was a forgery, well, hell, that sure explained why Hiss didn't remember signing it.

Closky reached in his pocket, pulled out the Zippo. He clicked the lid up and down, slow and quiet but it was enough to set my teeth on edge. Finally he put it away.

"Thing of it is, Joey, without Smith's testimony you don't have a link to Chambers. All you've got is a 'G. Crosley' in an old appointment book. Might not mean a thing."

"But Smith told me—"

Closky held his hand up, wagged a fat finger. "Hearsay."

160

"And the invoice? All right, forget Smith for a minute, here's the missing invoice everybody was so worked up about at the hearing, it's got the right serial number, it's got Hiss's name on it, but it's dated *three years late* if the title transfer is the real McCoy. I mean, at the very least we've got to explain that."

Closky leaned across the desk, slid the receipt out of Nixon's hand. Nixon didn't budge. Closky studied the receipt. Finally he set it down on the desk.

"I don't know. Misdated, maybe? How about that? Somebody types a nine instead of a six and then it got misfiled? Makes sense, doesn't it?"

I couldn't believe it. "Victor, are you serious? Look, on August twenty-fourth I'm handed a copy of a 1936 title transfer by a Chicago gangster who strongly hints he had something to do with Harry White's supposed heart attack. Signatures on it are from Hiss and Smith but neither of 'em remembers signing it. Then yesterday Smith tells me Chambers came to see him under shady circumstances in 1939. He was alone in his office long enough to use his notary seal. That same day somebody sold Hiss's Ford to Cherner Motor Company, but of course Smith doesn't know that. Yesterday he tells me everything he does know. And today the guy is dead."

"Suicide."

"What, on an inside stairwell? Jumpers like fresh air, Victor, you don't have to be a goddam psychiatrist to know that."

"Tell me this, Joey. If Chambers forged the title to sell the car in 1939—I mean, that's what you're suggesting, right? If he did that, why is the copy from the Motor Vehicle Bureau dated 1936?"

"Hell, I don't know. Because it's a forgery—"

"What, a forgery of a forgery?"

I didn't answer. Closky smirked. "Look, Joey, here's what we've got, okay? We've got a name in an appointment book nobody's ever going to look at. We've got an invoice missing from Cherner Motor Company." He frowned and looked at me. "Cherner didn't see you take it, you didn't give him a receipt?" I shook my head. "Okay. We've got an invoice missing from a file at Cherner Motor Company that nobody's ever going to look at either. And we've got a very

161

depressed civil servant who commits suicide over on Tenth Street. What's it all add up to?"

I stared at him. I wasn't going to give up. "Obstruction of justice."

Closky let out a little laugh, but there was an edge to it. "Obstruction of justice, Joey? Whose justice? Tom Clark's? The Democrats'? The Commies'? Let me tell you something, boy. Try to get this straight, okay? Alger Hiss is a dirty commie spy who sold his country and half the damn world down the river. And even if he wasn't, he's still a dishonest sonofabitch who's trying to make a monkey out of the Congress of the United States by lying under oath—"

"He wasn't lying about Crosley. He wasn't lying about the car—"

"Goddammit, will you shut up and listen to me? He's a lying sonofabitch who deserves to be put away for a long time. And let me tell you something else, okay? This man right here"—he pointed at Nixon—"has worked damn hard to bring Hiss to justice. His whole damn name is riding on this, Joey, his whole damn future, *our* whole damn future. If we blow this thing, if Hiss walks, there's not going to be a campaign '48, there's not going to be a campaign '50, there's not going to be a Senate seat and God knows what else after that."

I kept my voice calm, nodded at Nixon. "Fine. So it's up to him."

Closky stared at me, then at Nixon. "He's right, sir. It's up to you."

Closky picked up the receipt, folded it twice, set it in the glass ashtray on Nixon's desk. He reached in his pocket and pulled the Zippo out, thumb on the flint wheel, held it down next to the thin yellow paper. "Your call, sir. Just say the word."

Nixon looked to one side, then the other, like a trapped rat. He wiped his upper lip on his French cuff, stared at the paper in the ashtray. Finally his eyes met Closky's. His head barely moved, but if you wanted to take it for a nod I guess you could. Closky did.

He flicked the lighter on, touched the flame to the edge of the paper. He held it there while it caught and spread, paper unfolding and curling up again as the only piece of evidence I cared about in this whole damn case went up in a thin stream of powdery black smoke.

10

November 4, 1989

Two Moons told us to wait in the hall with the nurses while he talked to the plainclothes Stasi goon at the door, then ducked inside the room. A minute later he stuck his head out, waved us over. The Stasi boy took a step toward us. Two Moons held up an arm the size of a tree trunk and waved him back. He shot us a look but I guess he was too good a Kraut to ignore the three silver stars on Two Moons's shoulder boards.

Inside it was half hospital room, half condo. Shelf full of Western electronics against the far wall, Phillips color TV and Blaupunkt stereo setup. Heat cranked up near eighty, smell of alcohol and Vicks VapoRub. Geez, maybe the poor sonofabitch really did resign for reasons of health.

He was sitting up in bed, blue silk pajamas, copy of *Der Stern* clutched in bony fingers. Snow-white hair brushed straight back, thin face, horn-rimmed glasses. How old was Honecker now, seventy-seven? Born the year before the Boss, looked every day of it too. Guess it took guys like that more than a couple weeks to get used to the elder statesman role.

He set the magazine down but hardly gave Two Moons a glance. Then he spotted Closky and his face changed, soft smile spreading across the old hawklike features.

"*Na, alter Freund?*"

Closky drew his frail frame up to something that must've passed for attention at Allenwood's geriatric ward. "*Guten Morgen, Herr Generalsekretär.*"

Honecker held a limp hand out, didn't get up. Closky went over and pumped it. Honecker reached up and tugged on Closky's Hero of Socialism badge, grinned, mumbled something I didn't catch. Closky laughed. Then Two Moons stepped over and finished the introductions. There were a couple chairs on each side of the bed. Honecker motioned for us to sit down.

He stared at Closky, spoke in soft, Rheinland-accented German. "So, Preacher, you are back among us. I was happy to hear you gave your capitalist jailers the slip once again."

Closky nodded. "Nothing against capitalists, but four years was long enough, *Herr Generalsekretär.*"

Thin smile. "I spent ten in Brandenburg-Goerden, '35 to '45. That was long enough too."

There was an awkward pause, then Two Moons piped up. "Comrade Erich, as you know our visitors are here on a matter of some importance to our Republic. They are prepared to offer an extraordinary sum in *Devisen.* In return they want the documents we have discussed. Since time is of the essence, I took the liberty of already showing them the car."

Honecker's head jerked up, eyes flashed. "You had no authority to do that, Comrade *Generaloberst!*"

Two Moons shrugged. "I felt it essential that they know the merchandise is genuine."

Honecker's eyes softened. "You might have waited, but never mind. Now I suppose you want me to tell them the whole story."

Two Moons nodded. Honecker sighed, reached for a glass of mineral water from his nightstand, took a sip. He set the glass down, hand shaking. Then he shot a glance at Johnny and me.

"And I am to speak before members of Western intelligence?"

I held a hand up. "Government representatives, Mr. General Secretary. That's all."

Thin smile, hardly a smile at all.

"Very well." Honecker took a deep, wheezy breath. "The automobile you have just seen was given to me on June 10, 1946, by Walter Ulbricht."

He stopped to let that sink in.

"I was thirty-four years old and already a member of the Central Committee of the newly formed Socialist Unity party. That spring, at a conference in Brandenburg an der Havel, I was elected head of the Free German Youth. Ulbricht took me aside to offer his congratulations. He said the new position would require much work, and also much travel, even into the Western zones to build support among young people there. For that purpose, he said, I was to be given a car."

He started coughing and couldn't stop. Two Moons got out of his chair, helped him sit up straight, patted him on the back. One good whack of Two Moons's manhole-sized hand and I had the feeling Honecker would fly right through the Swedish shelving on the far wall, but Two Moons took it easy. Finally Honecker stopped coughing, pulled a Tempo tissue from the box on the nightstand, wiped his mouth. He waved Two Moons back to his chair.

"Ulbricht told me the Party had just acquired an automobile from the political commissar of the Soviet Berlin garrison. It was an old American roadster that had served as staff car for a Russian colonel during Zhukov's final offensive on Berlin the previous year. It was a Ford. The so-called Model A."

Wait a minute. "But how—?"

Honecker glanced at me, cold smile. "A gift to the Soviet government from their 'heroic' American allies, supposed compensation for their cowardly refusal to open a second front."

I damn near fell out of my chair. *"Are you talking about Lend-Lease?"*

Honooker nodded. "Yes. And if you expect me to be grateful, I'm afraid I must disappoint you. The Soviet peoples and the progressive forces of other nations made enormous sacrifices during the war against fascism, tens of millions giving their lives, and you Americans expect us to crawl on our knees because you sent us obsolete automobiles, pup tents, and Spam."

Johnny couldn't let that pass. "It was a bit more than that, sir. From October '42 to September '45 we sent your Russian friends half a million trucks, fifty thousand jeeps, seven thousand tanks, plus your assorted bombers and fighters, steam locomotives, machine tools, radios, food, fuel, paper, chemicals—"

Good old Johnny, our walking encyclopedia. I held up a hand to stop him. "Okay, but wait a minute, kid. We sent them Alger Hiss's *Ford* in the bargain?"

Johnny frowned. I could smell wood burning. "Well, Chambers did claim Hiss gave the car to a communist contact for use by a Party organizer *out West,* right? Let's say he really did, say the car ended up somewhere out on the Coast. Lend-Lease collecting point for shipments to Russia was at Auburn on Puget Sound, just north of Tacoma. We know the American Communist party called on members to donate what they had. And we're figuring at least one of them had a car."

Hmm. The rest of the crowd was glaring at us, so Johnny piped down. Two Moons turned to Honecker.

"Die Dokumente, Genosse Erich."

Honecker sighed. *"Die Dokumente?"*

I couldn't stand it anymore. "The K-documents, sir." Then I tried for a shot in the dark. "The papers you got from Whittaker Chambers when he visited Vienna in 1959."

Honecker frowned, stared at me for a good half minute. "I received no such papers."

Was he lying or just a forgetful old man? "We're pretty sure about that one, sir. Don't see how else it could've happened."

"You are very much mistaken. The documents you describe did not come from the man known to you as Whittaker Chambers."

Oh no? "Then where did they come from?"

He took a Fisherman's Friend cough drop off the nightstand, picked at the cellophane with a neatly manicured fingernail. He peeled the wrapper off and placed the lozenge carefully in his mouth. Finally he looked up.

"They were in the car."

I stared at him. "In the car?"

"In the trunk, under a rubber pad bolted to the floor. In a plain brown envelope."

Holy hell. I shot a glance at Closky. From the look on his face it was news to him too. Only Two Moons looked bored, like he'd heard this song before.

Honecker blew his nose. "My English was poor, but I understood enough to know the papers consisted of communications with a certain European embassy of the United States in the summer of 1939. Two of the names on the papers I recognized at once. The third I did not. That name was Alger Hiss."

He stopped and took a sip of mineral water, shifted the cough drop to the other cheek.

"It was clear to me that these papers were of a highly sensitive nature, that they had been deliberately hidden and then lost. In order to learn something about this man Hiss, I made discreet inquiries of Comrade Mielke, later to be our minister for state security. He informed me that Hiss was an aide to President Roosevelt who had been present at the Yalta Conference in 1945. He also determined that the so-called Dies Committee of the American Congress had begun an investigation into Hiss's alleged communist background some years earlier, but it had been abruptly broken off. He was, however, able to locate a former investigator from that committee in the American sector of Berlin, where he was serving as an army intelligence officer." He nodded at Closky. "Comrade Mielke also determined that this particular officer had a certain, shall we say, weakness. He recommended that I select an attractive young man from my FDJ staff and send him into the American sector to find out what he could. I did so. It ended badly."

Closky's jaw dropped. His face was chalk-white, his voice a whisper. "*You* sent him?"

Honecker shrugged. "When he did not return, I kept the documents to myself."

I leaned forward in my chair. "But you must have followed the case with some interest when it hit the news two years later, in '48."

"The internal affairs of capitalist countries are of no concern to the leadership of the SED. But yes, I did indeed follow the case, with some amount of amusement, I must say—although the documents themselves were of no use to me at that point. A historical curiosity. All that changed in 1961, of course."

Nineteen-sixty-one. The year Chambers died. The year he wrote the letter to Nixon. The year—

"The year you built the Wall," Johnny said. He used the German word, *Mauer.* I knew what was coming.

Honecker's head snapped toward Johnny like he'd just cursed in church. He drew himself up as best he could, face flushed, finger shaking. "The *Anti-Fascist Protective Barrier*—not 'wall,' young man, 'protective barrier'—has proven the greatest contribution to peace and stability in Europe. It has stood for twenty-seven years and will stand a hundred more if need be. It—"

Two Moons broke in. "It was a great accomplishment, Comrade Erich, *hyas mamook*, a great deed. All progressive forces of history will praise you for it forever, *wa.*"

Honecker caught his breath. He flopped back against the pillow. His voice got quiet. "It was a masterpiece of logistical organization. *Ein Meisterwerk, verstehen Sie?* Thousands of tons of equipment brought up to the border in complete secrecy, thousands of People's Police, workers' militia and NVA troops mobilized under the guise of practice maneuvers. Barbed wire, concrete, cinder blocks, masons' tools, cranes, all packed and shipped to collecting points for fictitious construction projects. Orders to the S-bahn, U-bahn, and Reichsbahn crews for the immediate rerouting of all rail traffic around Westberlin. Orders to the utility companies for emergency provision of water, gas, and electricity. Orders to the Volkskammer for the proper political preparations. All issued by *me* over Ulbricht's signature."

The room was dead quiet except for the sound of Honecker's breathing. He looked around like he wasn't sure where he was, hands twisting the sheet on his lap, face red. Just like Nixon, you had to let him talk himself out.

"I had established my headquarters in the police presidium at Alexanderplatz. It was Saturday night, August 12, 1961. At the stroke of midnight I telephoned Heinz Hoffmann to give the order. 'You know what's to be done,' I said. 'Move.' Work began at once. I drove to the construction site at Staatsgrenze-West. Crews were already unrolling the barbed wire at double-time, mixing concrete, setting the first posts in place. Throughout the night I drove along the border, stopping to encourage the troops and oversee construction. When dawn came the Western provocateurs had learned a lesson they would never forget, and the people of our Republic were at last free to build socialism, just as they are doing today."

Whew. I guess Honecker hadn't looked out the window lately. Only thing getting built out there now were barricades and protest signs far as I could see.

Closky was staring at Honecker, face still white. I started to talk but Honecker cut me off. He was sitting straight up now, face flushed, eyes wide behind his horn-rimmed glasses.

"The Western powers, of course, did nothing. Revanchist elements and warmongers urged action. 'Cut the barbed wire,' they said. 'Knock the barriers down.' But your president said no. Mr. Pay-any-price, Mr. Let-the-word-go-forth, the rich boy from Boston sat in his vacation home in Massachusetts and did nothing." Honecker's eyes got narrow, voice dropped to a whisper. "Wisely, I might add! Because he knew I had the papers, and he knew they would come to light *only* if the borders of the GDR were violated."

"And how did he know that, Mr. General Secretary?"

Sly grin. "Because I told him. I sent him a message through an old comrade that spring. And I'm sure he got it. Because whatever else he did, he always left our border in peace. He sent troops to

Vietnam, he bombed Laos, he enforced an illegal blockade of Cuba that took the world to the brink of war, but never once did he dare violate the sovereign borders of the German Democratic Republic. Never. And neither did any of his successors."

The room was quiet. Honecker fell back on the pillow. He was breathing hard, forehead shiny with sweat.

I decided to go for broke. "*Herr Generalsekretär*, a few weeks back we talked to a fellow who called himself Schmidt in the Office of Commercial Coordination. Victor gave him a message for you but I guess it was too late, you never got it. So here it is again. We're authorized to offer a total of two billion dollars for the papers in question, the ones you call the K-document. Five hundred million paid into your account at the Swiss Bankverein Lugano the minute we notify government contacts of your verbal agreement. Five hundred million when we notify them the document is in our hands. And one billion when we cross the checkpoint into West Berlin."

Of course I didn't really know if those numbers were good or if Closky had made the whole thing up. But he wasn't talking now anyway and it didn't seem like the time to chintz.

Honecker wouldn't look at me, stared straight ahead. "I am no longer the General Secretary. You should be talking to Krenz."

"Krenz doesn't know where the document is. Only you do."

Honecker smiled, shook his head.

Two Moons stood up, walked over to Honecker's side, leaned down. "The warmonger Kennedy has been dead for twenty-five years, Comrade Erich. The border is secure for all eternity. Now the document can serve a new purpose. It can save the Republic once again. By selling it to the West we can service the debt for five years at least, and with the remainder buy much wealth for the people, bananas and raisins, shoes and fashionable clothing, televisions, stereophonic record players, women's hygienic products. You can sweep Krenz aside like a paper doll, you can return to the Politburo in triumph, *wa*."

Honecker shook his head again. "Too late."

I gave it one more try. "Mr. General Secretary, I know a lot of folks are interested in this document, some of them for reasons I probably can't even guess at. But we were sent here to find it by a man who's very much like yourself, and one who didn't think too much of the rich boy from Boston either." This was a long shot. Honecker's eyebrows went up but he didn't squawk. I pushed ahead. "Humble beginnings, worked his way up to serve his country, made king of the hill but got canned by a crowd who didn't appreciate the good he did. Hell, the Berlin Agreements of '71 probably helped you and your country more than anything to come out of America before or since. Now he's looking for something you can help him out with, looking for that last Pumpkin Paper, *das letzte Kürbis-Dokument*. And he knows you can help him."

Honecker frowned. "Excuse me, are you saying *Kürbis*?"

I nodded. "*Ja, Kürbis. Die K-Dokumente, die Kürbis-Dokumente.* The Pumpkin Papers."

Honecker turned to Two Moons. Two Moons shrugged. Honecker looked back at me, puzzled look on his thin face. For the first time he spoke in English. "You mean to say, you are thinking all the time that the *K* is standing for *Kürbis*?"

I stared at him. "Well, sure. Or else it's *K* for 'Karl,' which amounts to the same thing, right?"

Honecker's frown softened, changed to a faint smile. He looked around the room from one of us to the other, shaking his head slowly. He switched back to German.

"Yes, it is the same thing. But both are wrong."

11

November 2, 1948

I spent most of the fall outside of Washington, which at least helped me put poor old Marvin Smith out of my mind for a while. Harry White too, for that matter. Closky worked on me for two months straight between campaign stops and I was even starting to convince myself he might be right. Sure, Chambers was no saint, hell, he'd probably lied to us more than once, but that didn't make Hiss a choirboy. Who's to say the main charges against him weren't true anyway? And old men get heart attacks, sure, and other old men get fed up and take the leap. Happens all the time.

Hiss came through with his suit, by the way, slapped a fifty-grand libel action on Chambers end of September, upped it to seventy-five when Chambers sassed him about it. That gave us some ink for a while, just like Closky promised, but Dewey never did jump on it. All for the best, anyway, since by now Dewey had a lock on the White House with or without our help.

So Nixon took off for the Coast after Labor Day, went on tour for the Dewey-Warren ticket, wowed 'em from California to New York and back again, same speech, Communist Menace, lock up Hiss and save the world. Halfway through he called us out for good measure, set Closky loose and I got to see firsthand how he'd earned his spurs in the primaries. Phony flyers, wiretaps, prank calls, even a burglary or two. All of it aimed at the poor Progressives, only ones to put up a fight in the twelfth since Nixon won both primaries in the spring. Upshot due in tonight, which would most likely be a landslide to send him back to D.C. for his second term, set to run for senator in '50 and after that, who knows?

Oh, and speaking of Senators, they came up short again, finished the season in seventh, forty games back of the World Champ Indians, missed knocking the Browns out of sixth by a lousy three games. So not every dream comes true, but tonight at least was going to be different.

It was close to midnight when the cab pulled up to the hotel entrance on Wilshire Boulevard.

I looked out the window. "The Cocoanut Grove? What the hell's he meeting us here for, Victor? I thought the action was at party headquarters."

Closky grinned, rubbed his crew cut. "No, they already left. Said to come here for a last-minute powwow, maybe a little early celebrating."

I winked. "You still got your money on Thurmond?"

Closky frowned. "Okay, so that didn't quite work out. We'll do fine with Dewey in the White House, don't worry about it."

We paid the cabbie and stepped across the sidewalk to the big glass doors. November in L.A., you couldn't beat it. Seventy degrees, balmy night air. Plus it probably did Closky good to be someplace where he wasn't the only one in a Palm Beach suit.

Inside it was cold, air-conditioned, I guessed, dark and smoky to boot, but the joint was pretty crowded considering it was the late show. Up on the stage Hildegarde the Chanteuse was working through a schmaltzy dragged-out version of that old Kraut tune "You Can't Be True, Dear." The maître d' gave us the eyeball but

Nixon spotted us in time and waved. We worked our way through the tables to the corner. He had his wife with him, plus some old college pals from Whittier I recognized from our last trip out.

"Come on over, boys." Nixon stood up. He was wearing a double-breasted light gray sport jacket and a blue silk tie, looked pretty sharp for a first-term congressman at the end of a long Election Day. He introduced us, then took Closky by the arm. "Excuse us for just a minute, Victor and I need to have a quick word."

Nixon and Closky walked over to a dark corner by the dance floor, went into a huddle. I felt like a horse's ass standing there but his wife finally asked me to sit down. That wasn't much better, but at least now it was easier for the three of them to ignore me. Nixon's Whittier pal said something about tipping Hildegarde off to the VIP in the crowd, took out his fountain pen and scrawled a note. He grinned, pointed at Dick over in the corner and put his finger to his lips. The two ladies smiled.

"You Can't Be True" was just ending, so he got up and slipped the note to the bandleader. He glanced at it, looked around. Nixon's pal pointed over to the corner. The bandleader nodded, passed the note up to Hildegarde. She studied it, smiled, leaned into the microphone.

"I've just been informed that we have a very special guest in the audience tonight, a wonderful congressman who's just been elected to his second term—"

Nixon jerked around like somebody gave him a hot foot. His eyes darted back and forth. The spotlight hit him and he caught himself, smiled and waved. Hildegarde held out her hand and Nixon climbed onto the stage and stepped up to the mike. His face was shiny in the spotlight, jowls dark blue with the day's growth of beard.

"I realize, folks, that most of you are probably Democrats thinking you're going to celebrate." The crowd laughed; Nixon kept it deadpan. "But that's okay. It just happens that I love Democrats. I even married one." He grinned and held a hand out to the table. "I'd like to introduce my beautiful wife, who was born on Saint Patrick's Day, and who was a Democrat when I married her."

Well, the place went nuts and why the hell not? Good ol' Dick. They cheered him and the missus too, and as Hildegarde struck up a chorus of "Buttons and Bows" the two of them hit the dance floor for a quick-step. Pretty soon other couples joined them and things were back to normal.

Closky came back and sat down. Dick's pals were up on the dance floor too so we were alone.

"What was that all about?"

Closky looked at his watch. "Long story. What time is it in Chicago, Joey?"

I stared at him. "Chicago? Two hours later, which makes it what, three in the morning?"

Closky nodded. "I gotta make a phone call. Couple irons in the fire back there and Mr. Big wants to know how it's cookin'." He jerked a thumb in Nixon's direction.

"Wait a minute. What the hell have we got cooking in Chicago that the Boss would care about?"

Closky winked. "A little get-out-the-vote with the help of our friends. See, if they can swing Cook County there's a good chance Dewey could carry Illinois."

"Chicago? Jesus, not Willie Marco—" Closky punched my shoulder and disappeared into the crowd.

Well, this was just great. I'd seen a lot in the past two months, seen enough to convince me there was more to elections than they taught you in high school civics class. The whole damn campaign was so crooked it made Boss Tweed look like Jimmy Stewart.

And even if it wasn't, even if it was all legit, it still wasn't kosher because Closky and I weren't supposed to be working for the campaign at all, we were supposed to be working for Congress. At least that's what our paychecks said. Still, all that was small change compared to actual vote fraud, if that's what we're talking about now. Holy hell.

Nixon came back and sat down. The ladies were laughing. A minute later Closky got off the phone and strolled back to the table. Big grin.

"Can't miss, folks. Willie says the early edition of the *Chicago Tribune* just hit the streets. They're calling it, all right. Anybody want to guess the headline?"

Nixon took a drink of Scotch, gave his wife a stiff hug. "We give up, Victor. Why don't you break down and tell us?"

Closky picked up his glass, held it high.

"It says: DEWEY DEFEATS TRUMAN."

November 4, 1989

The drive back from Wandlitz went pretty smooth, at least until we hit the crowds on Liebknechtstrasse. Looked like a combination of Nuremberg in '34, Times Square on V-J Day, and a Macy's white sale. Two Moons switched on the siren and we made slow but steady progress, finally bumped up on the sidewalk and took a shortcut across the huge pedestrian zone at Alexanderplatz straight to the TV tower. The crowd parted slowly as the big Mercedes rumbled across the paving stones.

"Is it me, Chief, or are they takin' their time getting out of the way?"

Two Moons got within a hundred feet of the tower and stopped the car. He didn't say anything.

We got out and waded into the crowd. Young couples and kids, teenagers and older folks, some of them with signs: CHANGE NOW, NEW THINKING, WE ARE THE PEOPLE. No argument there, at least from me, but then I wasn't on the central committee of the SED. Looked like folks were drifting in the general direction of the Rote Rathaus, the commie city hall.

I could tell from the looks we were getting they didn't much like the car, didn't like where we'd parked it, didn't like the Chief's uniform, and didn't like us. We stuck close to Two Moons as he shoved his way up the steps at the base of the tower, past the triple lines right up to the elevator doors. The middle elevator opened and a couple dozen people poured out. Before the attendant could let anybody on the empty car, Two Moons held his hand up.

"*Staatssicherheit*. State security." That plus his uniform was enough to part the waters and we slipped on. Just as the doors closed I heard somebody mutter "*Stasischweine*" but then the doors slid shut and the four of us were alone for the 699-foot ride up to the Tele-Café. My head was pounding and the pain was shooting down my neck. Closky was humming something I didn't catch at first. Then I got it. "Go Down, Moses." Terrific.

Johnny nudged me, pointed to the elevator hardware. "Look, Joe. Altimeters."

"Yeah, great, kid, a triumph of socialist technology." I turned to Two Moons. "Listen, Chief, I don't think you're risking our necks to show us the sights. What's up?"

Two Moons patted his gut. "Lunch. Best herring in town."

Oh, for—

Two minutes later the car stopped and the doors opened. Skinny maître d' in a polyester tux met us as we stepped out. Eyebrows shot up, then came down quick when he saw Two Moons.

"*Juten Tag, Jenosse Jeneraloberst.*" Berlin accent. He waved a leatherette wine list like a baton and we followed him to an empty table by the window.

We sat down and Two Moons held his hand up. "Great view. Platform rotates once every thirty minutes like a big aluminum shish kebob. Entire structure three hundred and sixty-five meters tall, tallest in Europe, except for Moscow, of course. All built on sandy soil of Berlin. Capitalists said it couldn't be done. Shining example of socialist engineering, *wa.*"

Wa. We were facing west at the moment, view along Unter den Linden out to the Brandenburg Gate and beyond, bare trees in the Tiergarten now, gray sky and mist making downtown West Berlin a dim silhouette a good three miles away. They still called this part of East Berlin *Mitte* even though it'd been on the far edge since '61, stubby panhandle bulging into the West. Which meant from here we could see Honecker's handiwork protecting us from the Fascists on three sides. It didn't look like that tough a hurdle from up here, more like a thick white chalk line. Or maybe more like a fault line. Only it never moved.

We did, though. Vibration probably no worse than the Graf Zeppelin dining room as we inched around in a clockwise direction. Pretty soon I had a clear view north through the gray Berlin air. Wandlitz up there somewhere, I guessed. If I'd had a pair of binocs I might've even spotted Honecker in his red-black-and-gold swimming trunks out in the garden taking the cure.

We were just far enough out in the bulge so you could see the graffiti-covered western side of the Wall, then the clean white-washed inside that ran west along Bernauerstrasse, cut south in front of the Reichstag and behind the Brandenburg Gate, past the green mound of earth where the Commies dynamited the Reichs Chancellory in '47 and built their damn monument up the street with the marble, Hitler's bunker down there somewhere. Then it took a sharp left south of Potsdamer Platz and headed east past Checkpoint Charlie, finally zigzagged back over to the Spree and down to the southeast. *Truly a Great Wall,* as Nixon once said elsewhere.

Two Moons picked up the menu. "The herring in cream sauce is good. Also the rouladen." A waiter hustled over to take our order. Victor still wasn't talking so Two Moons ordered herring for both of them, Johnny settled for a bowl of borscht and a *Bauernfrühstück.* My head was telling me I ought to be hungry but my gut had other plans. I compromised, went for the *Jägerschnitzel* and a glass of whole milk. The waiter raised an eyebrow again, then clicked his heels and disappeared.

But the people down there. Jesus. Hundreds of thousands, half a million? More? Staring down at the stormy sea from a steel-and-concrete crow's nest. They were still coming, pouring in from every direction. New Forum promised a million, biggest demo ever, they said, and the hell of it is, this time they were all volunteers.

I was sitting across from Closky and the Chief, Johnny on my left. Closky hadn't stopped humming since we left Wandlitz, hadn't said a word since our little visit, since Honecker mentioned the boy. Kai Beckmann, nineteen-year-old kid who died right here in Berlin, October 1947. Never did figure out exactly what happened, except that what happened wasn't pretty. Closky wouldn't talk about it either, not then, not ever. It was the one thing you just didn't bring up. Except now we had to.

"Victor—"

Closky stopped humming. He closed his eyes, leaned his head back. I knew that look from his old Gospel TV show.

> . . . *tell old*
> *Phar-a-o-h*
> *Let mah people go-o-o-o-o-o.*

He opened his eyes and looked at me. His voice cracked at first. "I know, Joey. I know. Life's full of surprises, isn't it? But see, that's how I always knew. I always knew Hiss was a spy, always knew he'd passed documents, not just because Chambers said so, hell, who'd believe that crazy sonofabitch? But I had it straight from the Commies themselves in '47, had it straight from that—" His voice caught and for a long time he didn't say anything. Head started a slow bob. Then he said, "Straight from that Beckmann boy."

Nobody said a word. It was the first time I heard Closky say the boy's name since the night before he died. And now the words came out.

"Hell, it was the last thing I expected, his pop was a Gauleiter and he still wore that damn Hitler Youth tunic every time we—" He cleared his throat, blinked, looked out the window. "But that night when I caught him on the phone, caught him talking about me, I had to find out what he knew. Hell, I thought the little sonofabitch was from the IG's office, thought somebody tipped 'em off to the black-market operation. When I found out the Commies sent him over from the Russian sector because I used to work for the goddam Dies Committee in '40 I didn't know what the hell to think. And now I find out it was Honecker himself that sent him and that bastard Mielke that put Honecker up to it." Closky's face was red. There were tears in his eyes, his voice so soft I could hardly hear. "Mielke will pay for that. I don't know how, yet, but that goddam commie sonofabitch is going to pay. Mark my goddam words."

Whew. Easier said than done. If anybody in the Zone was untouchable, it was Erich Mielke, legendary Grand Old Man of East German State Security, combination J. Edgar Hoover, Heinrich Himmler, and Beria all rolled into one. Probably about their combined ages, too. Not too much Closky could do to get back at him, at least as far as I could figure.

"I think I get it now, Victor. When you found out somebody in the Zone was sitting on documents from Hiss back in October '47, you figured it was time to bring the case out of mothballs. That's why you headed straight for Chambers when we flew the coop here, right?"

Closky sighed, straightened himself up. "Yeah. Took a while to get the fire lit but it turned out okay."

Well, it did and it didn't, I guess. "But wait a minute. Chambers told you back in '48 the boy was a spy, remember that? That day in August out at the farm? I thought he was blowin' smoke, but now it turns out he really knew. And if he really knew, that means he was still in touch with Honecker or somebody in the Zone back then, so his conversion from communism was phony."

Closky shook his head. "No, I don't believe that, Joey. I thought of it, but I don't believe it. The FBI knew about Kai and me, and Chambers talked to the goddam FBI every other day. Besides, if anyone was in touch with Honecker it was that sonofabitch Hiss. He sent the documents over."

While I was mulling that one the waiter brought our food. Tables around us still hadn't been served, folks staring at their tiny paper napkins, cobwebs forming on their cheap aluminum utensils.

Johnny slurped up a spoonful of borscht. "It didn't sound like that to me, Victor. It sounded like they were in the trunk of the car when it disappeared in July '36."

" '39," I said.

Johnny frowned. "What?"

Well, here we go. "It disappeared in 1939, kid, not 1936. I talked to Marvin Smith the day before he died. He told me about a visit he had in July '39 from a guy he later realized was Chambers. From the way he described the visit it sounded like Chambers used it as an excuse to use Smith's notary seal. So I drove up to Cherner Motor Company and sure enough, I found a sales invoice for a Model A Ford supposedly sold by Alger Hiss on July 23, 1939. Next day Smith was dead."

Johnny's eyes got big. "And the invoice?"

I looked at Closky. He stared back at me for a long time. Finally he set his fork down, reached in his suitcoat pocket, pulled out the Zippo. He flipped the top off, spun the flint wheel. A bright orange flame shot up.

Johnny closed his eyes and shook his head. "Jesus Christ, Joe."

I didn't say anything. Nobody did.

Johnny opened his eyes, poked at his borscht, finally set the spoon down. "So Hiss was framed after all. The poor sonofabitch gave the car to Chambers just like he said and three years later Chambers forged Hiss's signature to the title, faked the notarization by one of Hiss's buddies, and dumped the Ford at a commie car lot. What he didn't know was that the Commies would ship it to Russia to help fight the Great Patriotic War. And that it would turn up here."

I shook my head. It all made sense except for one little thing. "But what about the documents? Chambers wouldn't hide documents in the trunk if he was planning to dump the car."

"He would if he meant for the car to be found so it would incriminate Hiss."

"Yeah, but it wasn't. And why would he take a chance like that with the biggest bombshell of all, a document so hot that fifty years later we're offering the East Germans a couple billion dollars for it sight unseen? Which raises the question—"

I looked at Closky and Two Moons. They were shoveling herring into their mouths like a pair of oversized North Sea halibuts. I slammed my palm on the table. Glasses jumped. They both looked up. I kept my voice quiet. "Which raises the question, gentlemen, what in God's name *is* it? George, I doubt if you even know, but Victor, goddammit, you've been in on this from the get-go and it's about time you let us in on the little secret."

Closky set his fork down, wiped his mouth with a napkin. His blue eyes seemed brighter, face fuller. He'd been gaining weight in the past three weeks, no question about it now. Even the starched collar of his white shirt didn't seem to hang down so much, full Windsor knot of his red silk tie no longer at half-staff.

"Okay, Joey, you win. But don't say I didn't warn you. Don't say you wouldn't have been a lot better off not knowing, okay?"

He pushed his plate away, leaned back in his chair.

"Now, to be honest, I don't know exactly *what* it is either. But I do know who wants it, okay? So I do a little deduction. It goes like this. The CIA wants it. The FBI wants it. The Mob wants it. And we want it. Now I start going through things that interest all four of us. Things that start with the letter *K.* Castro doesn't start with *K.* Diem doesn't start with *K.* Hoffa doesn't start with *K.* Am I making sense to you yet, Joey?"

Holy, holy hell. Johnny's face was white. Two Moons even stopped eating. I felt butterflies in my gut, felt sick, felt my head pound. Because if there was one case I never wanted to see the inside of, this was it. I kept clear of it in November '63, kept clear of it ever since. And I liked it that way.

But now the sonofabitch was getting us all mixed up in it. Did Nixon even know? I stared back out the window. Half hour must've passed, because I was looking west again.

I tried to push it out of my mind, focus on something else, anything else. Anything but that. I stared down at the Wall.

August 1961. Yeah, it made sense all right. Really was a piece of work, too, no question about that. I tried to picture Honecker down there, middle-aged apparatchik, ex-roofer turned First Secretary for State Security, driving around in the dead of night, Sunday 13 Aug, hopping out of his car and cracking the whip. *Hurry up with that barbed wire, get those tank traps straight, your mortar's too wet, you set that block crooked, here, comrade, I'll show you—*

"Joe?"

Then it hit me. Jesus. Art of concealment. Completely natural, completely unexpected. I remembered Chambers's last letter to Nixon. "Overly conscientious practice of this art . . . 5 July 61."

I turned back and looked at them, looked each one of them in the eye. They were all staring at me.

182

"Hold the phone, boys. Hold dessert. Hold everything. I know where Honecker hid the K-document. I know where it is."

There was dead silence. I stared back out the window at the Wall. Ninety-nine and a half miles long, fifteen feet high, three feet thick, 23.6 million cubic feet of concrete, stone, and cinder block smack in the middle of the most closely guarded strip of earth on the face of the planet, stretching off in both directions to the horizon as far as you could see.

"I also know we'll never find it. Not in a million years."

12

December 1, 1948

Well, it sure as hell didn't work out the way we planned, I can tell you that much. Dewey went down the toilet, as Nixon put it, never mind whatever strings Closky's Chicago pals tried to pull, and half the Republicans went down with him. McDowell bought the farm out in Milwaukee, ditto Kersten and a half dozen others on the Committee. Thomas got re-elected all right, but two days later they hauled him in front of a federal grand jury on payroll kickbacks. He took the Fifth.

All of which brought us back to Washington in a lot less jolly mood than when we left a couple weeks before. Truman was back in the catbird seat, cocky as hell, swore he was going to shut the Committee down once and for all. Meanwhile the grand jury up in New York was still trying to figure out whether Hiss was a bigger liar than Chambers or vice versa so they could indict one of 'em for perjury. *Washington Post* column this morning hinted something was up, but then a United Press story in the *Daily News* said just the opposite, claimed the grand jury was getting nowhere fast, might even pull the plug for lack of evidence. For the hundredth time I thought about the evidence Closky torched right there on the Boss's desk but pushed it out of my mind. Hell, maybe they were right, maybe it didn't mean a goddam thing.

Nixon and I were alone in his fifth-floor cubby in the House Office Building on what was supposed to be his last day at work before he took off on vacation. Once he was out of the picture you had to figure any steam left in the case would leak out pretty quick.

Nixon leaned back in his chair, stared out the window. Tip of the Washington Monument poked up over the roof across the way, white against the gray winter sky. He swiveled his chair around, glanced at the half-eaten tuna sandwich on his desk and made a face. He hadn't been eating much lately, wasn't sleeping right either from the look of him. His white shirt was rumpled, blue polka dot tie crooked and loose at the collar. We were supposed to be catching up on his mail but so far he hadn't even looked at it. He picked up his sandwich, then put it down again.

"You're not married, are you, Pope?"

"No sir."

"Probably for the goddam best. Don't get me wrong, I love my wife and little girl. It's just—" He stared at the photo on his desk, young congressman and his pretty wife on bikes under the cherry blossoms, baby in a wicker basket on the handlebars. He sighed. Then he checked his watch. "Goddam boat sails from New York in twenty-four hours and I'm going to be on the sonofabitch, make no mistake."

I shrugged. "Probably do you good, sir. Cruise on down to Panama, get some sun, spend some time alone with your wife . . ."

Nixon kept staring at the photo. His face never changed, hadn't for the past hour. "Yeah, like hell."

There was a loud knock at the door and before we could say anything it flew open.

It was Closky, of course, topcoat hanging open, red silk tie half out of his crooked gold tie clip. His face was bright pink and he was out of breath. He had a young dark-haired guy with him I didn't recognize.

"Afternoon, sir. Hi, Joey. Wasn't sure you'd still be here. Some-body I think you ought to meet. Nick Vazzana, one of the lawyers Mr. Luce hired to help Chambers out."

Nixon stood up, shook hands with Vazzana. He shrugged at the chairs and we all sat down.

Vazzana grinned, sat back and crossed his legs, brushed a piece of dust off his forty-dollar Florsheims. "Officially, sir, I'm just drop-ping in to say hello." Nixon stared at him. Closky cleared his throat.

"Well, hell, Nick, you could've said hello to us on the goddam phone. I thought you said you had some news."

"Might have some, might not." He smirked, half covered his mouth with his hand, lowered his voice. "Can't talk or I might be held in contempt of court."

Well, holy hell. Closky and I looked at each other, then over at Nixon. He wasn't in any mood for bullshit, I could tell that much.

Nixon slumped back in his chair. His voice was low and soft. "Why don't you just tell us what you have to say, Mr. Vazzana?"

"I can't discuss it in detail, Congressman. But I can tell you it has to do with the libel suit. And it concerns documents."

At the word *documents* Nixon perked up. We all did. He leaned across his desk, shoulders hunched. "Do you mean to say Chambers has some sort of documentary evidence he's just introduced? Some-thing against Hiss?" Nixon's eyes darted around.

Vazzana raised his eyebrows, moved his head in a way you could take for a nod or a stretch.

Nixon frowned. "You were *there*? You saw it?"

"No, but I was at Richard Cleveland's office in Baltimore when they all came back from giving a deposition at Marbury's."

"When who came back?"

"Chambers and his two attorneys, the ones in the libel suit. Cleveland and Macmillan. They were just returning from the pre-trial hearing at Marbury's."

"Marbury is Hiss's lawyer now?"

"And his friend, but maybe not for long. Cleveland said he was pretty shaken when he saw—well, I can't spill the beans, but let's just say it's getting tougher even for Hiss's friends to believe him now."

Nixon stood up. "But you're telling me the sonofabitch had *documents*?" He turned to Closky. "He never told us he had any documents."

Closky shrugged. "We never asked him."

"We never—?" Nixon sank back down in his chair, rubbed his face. "Jesus Christ in heaven."

Vazzana grinned. "They tell me Marbury said something like that when Chambers laid the envelope on the table."

"But why? Why would he wait this long? He could've saved us the whole goddam investigation, hell, he could've cracked the case wide open ten years ago."

Vazzana shrugged. "He claims he was trying to shield Hiss. Didn't want to hurt him any more than necessary."

Nixon shot a glance our way. "Well that doesn't make any goddam sense, does it, boys? The man's declared a holy war against communism and he's pulling his punches, shooting blanks? Why the hell would he do that unless—"

I chimed in. "Unless the documents are fakes?"

Nixon shot me a look like he was about to slug me. Then he caught himself, shook his head real slow. He started pacing. Nothing to do now but give him his head. "You know, Chambers already gave a deposition to the FBI about his—his homosexuality and so forth. Just between us I got hold of a copy and it's pretty seamy stuff, the whole New York scene, you name it. Of course it all happened before he broke with communism and the man's married now, father of two fine kids, but hell, that's the whole point, his life is changed and that's all to his credit. But now Hiss, well, you can't look at the man and tell me you don't think—"

Closky cleared his throat. "You can't really tell that by lookin', sir."

Nixon stopped pacing. "Right, I forgot you were a goddam expert, Victor."

Vazzana coughed, straightened his tie. "Look, I don't see any point in speculating about Chambers's motive. The crucial thing is

187

you've got a reason to keep the case going. You gentlemen have got to keep the heat on."

"So where are the documents now?" I asked.

"The originals are with Marbury. We have copies, of course. I also understand Marbury turned photostats over to Justice on November twenty-first."

Nixon frowned. "Why the hell would he do that?"

"He talked to Hiss, Hiss said they're forgeries. Marbury believes him, figures he has nothing to hide, wants to clear his name."

Nixon snorted, shook his head. "So now everybody has the goddam things but us. Terrific. And you can't tell us what they are?"

Vazzana shook his head. "That's where I draw the line. Look, I can be cited for contempt of court just for being here."

I was about to bring that up myself. "So why *are* you here?"

Vazzana pointed at the *Daily News* on Nixon's desk. "I read the same papers you do. Way things are going there might not be a Hiss case this time next month. Hell, there might not be an Un-American Activities Committee. Not unless you fellows get off the dime."

Closky stood up. "I say we drive up there, sir." He checked his watch. "Hell, we can be in Westminster by four o'clock. Put the heat on, make the sonofabitch come across with the truth. We can do it, I know we can."

Nixon walked over to the low window, stood there looking down at the courtyard with his back to us. "What are you suggesting, Victor, we all go up there and beat the crap out of him? Chambers is under the same sonofabitching injunction Vazzana is. He can't tell us a goddam thing or he'll end up in contempt too."

We didn't say anything. Finally Nixon turned around.

"Listen, boys, I'll be honest with you. I'm going on vacation tomorrow. Period. I, uh, I promised my wife and if I break that promise one more time she's going to have my balls, okay?"

The Boss never did have much luck trying to sound like one of the boys, but we forced a chuckle anyway. Closky wouldn't give up, though. He walked straight over to the window, topcoat flapping, bright pink face a foot from long dark jowls now. His voice got soft.

"I'm not talking about tomorrow, sir, I'm talking about right now—"

Nixon threw his hands up. "Jesus Christ, Closky, are you deaf? I've got a million goddam things to do, I don't have time for another goddam wild-goose chase up to that shitass farm and if I did I sure as hell wouldn't go there with you assholes. I'm so goddammed sick and tired of this case I don't want to hear any more about it. I'm going to Panama, and to hell with it and you and the whole damn business!"

Closky was tensing up, I could see it. Fists clenching, big neck straining against his starched white collar.

"Okay, sir, how about this. This might even work out better, okay? You go ahead, you go on the cruise. Tomorrow after you're gone we'll slap a subpoena on the sonofabitch, ask for anything and everything he's got related to the case that he *hasn't* turned over to Justice yet. Hell, he can't be held in contempt for that, can he? Once we get it, we'll check it out. If it looks good, we'll call you back."

Nixon frowned. "What do you mean, call me back?"

"You know, bring you back from the cruise. Send you an urgent radio message, fly you up to Washington to reopen the hearings."

Nixon shook his head. "How the hell are you going to fly me back from a goddam boat?"

"Hell, I don't know. Get the navy on it. Or the Coast Guard. Don't worry, sir, we'll think of something. All you have to do is be ready to leave the boat when you get the word from us."

Nixon glared at Closky. He folded his arms, looked over at Vazzana and me, stared into Closky's face for a long time. The room was dead quiet except for a low whistle from the radiator by the window. Finally Nixon took a deep breath, blew it out. He picked up the tuna sandwich off his desk, gnawed off a slab, tossed the rest in the trash, wiped his mouth on the back of his hand.

"All right," he said. "If it'll shut your goddam mouth, I'll do it."

November 9, 1989

We were back at Stasi HQ in Two Moons's private office, good-sized room on the third floor with a window that looked out on Normannenstrasse. No Biedermeier this time, sleek Swedish office furniture like Schmidt's place only bigger. Map of Berlin Hauptstadt der DDR mounted on one wall, couple of Paul Klees on the other, originals I figured. All pretty tasteful except for the portrait of Lenin at the far end, cheeks airbrushed, eyes fixed on some spot beyond it all like a nineteenth-century Jesus. Only trace of the Chief's past was the old deer's hoof rattle on his desk. He'd managed to salvage that, I guess.

We'd spent most of the past four days here, kept a roomful of Stasi clerks busy dredging up the names of every ex-Vopo, People's Militia member, or NVA construction type who worked on the Wall in August '61 and might have crossed paths with Honecker in the bargain. Which went pretty quick here compared to home, I'd say that much. Stasi had complete files on just about every citizen, plus a secret police force that could hop in their Volvos and bring folks in to answer questions, then send 'em home again and know there wouldn't be any complaints to the commissioner. Something like what Closky used to picture for his perfect world.

Closky, geez. There he sat over in the corner, fresh Palm Beach suit fetched from Blunt's place by the Stasi shopping squad, long since bored with it all, humming Negro spirituals and reading a *Tagesspiegel* Blunt stuck in the pocket for him. Headline: ENTIRE POLITBURO QUITS, all twenty-three of 'em, fired and sent packing in a shake-up that would've been a sensation a month ago but now was probably too little and too late.

Johnny was staring out the window, mulling it all over for the hundredth time. "It really is the perfect hiding place, Joe, no question about it. Honecker takes an envelope, a can of microfilm, whatever, and drops it inside a single cinder block. Then he slips that cinder block in with forty million other cinder blocks, cements them all together into a ninety-nine-and-a-half-mile-long wall and issues shoot-to-kill orders to the guards. Now try to figure out which one it's in. Or get at it once you do. Brilliant."

That was the theory, at least. In the past three days Two Moons, Johnny, and even Closky had come around to figuring I had to be right, it was the one place Honecker would pick, and it fit in with Honecker's boast and Chambers's letter to Nixon. It all fit, or at least we thought it did. But now, as Johnny said, try to find it.

Two Moons's phone rang and he picked it up. "*Ja?*" I checked my watch. It was close to nine at night, and we'd been at it since seven this morning. Steady stream of unfortunates rousted by the windbreaker brigade, brought in for a chat and sent packing. This had to be the last one for today. Two Moons said "*Gut*" and hung up. A second later the door opened.

It was Blondie again, decked out in an NVA captain's uniform this time, bandage off, head looking better for what that was worth. Overweight middle-aged guy at his side, thinning gray hair, cheap plastic specs. Eyes bugged out at the sight of Two Moons's scarred face but he got a grip real quick when he saw the lieutenant general's stars on his shoulder boards.

Blondie handed Two Moons the file, saluted. Two Moons nodded and Blondie turned on his heel and left.

Two Moons turned the file sideways, read the name. "Heinz Koepke?"

Slight pause. "*Jawohl, Genosse Generaloberst.*"

Koepke was standing at something less than attention, and even if the title was right there was something in his tone, something that said maybe he'd been carrying a sign at the Alex last Sunday. But then that was probably in the file already too.

Two Moons opened the folder, started rattling off the questions. By now we knew them by heart.

"Current address?"

"Frankestrasse thirty-six."

"Occupation?"

"Manager, VEB Elektrowerk, here in the capital."

"Membership in the SED since—?"

"October 12, 1958."

"Herr Koepke, you were involved in operations to secure the border in August 1961?"

Koepke stared at Two Moons, didn't answer.

"Herr Koepke?"

"Sagen Sie, Sie sind wohl Chinese, oder?"

Wow. Granted Two Moons didn't look like your run-of-the-mill Aryan but it sure as hell wasn't SOP to change the subject on a lieutenant general in a Stasi hearing, much less ask a personal question. Two Moons drew himself up in the chair. I watched his big knuckles get white as he gripped the rattle, then relax and let it go.

"I am a member of the international proletariat like yourself, Comrade Koepke. I am also a lieutenant general in the National People's Army investigating a matter of extreme importance to the security of our Republic, and require your cooperation."

Koepke shrugged, glanced at the headline on Closky's paper.

"Times are changing, Comrade Lieutenant General."

"They are not changing so quickly that traitors cannot be dealt with. Do I make myself understood?"

Koepke didn't answer but you could see from his eyes that he got the message.

"Good. Now I repeat, you were involved in securing the border in August 1961?"

"Jawohl, Genosse Generaloberst."

Slow nod. "I understand that in that capacity you saw—" Two Moons checked the file, eyebrow came up. "No, you actually *spoke* with Comrade Erich Honecker at the border, is that correct?"

Koepke swallowed hard. They were all suspicious on this one, and why the hell not? Honecker got cashiered three weeks ago and now here they are hauled in front of a Stasi general because they helped him build the Wall in '61.

Finally Koepke answered. "That is correct, *Genosse General-oberst.*"

"Tell me about it. Describe the circumstances."

Koepke shifted from one foot to the other. "I was a sergeant in the People's Militia. I had a squad of five men to secure the border in the block just southwest of Chausseestrasse."

"This was the night of August 13, 1961?"

"No. It was the following week. August twenty-second, when the first concrete slabs were delivered. The posts had been set the previous day. The crane had moved into position and we were setting the slabs. One and a quarter by one and a quarter meters, thirty centimeters thick. Much too heavy to lift, but we guided them into position and mortared them in place."

This was old news. Two Moons was tapping the rattle on the desk. "Describe your meeting with Comrade Honecker. When did he arrive?"

"It was close to midnight. Perhaps eleven-thirty. A black ZIL limousine drove up from the direction of the Stadium of World Youth, parked with the lights on and motor running. A small, middle-aged man wearing spectacles and a gray suit got out. It was obvious he was a high Party official. Only later did I learn that he was First Secretary for State Security, Comrade Erich Honecker."

I jumped in. "You're sure it was Honecker?"

Koepke gave a half smile. "Comrade Honecker's picture has been in the newspaper and on television twenty times a day for the past eighteen years. Yes, I'm sure."

For the first time Closky set the newspaper down. Two Moons stopped tapping the rattle. The room was quiet. "Go on."

"I came to attention, saluted, stated my name and rank. He was carrying a white plastic construction helmet of the type we were all wearing. He nodded and placed it on his head, walked over to the men setting the blocks in place."

"Was he carrying anything else?"

"No."

"You said he was wearing a suit. With pockets?"

"Yes. A gray suit and a tie."

"Go on."

"He held his hand up to the crane operator, signaled him to stop. Then he ordered the men away, sighted along the line of blocks we had just set, placed his hands on top as if to test them. There was a mason's trowel resting on the block beside him. He picked it up. Then he looked over his shoulder and noticed me."

"How close were you standing?"

"Three or four meters away. He called me over, showed me the trowel. 'How can you work with this?' he shouted at me. 'This trowel is filthy.' "

I leaned forward. "Was it?"

Koepke frowned, looked at me like he was surprised by the question. "No, it was not. But he ordered me to fetch another one from the supply truck. When I came back a minute later he seized it from my hand and began smoothing the mortar between the blocks. It was absurd. The man was a roofer. What did he know about masonry? Even in the short time I was gone he managed to make a mess of it."

"What do you mean?"

"His hands. When I came back from the truck his hands were covered in wet concrete, as if he had tried to smooth the mortar by hand."

My throat felt dry and my heart was pounding. Two Moons's eyes were locked on Koepke's. His voice was quiet and slow. "Do you remember the precise location at which this happened?"

Koepke looked around at us like he was trying to figure it all out, like maybe it was a trap after all. Finally he shrugged. "You can't approach it now, of course, but yes. It's just south of the Chausseestrasse control point, where the border runs east, then abruptly turns north for a hundred meters. I passed the spot with my children once and told them, 'There is the block that Comrade Honecker set for us.' I assumed they did not report me, but perhaps that is in your files too."

Two Moons ignored the crack, stood up, walked over to the map on the wall. We got up and followed him. He waved Koepke over. "Show us."

Koepke pointed to a spot on the map about a mile north of the Brandenburg Gate. It was a little bulge on the bigger downtown bulge, maybe half a square mile of wall around the Stadium of World Youth that jutted northwest toward the Wedding District in West Berlin. Koepke leaned closer until his glasses were a couple inches from the map. He moved a pudgy finger a half inch and stopped.

"It was right here. At this corner, just west of the police hospital."

Two Moons studied the map. Then he turned to me. "The one-point-two-five-meter wall was erected between August and October 1961. It was later replaced by a wall of three meters, then by the present one of five meters." He pressed his hands together, fingers straight out. "Each time the previous wall was encased within the new structure."

"Meaning it's still there."

"Perhaps."

Two Moons walked back to his desk, picked up the telephone, dialed a number. "This is Mann. I want a border security maintenance crew and truck here at once. Full equipment, including measuring gear. *Ja, sofort.*"

He listened for a second, reached under the desk, pulled up the old briefcase. He looked inside, then snapped it shut.

"*Gut. Und vor allem den Presslufthammer nicht vergessen!*"

He slammed the receiver down.

Presslufthammer. "Pneumatic drill."

Good thinking, Chief.

13

December 2, 1948

Nixon left for New York on the eight o'clock train, and if I thought that was the last we'd hear from him in a while it was only because I didn't know Pennsy had radio phones on their express trains now. Sure enough, an hour later the phone rang and there he was, wanted to know if we'd made any progress on the subpoena.

Well, we had, or at least Closky'd managed to phone Chambers in Westminster a few minutes before. Found out he was on his way to Washington to testify at a loyalty hearing over at the State Department. We asked him to stop in on his way home and he agreed.

All of which made for a pretty long afternoon. Closky was sitting at Nixon's desk, feet up on the big green blotter, Pall Mall smoldering in the cut-glass ashtray where the Cherner invoice went up in smoke a couple months before. I was perched in a green leather armchair off to the side with a bottle of Coke and a honey-glazed doughnut balanced on my knee, staring out the window at the tip of the Washington Monument poking up over the roof next door.

"So where do you think he is now?"

Closky checked his watch. "Well, assuming he really did sail at one, I'd say he's somewhere off the coast of North Carolina. Probably playing shuffleboard in his wingtips."

I took a bite of my doughnut, washed it down with a mouthful of Coke. "Tell me something, Victor."

"Shoot."

"What do you really think of him? I mean, half the time you make fun of him, but then you act like he's some kind of political genius. Which is it?"

Closky picked up the photo on the desk, held it up to the light, studied it. Dick and Pat on bikes under the cherry blossoms, little girl perched in the basket. He dusted it off with his shirtsleeve, set it back down, shifted his huge bulk in the creaky desk chair, gave his crew cut a good rub.

"I think, Joey, that right now he's our best hope, okay? Maybe our only hope. He's smart, he's sly, he's well funded, and he'll do what he has to do to get things done. Sure, he needs a little push now and then, but that's what we're here for."

He swung his legs off the desk, pulled the chair in, folded his hands on the blotter and leaned over at me like some shrink about to crack an especially tough nut.

"Okay, last year in Berlin, trying to bring Hitler back, sure, I talked him into that, twisted his words so it sounded like he gave his okay. That was crazy, I'll admit that. And Strom, well, that was my bright idea too, didn't work out. Hell, even Dewey didn't work out."

He tugged a new Pall Mall out of the pack, flicked the Zippo on, set the smoke down alongside the one still lit in the ashtray.

I brushed the doughnut crumbs off my lap. "So what are we busting our beezers for? What good's it going to do us to convict Hiss at this point if we're looking at four more years of Truman anyway?"

"Oh, Joey, don't say that, don't let me hear you say that. Hiss is our ticket to the big time, don't ever forget it. Before Hiss came along we were working for a thirty-five-year-old first-term congressman nobody'd ever heard of. Now he's a national figure, re-elected by a landslide, dough pouring in like you wouldn't believe. A year from now he'll run for the Senate. He'll make it, too, take my word for it. Two years after that, well, probably a little early but by '56 at the latest he's going to be somebody's vice president, Taft's maybe, shoot, what's the damn difference, right?"

He leaned back in the chair, clasped his hands behind his head, stared up at the high ceiling.

"In 1960—you remember this now, I'm calling the shot right here and now—in 1960 that sonofabitch is gonna be elected president of the United States, mark my words. And when he is we'll be moving right down Pennsylvania Avenue with him and then it'll be time to clean house for sure. You think the goddam Democrats know how to use the Justice Department to cover up for their friends and screw their enemies, hell, you ain't seen nothing. We'll use the FBI, the CIA, we'll set one off against the other, shoot, I was just talking to him last week about this idea I had, you'll love this, Joey. You get some pinko journalist giving you bad ink, you call the IRS and you get his ass audited. How about that? We'll put wiretaps on all the Commies, we'll read their damn mail if we have to. By then we're not going to be working out of some goddam warehouse, either, maybe build a complex over in Virginia, bring everything under one roof, operate everywhere against everything and everybody. Man, it would be paradise." He smiled and shook his head. "Absolute paradise."

I stared at him. His fat, pink face was lit up like a little kid's at Christmas, eyes twinkling, staring off at some vision a million miles away.

I leaned forward, tapped a finger on the desk. "But first we've got to fill out the subpoena."

He snapped out of it, glanced at his watch. "Geez, you're right, it's five-thirty. Damn." He pulled open a desk drawer, rifled through some papers, slammed it shut and pulled out another one. "Well, where the hell does he—" Bingo. Closky laid the paper on the blotter, reached into the inside pocket of his Palm Beach suitcoat, pulled out his Parker pen. He unscrewed the cap, limbered his wrist and scrawled out the words.

"Date?"

I glanced at the calendar. "December second."

The pen scratched across the paper. Finally he finished writing, leaned back and studied his handiwork. "And now, the signature. Let's make it Martin this time."

I watched his big hand slowly trace the letters, craftsman at work, until the paper bore the unmistakable signature of House Speaker Joe Martin.

Closky screwed the cap back on his pen, shook the paper in the air to dry.

There was a knock on the door. Closky stood up, winked. "See? Just in time."

He folded the paper in thirds, slipped it halfway up his right sleeve, walked over to the door. I got up and followed him.

We opened the door and sure enough there was Chambers, shoulders stooped, tweeds rumpled, stained tie at half-mast. Only thing standing up straight was his cowlick.

"Hello, Victor—"

"Whittaker, thank God you could make it." Closky stuck his hand out. Chambers reached out to shake it and Closky slipped him the subpoena.

For a second Chambers's face went blank. Then he heaved a sigh. He unfolded the paper, took a minute to read it. " 'All paper, documents, and other matter . . . relating to testimony before the Committee.' All right, gentlemen, you win. I'll give you what I have. It's at my home."

Closky grinned. "That's great, Whittaker. We can drive you."

Chambers frowned, thought a minute. "Actually, my car is in Baltimore at the train station. But if you could give me a lift there, you can follow me the rest of the way out to Westminster."

"Fine. C'mon, Joey, let's give Mr. Chambers a ride to Baltimore."

We tugged on our topcoats and headed out the door. "Aren't you going to tell Stripling what's up?"

Closky made a face. "What, and let that sonofabitch take all the glory? Let's go, gentlemen, time's a-wastin'."

We tried to pry some dope loose from Chambers on the ride up Route 1 but he wasn't buying it, said we'd find out what we needed to know when we reached the farm. So we switched on the radio, caught the news on CBS. No mention of the Hiss case but they did have a big piece on the airlift, twenty C-47s every hour now flying coal to Tempelhof for the Berlin winter if you can believe that, Rooskies claiming it couldn't be done, Uncle Joe said we'd call it quits in a month or so, pack up and leave. Guess we'd see about that.

It was seven-thirty by the time we got to Baltimore, rush hour long over. We made pretty good time going up Charles Street, got to the parking lot behind Penn Station a little before eight. We pulled up next to Chambers's Pontiac and he opened the door to get out. It was dark now and cold, air damp with a misty rain.

Chambers stood holding the door, poked his head in. "The quickest way is straight up Charles, then left on Twenty-ninth, around Druid Hill Park and out Reisterstown Road. I suppose you might as well follow me, but if we get separated I'll meet you at the farm."

Closky clicked the radio off, shot him the thumbs-up. "Don't worry, Whittaker, we'll be on you like Wallis on the Duke o' Windsor."

Chambers gave Closky a pained smile, waddled over to his car and climbed in. We waited for him to back out of the parking space. Then Closky put it in gear and we headed north through town.

"Well, Victor, you really think this is it?"

Closky settled in behind the wheel, tugged his topcoat across his lap, adjusted his vent a crack. "Yeah, Joey, I do. I think this is it. Because whatever it is, we're going to play it right. Strip said he can even put a call in to Forrestal if he has to, try to get a flying boat down to the Caribbean to nab Nixon off that damn cruise ship. You can just see that in the newsreels, can't you? It's going to be beautiful."

"What is, Nixon climbing off a rubber raft in his suit and wingtips?"

Closky laughed. "Yeah, well, that'll be beautiful too, I guess. But I mean the sheer theater of it, the timing, the drama. Whoo-ee, this is going to be rich, wait'll you see."

I still wasn't convinced. "What if the documents are duds?"

Closky frowned. "How could they be duds?"

"I mean, what if they aren't important? Or what if they don't prove a link to Hiss?"

Closky shrugged. "Why would that matter, Joey, tell me why that would matter? What, you think we're going to call a press conference and read the goddam things out loud? You think we're going to ask the *Post* to run 'em verbatim in a special pull-out section? You think we'd do that with secret documents? *Secret,* Joey, that's the whole point. So secret we can't even reveal 'em now, too touchy, compromising sources, all that shit." He punched my leg. "*Top* secret, why don't we say that, okay?"

"And you really think the press will buy it?"

The smirk. Even in the dark I could pick it up. "The press will buy it, Joey, and the grand jury will indict him. Then we'll make damn sure he's convicted and when he's made the trip up the river we'll have a hero on his way to the Senate, you wait and see."

We were passing Druid Hill Park, the place where Hiss used to come as a boy to fetch springwater, or so he said at the hearing a few months back.

"Hiss's old stomping grounds, right?"

Closky nodded, pointed back over his shoulder. "Family had a house down there on Eutaw Place, fancy brownstone. And Chambers"—he peered through the windshield in the dark as we passed a block of three-story brick row houses opposite the park—"Chambers settled in one of these after he quit the Party in '38. Forget which one."

"Small world."

"Ain't it?"

Closky turned the radio back on and we picked up CBS news out of Baltimore. Berlin back on the air, trouble again, of course, new commie mayor set up by the Russians yesterday but of course his writ didn't go past the sector line. Looked like the town was going to be split in two for good. Meanwhile every damn plane in the Bizone was grounded by fog, so the airlift was on hold, who knew for how long.

"Doesn't sound too good, does it, Victor?"

Closky shrugged. "Let 'em take half of Berlin, we'll roll the sons-ofbitches back one of these days, you wait and see. Nothin' lasts forever." I wasn't so sure. Sounded like we were in for a long haul at the very least. Closky spun the dial to ABC and we picked up the tail end of Abbott and Costello, then switched to NBC for Burns and Allen, drove the rest of the way without saying much as the big Plymouth roared past the city limits and out into the Maryland countryside, good hour and a half locked onto the Pontiac's taillights over the dark, winding blacktop. We blew through Westminster around nine-thirty, rumbled over the railroad tracks on Main Street, headed north on Bachman's Valley Road out to the farm. It was quarter of ten by the time we made the left onto East Saw Mill Road and bumped up the dirt driveway to the farmyard.

We pulled up alongside the Pontiac next to the red barn. Chambers and Closky both killed their lights and engines at the same time. Dark and quiet pretty near total. I pushed the door open and climbed out.

It was colder than Baltimore too, a lot colder. Still a chilly damp mist in the air, and as my eyes got used to the dark I could barely make out the pump with the metal cup on a chain and the wood slat fence just a few feet past that.

"Over this way, gentlemen." We heard Chambers's voice but couldn't see him. I took a couple steps in the dark and finally spotted him over by the fence.

"Where the hell are you, Joey? I can't see a goddam thing."

"Right here, Victor."

Finally Closky loomed up out of the mist like a freighter coming out of the fog, flashed a grin, winked. We felt our way over to where Chambers was standing.

For a long time nobody said anything, only sound was Chambers's deep breaths, like he was getting ready for something. Finally he said, "This way, Victor. You wait here, Mr. Pope."

I wasn't too thrilled about that, but I stood at the fence while Chambers pushed the gate open and waddled into the yard behind the barn, Closky holding on to his rumpled topcoat sleeve like

202

a blind man. I heard Chambers say "Watch your step" and heard Closky curse. I stooped down, peered through the fence slats. Ground covered with a tangle of wet vines and rotting pumpkins. Chambers and Closky disappeared into the dark fog at the other side of the yard. Then I heard Chambers's voice counting, like he was pacing off steps. I couldn't make out the numbers. Finally I heard them coming back, saw the two of them appear out of the mist like a vision. Chambers was holding a pumpkin in his arms. When he reached the edge of the yard he set it on a fencepost.

Closky stared at the pumpkin, then at Chambers. "What the hell is this, Whittaker, Dick Tracy?"

Chambers didn't answer. He placed his fat hand on the stem of the pumpkin and pulled up. The top came right off, sliced and hollowed out like a jack-o'-lantern. He dropped the lid on the ground, reached inside.

When his hand came out he was holding a wax paper package. He unwrapped the paper. Inside were three small metal cylinders wrapped in black electrical tape. He held them out to me. "I think this is what you're looking for."

November 9, 1989

It was after ten by the time we got in Two Moons's Mercedes and linked up with the maintenance truck. I rode shotgun next to the Chief, old briefcase on the seat beside us, Koepke in the back sandwiched between Johnny and Closky. He hadn't said a word since we left Two Moons's office, but you had to figure he wished he'd kept his big mouth shut, let himself get sent home with a frown and a *Dankeschön*, let that be the end of it.

Traffic was light in the outskirts and we made good time. I tried to relax but my whole body was stiff from sitting down all day, neck ached, gut churning. I checked the dash. The Cheez-It box was empty.

Two Moons glanced over. "I told Strohmeyer to replace that. Guess he forgot. Have to talk to him."

Forgot my ass. Score one for Blondie. I buzzed the window down a crack. Night air felt good, cold but dry for the first time in three weeks. I could hear Closky humming again from the backseat, couldn't place the tune. I turned around. "What's on the hit parade tonight, Victor, more of that gospel music?"

Closky shot me a smirk, threw his head back, wisps of white hair fluttering in the breeze. Voice as sweet a tenor as it ever was, even now, slow 4/4 time.

> *Joshua fit the battle of Jericho, Jericho, Jericho*
> *Joshua fit the battle of Jericho*
> *And de walls come a-tumblin' down.*

Two Moons frowned, shook a finger. "Not that song, Six. *Streng verboten.*"

Closky grinned. "Things are changing, George. Koepke here even said so." Closky laughed, poked Koepke in the ribs. "Might be number one on Radio DDR this time next week, who knows? It's Rollback, George, and we're rollin' back the Red Tide, make no mistake. A little late, but it's Rollback. Red Tide, Red Sea, parting of the waters. Might be time to think about changing partners again."

Two Moons shrugged. "Yin and yang." He flipped the radio on, tuned it in to RIAS. It was a taped replay of Schabowski's press conference from earlier today. Old news too by now, but a blockbuster anyway, claimed the Vopos had orders starting tomorrow to issue visas to just about any GDR burgher who wanted one, let them come and go as they pleased for the first time in twenty-eight years.

"You think it's really going to happen, Chief?"

Two Moons shook his head. "Too many people against it. Brünner told me he was going to seal the border with NVA troops on his own authority if Krenz and Schabowski go too far. If necessary, *Putsch.*" His hand came down on the steering wheel. "*Skookum.*"

We were close to the center of town now, sidewalks full of people headed in one direction. No signs this time, no luggage either, just a steady march westward.

I pointed out the window. "Guess somebody better tell *them*."

Two Moons didn't answer, just reached in his pocket and gnawed off another plug of Bazooka.

I didn't know if Koepke understood English, but it seemed like we were running out of time and there was still something I had to know.

"Listen, George, if this all works out we might be parting company pretty soon, maybe even tonight. You'll have what you want and we'll have what we want. But what's in this for you, anyway? Another Hero of the DDR badge, or are you after something more?"

Two Moons shrugged. "Gaining great wealth for the tribe is honor enough, *wa.*"

"And great wealth for yourself?"

No answer. Of course, I could've asked myself the same damn question. What was in it for me, anyway? Did I really think there was a document on the face of the earth that could help Richard Nixon stage a political comeback at this point? And if there was, did I really want to find it? Ah, hell.

We took the half right turn off Wilhelm-Pieck-Strasse onto Chausseestrasse and headed for the control point. Crowds were spilling off the sidewalk into the street. Geez, Schabowski said they'd be processing visa applications tomorrow. Looked like a real struggle to be first in line. A block ahead, the street was packed with people, shoulder to shoulder. Gridlock.

"No way you'll get through, Chief, siren or no. This is worse than Sunday."

Two Moons checked the mirror, flashed his lights on and off. Then he flipped on his right-turn signal and slipped onto a side street. It was less crowded but now we were headed the wrong way.

"Shortcut?"

He didn't answer, just hung a quick left and a minute later we came out at Invalidenstrasse maybe a mile back of the checkpoint. There were folks in the street here too, but not as many, and we made it across with a couple toots of the horn. I checked the sideview. Maintenance truck sticking to us, couple yards off our bumper.

We were near Bernauerstrasse, charming piece of real estate where the old sandstone row houses looked straight out onto West Berlin except the windows were bricked up and the houses empty. No-man's-land dead ahead.

Two Moons didn't even slow down, drove past the warning signs straight into the floodlit area they called State Border West. Narrow blacktop road led through the plowed earth and tank traps, light so bright now you didn't need headlights. A two-man Vopo patrol with machine pistols and a guard dog were walking along the side of the tarmac, headed for us. Two Moons slowed down just enough for them to get a look at the car. They snapped to attention and saluted, jerked the dog's leash like he was supposed to do a trick too but we were past them before he had a chance.

The Wall was smooth and white on this side, almost hurt your eyes as you got up close. Something else was different too, something besides the light and the emptiness and the starkness of it all. Then it hit me. The car wasn't shaking. There were no potholes. The road was in perfect shape, smooth as an airport runway. Only one in the whole damn town that was.

"Nice road, Chief. Too bad you can't use it more often."

He jerked his thumb over his shoulder. "Crew does a good job. Fine men."

Two Moons kept it at a steady 60 kmh as we took the straight shot north along the stretch of wall that paralleled Chausseestrasse a good block to the west. Clear sailing all the way, felt like you were zipping along the warning track at the outfield fence for the trip in from the bullpen. Sharp turn dead ahead as the Wall jogged southwest toward the checkpoint. We slowed down and made the turn, then took it easy as the tarmac road crossed Chausseestrasse between the Vopo checkpoint and the sector boundary.

A few hundred feet back a half dozen Vopos stood at the lowered candy-stripe pole inside the maze of concrete monoliths, thin gray line in front of a solid mass of folks that stretched from the arc lights of the border zone as far as you could see back up the street, back into the dark. How many were there on this street alone, a hundred thousand? Millin' around like souls out of purgatory waitin' their turn at the gates. Unreal city.

Two Moons didn't even look, just slowed down and drove a little closer to the Wall as we headed past the checkpoint. Stadium of World Youth was a block to our left, police hospital straight ahead.

Two Moons braked to a stop. "All right, Herr Koepke. Where?"

Koepke leaned over the seat. He pointed through the windshield.

"At the corner, where it makes the turn up to Boyenstrasse. Right up there."

We eased on ahead, pulled over, parked and killed the engine. We were so close to the Wall I barely had room to open the door and get out. I stood at the base of it and looked up. It was high enough, all right, fifteen feet but looked like fifty, smooth white monolith lit up like the wall of a nuthouse. Which I guess it was. I ran my hand over it. Rough and cold.

"Here it is, Joey. Here's what it was all about, eh?"

Closky was at my elbow, funny grin on his face. He looked up at the wall. "Us and them, Joey. That side us, this side them. Line down the middle. Geometric. Perfect symmetry."

Behind us the crew was climbing out of the truck, opening the back and bringing out their tools. Two Moons waved them over. He had the old briefcase in his hand, set it down on the hood of the Citroën. Then he turned to Koepke. "Show me."

Koepke looked around like he was getting his bearings, trying to remember what a twenty-year-old militia sergeant saw one night at a construction project on a downtown city street. He walked over to the corner, stood facing the wall, took a sidestep to the left, then another. He reached out and put both hands on the wall just below chest level.

"Here."

Two Moons stood next to him. "You are sure."

"Yes."

Two Moons turned to the crew chief. *"Messband!"*

The crew chief fumbled in his overalls pocket, pulled out a metal tape measure, handed it to Two Moons. He slid the tape out, set the end on the ground at the base of the wall, measured up one and a quarter meters. The crew chief stepped up, held the tape in place. Two Moons reached in his pocket, pulled out a black felt-tip pen, flipped the cap off and let it fall to the ground. He traced out a black rectangle on the wall, maybe four feet long and two feet high, tossed the pen on the ground too. He turned to Koepke.

"So?"

Koepke nodded. "*Ja, so.*"

For a minute everybody stared at the black rectangle on the clean white wall. It was quiet except for the noise of the crowd a block away, dull rumble, muffled mutterings and the occasional shout you couldn't quite make out.

Then Two Moons turned to the maintenance crew chief. "*Kompressor anlassen!*"

He ran to the back of the truck and a second later I could hear the little gas engine crank and catch. A couple of the crew boys came out from behind the truck with the jackhammer on a long, dirty red hose.

With the noise of the compressor running I didn't hear the car drive up. Nobody did. But out of the corner of my eye I saw something moving behind the truck. I looked over. It was a Citroën, lights off, front doors opening. Young guy in an NVA captain's uniform.

Well, what do you know, it was Blondie, but somehow I didn't think he'd rushed over here to bring me a new box of Cheez-Its. When I saw who was with him, I knew I was right.

"Howdy, Pope, Victor. *Kla-how-ya*, George. Looks like you guys are out to do a little remodeling."

He still had the Ray-Bans on. Finally found something to cover the suit, though.

I stared at him. "Nice trench coat. You get it at Wertheim's like I told you?"

I couldn't see his eyes, of course. Johnny stepped up next to me. "Your pal from the restaurant?"

I nodded. "This the rogue agent you were talkin' about, Victor?"

Closky was humming under his breath. Finally he stopped.

"The very same, Joey. Jack Marco as I live and breathe. Long time no see, greaseball. No need to tell me how you got over here, you just picked a crack in the Wall and slid on through, right?"

Closky was grinning. Marco's face didn't move but I could see him swallow hard.

Marco reached up, adjusted his Ray-Bans. With the arc lights glaring off the white wall it was probably the first time he really needed them. "Rogue agent. That's a good one, Pope. I'd say we were all rogue agents, don't you think?"

Two Moons folded his arms, glared at Blondie. "*Und du, Strohmeyer?*"

Blondie grinned. "*Jin und Jang, Genosse Generaloberst.*"

Marco took a step forward. "Strohmeyer's been working with us for a while now, George. He'll be coming with me when I leave, which will be just as soon as you hand over what we came here for." He held his trench coat open. "Now, you'll notice I'm not armed and neither is he. You'll also notice we don't look worried that you'll have us arrested and carted away for an extended stay at Bautzen. Let me explain to you why that is."

I figured I was losing the title for biggest wiseass of all time, but I wasn't about to contest it until we'd heard him out.

Marco pointed to a stretch of the Wall about a hundred yards away that ran perpendicular to the section where we were standing, far end of the three-sided bulge that hemmed us in like a squash court. "Just over there on the Western side of Boyenstrasse there's a wooden observation platform. We've got the steps sealed off at the bottom, but up top there's a man in a West Berlin police uniform looking this way. He can see us now—in fact, he can see us real good. The reason he can see us so good is he's looking through the scope of a Remington Sendero 7mm Magnum. He'll keep looking while you drill into the wall and get the canister out. He'll still be looking while you hand it to me and give me an escort through the checkpoint. Once I'm back in West Berlin he'll stop looking. But if he sees me give the signal, or if he sees you try anything funny, he'll take the four of you out. You first, George, then Victor, then Pope, then whoever's left." He nodded at Johnny. "He can take out all four of you before the first one hits the ground."

Well, this was crazy. "Listen, Marco, are you out of your goddam mind? You're going to fire shots into East German territory to take out a lieutenant general in the NVA? What are you trying to do, start World War Three?"

"If we have to, so be it. So don't screw up." He grinned. "Besides, George ain't really in the NVA, probably bought that uniform at a KoKo garage sale, right, George?"

Two Moons stared at him. If Marco was getting under his skin, the stone face didn't show it.

Johnny stepped up next to me. "How do we know you aren't bluffing?"

"Good question. Let me explain that one too." He bent down, picked up the felt-tip marker, walked over to the Wall just next to the rectangle. He sketched the outline of a human silhouette from the waist up. Then he stepped back. He stared up into the darkness over the top of the Wall, head gave a slight nod. Then he looked back at the target.

All of a sudden there was a whoosh in the air a foot above my head, then a noise like a sledgehammer pulverizing rock, nothing more than that, cloud of whitish-gray powder shot out from the wall. Middle of the target's head had a baseball-sized hole.

Marco's face still didn't change. "AWC Thundertrap silencer. Very effective."

The maintenance crew chief was staring at Two Moons, waiting for an order. I doubted if he understood much English, but he understood enough to know this wasn't just another routine service call. Two Moons looked at the jackhammer, then pointed to the rectangle on the wall.

"*Da 'ran!*"

The crew chief shook his head. "*Geht nicht, Genosse Generaloberst.* The hammer is not made for drilling into a vertical surface. Too heavy."

Two Moons's scarred stone face twisted into something like scorn. He shook his head, muttered *"Tenas klooshman."* Then he tugged off his officer's topcoat, folded it once. He started to hand it to Blondie, then set it down on the ground. He unbuttoned his tunic, peeled it off and laid it down on top of the coat.

Under his thin white shirt his upper body looked as thick and strong as a century-old cedar. You had the feeling nothing could stop him, maybe not even a bullet, but he didn't look like he wanted to take a chance on that. At least not yet.

He picked up the drill with his right hand, swung it up and cradled it in his left like a tommy gun. He squeezed the hose to check the pressure. Then he set the bit against the upper right-hand corner of the rectangle. He turned to Koepke.

"You are sure."

"Yes, *Genosse Generaloberst.* I'm sure."

Two Moons's huge right hand squeezed the trigger on the drill handle. It jumped to life in his arms, pounding the pure white cinder block, sending a shower of dust and shrapnel into the air, shaking the Chief's arms and body so hard and fast he looked like a blur.

Johnny was shouting something in my ear. I couldn't hear him, shook my head. He leaned closer.

"Tukamonuk tillakum mamook tlkope stone. Remember that one, Joe?"

I remembered all right. "A hundred men worked to cut the stone." This wasn't the first time Two Moons had jumped into history with a jackhammer. But that was long ago. This was now.

He worked in short bursts, shut the drill off, moved it a half foot along the line, then started it up again, slowly opening a crack in the Wall Honecker had built to last a hundred years.

December 12, 1948

I found a space in the lot behind the warehouse and switched the ignition off. The inside of the Hudson smelled like new leather, shiny brown calfskin briefcase on the front seat beside me. I checked out the key tied to the handle one more time, opened it up. White tissue paper inside, price tag tied to the handle. I made sure the receipt was still in my shirt pocket. Twenty-five bucks seemed like a lot, but it was no skin off my beezer as long as I got reimbursed.

Outside it was cold and raw, snow flurries in the air again but they said it wouldn't amount to much. I held my topcoat closed as I walked across the parking lot against the wind. Closky's red Plymouth was parked next to the door, Nixon's Ford right behind that.

It felt good to get out of the cold, and I headed up the concrete steps in the stairwell two at a time. When I got through the fire door I smelled fresh coffee. Closky's office was down the hall. I could hear his voice, the sound of his high-pitched laugh, then Nixon's baritone. The door was open. Closky had his size thirteens up on the desk, white shirt open at the collar, red silk tie askew, fat face red with laughter, crew cut down an eighth of an inch since last week. Nixon sat in a chair across the room, double-breasted jacket buttoned up, legs crossed. For the first time since I could remember he was grinning from ear to ear.

I tapped on the door frame. Nixon stood up. "Well, what do you know, here's our propman now." He took the briefcase, ran his hand over the smooth leather. "Nice one. Good quality."

I nodded, looked around the room. Bulletin board next to Closky's desk was plastered with news clippings from the past week, wirephoto of Nixon hopping off the flying boat, grainy black-and-white shot of the pumpkin patch, Nixon and Stripling eyeballing a couple frames of film through a magnifying glass. Never mind that you couldn't actually read microfilm that way. Headline: PUMPKIN PAPERS PROVE SPY LINK, COMMITTEE MEMBER SAYS.

I pulled the receipt from my shirt pocket, dropped it on Closky's desk. "If it's not right I can take it back." Closky glanced at the receipt, then looked at Nixon. Nixon shook his head. "It's fine." Closky reached in his suitcoat, pulled out a roll of bills. He peeled off two tens and a five, tossed them on the desk. I slipped them in my pocket.

"So what's it for?"

Nixon and Closky looked at each other like they were both in on the biggest joke in the world. Then Closky said, "Nothing."

I stared at them. Finally Nixon said, "I'm taking the documents to the grand jury in New York tomorrow. Once they see them, Hiss is finished. So I wouldn't be a bit surprised if Justice doesn't try to stop me, hand me a subpoena as I'm walking up the courthouse steps, maybe even hire some goddam goon to steal them on the way." He took the briefcase by the handle, held it at his side. "So I'll be carrying this, but here's the trick. It'll be empty. A decoy. The actual documents will be in your pocket. Victor's idea."

Of course. Closky gave an aw-shucks grin, held out his hands palms up. I frowned. "Well, geez, sir, that's great, I'm honored, I really am. But are you sure we can fit all that paper inside my coat? Or maybe you want me to wear Victor's."

Nixon chuckled and sat down again; Closky made a face. He picked up a small stack of papers off his desk, eight and a half by eleven, maybe a half inch thick. "Any problem with this?"

"That's it? I thought you told the press we had a stack of documents three feet high."

Nixon shrugged. "Poetic license. Besides, we also said most of them were too hot to release to the public."

"Meaning they're actually worthless."

Closky flipped through the papers. "Oh, I'd say there's enough here to cook Hiss's goose, wouldn't you, sir? 'From the embassy in Paris to the Secretary of State, strictly confidential . . .' 'From the embassy in Berlin to the Secretary of State, strictly confidential . . .' 'From the embassy—' "

Here we go again. How many times in the past ten days was I treated to this performance? "Okay, Victor, okay. I'm trying to believe this, I really am. Sir, don't get mad at me again. So we show the grand jury the microfilm. We show them the copies of confidential cable traffic from foreign embassies in the late thirties. We remind them Hiss had access to those cables. But hell, so did fifty other guys at the State Department. The fact that Chambers had microfilmed copies of documents in 1948 doesn't prove he got them from Hiss in 1938. For that matter, Chambers always swore he broke with communism in '37. Now he turns up with these papers from '38 and he says, 'Oops, guess I was a year off.' You really think a jury's going to buy that?"

Closky held up his hands. "Joey, you're still not seeing the whole picture, okay? I mean fine, what you're saying is true as far as it goes. But the microfilm means a lot more than that. Number one, it's *microfilm*, for God's sake. To John Q. Juror that says Spy Scandal right off the bat, okay? Number two, the grand jury's already seen the so-called Baltimore Documents, the papers Chambers turned over to Hiss's lawyers last November. And Ramos Feehan from the FBI has already told 'em the typing on those copies matches the typing samples from Hiss's private correspondence at home. So it all adds up."

Nixon held up a hand, waved Closky off. His face was serious, he leaned toward me, hands folded between his legs. "Tell me something, Joe. Do you really believe it's possible that Hiss is being framed? Is that what you're getting at here?"

It was the first time Nixon ever called me by my first name, and it caught me off guard. I backed down. "No sir, I don't. I just think something's going on we haven't figured out yet."

He ignored me. "Because if you think that, you've always got to come back to the question of Chambers's motive. Why would he do it? Why would he throw away a thirty-thousand-dollar-a-year job as senior editor at *Time* magazine, why would he open himself up to perjury charges, why would he ruin a life he worked so hard to build up just to frame Alger Hiss? Anti-communism? Some jealous grudge? Sure it's possible, but it's not enough. There's no goddam motive in the world you can come up with that would make sense. So he's got to be telling the truth."

Well, he was probably right about that, although I couldn't help thinking of the severance check Chambers got from Henry Luce last week. Probably more dough than I'd ever see in my lifetime. Still, it didn't explain anything.

What could I say? I smiled. "So what time do we leave?"

Nixon grinned, gave me an atta-boy punch in the arm. Then he clicked the latch on the briefcase shut, grabbed his topcoat and hat from a rack in the corner. "Seven forty-five from Union Station. Meet me at the office at seven. We'll take a goddam cab."

He shot us the V sign and ducked out. I walked over to Closky's desk, flipped through the papers. "You really think this is going to do the trick?"

Closky shrugged. "This, or maybe this plus something else."

He had that look on his face. "Something else, Victor?"

Full-blown smirk now, hint of a smile around the eyes. He swung his feet off the desk and stood up. "You been down to Blunt's lately?"

I shook my head. "Not in the past month or so. Why, he's up to something?"

"You might say that. Come on."

We left Closky's office, headed downstairs to the basement. The file room looked more crowded than usual.

"You hire more people again?"

Closky looked around. "Couple more, yeah. Still not the big breakthrough yet. I'm trying to get the dough for a move out of this dump to a place across the river. We'll see."

Guess we will. Blunt's office was in a walled-off corner of the old warehouse basement, frosted glass door, bright light inside. Closky turned the knob. It was locked. He rapped on the glass.

"Hey, Ed, open up. It's me."

I saw Blunt's hulking silhouette against the glass, then heard the lock turn. When the door opened it smelled like coffee and sewing machine oil. We slipped inside.

Blunt's workroom looked like an explosion in an office machine factory. A dozen busted-up typewriters on the floor, cardboard boxes full of parts, keys, spools, ribbons, platens, plus a hundred other pieces of grimy metal. There was a clean white sheet over Blunt's desk, half-assembled guts of something in the middle, goose-necked lamp with a five-hundred-watt bulb shining on it. Oily brown bag on one corner, white mug half full of Blunt's trademark beige coffee, couple of typewritten papers alongside that. I glanced at the first lines. "From the embassy at Paris the quick brown fox jumped over the lazy Secretary of State ran away home, strictly confidential . . ." Blunt set something down on the table. I looked closer. A jeweler's eyepiece.

He was wearing a white lab coat over his rumpled sergeant's uniform, had a half-eaten doughnut in one hand, other half tucked somewhere in his fat cheek. "Howdy, Colonel. Hi, sir. Come down to inspect the troops?"

Closky walked over to the desk, bent over the machine in the middle. "How's it coming?"

Blunt crushed the doughnut in his mouth, gulped it down. "Not bad. Parts aren't a problem, Woodstock people have been real good about that. Machining the type down to match the documents is tough, but it's kind of fun when you finally get it right." He pointed to a cardboard box full of broken type. "Those are the ones I messed up."

Closky nodded. "You think you'll have it ready for the trial?"

Blunt stuffed the rest of the doughnut in his mouth, wiped his lips on his sleeve, walked over to a sink in the corner to wash his hands. "Should be no problem. You're figuring what, a month or so?"

"Maybe. Once Joey and the Boss get the goddam grand jury off the dime tomorrow it could be sooner than that, though."

Blunt finished drying his hands on a clean white turkish towel, came back over to his desk and sat down, screwed the jeweler's glass into his eye. "Guess I'd better get to work then."

I couldn't believe it. I looked at Blunt, then at Closky. "Let me get this straight, Victor. We're building a typewriter to match the documents Chambers claims he got from Hiss?"

Closky grinned. "Bingo, Joey. Which in turn match the Hiss standards."

"Meaning the papers Hiss turned over as samples of the machine he had at home in the thirties?"

"Right. Which is pretty incriminating in itself. We already know copies of secret State Department documents were typed on Hiss's old machine. Having the actual machine itself will clinch it, though."

"Yeah, but Jesus, you say we're not framing the sonofabitch and here we are manufacturing evidence in a federal perjury case?

216

Doesn't that bother you a little bit, Victor, at least the irony of it? Not to mention what'll happen to Nixon and us if it backfires? Hell, don't you have enough of a case already without throwing in a fake typewriter?"

Closky shook his head. "What's fake, Joey? What's real? You can counterfeit anything, and if it's perfect, what's the difference? Who's going to ever know?"

I turned to Blunt. "You got an opinion on this one, Ed?"

Blunt was hunched over the typewriter, tiny screwdriver in his fat hand, face more lumpy than usual in the bright light. "I just work here, sir, know what I mean? Just work for the government like you and the Colonel and everybody else."

Closky clapped me on the back, damn near knocked me over. "Besides, Joey, you're missing the main point." He put his arm around my shoulder, thin lips brushing my ear, hoarse whisper. *"Hiss is guilty so it doesn't matter."*

I pulled away. "And what makes you so goddam sure of that?"

Closky was quiet a long time. "I can't tell you that, but trust me. I just know, okay? Trust me."

I stared into his fat, pink face. He was doing his best to look solemn but it wasn't coming off, just a real smart guy in his late twenties who was headed up so fast he didn't have time to think about anything else. He'd be in for a fall again someday, I knew that much, just didn't know how soon or how far. I turned to go.

Blunt looked up at me, black cylinder still screwed into his eye. "Sir?"

I stared back at him. He reached across the table, picked up the oily brown bag, handed it to me. I looked inside. A doughnut.

"Saved a cruller for you this time. Make you feel better."

November 9, 1989

The hole in the wall was about four feet wide and two feet high, block of whitewashed concrete set on the tarmac alongside it. I bent down and peered in. Looked like the Chief went clear through

217

in one spot, six-inch crack of Free World moonlight shining through in the back. Two of the maintenance crew boys were chipping away at the rest with a crowbar and sledgehammer. Finally Two Moons gave the word for them to step aside.

He reached in, brushed some dust away with his bare hand, turned back to us. "The original concrete blocks. Joint is right here." He waved Koepke over. "*War's hier?*"

Koepke took a step back. "*Jawohl.* We had set two blocks from the corner there. The third one had just been put in place and we were applying the mortar."

Two Moons held out his hand. "*Messband!*" The crew chief handed him the tape measure, held the end as Two Moons pulled it out and held it to the wall. "*Zwei Meter fünfzig.* This is the second block." He set his hand on top of the concrete block inside the wall. "And this is the third. So between here and here—" He turned to the maintenance boys. "*Hammer und Meissel!*"

We watched as they chipped away at the mortar with a hammer and chisel, chips flying as they worked their way down between the blocks. So far, nothing.

Then we heard the voice.

"*Um Gotteswillen, was geht denn hier vor?*"

Great, more company. I turned around. It was a Vopo captain and two guards with machine pistols, must've come over from the checkpoint. Two Moons drew himself up to his full six feet, five inches, stared down at the captain. "State security, *Genosse Hauptmann.* These men are under my command."

The captain didn't know what to make of Two Moons's face, but he had enough sense to salute the red general's stripe on his britches. He wasn't buying the rest of it, though, I could tell that much.

"Begging your pardon, *Genosse General—*" Two Moons scowled. The Vopo captain glanced down at the tunic on the ground. "*Genosse Generaloberst.* I have been in constant telephone contact with the Ministry for State Security. There is no maintenance operation scheduled for this sector tonight."

I glanced at Marco. So far he hadn't looked at the captain. But now he did, turned and stared at him long and hard. Then his head slowly rotated toward the darkness at the top of the far wall. Slight nod. Oh holy hell.

Then I heard it. In spite of everything, the dull roar of the crowd behind the barricade, the sputter of the little gas engine behind the truck. I heard it, or I thought I did, a muffled *click-click-click* coming from Closky's trench-coat pocket. He stepped forward until he stood directly between the captain and the dark at the top of the far wall. Marco stiffened, didn't move. The captain stared at Closky. Closky's head started a slow bob and weave. Weak smile.

"Jenosse Hauptmann, isses wirklich meeglich, dass Sie mich nicht erkennen?" Berlin accent this time, voice a half octave lower than usual. What the hell?

The captain stared at Closky. Flicker of uncertainty on his young Saxon face. "No, I am afraid I do not recognize you."

Closky looked around the group with a smile, shaking his head like the whole thing was just too damn funny for words.

"May I?" He held a hand up, palm out, opened his coat with the other, reached in slowly, pulled out a pair of horn-rimmed glasses I'd never seen before, slipped them on. Then he reached in again and came out with an oversized brown leather wallet I'd never seen before either. Embossed gold Zonal seal flashed in the bright lights, hammer-and-calipers of the first worker-and-peasant state on German soil. Closky opened it and flipped through a couple papers bound inside, finally unfolded a document, big one, parchment it looked like, and there was that damn seal again, red and gold this time, and a worn color photo pasted and stamped in the corner. It was Closky all right, same glasses he was wearing now. Or was it? Actually looked even older than he was, looked more like a cross between him and—

"Genosse Armeegeneral Mielke! Verzeihung! Ich—" The captain was standing at attention, his face white, lips stammering without making a sound. The two boys with machine pistols behind him hesitated, then followed suit and turned to stone.

I took a half step closer and risked a glance over his shoulder at the document. State Security ID, luxury edition, Serial Number 1. Geez, what a piece of work. Guess Closky's Palm Beach suit had deeper pockets than we thought. Good old Blunt. Then I read the name under Closky's photo. Sure enough. Holy hell.

"Erich Mielke." Hoover, Himmler, and Beria all rolled into one. Well, this was it, I guess. Closky's revenge on the commie sonofabitch he blamed for sending poor Kai Beckmann to his doom and twisting Closky's soul into a spiritual pretzel in the bargain. But what the hell was he going to do?

Closky screwed his face into a scowl. Wisps of white hair floated in the cool night breeze. He adjusted his phony glasses, folded the document and shoved the leather case back into his pocket.

"What you have heard from the *Genosse Generaloberst* is correct, Captain. This is a State Security matter and does not concern you." He checked his watch. He held it six inches from his face, blue eyes bugging out behind the thick lenses, face half maniac, half senile old man. His voice rose an octave. "What should concern you, however, is the performance of your duty at *Staatsgrenze-West Kontrollpunkt Chausseestrasse!*"

As Closky spat out the words the captain stiffened until it looked like he was going to snap like a violin string. Closky eyed him up and down, started pacing.

"Why do you think these people are gathered here? For a soccer match?" He gestured at the dark and empty stadium a block to the south. "Have you misunderstood today's order from Comrades Krenz and Schabowski? Have you failed to incorporate the words *glasnost* and *perestroika* into your socialist German vocabulary, as Comrade Gorbachev has ordered?"

Holy, holy, holy hell. I finally got it. Finally figured out what he was up to. A little earlier than he planned, a little off schedule, but if he could neutralize Marco in the bargain, so be it. Looked like the Chief and his pal General Brünner weren't going to have their putsch tomorrow after all. Looked like it was Rollback, forty years late. But could Closky really pull it off?

One look at his face and I knew he could. He drew himself erect, clutched his trench coat with a bony hand. "Follow your orders, Captain! Open your gate! Open this control point and let our people pass freely among the rooms of our Common European House! Open it *now!*" The captain's face was white. His lip was still trembling. "Sir, I have received no such orders—"

Closky exploded. In a half second his face turned bright red, flecks of spit on his thin lips, transformation from sweet reason to psychopath like somebody threw a switch. His voice was shrill, lips curled in a snarl, head shaking.

"You are receiving orders from me, do you understand? Me, Erich Mielke! I battled for communism before you were born, before your parents were born! Do you think you can question me because you stand here with two armed policemen at your side? I can brush you all aside like flies! I can crush you like worms!" He held two bony claws up in the air, shook them in the captain's face. "With these bare hands I dispatched two fascist policemen right here in the capital and I will do it again if you dare oppose me! Now follow me and do your socialist duty. *Do your socialist duty!* Open your gate!" He stepped past the captain, set his hands on the shoulders of the two guards. They shuddered, but Closky's voice suddenly got soft again. *"Kommt, Jungs, an die Arbeit!* C'mon, boys, let's get to work."

They shot a glance at each other, then turned together and walked with him, Closky's arms around each of their shoulders. The three of them marched in lockstep for a dozen yards or so, then Closky raised his arms to the sky and stepped ahead of them to lead the way. The captain hesitated, then ran after them. I heard Closky's sweet tenor rise above the roar.

> *Völker, hört die Signa-a-a-l-e,*
> *auf zum letzten Gefecht!*
> *Internation-a-a-a-l-e*
> *erkämpft das Menschenrecht!*

The guards sang with him for another verse, then they stopped and I could hear Closky shouting *"Macht den Schlagbaum auf,"* "Raise the barrier," over and over again until he was too far away to hear.

Two Moons shook his head. *"Pelton. Boss sick kopa la-tate."*

I muttered, "Yeah, *pelton* like a fox."

From a block away I could see Closky's white trench coat fluttering in the wind, big dome of a head gleaming in the arc lights. We couldn't hear him anymore but saw his arms waving upward. The crowd surged as he approached, wave rippled through them, poised on the brink like the Israelites at the Red Sea and Moses about to say the word. The two guards marched on either side of him a step behind, the captain still running to catch up.

Finally they reached the gate. Closky stood still facing the glassed-in guard post, his back toward us. His arms went up. Once. Twice. Three times. For the first time all night the crowd was quiet.

Then it happened.

I heard Marco whisper, "My God, they're doing it."

The gate came up.

The red-and-white turnpike with the chain-link mesh hanging from it rose up just as smooth as a railroad crossing gate, hung there pointing up at the night sky. And for a second everything froze, Closky with his arms up like Moses, the crowd, the gate, all washed in that unearthly white light like they were standing on the damn moon.

Then a roar like the crashing surf, folks up front took a step, held back, then surged forward as a cheer went up that drowned out everything. How many were there? A hundred thousand? Two hundred thousand? They were packed shoulder-to-shoulder on the six-lane boulevard as far back as you could see, and now they were surging forward. Already the first ones were passing through the Wall to the other side, faster now, and a second roar went up from the West as folks waiting over there saw what was happening.

We all just stood there, didn't say a word. I looked around. Marco's mouth was hanging open, Johnny smiling. Only Two Moons's face was still a mask. Then I looked at the East German

222

repair crew and saw a look on their faces I hadn't seen in this town since I'd been here.

Joy.

All of a sudden the crew chief dropped the hammer and chisel on the tarmac. He started walking straight ahead toward the crowd. His two buddies hesitated, then followed him. Two Moons shouted for them to stop but they didn't react, kept walking, all three of them together, then they broke into a run, finally disappeared into the crowd moving through to the other side. I looked back for Closky, didn't see him, then caught a glimpse of his white trench coat, arms waving above the crowd. Then he was gone.

Two Moons picked up the hammer and chisel. He muttered something in Chinook, then started chipping at the mortar again.

There was another surge from the back now as people started spilling off the street. It was a bottleneck, no way they could get through the checkpoint fast enough to suit folks in the back and pretty soon they were scrambling over the tank traps and concrete vehicle barriers, pushing toward the narrow exit, pressing against the Wall beside the checkpoint, filling in the empty space between us and the street.

Then even that wasn't room enough anymore and they surged toward us, folks running now to keep from getting crushed or trampled. There were screams. A couple people hit the Wall and stood on each other's shoulders to try to reach the top, and when the crowd saw that they all broke loose and headed our way. We started to move back but they were all around us, trampling Two Moons's uniform, climbing over the Mercedes, the Citroën, the truck and trailer, laughing, shouting, singing. They were all ages, young folks and old, children among 'em, mothers with babies, and they were all around me now, pressing against the wall, pushing and jostling, slowly moving toward the opening as sure as the current pulls you to the break in a burst dam.

There was a scuffle now, and different shouts, somebody got sore and gave a hard shove and I fought to keep my balance but I couldn't, went down among a thousand feet, couldn't hold on to anything, couldn't get up. I felt the pain and the panic, crowd still moving and the ones who saw me fall long gone, nobody knew I was down here now, heavy shoes pressing into my arms, my chest, my face, and I muttered "Jesus" and tried to cover my head.

Then I felt something else, felt the bodies above me brushed aside like twigs on the water, saw a big hand come down, felt it clamp onto my arm with the strength of ten men, felt myself pulled up and back on my feet like Saint Pete himself on the Sea o' Galilee. Two Moons shoved something into my chest and I grabbed it without thinking, held on to it like a life vest, felt the crowd tug at me again and pull me away. For a split second I saw his scarred face above the crowd, saw his arm reach out in a wave, flicker of a smile through the stone, a shout I couldn't hear but I knew it was "*kla-how-ya*," and then he was gone.

I couldn't see Johnny or Marco but I stayed on my feet, worked my way along the Wall with the crowd, didn't fight it now, nowhere else to go but out, slow progress toward the gap. I couldn't tell how long it took, couldn't bring my arm up to see my watch but we kept moving and finally we were there and we made the turn and broke through to the other side.

There was room again, lots of it, room to move, room to breathe, and the crowd fanned out, slowly at first, but we were in the West now and there was more cheering and singing. It got darker past the border area but the West Berliners lining the streets were holding up their lighters, hundreds of flames, thousands of them, and the Krauts East and West were calling to each other, tears in their eyes and shouting "*Brüder, Brüder,*" and then somebody struck up "*Deutschland über Alles*" and I bailed out.

I stumbled off the street about a half block from the Wall, got away from the main crowd that kept moving west. I was drenched in sweat. When I got loose from the crowd I felt the chill and started shivering. Finally I found a spot on an empty packed-dirt lot and fell to the ground.

My arms were still locked in front of my chest, and when I looked down I saw I was holding the old leather briefcase. I clicked the latch open and pulled the top apart. Then I looked around, looked back at the Wall. It didn't look real.

People were actually on top of the damn thing now, balancing, waving their arms, walking along like acrobats. A gang of young guys with shaved heads stood at the foot of it, right at the spot where Two Moons drilled through. One of them had a tire iron and was whacking at the wall, stone chips flying, couple people picking them up and putting them in their pockets.

I looked back at the briefcase, peered inside. Our money was still there, ditto the papers and envelopes from Saddle River HQ. Honest Injun, huh? But there was something else too. I slid it out.

It was the cardboard box Two Moons pulled off the shelf at Honecker's garage, carried it with him ever since. I tore the packing tape off and opened one end.

Metal box inside, cut wires poking out. My gut leaped up into my throat. Jesus Christ, was it a bomb?

I damn near dropped it and ran but something made me stay there, something that told me he wouldn't save me from getting trampled just to blow me up ten minutes later. I slid it out of the carton. It was a metal box all right. Wires. Glass dial. Plastic knobs. Chrome buttons.

I laughed out loud. I couldn't help it. "Holy hell," I said. "It's my Volumatic."

14

January 26, 1950

Well, the grand jury swallowed the Pumpkin Papers all right, swallowed 'em hook, line and sinker, brought back an indictment of Hiss on 15 December '48, two days after Nixon dragged me up to New York with him, and if you want to see how it looked to history, well, there was that World Wide Photos shot that ran in all the papers, poker-faced young congressman coming up the courthouse steps in his new blue suit and pearl-gray snap-brim hat, yours truly a half step behind like Prince Philip himself, crowd at a respectful distance too, all eyes on the briefcase, of course, shiny and new in the congressman's right hand, Nixon doing his best to look like the damn thing felt heavy, which of course it didn't.

But even after the indictment it wasn't easy, never mind the microfilm and Blunt's ersatz typewriter and Nixon's secret pipeline to the prosecution via the New York *World-Telegram* and his letter to Felix Frankfurter and Closky's shenanigans and a dozen other marked cards in a well-stacked deck. Closky kept saying the climate wasn't right, and I guess it wasn't. Russians finally lifted the blockade in Berlin that June and folks were saying maybe the Commies weren't such a threat after all. So the first trial ended with a hung jury, eight to four for conviction, 7 July '49, and you should've heard Nixon wail the day *that* news broke. Damn near called the jury foreman a Commie, claimed we ought to appoint a special prosecutor, said the Demos were trying to make the case political, which it clearly was not. (That's irony, as Blunt would say.)

But then things started to break our way. Mao sent Chiang packing across the Formosa Strait, Uncle Joe set off his first A-bomb, not that Closky had anything to do with either of those, mind you, but next thing you know folks were thinking, hey, better safe than sorry when it comes to commie spies in the government. So when the second trial came up last November the climate *was* right, although I'd be lying if I said we didn't help things along here and there. Got ourselves a judge left over from the Harding administration, plus a jury forelady who was a member of the church where the judge was vestryman and damn near thought he was Jesus Christ himself. Oh, and another juror who was married to the court bailiff, plus three more with relatives in the FBI, and on and on and on.

Looking back on it though, I'd have to say the clincher was that damn typewriter, even if Blunt did stamp the wrong serial number on it after all that, but the FBI hushed it up and it never dawned on Hiss's lawyers to check. So there it sat in the courtroom the whole time, our mute star witness made of metal and rubber and ribbons, FBI man careful not to perjure himself by swearing it was the right machine, everybody else just assuming it was because why else would we've schlepped it into the courtroom in the first place, prosecutor even going so far as to tell the jury they should let Hiss walk if they so much as suspected any of the evidence in the case had been "manufactured, conceived or suborned by the government." Whew.

But they didn't, so after two trials, two judges, and two juries they finally found Hiss guilty last week on two counts of perjury. Once for lying when he said he never saw Chambers after '37 and once for lying about passing documents. Statute of limitations on espionage was up or they'd have nailed him for that too.

Now that it was over, of course, I had to admit it didn't make any more sense to me than when it started. Hiss never budged an inch from his story, claimed to the bitter end Chambers dreamed the whole thing up, framed him for some crazy reason Hiss couldn't even guess at. And yet even his own lawyer couldn't keep it from sounding like something was fishy, like Hiss was holding back, covering his tracks, and try as you might you couldn't help thinking that here was one sonofabitch who had to be hiding *something*.

So Judge Goddard sentenced him yesterday, two concurrent five-year terms in federal prison. If he was lucky he'd see daylight in a little over half of that.

Needless to say, the mood in Closky's office was pretty chipper. We'd even managed to get clearance for a move to new digs again, fancy joint across the river he'd had his eye on for the past year or so. Movers showed up this morning, tromping up and down the narrow hall with furniture and filing cabinets. Half the stuff in Closky's office was packed in cartons, art crated up, balsa wood Luftwaffe wrapped in tissue paper up on the filing cabinet, never did get strung from the ceiling like it was in Berlin. Maybe at the new place he'd feel more at home.

And Closky, well, there he sat, whistling to himself, pecking away at the machine on his desk, one of Blunt's failed prototypes no doubt. His crew cut had grown in a good eighth of an inch, still pure whitewalls around the temples, though, new red silk tie neatly knotted under a starched white collar straining against his fat neck, gold tie clip at a sharp right angle to his gig line. Every so often he stopped and looked up at me or over at Nixon, shook his head and grinned like he was savoring the moment.

"Five years in Lewisburg. Hoo-ee. It's tough there, but the sonofabitch deserves it. Up the lazy river, buddy."

I shrugged. "It ain't the Harvard Club, that's for sure."

Nixon looked up from across the room. "You're damn straight it isn't." He was hunched in the corner scribbling on a yellow legal pad, topcoat draped over the back of his chair, briefcase on the floor by his feet. Tomorrow he was addressing the House, had a four-hour speech planned, called it "The Hiss Case—A Lesson for the

American People." He sat up, cleared his throat. "How about this for the blowoff, boys: '*In 1945, when Alger Hiss was making postwar agreements for the United States, one hundred and eighty million people were in the orbit of Soviet totalitarianism. Today that figure has grown to eight hundred million. That is the true cost of the Hiss treason and cover-up. We owe a solemn duty to expose this sinister conspiracy for what it is, to roll back the Red Menace.*' "

Closky didn't look up, kept typing. " 'Tide.' "

Nixon frowned. "Say again?"

"Red Tide, not Red Menace. More of a ring to it. Plus it sounds biblical, know what I mean sir? Red *Sea*, Red *Tide.*"

Nixon scratched out one word, wrote in another. Red Tide it was.

Through it all, Closky's typing never stopped. What the hell was he doing anyway? I glanced at the book propped up on his desk. *U.S. Department of State Telephone Directory.* Guess he'd tell us soon enough.

Oh, and the Boss was running for Senate now along with everything else, have I mentioned that? Formal announcement came last November after the California crew spent the better part of the summer lining up the dough, Republican primary still four months away but things were looking pretty good. I didn't know whether that meant our Chicago friends were out of the picture now or not, and I didn't have the stomach to ask. I had my fill of poking under that rock after Marvin Smith died, even kept my mouth shut that December when another of Hiss's pals took a fall, ex-State Department boy name of Laurence Duggan, sailed out of a Manhattan skyscraper window a couple days after his name came up in Committee testimony. That made two very depressed individuals, as Closky put it, three if you count Harry White, but of course who could prove the three deaths were linked—and, at this point, who cared?

For about the tenth time Blunt poked his head in. His rumpled uniform sleeves sported the freshly sewn-on chevrons of a first sergeant. Congrats, I guess. Behind him stood a couple oversized army privates, dirty fatigues stained with sweat. "Okay to start in here now, sir?"

Closky looked up. "Give us another half hour, Sergeant."

Blunt shot the thumbs-up. "Check." He motioned to the movers and they disappeared down the hall.

Finally Closky pulled the last sheet out of his typewriter, put it with the others, evened them up and clipped them together. "Here you go, sir, all ready for tomorrow."

Nixon set his speech down, got up, took the papers from Closky's hand. "What the hell's this?"

Closky grinned. "It's a list of two hundred and five employees of the State Department who happen to be card-carrying members of the Communist party. Acheson knows all about 'em too, don't let him kid you."

Nixon's eyes popped. "Two hundred and *five*? You can't be serious. How in the hell could there be two hundred and five Commies in the goddam State Department?"

Closky shrugged. "Let's just say there are. What's the difference? You get up in front of the House tomorrow, you wave this list, you say '*I have here in my hand a list of two hundred and five Communists in the State Department.*' Folks'll go nuts, I guarantee it, and with Hiss in the bag they'll be too damn scared to question it. It's a can't-miss proposition, sir; it'll put you over the top once and for all. Guaranteed."

Nixon was frowning, reading through the list, flipped from one page to the next. Then he looked down on the desk, saw the phone directory, picked it up.

"You were typing from this?"

Closky nodded. "Yeah, that's totally up-to-date, just came out first of the year."

Nixon looked from the papers to the phone book and back again. "I'm missing something, Victor. How do you know these two hundred and five people are Communists?"

"Sir?"

"In other words, you have some way of identifying—I mean, you can't just pick out two hundred and five names at random and type them—"

Closky grinned, touched a finger to the tip of his nose, winked.

Nixon threw the book and papers down. "Oh, for Christ's sake, Closky, of all the stupid-ass, harebrained tricks you've tried to sell me this is the most screwed up of all. You want me to read a list of names of State Department employees, claim they're sonofabitching Commies, and you just typed the goddam thing up at random?"

"Not *read* it, sir, I never said that. Just wave it around, make the charge, let 'em sweat for a while. This time next year you'll be in the Senate, I guarantee it."

Nixon laughed. He was pulling on his topcoat, shaking his head. "Closky, you are out of your goddam mind. What senator, what member of Congress would be so flat-out stupid that he'd try to pull a stunt like that and think he could get away with it?"

Closky's face was red. He bent down, picked the papers off the floor, put them back in order.

"So you're saying you don't think somebody else would jump at the chance to use this?"

Nixon rolled his eyes. He slipped his speech into the briefcase, put his hat on, patted Closky's arm. "Tell you what, Victor. You find somebody who wants to use it, you go right ahead and give it to him with my compliments, okay? Don't feel like I want to monopolize your goddam talents." He checked his watch. "I'll see you boys on the Hill tomorrow. Got some backers I can't keep waiting." He shot out into the hall, dodged a pair of movers, and was gone.

Closky folded the papers, put them in an envelope. "Well, you heard him, Joey, he had his chance."

"You really going to peddle that to somebody else, Victor?"

"I got some ideas, sure."

I thought about that for a minute. "Which means we're not working for Nixon anymore? At least, not exclusively?"

Closky laughed. "Oh, hell, Joey, sure we are. Always were, always will be." He cocked an eyebrow. "At least, in a way we are."

"And when we move to Virginia? No more junior assistant investigators then, I guess, hell, no more HUAC once he makes it to the Senate, right? What are we doing, joining the goddam CIA?"

Closky shook his head. "Negative. See, Joey, the problem with the CIA is, their budget's a secret but they're not. That's only half the trick. Now you take us, hell, nobody knows we even exist. It's perfect."

"And yet we seem to have a budget."

Closky winked. "Correct. Because funding is never a problem, Joey. Never. I've told you that before. It comes from the campaign, it comes from Congress, it comes from private sources, you name it."

"So from now on when somebody asks, we say what, we just work for the government?"

Closky thought for a minute. Then his fat face broke into a big grin. "Yeah. I like the sound of that. *The government.* That's exactly what we'll say, Joey. Let's just call it that."

November 12, 1989

It was dark when we finally turned off Chestnut Ridge Road onto Elden, then hung a left on Charlden Drive and took it to the dead end. I eased the T-bird off the road and waited for the low iron gates to swing open. Motion sensor picked us up and the quartz lights came on. TV cameras up in the pine trees whirred around, zoomed in on us. I stuck my head out the window and waved. A pair of lenses eyeballed me from inside two oversized birdhouses. Finally somebody inside got the message and the gates opened. I pulled up the driveway into the carport behind the limo, switched the Volumatic off.

"Neighbors must love him, don't you think?"

Johnny mumbled something, stretched. The kid slept through most of the drive up from Dulles, ditto the flight back from Berlin. Not that I blamed him, hell, I was planning to catch my share of shut-eye once I got finished letting the Boss chew me out for screwing up. Which would probably take the better part of the night.

I rubbed my cheek, felt the three-day growth of beard starting to cover the footprint. It'd be a while before things were back to normal, that's for sure. We got out and I popped the rear deck, grabbed the briefcase. At least we salvaged that. Shovel too, for that matter. I pointed to it and Johnny pulled it out, tapped the dirt off on the driveway, heaved it to shoulder arms as we headed for the front door.

The house was dark except for a light in the big flagstone foyer. I peeked through the leaded-glass pane and saw him padding down the hall, blue flannel shirt and maroon cardigan, gray pleated slacks, carpet slippers. Burning the midnight oil waiting for his boys to come home.

He opened the door.

I held the briefcase out. "Here you go, sir, none the worse for wear. We even brought back the change."

He stared at the briefcase. He wasn't smiling. "Get the hell in here." Then he looked at Johnny. "And leave that goddam shovel outside."

Johnny leaned the shovel against the wall by the door. We came in and Nixon shut the door behind us, looked at Johnny first, then at me. "Gentlemen, that has got to be the most fucked-up operation this sonofabitching outfit has ever undertaken."

I could think of at least a half dozen that were worse, including the one that sent him on a permanent Jersey vacation, but I wasn't about to bring that up now. Not with the Comeback of the Century down the hopper. All I said was, "Yes, sir."

Nixon stomped down the hall to his office. We followed him. He walked in the door, then turned around.

"Oh, hell, come on in and sit down." He picked up a can of Tab from his desk, handed it to me. "Been saving this for you, Joe. Everyone's asleep or I'd have them fix you something else." He turned to Johnny. "You want anything?"

Johnny shook his head, swallowed a yawn. "I'm fine, sir."

Nixon sat down in the overstuffed chair behind his desk. Office was smaller than the one down the road, more like a private study. Big globe in one corner, silver jug from the Shah on a bookshelf.

I popped the top on the can, took a sip. Room temperature but better than nothing. Good ol' Dick. I reached into my shirt pocket for the last couple Advils and sloshed them down. Nixon watched me. "How's that neck?"

I shrugged. "Comes and goes."

He nodded. "Know what you mean." He rubbed his leg, stretched. "Oh, hell, boys, I'm not blaming you. Hell, when I got the word from Deng a month ago that the goddam East Germans were holding some hot document from the Hiss case, well, I didn't know what it meant. First I thought, how in the hell can that be? Figured maybe that Kraut commie sonofabitch Eisler took it over, you know, the one who told the Committee to kiss his commie ass, then jumped bail and defected to the Russian Zone in '47. But that didn't make any sense, so I started thinking about Chambers. Spoke fluent German, had contacts there in the Party and so forth. Plus he wrote me that damn letter in '61, which you could take to mean he knew about it. Why not, right? But he didn't do it either, did he?"

I shook my head. "Nope. They were in the car the whole time."

Nixon stared at me. "That's the part I'm still trying to take in. You *saw* the goddam thing?"

"We all saw it. I read the serial number on the engine block. It was Alger Hiss's Model A Ford."

"In Erich Honecker's garage."

"Correct."

Nixon closed his eyes, rubbed his face with his hand. "You know, I never met Honecker. Let me say it would've been a logical next step after Mao in '72 but . . ." His voice trailed off. He blinked a couple times, then slammed his palm on the desk. "Well, the hell with that shit. I guess the question is, who put the goddam documents in the car in the first place?"

"That's one of the questions, sure. And believe me, we've been mulling it over."

Johnny nodded. "You've got to think it was Chambers, sir, since he's the one who probably sold the car to Cherner in July '39."

Nixon's eyebrows shot up, he looked at me. I shrugged. "Told him about the receipt we burned, sir. Told him the whole story."

Nixon puffed his cheeks, blew out some air. "Well, what's the goddam difference? We never did anything the Democrats didn't do first; hell, Roosevelt and Truman covered up the case for ten goddam years, God knows how much evidence they eighty-sixed to do it. Hell."

"But getting back to the car, sir, the question is, why would Chambers hide such a hot document in the car and then get rid of the car?"

Nixon frowned, pressed his fingertips together. "He was using the car to transmit the document? Like the goddam French Connection? Damn thing ended up in Russia, after all."

"Yeah, but only by accident. Nobody in Russia knew the document was in the car. It was still there when Honecker found it in 1947. Or so he said."

"And you think Honecker buried the document *in the Berlin Wall?*"

"I'd bet the farm on it, sir. Of course, we never found it—"

"Any chance you still might?"

I shrugged. "Total chaos over there now. A million people crossing back and forth, traffic in complete gridlock, new Politburo getting elected and fired every half hour. All that confusion might provide some cover, but the truth is, if it's not at the spot in the wall where Two Moons thought it was, there's no telling where it could be."

Nixon shook his head. "Damn. That lousy red-skinned sonofabitch, working for Stasi after all those years. Christ, I thought he was dead, even felt sorry for the bastard."

"Well, he's not. And he's flown the Stasi coop too, for that matter. He was talking about opening an art dealership in West Berlin with Closky and Blunt when we left."

"Figures. Victor's still over there too?"

I nodded. "Not likely to come back soon, either. Not unless government's ready to get his sentence commuted, maybe set him up somewhere with a pension."

Nixon laughed. "Don't hold your goddam breath."

"Hell, sir, we could afford it, I'd imagine. We were ready to shell out a couple billion for the damn document."

"What are you talking about?"

"The price for the K-document. Two billion dollars."

Nixon's eyes got big. *"Two billion dollars?* Why in the hell would we pay that much? Two *billion* to the East Germans for a fifty-year-old intelligence document? What kind of crazy bullshit is that? A million maybe, maybe two."

I glanced at Johnny, then back at Nixon. "You mean, you didn't know?"

"Didn't know what? That Victor's off his nut? Yeah, I knew that, but I didn't know he'd go promise Honecker a billion—"

"Two billion."

"—All right, two billion dollars for a scrap of paper that proves Roosevelt was a commie spy. Now who in the hell—"

"Wait a minute, sir. You think the papers the East Germans call the K-document are something that links FDR to the State Department spy ring?"

Nixon nodded. "Or that he knew about it and looked the other way, sure. Hell, I figured that one out long ago. What the hell else could it be?"

I shook my head. "Not even close, sir."

So I told him what we knew. Told him Honecker's story, and his wisecrack that the *K* didn't stand for *Kürbis* after all, and how he bragged that having the document in '61 meant he could build his wall and know the West wouldn't knock it down. I told him about Marco and his ties to the Mob and the CIA, about Closky's little lesson on things that start with *K* and how the folks who were nervous about the document's being found were the same folks who'd been nervous since November '63.

Nixon was on his feet after the first couple sentences, never stopped pacing, face a scowl, grinding his fist into his palm. Finally I finished. He stopped pacing, stood hunched in the corner, hand stroking his chin, elbows tight against his sides. He looked up.

"Get your goddam coat on, Joe. We're going for a ride."

I checked my watch. "Sir, it's after midnight."

"I don't give a shit what time it is, get your goddam coat on!" He kicked off his slippers, jammed his feet into a pair of shiny black tasseled loafers, stomped on the hardwood floor to force them on. Then he turned to Johnny. "You stay here, guard the goddam fort."

Johnny stood up. "You sure, sir? You might need some muscle."
Nixon thought a minute, then shook him off. "Not too goddam likely." He grabbed his topcoat and stormed out the door to the hall.
Johnny shot me a look, eyebrow up. I gave him a slow nod, then took off after Nixon.

A minute later we were outside in the carport, climbing into the T-bird. I fired it up, drove around the circle past the limo and down the drive. The gates swung open just in time and we bumped onto the dark street.

Nixon hunched down in the seat. "Goddam sonofabitch! Goddam commie bastard!" He pointed through the windshield. "Right at the corner. Then left. Garden State south, Route Three to the Lincoln Tunnel. Shit. Damn."

He didn't really have to tell me. There was only one possible place to go now. I still couldn't believe he'd actually do it though. Not now.

Not after forty-one years.

May 22, 1950

The phone rang. Nixon picked it up.

"Yes?" Puzzled frown. "Well, of course, Rose Mary, send him right in."

He stood up, came around to the front of his desk. The door opened.

"Good morning, I, ah, hope I'm not catching you at a, ah, bad time."

It was Jack Kennedy, no blond bombshell on his arm this time, suit hanging loose on his emaciated frame.

He shook Nixon's hand. "Congratulations on the, ah, primary win. I'm sure you'll wage a hell of a campaign against Helen, but just in case . . ."

He reached inside his suitcoat pocket, pulled out a white envelope. Then he glanced at me. Nixon gave a wave like I was okay. He took the envelope.

"My, ah, father wanted you to have this. Strictly confidential. Wouldn't do to advertise the fact that we're supporting a Republican. But for all the good work you've done. And if you need more . . ." He flashed a grin, teeth gleaming white against his yellow skin.

Nixon's eyes darted around. He took the envelope, held it in both hands. "Thank you very much. And let me say—"

"Don't mention it. And good luck to you. Perhaps we'll meet in the Senate someday. Dad wants me to run in '52." He glanced at his watch. "Uh-oh, gotta run. Can't keep a lady waiting." The toothy grin again. Then he was gone.

We stood there for a minute, didn't say anything. Nixon picked up a letter opener, slit the envelope and reached inside.

It was a check for a thousand bucks, made out to the campaign. I looked at Nixon. "Now, why in the hell would Jack Kennedy contribute a thousand dollars to *your* Senate campaign?"

Nixon sat down. "He said it was from his father, didn't he?"

"Okay, so why would *he* contribute a thousand dollars to your Senate campaign?"

Nixon stared at the check, then stared at me. There was a look on his face I'd never seen before. It was genuine, complete bewilderment.

"I'll be goddamned if I know."

"Guess that makes two of us, sir." I leaned over his shoulder, took one more look at the check.

Sure enough. It was signed by Joseph P. Kennedy.

November 13, 1989

He pushed the buzzer. No answer, of course.

"Sir, you know it's one in the morning, right?"

Nixon didn't say anything, just pushed the buzzer again. And again.

Finally a light came on. A voice crackled on the intercom. *"Who's there?"*

Nixon leaned toward the speaker, spoke his name.

Silence.

"Your joke is as stupid as it is unimaginative. If you do not leave at once I shall call the police."

Nixon's eyes darted around. He fished a hankie out of his topcoat pocket, wiped his upper lip. He leaned toward the intercom, pulled back, then leaned in again. "On August 25, 1948, we spoke privately for the first and only time. You were seated at a table in the caucus room before the hearing began. Your attorney was conferring with someone at the other end of the table. I passed by on my way to the rostrum. It occurred to me to make some gesture that would help keep our relationship from deteriorating further. I leaned down and said, 'I'm sorry your wife had to make that long trip last week.' You responded, 'It is kind of you to say so.' Those were our exact words, and that was the extent of the conversation."

Long pause. Then the sound of a dead bolt being pulled back, key turning in a lock. The door opened.

He was eighty-five years old now. Thin white hair, thick glasses. But he stood erect, tall and slim as ever, hand clutching the lapel of a silk bathrobe. When he caught sight of Nixon you could almost see his jaw drop.

"Good God. It really *is* you."

Nixon stuck his foot in the door like a salesman. "I need to speak with you at once, Mr. Hiss."

Hesitation, ancient face still in shock. Then he stood aside, held the door open and we walked in.

There was a single table lamp lit near the staircase. Leather sofa, two easy chairs, mirror on the far wall. Bookshelves, lots of them.

He closed the door. From upstairs, a woman's voice. "Who is it, Alger?"

Hiss looked up the stairs, then looked at Nixon. "It's—" The words wouldn't come out. Finally he said, "It's all right. I'll be a few minutes. Go back to bed."

So there they stood, face-to-face for the first time in forty-one years, Alger Hiss in his bathrobe, Richard Nixon in a herringbone topcoat thrown over a blue flannel shirt, sweater and pleated gray slacks. They both needed a shave, Nixon's five-o'clock shadow past midnight now, tinged with white and gray.

For a long time nobody said anything. Then Hiss remembered his Harvard Club manners. "Do sit down. And take off your coats if you like."

We took off our coats. We sat down. Nixon introduced me to Hiss but we didn't shake hands. If he remembered me from '48 he didn't let on. More silence. Finally Hiss said, "You wished to speak with me."

Nixon shifted on the sofa. The leather creaked. He had his temper under control now, thank God for that. He frowned, like he was collecting his thoughts. Then he said, "Last month, you may have heard, I visited China. During a private talk there, Deng Xioping informed me of a personal message left for me by the visiting East German delegation to Beijing two weeks before. The message was cryptic, but I took it to mean the East Germans knew the location of documents that had been transmitted to the Communists by"— he hesitated—"by the so-called apparatus associated with Whittaker Chambers in the 1930s."

Sour grin from Hiss. "More fire extinguisher manuals, no doubt."

Nixon pressed his lips together, face red. "Please let me finish. Since I no longer serve in any official capacity, I asked an old friend—I asked Joe here to take a few men and look into it for me. For the past three weeks he's been in East Berlin—"

Hiss's eyebrows shot up.

"—where he contacted elements in the Ministry for State Security. They confirmed that the documents existed and were prepared to sell them to U.S. intelligence agents for hard currency. Their price was two billion dollars."

Hiss laughed. "I'm sorry, but this is all too absurd. Even if what you say is true, it has nothing to do with me—"

I interrupted him. "Maybe. Except that we found your car."

Hiss was still smiling. "I beg your pardon?"

"We found your car. The Model A. Slightly collegiate model with a sassy little trunk, remember? Serial number 2188811. It's in East

Germany. In an underground parking garage in the Politburo compound called Wandlitz. Part of an antique car collection that belongs to Erich Honecker."

Hiss shook his head. "You are surely joking."

Nixon leaned forward. The edge was back in his voice. "I ask you to consider this, Mr. Hiss. Do you really think that after forty-one years, after all that you and I have been through, I would come to you in the middle of the night for the purpose of telling you a joke?"

Hiss stared at Nixon for a long time. "No, I don't suppose you would. But still, it's fantastic. How could the car possibly have ended up there?"

Nixon slumped back in the chair, gave me the nod. I took a deep breath. "Long story, Mr. Hiss. Starts in 1935, the year you testified you gave the car to Chambers."

Hiss waved his hand. "Or let him have the use of it, I really can't recall."

I smiled. "Let me help you out. You let him have the use of it. Maybe he kept a key, maybe he managed to filch the title from you, but you never signed it over to him. Because you still had the car in your possession in July 1939."

Hiss smiled back. "Is that so? I thought you were the ones who were so proud of finding the title transfer that showed I sold the car in 1936."

"That's true. But let me tell you about that title transfer, Mr. Hiss. That particular document was handed to me the day before the August twenty-fifth hearing by a man named Willie Marco, long-time associate of Al Capone and later of Sam Giancana. Political fixer for the Chicago Mob. It was a forgery and you knew it."

"Very interesting. And how do *you* know it, Mr. Pope?"

"I know it because your pal Marvin Smith tried to tell me, only the next day he ended up dead. But he told me enough to point me in the right direction, and the day before he died I actually found the receipt at Cherner Motor Company that proved the car was sold in 1939, not 1936."

"And this receipt—?"

Nixon stared Hiss straight in the eye. He was long past cover-ups, long past stonewalling, I could see that. He spat out the words. "We burned it."

Hiss laughed, shook his head. "You *admit* this?"

I ignored him and pushed on. I told him how I figured out Chambers forged the title transfer with Smith's notary seal, how he drove the car to Cherner in July '39, sold it in a shady deal to frame him. I told him about Tacoma and Vladivostok and Lend-Lease, how the car made it to Berlin after the war and ended up in the hands of a German Communist Youth organizer named Erich Honecker, and how Honecker cleaned out the car and found the papers Hiss had hidden eight years before.

For the first time Hiss didn't have a snappy comeback. I could see him tense up. "And you actually saw these papers?"

I looked him straight in the eye. "No."

He relaxed again. "I thought not. You see, it has always been just as I've said. The question is not what happened to my automobile or where I lived or how well I knew a man who called himself Whittaker Chambers. The question is whether I was ever a Communist."

I shook my head. "No, Mr. Hiss, that was never the question. We thought it was, and we wasted a lot of time trying to prove it. But we were wrong. You were never a Communist, I'm convinced of that now."

Nixon looked at me, started to say something. I held my hand up.

"You *were* framed, Mr. Hiss. Framed by Whittaker Chambers, framed by the FBI, framed by the federal prosecutor, framed by us. So no, the question is not whether you were a Communist, because you weren't. The question is something else entirely. Something you've been covering up for the past fifty years. Something you've been more afraid of than losing your job, going to jail, or living a life in disgrace."

Hiss's face was white. He said nothing. I went on.

"Yes, you had access in the late thirties to cable traffic and other messages between the State Department and U.S. embassies. Confidential messages to and from ambassadors in Paris, Berlin, Rome, and Tokyo came in all the time, and you could have intercepted hundreds of them if you'd wanted. But you didn't. You only intercepted one. A message to the ambassador in London.

"In the summer of 1939 Joseph P. Kennedy had been ambassador to England for just over a year. In that time he'd come out in support of Mussolini's invasion of Ethiopia, made himself a regular at Lady Astor's weekly pro-Nazi luncheons at Clivesdale, and told Roosevelt the U.S. would eventually have a fascist government. All of which helped to grease the skids that sent him on a permanent vacation to Hyannis Port in 1940.

"That was bad enough, of course. But there was never a shred of evidence that it went any deeper than that. Never any proof that Kennedy's fascist leanings led to anything illegal or treasonous. My wager is you found that proof. Am I right, Mr. Hiss?"

Hiss was quiet for a long time. I could hear a clock ticking in the next room and counted the ticks. Almost a full minute went by. Finally he said, "I assume you are not wired? Is that the word? No hidden microphones or taping systems?"

I was wearing my blue Harry Truman shirt, the one with the palm trees, and thin khaki slacks. I stood up and patted myself down, held my arms out. Then I looked at Nixon. He rolled his eyes, finally got up and peeled off his cardigan, stood there in his flannel shirt and slacks. "Let me say, Mr. Hiss, that if I were wearing a concealed microphone I would not have admitted to you that we destroyed evidence in 1948. Surely you can appreciate the logic of that."

Hiss smiled. "Yes, I suppose you've learned your lesson on that score, haven't you?"

Nixon's teeth clenched. Hiss kept smiling. "Very well. First of all, you must understand that security precautions at the State Department in those days, even on the eve of war in 1939, were incredibly lax by today's standards. The sorts of documents Chambers dredged up to incriminate me could have been pinched by any one of dozens of people. I have always maintained that."

Nixon snorted, rolled his eyes. Hiss ignored him.

"The same standards, or lack of them, were applied to the receipt and dispatch of what ought to have been handled with the utmost care and discretion—diplomatic pouches. And so it happened that one day in July 1939 I went to retrieve an overdue packet of confidential messages, sent by pouch from the chargé in Berlin, which I urgently needed to complete a report for my superior, Assistant Secretary Francis Sayre.

"When I arrived at the pouch room I found the clerk speaking on the telephone. He looked up, nodded in recognition, opened the Berlin-Washington pouch—one hand still clasping the telephone receiver to his ear—and brought forth a half dozen envelopes, which he handed to me without so much as pausing in his conversation.

"I daresay I was as annoyed by his casual attitude as by the delay and, arriving back at my desk, tore the envelopes open without even a glance at their exterior.

"There were six in all. The first five contained, as expected, confidential information on German plans for economic cooperation with Japan. The sixth did not. It was a handwritten letter on the stationery of a Berlin hotel. I needed read no farther than the salutation to realize that, in my haste, I had inadvertently opened someone else's personal mail. Angry at my own carelessness, I reached into the waste can and retrieved the envelope. When I read the name of the intended recipient, my anger changed to astonishment.

"The envelope was addressed, in longhand, to 'Joseph P. Kennedy, Ambassador.' Below that were the words 'Personal and Confidential.' The return address was imprinted with the name of the Hotel Excelsior in Berlin. Above it the sender had written the name 'Kennedy' again.

"Clearly the letter had been placed in the wrong pouch before it even left Berlin. Such things happened in those days, of course, but I found it no less galling that this particular bit of stupidity should cause me embarrassment, perhaps even cost me my job.

"I glanced at the letter. It was a personal note to Ambassador Kennedy from his son Jack, who was traveling in Europe after having graduated from Harvard. The young man had been to Paris, Rome, Budapest and Prague, and now, in the summer of 1939, he'd reached Berlin. I knew that Ambassador Kennedy had subjected the Foreign Service to his son's inane 'reports' over the past few weeks, and I had no reason to believe this letter would contain any more than the usual—puerile political analysis, coupled this time perhaps with travelogue or an urgent request for money. And I had no intention of reading it.

"But a phrase caught my eye. I skimmed the first sentence, then the second. What I found took my breath away. It was fantastic. I knew I should take the letter at once to Assistant Secretary Sayre. But then I would need to explain how I came to open the envelope. By this point I had become extremely agitated. The simple truth—that I had received and opened the letter by mistake—suddenly seemed preposterous. Surely I would be suspected of sinister involvement myself—or, at the very least, be subjected to endless rounds of official interrogation that would leave a permanent cloud over my career.

"I put the letter aside and tried to think. I could simply destroy it, of course, at once ending my own involvement and perhaps thwarting the plan it appeared to describe. I could attempt to expose it by sending it to the press anonymously—at the risk of its being dismissed as a hoax or, worse, suppressed by someone sympathetic to Kennedy or his views. And even if I were certain of the outcome, making such an explosive matter public would, I reasoned, have greatly harmed the United States's international reputation at a time when she could least afford it.

"That left the option of taking matters, for better or worse, into my own hands. I was thirty-four years old, and fool enough to imagine myself a match for a man as cunning and ruthless as the fascists he so greatly admired. So I made a decision. A decision I have had precisely half a century to regret."

Nixon leaned forward. "Do you mean, Mr. Hiss, that you tried in some way to blackmail Joseph Kennedy?"

Hiss stiffened. "No, Mr. Nixon, I did not try to 'blackmail' him. I did something you will no doubt consider much more foolish. I tried to render him harmless.

"Yes, I kept the letter. Stole it, if you will. The next day I wrote to Kennedy. I explained that I had intercepted the letter of July twelfth from his son in Berlin. I told him I would surrender it to him or his agent on two conditions. First, that he resign the ambassadorship within seven days and return with his family to the United States. And second, that he permanently and completely withdraw from public life. Otherwise, I would make the letter public. It seemed a fair exchange, given the nature of the document."

"The price has since gone up," I said.

"So it seems. In any event, I made sure to place my letter in the correct pouch, and waited. The ambassador's response came two days later, in the form of two men knocking on the door of my apartment on Volta Place at seven o'clock on a Sunday morning. From their look and manner I could describe them as nothing other than common gangsters. Of course I was vaguely aware of rumors that Kennedy had made his fortune in bootlegging, but the idea that the ambassador to the Court of Saint James's would have traffic with such men was at first inconceivable to me. Yet I was soon forced to accept it.

"They demanded the letter. I lied and told them it was not at my apartment, that I had hidden it in a place where it would soon be discovered should anything happen to me. They gave me a simple warning. I was to return the letter within twenty-four hours to an address in Georgetown or I would be 'destroyed.' That was the word they used, and they used it several times. Then they left.

"I panicked. It was obvious to me that making the letter public now would be dangerous, perhaps fatally so. I needed time to think. But first I would hide the letter somewhere outside my apartment. I looked out the window. And I saw the car. Not my new Plymouth, the old Model A."

Nixon rubbed his chin. "Didn't you realize, Mr. Hiss, that they could search your car as well as your home?"

"Yes, but I didn't think I would keep it there for long. Besides, the Model A looked very dilapidated. Hardly the place you'd expect to find anything of value."

I shrugged. "And then?"

"When I was sure they were gone I took the letter and a copy of my note to Kennedy and went out onto Volta Place. I opened the

246

trunk and was prepared simply to stuff the papers in a corner when I noticed the edge of the rubber mat was loose. I slipped them under the mat. Then I got a screwdriver and screwed the mat down tight. I felt very pleased with myself."

"What happened then?"

"The next day, nothing. The day after that, the car was gone."

"July 23, 1939."

"Yes. Of course I assumed I had been outwitted. I felt like a fool."

"But that can't have been the end of it."

"No. The following day the two men reappeared. They again demanded the letter. I was so taken aback I didn't have time to think. I blurted out that they must already have it, since it was in the car they stole. They looked at each other. Then they pushed their way past me and ransacked the apartment. I was, frankly, terrified. My wife wasn't home, thank God, but when she returned she was understandably agitated. She knew nothing of my dealings with Kennedy, and she could not understand why I insisted we not call the police. We did not, of course.

"My life slowly returned to normal. My career in the State Department brought me advancement far beyond my own expectations, first as an aide to President Roosevelt at Yalta, then as the first secretary general of the United Nations in San Francisco, and ultimately as chief of Special Political Affairs at the State Department. In all modesty, there were many who predicted that in the next Democratic administration I would become secretary of state. But soon after Roosevelt's death, under circumstances whose origins I learned only later, I came under increasing pressure to resign. When at last I did so in 1947, the mantle of heir apparent passed to my successor."

Bingo. It fit. "Dean Rusk."

"Precisely. That same year, the man who would head the next Democratic administration had just won his first seat in Congress—or, I should say, had just had a seat in Congress purchased for him by his father. But at the time I took little note of young Kennedy's success, except as an ironic reminder of my ill-fated attempt at playing the hero in 1939.

"Then, on August 3, 1948, I read in *The New York Times* that a man calling himself Whittaker Chambers had alleged I had been a member of a communist cell with him in the 1930s. It was preposterous, and I came forward at once to deny it. At first I had no doubt of my eventual exoneration. But as the days passed and the web spun around me grew ever tighter, I remembered Joseph Kennedy's threat: I would be destroyed. I now understood that he was at last making good his threat. But of course, I could never prove it—even had I wanted to risk my own safety and that of my wife and children by revealing what I knew. And so I went to jail."

Hiss paused. The ticking of the clock in the next room sounded like whacks on a snare drum. I glanced over at Nixon. If he'd been any closer to the edge of his seat he'd have been sitting on thin air. His face was set in stone, eyes burning into Hiss's, as the enormity of it all slowly dawned on him. The incredible, ironic enormity of it.

Hiss took a deep breath. "I didn't learn the whole story until I'd been in Lewisburg Prison for nearly a year. At that time Frank Costello was there as well, serving a brief sentence for contempt of Congress. One day I was informed by an inmate that 'Mr. Frank' wanted to see me. I went to the exercise yard with two of my friends. Costello brought two Italian-American associates and formal introductions were made. Then he and I walked around the cinder track together, as the inmates did when they wished to speak privately. He was very respectful. I was astonished at that. He called me 'Mr. Hiss.' We offered each other mutual sympathy about the miscarriages of justice that had brought us together. He told me the political figure he admired most was, curiously, Eleanor Roosevelt. Then he asked me if I knew why I was really there. I said the answer to that seemed to depend on one's point of view. He shook his big, brutal head, stopped walking, and laid a hand on my shoulder.

"Then he said, in words I shall never forget, 'You're here because you screwed with old man Kennedy.'

"I felt a curious sense of elation and relief. For the first time I'd heard spoken what I had secretly suspected. And as Costello spun out the details for me while we slowly walked around the track in the prison yard, at last it all made sense.

248

"He began by telling me, as an aside, that there was no love lost between him and Kennedy. He claimed to have actually had a 'contract' on him owing to some difference of opinion stemming from Kennedy's Hollywood days, but matters had been patched up by a colleague in Chicago. Someone named Sam Giancana.

"He said that when Kennedy got my letter in July of '39 the Ambassador immediately placed a transatlantic call to Henry Luce in New York, a close friend and fellow anti-Communist, although their relationship was complicated by the fact that Luce's wife, Clare, was Kennedy's mistress. Kennedy asked Luce if he had ever heard of a State Department employee named Alger Hiss—and, of course, at that time Luce had not. Kennedy then told Luce he had reason to suspect this fellow Hiss was a pro-Soviet leftist plotting to steer Roosevelt and the Western democracies into a war with Germany. He needed a favor. Was there anyone on Luce's staff at *Time* conversant with pro-Soviet elements in Washington? And, of course, there was.

"Luce knew that his senior editor, the man now calling himself Whittaker Chambers, was a former Communist when he hired him. Chambers had admitted as much, although he had not yet admitted to espionage, and when he did in 1948 it would cost him his job. Luce asked Chambers if he knew of a 'leftish' State Department official named Alger Hiss. Chambers said he did. He had interviewed me about my work for the Nye Committee, and as a result of that acquaintance—and *only* that acquaintance, as I testified under oath—he sublet an apartment from me, using the name George Crosley.

"This was just what Kennedy was looking for. When he got the information from Luce, he placed a second call, this time to his old bootlegging pal Frank Costello. The message was simple: 'Use Whittaker Chambers to destroy Alger Hiss.'

"Costello knew Chambers as well, or at least he knew of him. He told me they had a file on 'every Commie and queer in New York,' as he put it, the result of working together with the FBI. That shocked me in 1951. Today, well . . ." He shrugged. "So Costello's men made Chambers one of their notoriously difficult-to-refuse

249

offers. And Chambers, reluctantly at first but with obviously growing enthusiasm, obliged."

Hiss paused. I turned to Nixon. "Well, there it is, sir. The motive. 'What possible reason could Chambers have for giving up his privacy, his reputation, his thirty-thousand-dollar-a-year job?' Chambers threw that in our face so often we believed it ourselves. And now there's the answer."

Nixon's eyes never left Hiss's face. His voice was a whisper. "Go on."

Hiss shrugged. "So Chambers, in July 1939, began preparing for the role he would play for the remaining twenty-two years of his life. He memorized details of my private affairs reluctantly provided by our colored help to Costello's men. He used his key to steal my old Ford and turn it over, forged title and all, to his ex-comrades at Cherner Motor Company. And several weeks after that he managed to get an appointment with Adolf Berle at the State Department to make his now-famous denunciation. Except that along with the names of his *actual* contacts in Washington, he now included mine.

"Of course, I knew none of this, except that my car was missing. And by that time war in Europe had broken out and the State Department had other concerns, so the immediate effect was somewhat less dramatic than Kennedy would have wished. In fact, when Kennedy tried to help matters along by hinting to Roosevelt about a witness to treason in the State Department, it had the opposite effect. By that time Roosevelt's disenchantment with Kennedy's defeatism had reached the point where he actually ordered State and Justice to ignore Chambers. And as long as FDR lived, they did.

"The first time I ever heard the name Whittaker Chambers was nine years later, when I read the newspaper account of his testimony before your Committee accusing me of being a Communist. It was days before I linked the name of Chambers with the man I had known as George Crosley, and weeks before it dawned on me that Chambers-Crosley could be somehow connected to my brief, terrifying dealings with Kennedy nine years before. Even then it seemed preposterous. Why then, after all?"

I interrupted him. "I can answer that one for you, Mr. Hiss. Because in 1947 Erich Honecker finally found the letters in the trunk of the Ford. When he realized what they were, he sent a young agent into the American sector of Berlin to spy on an army intelligence officer, a fellow named Victor Closky, a former Dies Committee investigator who knew the case and knew Chambers's testimony. Only it backfired; the boy ended up dead and Closky ended up with the garbled information that the KPD was holding 'documents from Alger Hiss.' He assumed that meant Chambers had been telling the truth in '39, that you really were a spy and had even passed documents to the Communists. So when he left Berlin he headed straight for Chambers. Which is what got the whole thing rolling again. Only this time it couldn't be stopped. Harry White and Marvin Smith didn't understand that. Neither did Laurence Duggan. It cost them their lives."

At the mention of his old pals Hiss's eyes got wet. He cleared his throat, adjusted the sash on his silk dressing gown. "That's quite correct. Any one of the three might have cleared me. White knew Chambers was a fraud. He was quite adamant about it, as you'll recall. Had he lived to continue testifying, I doubt that even your Committee would have been able to overlook the flaws in Chambers's story. Marvin Smith, of course, even had the proof, but his fatal error was in trusting the telephone to summon you. And Duggan spoke with me the week before he died. He said he was fully prepared to corroborate my story of Chambers posing as Crosley the journalist in 1935. So he was doomed as well."

Nixon frowned. "Just a moment, Mr. Hiss. Doomed by whom? Costello was strictly New York, I understand, but the boys we were—uh, the boys who got mixed up in the case in '48 were from the Chicago outfit."

Of course. "I can answer that one, sir. Somewhere between '39 and '48 Costello had his falling out with Kennedy, so the old man called on his Chicago connections to close the deal. Which meant Giancana and Marco Senior took over. Because it was Marco who filched the old title transfer from Motor Vehicles, then had a Mob forger alter the date from '39 to '36 to jibe with Chambers's story.

251

And when even that didn't do the trick they helped Chambers 'remember' the hidden documents he claimed he got from Hiss. Also forgeries. Bad ones at that, but it didn't matter because we covered their tracks by building a typewriter to match them."

Hiss's jaw dropped. "Why you—you *bastards*! So it *was* you who—"

I cut him off. The typewriter was the least of it at this point. "Closky tried to keep up with them for a while, thought they could do for us in Cook County what they eventually did for the Democrats in 1960, but he was in over his head and they dropped him. Meanwhile the Kennedys were racking up a debt to the FBI and the Mob and folks that later ended up in the CIA and government and God knows where else. A debt they welshed on when JFK blew the Bay of Pigs and then set Bobby loose on organized crime. And we all know where that led."

Nixon coughed, cleared his throat. "Mr. Hiss, do you still have a copy of the letter itself?"

Hiss didn't move. He was still thinking about that damn typewriter, I could see that much. Finally he shook himself out of it. "Of course. I wrote out a copy in longhand before I hid the original in the car."

Hiss stood up, went to the bookshelf.

"I still move it around every few days. Don't suppose it matters now."

He pulled down a copy of *Darkness at Noon*, slid out a piece of folded paper, opened it carefully. He handed it to Nixon. I leaned over and Nixon held it so we could both read. The paper was yellow and worn, the handwriting neat and clear.

HOTEL EXCELSIOR
BERLIN

July 12, 1939

Dear Dad,
    Carried yr message to Ribbentrop at Wilhelmsstrasse at 10 this morning. After twenty minutes he took me in to see Reichs-

chancellor Hitler, who reminds you this is the *third* time he has invited you to Berlin + now expects you will come.

H. says he accepts yr proposal, offers following specifics: Germany will push Poles to brink of war by late August. Ultimatum demanding return of Danzig + corridor through the Corridor. You fly to Berlin as mediator August 31. After talks with you, H. will *drop* his demands, offer non-aggression treaty to Poland, U.S., Britain + France.

Hitler agrees yr perceived success at preventing conflict will make you strongest possible candidate against Roosevelt next year, virtually ensuring your election. He stresses it will not be "second Munich," i.e., Germany to actually make strong concessions after meeting with you.

Further as per yr proposal, Hitler to delay action against Poland + Russia until after Kennedy inauguration January 1941. Germany—free hand in Europe. U.S.—British colonies after defeat of England.

Respnd by diplomatic pouch if agreed.

(Dad—you know from our recent talks that I cannot share your faith in Herr Hitler's word—Austria, Sudetenland + Czecho, etc. Please be careful!)

Will remain in Berlin as instructed until I hear from you.

Jack

Holy, holy, holy hell. Question of character, eh? Jesus. I looked at Nixon. His face was white. And no wonder.

Christ, the irony of it was sickening. The whole reason for nailing Hiss in '48 was to jump-start Nixon's career. So what if we told a few lies, cut a few corners? So what if a few guys died? It worked, after all, at least for a while. But if we'd *really* cracked the case in '48, if we'd really learned the truth, that would've been the end of it. No Senator Kennedy in '52, no Candidate Kennedy in '60. Nixon runs against Johnson or Stevenson, beats either one easy. Puts us in the White House eight years early, right on Closky's schedule. No Vietnam, no Watergate, maybe even no Berlin Wall. Talk about rewriting the history of the twentieth century. *If* we hadn't burned that goddam receipt. And to think all we got out of it was a lousy grand from old man Kennedy.

Nixon was still staring at the letter. He didn't move. Then I thought of something else. I turned to Hiss.

"Didn't it ever occur to you, Mr. Hiss, that you're a goddam hero? If you hadn't intercepted that letter, Joe Kennedy might well have taken Hitler up on his offer. Then he gets elected president while the Nazis overrun half the world, not to mention the United States at the mercy of a bunch of gangsters and crooks that would've made—"

Nixon shot me a sideways glance. I dropped it.

Hiss sighed. "Of course it occurred to me. Acting admittedly in a foolhardy and amateurish fashion, I succeeded in accomplishing a great good. But who will ever know? Even if I wished to endanger myself and those I love by revealing what I did, who would believe me now? Where is the proof? So for the past forty years I've had an 'understanding' with men who hold my life and the lives of my family in their hands. I steadfastly maintain my innocence, I take this secret to my grave, and they permit me to reach it at my own pace—as they are fond of reminding me when they come to visit. They even keep a key to my apartment. I assure you it has not been pleasant."

Hiss gently took the letter from Nixon's hands, folded it up again. He put it back in the book. "I don't suppose you have any indication as to where the original might be?"

"As a matter of fact, we do," I said. "We think it's buried in the Berlin Wall."

Hiss's face went blank. He repeated the words like he didn't understand: "The Berlin Wall."

I nodded. "When John Kennedy became president in January 1961, Honecker was East German minister of defense. He still had the letter, only now it was more than a historical curiosity. And he was ready to use it in a shakedown scheme with stakes a lot higher than 1939. When he started to build the Wall eight months after Kennedy took office, his message to Kennedy was simple: 'Let the Wall stand, and your letter will never see the light of day. Knock it down and—' " I shrugged. "Well, he didn't knock it down, did he?"

"But for Honecker to conceal it, literally, inside the Wall?"

"Well, don't forget, Honecker was hiding it from his cronies as much as from us. There were rumors in East Germany that Honecker had something on the West that made him untouchable, but if anybody thought of using Stasi for a covert search of Honecker's digs, they'd never have found it. It was perfect. Of course, when the East German economy started to hit the skids early this year, demand for anything with a cash value in hard currency went way up. My guess is the secret Politburo meeting of October eighteenth revolved around one subject: Tell us where your so-called K-document is or you're headed for the dustbin of history. Honecker was stubborn. He still is."

"K-document? *K* for Kennedy, I presume?"

"Right. That took me a while, but it can't be anything else. Funny to think the damn thing went clear around the world to end up cemented into a wall a couple blocks from the hotel where a twenty-two-year-old John F. Kennedy wrote it fifty years ago."

"But after Kennedy died? Surely the letter's value would drop when it was no longer useful for blackmailing the U.S. president."

I looked at Nixon. He pulled a hankie out of his topcoat pocket, blotted his upper lip. His hand was shaking. Finally he nodded. I looked back at Hiss.

"The letter by itself would be explosive. Or maybe not, maybe it would just be one more stunning revelation about a president the American public has long since known was no saint. Sure, it would be a hell of a blow, probably the final blow to what was left of Kennedy's reputation. But that's all it would be.

"Put that letter alongside the copy of your note to Kennedy's father, though, and you've got a whole new story. Now you've got an answer to the question 'What was Alger Hiss covering up in 1948?' And the answer to that is, a link between himself and the Kennedys, a link that explains why he might have been framed, who might have done it and with whose help. And *now* you've got what all the so-called conspiracy theorists have been unable to dredge up since 1963. Proof of that unpaid debt Kennedy owed to the elements that finally did him in. It's a trail that leads from Berlin to Dallas by way of London, Washington, and Chicago. And I couldn't begin to tell you how many people want that trail covered up."

We all heard it at the same time. A key in the lock, then the front door opened. First thing to come in was a sleek new Thundertrap silencer somebody'd managed to screw onto the barrel of a Makarov. Behind it, skinny guy in a three-piece suit, wavy black hair, olive skin. Still wore the Ray-Bans, even at night.

Holy hell.

I tried to stay calm, nodded at the gun. "Looks like you've been to a few KoKo garage sales yourself, Marco."

His face didn't move, eyes still hidden by the shades. How could he even see through the damn things? He muttered one word. "Wiseass."

I shrugged but my gut was churning. He kept the gun pointed in my direction, looked over at Hiss. "You played the game pretty good for forty-one years, Alger. Too bad you couldn't have held out a couple more." He tossed the key onto the coffee table. It clattered on the glass. "Won't be needing to visit anymore, I guess." He nodded at Nixon and me. "Won't be needing to visit any of you."

Hiss's face was white, beads of sweat on Nixon's upper lip. I stared at the gun.

"Marco, I thought you were out of your goddam mind in Berlin, but this sure as hell beats that. What are you going to do with that thing, pull the trigger? You have any idea what kind of heat's going to come down when they find us?"

His face still didn't change. "Who said anybody's going to find you?"

That gave my gut another turn but I tried not to show it. "Jesus, Marco, you're not as dumb as you look, right? Okay, so you dump us in the river. Are you really having that much trouble imagining the headlines when these particular gentlemen turn up missing on the very same day? These gentlemen, Marco?" I pointed at Hiss and Nixon. "You don't think somebody's going to make a connection?"

"Doesn't matter. We got no choice."

"Yeah, I bet. Just like your pop and his friends had no choice with Harry White. No choice with Marvin Smith either, or Laurence Duggan. They all knew, didn't they, figured out part of it one way or another and wouldn't keep quiet. And Chambers himself, the poor fat sap, tried to come clean in '61 and two days later *he* had a heart attack. Just like Harry White. Not much imagination there, Marco. Didn't you boys get tired of giving old men heart attacks?"

Marco grinned. "When we did we switched to strokes."

That took me a second. Then the nickel dropped. JFK in the White House, 1961. Chambers tries to rat on him and gets a one-way ticket to the pumpkin patch. A month later Honecker's Wall goes up. Then old Joe Kennedy has a stroke. Never talks again. I didn't see that one coming but it fit. It all fit. Every bit of it.

Of course, that wasn't all. I wondered how much Marco really knew, decided to give it a shot. "So I guess when *your* pop's turn came they were back to heart attacks, right?"

A twitch. "Shut up."

Bingo. I pushed ahead. "What, you're telling me you never even thought about it? November '65, FBI tries to bust The Wheelman on a weapons charge—a *weapons charge,* Marco?—then they claim he has a heart attack resisting arrest? And you're still on the payroll, you can still look yourself in the eye every morning?"

The gun was shaking. "I said shut up!"

I had him now, I knew I did. Just needed a little more edge, a little more time to make up the difference in reflexes between me and a guy half my age.

"Okay, I'll shut up. But the Secret Service boys back of you there might want to have a word before you go."

Marco smirked, shook his head. "Don't be an asshole. He doesn't use Secret Service. Only one who—"

But he looked. Damned if he didn't look. Just for a split second, just a quick glance, but it was enough, and I aimed a Hail Mary at the Makarov, aimed a kick that felt like it was in slow motion and probably would've been too if it hadn't been for that last Tab, but it connected and the pistol sailed across the room, bounced off the wall with a loud thunk, and I was on top of him and we went down together.

I tried to use my weight to pin him but he recovered quick, aimed a knee at my groin and missed, then got enough leverage to roll me over on my back. I ripped his Ray-Bans off and was about to go for his eyes but all of a sudden I felt somebody pull him off me, heard a voice so strained, so twisted with blind rage it took me a second to realize whose it was.

"You goddam dirty dago sonofabitch, you and your Mick asshole friends saved Kennedy's ass and ruined my career! You ruined it! Ruined my goddam life, ruined my place in history!"

Nixon had his arm around Marco's throat, yanked his head back, kept punching him in the side of the face, muttering "My place in history" over and over through clenched teeth. I thought he was going to kill him with his bare hands.

And maybe he would have, but next thing I knew Marco was getting pulled the other way.

"Your career? Why you smarmy, pious, self-righteous bastard, you deserved everything you got! Your career! What about *my* career? What about my friends, what about the men who died because these fascist Mafia-CIA hoodlums were protecting the biggest fascist of them all!"

Hiss dug his fingers into Marco's throat, shook his head back and forth. When Marco finally got over the shock he shook Hiss off, grabbed for Nixon. I managed to crawl out and retrieve the Makarov, held it by the barrel, swung it and landed a blow on the back of Marco's skull. He went limp. I stood up, stuffed the pistol in my belt. It wasn't over yet, though, because now Hiss and Nixon turned their fury on each other, two bitter old men, two enemies whose hate was so deep and so ancient it made Achilles look like Will Rogers.

Nixon rolled off Marco, grabbed Hiss by his silk bathrobe lapels. "You lying communist sonofabitch, if you'd have told the truth in the first place none of this would've happened!"

Hiss batted at Nixon with his frail arms, thin face red with rage. "The *truth*? You wouldn't know the truth if it walked up and spit in your shifty eyes! All you've ever done with the truth is twist it around to serve your own despicably crooked ends!"

Hiss finally connected with a soft punch to Nixon's nose. It wasn't much but Nixon yelped and a trickle of blood ran down one nostril. I figured I'd better hit the bell. But another voice in the room beat me to it. A woman's voice.

"Alger! What on earth is going on?"

Hiss's wife stood in the hallway, blinking in the light, clutching her dressing gown. She glared at me. Then she saw Nixon on the floor. His nose was bleeding, gray hair tousled, cardigan askew. But she knew him all right. Knew him straight off. Hell, who wouldn't? Her voice dropped to a whisper.

"My God, it's—"

Hiss let go of Nixon's throat, helped him up. I stood up with them. Marco stayed down. Nixon coughed, tugged his cardigan back into place.

"Just let me say I, uh, I'm sorry for the disturbance, Mrs. Hiss." He was breathing hard, dabbed his nose with the side of an index finger. Hiss pulled a monogrammed hankie out of his dressing gown, held it out. Nixon took it, wiped his nose. "Thank you." He turned to me, took a deep breath. "We should probably be going."

I nodded. Hiss pointed at Marco.

"What about him?"

I poked at him with my foot, rolled him over onto his back. "We'll drop him off with the CIA boys downtown; they'll know what to do. He blew his big chance, won't be much use again. Lucky for us he was dumb enough to come alone."

The voice came from the half-opened door. German accent. *"But he wasn't, Grandpa."*

Oh hell, here we go again. I glanced over. It was Blondie all right, 7mm Beretta resting easy in his big hand, windbreaker traded in for a wash-'n'-wear Company suit, bandage gone too, hardly a bruise now where Closky kayoed him three weeks ago. A lot bigger than Marco, better shape too. As for me, I was soaked in sweat, puffing like a locomotive, and my neck felt like it was about to snap off. Plus I was running out of wisecracks.

Blondie pointed at the Makarov in my belt. "Grasp the gun with your left hand and lay it on the table."

I pulled it out like he said, laid it down.

Then he waved his Beretta down at Marco. "Pick him up and put him on the couch."

That was a tougher one. Skinny as Marco was, I wasn't sure my back could take it. I stared at Blondie. "Shouldn't you at least shut the door first?"

Faint smile. Another wave of the gun. "You do it."

I was stalling for time and he knew it, but he didn't know why. I had him there at least, or hoped I did. All in the timing now. I took a careful step toward the door, hands raised, palms out. Blondie stepped back to let me past, gun still pointed my way.

All of a sudden there was a whoosh and a flash of steel, loud crack and a gong and the Beretta went flying, Blondie's face like he was about to ask one last dumb question before he crumpled to the floor. Hiss's wife shrieked.

Johnny sauntered in, leaned the shovel against the wall.

I picked up the two pistols. "Not bad, kid. Learn that trick from Victor, huh?"

Johnny grinned, shot Nixon the V sign. "Commandeered the limo, sir. Hope you don't mind."

Nixon let out a whistle, shook his head. "Not a goddam bit."

The room got quiet. I looked at my watch. It was three in the morning. I'd been awake for almost forty-eight hours but I didn't feel tired. I glanced at Nixon. Bloody nose, shoulders slumped, jowls drooping, looked as bad as I'd ever seen him, worse than he did at the end in '74. Hiss broke the silence.

"You won't be mentioning any of this in your next book, I don't suppose."

Nixon straightened up, shook his head. "No. Nor will you at your next speaking engagement."

"No."

Johnny was kneeling down to snap a pair of hand irons on Blondie and Marco. I held Nixon's topcoat for him. "That leaves the two letters themselves," I said. "It's possible they could be found tomorrow. Or in a year. Or in a hundred years. Or never."

The two men stood facing each other. For a second it looked like they might shake hands, but they didn't.

Nixon buttoned his topcoat, turned the collar up. "Well," he said, "at least they're not going anywhere, that's for goddam sure."

EPILOGUE

January 28, 1990

Temperature a balmy seventy-two at noon, Fighting Conchs taking their warm-up tosses on the practice field, young Conchettes on the sidelines in pleated skirts and white cowboy boots, tight formation, flash of chrome batons. I was sitting in the bleachers with a shrimp sandwich and a fruit-a-bomba shake letting the sun bake out the rest of the pain. News of the New World Order still rolling in. Pinochet, Noriega, and Egon Krenz join Honecker in the unemployment line, Ceaușescu should have been so lucky. Erich Mielke under arrest, charged with killing two Berlin cops in 1931, it sez here. Meanwhile a hundred thousand disgruntled GDR burghers storm Stasi HQ on Normannenstrasse, tear the place apart, trash documents and files going back to Marx himself. If George and Victor had any hope of picking up the search where we left off, well, good luck to 'em.

And just in case they did get that far there was this of course, in today's *Herald*, 28 January 1990, page 3:

BERLIN WALL DISMANTLED
FOR SALE TO WEST

WEST BERLIN, Jan. 25—The Berlin Wall, for twenty-eight years the symbol of Europe's Cold War division, is being dismantled for sale to the West.

Intact sections of the former wall go on sale today through the East German import-export firm Limex. The price of a three-ton, four-by-twelve-foot slab ranges from $60,000 to $300,000, with museums eligible for bulk discounts on purchases of three or more adjacent pieces. According to a Limex spokesman, each slab will be stamped, numbered, and accompanied by a certificate of authenticity. Wall sections against which would-be escapees were shot will not be sold, he emphasized.

So far most orders have come from Japan, the United States, and western Europe, but sections of the former wall are also being shipped to Latin America, Malaysia, Australia, India, and South Africa. Buyers are responsible for delivery costs.

The West Berlin newspaper *Der Tagesspiegel* estimated that selling the Berlin Wall could net the East German government as much as $3 billion over the next three years.

Zonia delenda est, eh? That's irony, I guess. No word as to whether the Limex spokesman was a giant Indian or a semi-demented, multilingual Mielke double, but I'd lay odds it was one or the other. Maybe both, who knows, stranger things have happened.

Sharp whistle on the field, batons at shoulder arms, high kicks, narrow feet held firm in tough white leather.

I slurped up the last of my shake, glanced back at the paper. Malaysia, huh? Well, at least they were numbering the damn things. Not that I had plans to go back on the road again any time soon.

But then with the government you never know.

AUTHOR'S NOTE

Richard Nixon, Whittaker Chambers, and Alger Hiss are historical figures. Their public words and actions in the period from 1948 to 1950 are a matter of record and are incorporated into this novel with no significant changes. The fictitious re-creations of the hearings of the U.S. House of Representatives Committee on Un-American Activities (HUAC) of August 8 and August 25, 1948, are based on the transcripts of those hearings, which I edited for space and, in some cases, for clarity. Representatives Karl Mundt (R-S.D.), F. Edward Hébert (D-La.), John McDowell (R-Pa.), J. Parnell Thomas (R-N.J.), and "Lightnin'" John Rankin (D-Miss.) were members of that committee, as was freshman congressman Richard Nixon (R-Cal.). Robert Stripling was the committee's chief investigator. Ben Mandel was research director. The main developments of the Hiss case, from August 1948 to January 1950, are told here as they occurred. Alger Hiss's colleagues Harry White, W. Marvin Smith, and Laurence Duggan died under the circumstances described here; foul play was suspected but never proved. The explanations I provide for these and other still-controversial questions, such as the whereabouts of Alger Hiss's Model A Ford and the origins of the Woodstock typewriter that helped convict him, are fictional.

Joe Pope, Victor Closky, Johnny Reed, Ed Blunt, and George Two Moons are fictional. When these characters interact with historical figures, the dialogue and action are the products of my imagination—or, in a few cases, are adapted from actual conversations those figures had with someone else.

Nixon's 1989 China visit did take place immediately after the East German visit by Erich Honecker's deputy, Egon Krenz, although Nixon actually went in late October, not early October. The chronology of events in East Germany from Honecker's resignation on October 18, 1989, to the opening of the Berlin Wall on November 9, 1989, is based on the well-known published accounts. Erich Honecker's underground economic empire, the East German Office of Commercial Coordination (KoKo), functioned more or less as described. It was run by Alexander Schalck-Golodkowski under Honecker's close supervision.

Readers familiar with the Hiss case will know that many details were omitted from this novel. The case involved at least two other suspicious deaths, a second car, a second farm in Westminster, three apartments, four identical Persian rugs, and conflicting testimony from dozens of witnesses. Despite these omissions, and despite a good deal of fictional meddling by the fictional characters, nothing in the novel is deliberately inconsistent with the known facts of the case.

Some of the strangest events depicted here are true. Whittaker Chambers really did lead committee investigators to his farm in the dead of night to pull the incriminating microfilm from a hollowed-out pumpkin. Alger Hiss really did meet Frank Costello at Lewisburg Prison, at Costello's request. Erich Honecker really did have a fleet of twenty-three automobiles for his personal use. Young John F. Kennedy really did visit Nazi Germany just weeks before the outbreak of World War II. And Richard Nixon really did receive a $1,000 campaign contribution from Joseph Kennedy in 1950, delivered to Nixon's office by young JFK.

As of this writing, many questions about the Hiss case remain unanswered. It is possible, however, that documents from some Russian archive may soon reveal the "truth" about whether or not Alger Hiss was a spy. If that happens, you may consider this story another "Case Closed." Which is, of course, exactly what *they* want you to do.

ABOUT THE AUTHOR

BOB OESTE has worked as a military policeman, an Arthur Murray dance instructor, a high school teacher, and an interpreter for the U.S. State Department. His articles on the lighter side of history, politics, and the contemporary scene have appeared in the Baltimore *Sun* and newspapers of the *Los Angeles Times* syndicate. He lives in Baltimore with his wife and three children.

ABOUT THE TYPE

This book was set in Caledonia, a typeface designed in 1939 by William Addison Dwiggins for the Merganthaler Linotype Company. Its name is the ancient Roman term for Scotland, because the face was intended to have a Scotch-Roman flavor. Caledonia is considered to be a well-proportioned, businesslike face with little contrast between its thick and thin lines.